D0369104

A Time to Sing

A Time to Sing

Sally Mandel

McGRAW-HILL PUBLISHING COMPANY
New York St. Louis San Francisco Toronto

1 2 3 4 5 6 7 8 9 DOC DOC 8 9 2 1 0 9

ISBN 0-07-039860-7

LIBRARY OF CONGRESS CATALOGING-IN-PUBLICATION DATA

Mandel, Sally.
A time to sing / Sally Mandel.
p. cm.
ISBN 0-07-039860-7
PS3563.A446T56 1989
813′.54—dc19 89-2753
CIP

Book design by Eve L. Kirch

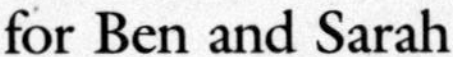

for Ben and Sarah

A little time for laughter,
A little time to sing,
A little time to kiss and cling,
And no more kissing after.

Philip Bourke Marston
(1850–1887)

The difference between American and English cocktail parties was the aroma of the cigarette smoke. Karen Wells sniffed, coughed, and moved closer to the window. Flat slices of dank London winter slid from cracks in the frame. Karen sucked in a deep breath. Nicotine and tar were hell on the vocal cords.

There was a hospitable charm to the room despite the lofty ceilings and formal chandeliers. Thick Oriental carpets softened the floor underfoot, overstuffed furniture stood in friendly clusters, and fireplaces at either end glowed and crackled. Karen estimated that the guests numbered close to two hundred, but somehow the place achieved a sense of intimacy.

Thus far, she had remained unnoticed, though perhaps the news of her recent triumph had not yet penetrated this particular circle. The focus of attention here was Sir William MacIntyre, whose shiny bald head bobbed above the crush of European luminaries like a genial balloon. It was rumored that Sir William's latest epic film, *Sleeping Giant,* might earn him a Berne Peace Prize for its devastating portrait of apartheid in South Africa. The crowd unraveled for a moment, permitting Karen a clear view of the guest of honor as he leaned against the marble fireplace. The top of his face was round and smooth, but the bottom sagged as if tugged by powerful fingers of gravity into pockets under the eyes, pouches beside the mouth, loose sacks beneath the chin. Karen remembered a game she used to play with her brother, Michael, where you had to match the halves of people's faces. It looked as if somebody had gotten Sir William's mixed up. Words began to swim in Karen's head: *You're two-faced, baby, but it's fine / Long's I know both halves are mine . . .*

She could imagine Tony's voice prodding her to socialize. He had wangled an invitation with the notion that someday soon Karen might need contacts in the film world. Her acting experience was thus far limited to an appearance as one of the Three Kings in her fourth-grade Christmas play, but such technicalities never daunted Tony. Karen could sing; it stood to reason that she could act as well.

A waiter passed by with a tray, and Karen snagged a glass of champagne, her second. She knew she should be chatting and mixing, at the very least making an effort to meet the guest of honor. But after the hysterical madness of her success in France last week, she was feeling a kind of blissful exhaustion, an inertia that kept her at the fringes of the party, smiling complacently like a woman with a delicious secret. In her lifetime, Karen had felt the exhilaration of holding an audience with the power of her voice, but at the Midem festival, she had set them on fire. Tony had told her there was always one artist who blew the place apart. This year it was Karen Wells. She had stood on that stage, the floor glistening with her sweat, and stared out at acres of people on their feet, screaming, stamping, howling for more. The news of her performance had preceded them to London. The hotel suite overflowed with flowers, journalists, and miscellaneous hangers-on, while the incessant ringing in Karen's ears was the telephone, which knew no mercy. It had been so crazy that, in a way, tonight's party was almost a reprieve. Surely she was entitled to rest on her laurels in a quiet corner.

She spotted a journalist acquaintance and turned her head so as not to be recognized. Ignoring Tony, she had dressed conservatively except for the mismatched earrings and the sprinkling of glitter in her makeup. Such defiance of her manager was uncommon, but tonight it had seemed born from an instinct for self-preservation. The relationship had reached such an intensity that when she opened her mouth, she half expected to hear Tony's deep voice emerge from between her lips.

Karen watched the worshipful surround the legendary Sir William. Some were awestruck and stared silently at his mouth, nodding uncomprehendingly at the transfixing spectacle of famous lips moving. Perhaps a glimpse of root canal work might provide some titillating hint of human imperfection. A compulsive talker stood at Sir William's elbow. There would be no stemming the flood of autobiography, Karen knew. (She herself had been stunned by the personal revelations that poured from such faces. Out of the mob at the Carlton Hotel in Cannes, a middle-aged woman shoved her way forward to proclaim that Karen's song, "You Give Me," had induced the first of many multiple orgasms.)

There were bored and disenchanted faces here, too. These were the journalists. Like weary gold prospectors, they sifted endlessly through the dirt in search of a speck of precious metal that might prove valuable in tomorrow's edition.

"Hiding, darling?" The voice belonged to Guy Burlingame of *Orbit* magazine. Karen allowed herself to be kissed on both cheeks. Then Guy handed her a glass of champagne.

"Just saving the cords." Karen waved her hand in front of her face. "Haven't these people ever heard of cancer? Whew, my third glass." She touched the handkerchief that poked crisply out of Guy's vest pocket. "Such a fashion plate. Don't you get wrinkled like regular people?"

"Not often enough." His upper lids drooped over pale eyes, lending him an expression that was at once mysterious and plaintive. Karen had met very few people in her lifetime who did not provoke in her a physical response, however slight. Attraction or repulsion, there was always something. Back home in the country, Karen had occasionally even felt the impulse to throw her arms around the trunks of certain trees. But Guy was a rare specimen in that her reaction to his presence was completely neutral. She regretted her lack of sexual interest, knowing that Guy's concern transcended professional curiosity.

They had met years ago, after a performance in an East Village bistro. Guy sought her out, leading her through the sticky puddles of spilt beer into a quiet corner near the rest rooms. As he questioned her, she kept repeating to herself: This is it, this is it, an interview with Guy Burlingame, prominent journalist, syndicated, no less. This wasn't it, of course; there were more years of obscurity ahead. But Guy always did what he could, consistently dropping her name in his columns and passing the word that Karen had a special gift.

He took her hand in his dry, paper-light fingers. "I caught your act at Midem," he said.

"And?"

"Your time has come."

"You really think so?"

"No doubt about it," Guy said. "Nobody's had that kind of impact since Hildy Watson."

"Lord," Karen said. Hildy, unable to cope with the stresses of fame, had overdosed shortly after her Cannes debut.

"You're too sensible for that trip," Guy said. "Doing *Britvideo* while you're here?"

"Tomorrow." She took a long swallow while Guy made his customary inspection.

"You've lost weight. Four pounds, I'd say."

"On the button. How do you do that? Is it something you're born with, or does it take practice?"

"Comes from years of observing Elizabeth Taylor. Are you going to give me a real interview while you're in London?"

Karen hesitated. The last time she had been alone in a room with Guy, he had found an excuse to catch her around the waist. She had made a joke of it and managed to dance herself free without injuring his ego.

Guy's face pleaded with her. That particular expression—silent entreaty—never failed to move her. She averted her eyes but was already snared in the memory of her brother, Michael, sitting on the bank of the creek, rocking back and forth in agony as the sluggish brown summer water slid past them through the cow pasture. He and Karen had been fishing, and somehow Michael managed to plant a tanned bare foot squarely on his fishhook. It had passed through the soft pad of his sole up near the big toe.

"I'll get Dad," Karen had said. The river, and then everything else, swam into shades of gray and beige. She gripped the tree trunk to keep herself from passing out.

"No. You have to take it out," Michael said. His thirteen-year-old face had suddenly seemed much younger. There were salty tracks down both cheeks. Her big brother, in tears.

"I can't," Karen said. Michael gave the hook a tug and moaned. Karen swayed and tried to concentrate on the chapped birchbark beneath her fingers.

"Dad's downtown," Michael said. Sweat had gathered in a jeweled mustache above his lips.

"Mother, then."

"Oh, her."

Karen imagined her mother's fluttering hands and her breathy disconcerted exclamations.

"You've got gentle fingers, Kar," Michael whispered. "Please. It's got to come out."

So Karen raced to the house, retrieved a pair of wire cutters, the pliers, and a bottle of peroxide. When she got back to him, Michael's wound had swollen around the hook in an angry knob. It was hard going, maneuvering the wirecutters. Michael kept very still, but every now and then she would hear him gasp. It took almost twenty minutes for her to work the hook free. Then she dosed the puncture with peroxide, crawled over behind the birch tree, and threw up.

"Just an hour," Guy was saying. He was stroking the back of her hand and looking as if his future hung on her answer.

"Sure, of course," Karen said. "I read the piece you did on Cannes, Guy. If it weren't for you and your kind remarks about my pipes, I'd still be working those dingy clubs in the Village. But you'd better check with the boss for timing. My schedule's been nuts since Midem. As a matter of fact, I've got to run this minute."

The covert pain in Guy's face flickered into panic. Suddenly he grabbed her and kissed her full on the mouth. His lips were smooth and wet. Karen stood perfectly still until he released her, then she touched his cheek with her finger and walked quickly away.

Edward Vaughn huddled on a chair near the radiator with his long legs jackknifed over his tweed sports jacket. What a farcical posture for a professor of twentieth-century lit, crammed into the corner of a star-spangled gala in a Mayfair penthouse. Edward assumed it was star-spangled, but there was no one he recognized. He was no film buff, and if it had not been for his sister, Persis, he would never have been induced to come. Persis's curiosity about the famous baffled Edward. She had received an invitation through a London contact but was stuck in New York for the bound galleys of her latest volume of poetry. With Edward in London on sabbatical, however, all was not lost.

"It'll be good for you," she had said over the telephone. It had been one of those awkward satellite connections where you heard yourself repeated a second after you finished your sentence. They had learned to punctuate their remarks with long pauses. "You're such an old fart," she had gone on. "And you really ought to shave that beard. You'll look like a deranged monk."

"Rasputin?" Edward had asked hopefully.

Persis had ignored him. "Just go. Then write me a ten-page letter, single spaced. Please try to remember what people wore." This from Persis, whose wardrobe consisted solely of sweatpants and turtleneck jerseys.

So he had shown up with Persis's friend's invitation. It would be tough to manage one page, let alone ten, he thought. Except for the clothing, it might have been the usual dull faculty party back at Columbia University in New York City. But here, half the men wore dark suits with pinstripes like tailor's chalk. The others were self-consciously bizarre. Edward watched, bored, as two men with screws through their ears and shaved heads necked beside the bookcase. The trouble is, he thought, I have lost my capacity for wonder. In fact, this pervading sense of staleness had prodded him into a sabbatical in the first place. Persis had diagnosed male menopause. Edward was, after all, fifty last month, and sometimes he looked older than that. As Edward had climbed into the back seat of the London taxi outside Heathrow, he experienced the customary sensation of reassurance, almost like a homecoming, yet six months in England had not produced a resurgence of vitality.

Perhaps it had to do with his research. The Bloomsbury group bristled with such lively nonconformists that modern society seemed pitifully prosaic in comparison. Or maybe it was his family. The

Vaughns were peculiar, a sprawling assembly of eccentrics. Edward remembered the month his mother took to wearing swim fins around the house in order to preserve the muscle tone of her legs and prevent varicose veins. His father had been so devoted to his goldfish that he had each one stuffed upon its demise and hung in the mobile above his desk in the study. After growing up in such a household, Edward found most outsiders of minimal interest. The trouble was, lately, nothing else much interested him either, not even his work. Edward tried not to dwell on the implications of such a fact. He had never been the depressed type. But he had awakened from a dream just last week, the image of a tombstone lingering. On it were inscribed the words: *This is all?* Complete with question mark. Edward shook his head and tried to focus on the party.

The two young men with the screws in their ears had become entangled. The business end of one screw had caught in the fabric of his partner's sweater. A small crowd gathered to offer advice and encouragement, but Edward managed a clear glimpse of the man in the sweater reaching out to touch the bare neck of his lover. Edward was struck by the tenderness of the gesture. Who are we to judge? he thought. Those two may share a love more passionate and enduring than Antony and Cleopatra, Solomon and Sheba, Romeo and Juliet. Perhaps contemporaries of those legendary pairs snickered at them as well. Romeo and Juliet were mere adolescents, after all. *Look at those silly bambinos!* the Veronese must have said. *Puppy love! Ridicolo!*

Edward had always suffered from a suspicion that he himself might just be faintly ludicrous. Ensconced within the wood-paneled high-ceilinged rooms of the Vaughns' rambling apartment on West Eighty-fourth Street, he felt normal enough. Even as children, Edward's brother and sister were stringy and nonathletic like him, the family sport being chess. Their extreme myopia that lent them a rather tentative demeanor in unfamiliar territory did not apply at home. Edward could negotiate the cluttered rooms in pitch dark, neatly side-stepping Victorian armchairs, dilapidated needlepoint sofas, and assorted gimcracks on pedestals. It was outside that posed the problem. Once thrust into the glare of Upper Broadway, Edward's nine-year-old heart would begin to pound, his mouth grow dry, and he would watch with a mixture of awe and contempt as troops of boys clambered off to Central Park with their baseball gloves.

Academic achievement was all very well and good at the public school on Seventy-ninth Street. There was a certain respect for "those brainy Vaughn kids." But one had to pass through the cruel years when anybody deviating from the norm in any significant way was subjected to the most virulent abuse. The uncool shoes, a geeky shirt, a nerdy jacket, a lack of finesse in the gymnasium, of all of these things Edward was pronounced guilty. He comforted himself by clinging to his siblings and to the certainty that the intellect shines like a pure beacon, illuminating and, in the long run, triumphing over human stupidity. (In Edward's fantasies, even the flaxen-haired Kelly O'Brien, who in the sixth grade had nicknamed him Ichabod, would ultimately see the light. He imagined her in later years saddled with the football star of model physique and small brain and several children who had inherited their father's mental midgetry and would never amount to a thing, lying awake at night, muttering to herself that it had all been a foolish miscalculation. Here she lay, trundled beside this numbskull, when she might have had someone of rare intellectual acuity like, say, Edward "Ichabod" Vaughn.)

It wasn't until later, when Edward was well into his college years, that he discovered that women liked him. There was, for instance, the wife of a French lit professor. At one of the early "at-homes," the hostess spent most of the evening on a couch with Edward discussing nineteenth-century female writers. By the time she got to Emily Brontë, she had removed her shoes and crossed her legs so loosely that Edward could see her peach-colored lace panties. Her attentions eventually blossomed into an affair, with Edward guilt-ridden and the professor's wife all the time insisting that true sexuality transcended the barriers of conventional morality. "Would Heathcliff have cared?" she would whisper. "Would Catherine Earnshaw?"

At first, Edward presumed she was a sexual deviant, a nymphomaniac. But to his continual surprise, he began to realize that many women responded to him, confided in him, let their hands brush his leg, and leaned forward with blouses unbuttoned precariously close to the navel. Persis explained that it was because he never condescended to women and that there was nothing more sexually stimulating than a man who actually regarded women as human beings.

"I must symbolize something," he would theorize, shaking his head.

"You take them seriously," Persis said.

"But why wouldn't I take them seriously?" Edward protested.

"See there?" Persis responded.

The party had escalated to the point where Edward's ears were defending themselves by generating a low-pitched steady hum. A pleasant-looking woman with a round face and a long Margaret Thatcher nose pulled up a chair beside him. "Are you anybody?" she shouted. She was encrusted with jewelry that seemed too outrageously opulent to be real.

"No," Edward replied.

"Me either. It's *such* a strain. How lovely in the corner away from the maddening crowd."

"Madding," Edward corrected her automatically. "What are you doing here if you're not anybody?"

She sighed. "I'm just one of life's observers. I have tons of money, you see, and they all think I'm bound to put some of it into the movies. I always get invited to these things, but they don't pay proper attention to me." She touched her hair, and the sparkle from her bracelet made Edward wince. She regarded him carefully. Edward saw her calculate, then arrive at some decision. "You look frightfully creative. Are you a starving artist?" she asked. Her voice held only mild curiosity.

"Teacher," he replied.

"Well, then, I'm certain you teach something frightfully exotic like the sexual practices of the aborigines. Oh, I suppose the Americans wouldn't go for it. They're such sillies about sex."

"I am."

"I beg your pardon?"

"A silly about sex," he said.

"Quite."

He waited, but she did not ask for particulars. Her eyes scanned the room. "Karen Wells is here," she said.

"The, uh, actress," Edward guessed.

"Oh, my God, the *singer*. This year's Barbra Streisand, Melissa Manchester, Linda Ronstadt."

"I've heard of Barbra Streisand," Edward said.

"I got up my courage and spoke to her. She was frightfully charming and looked as if she couldn't wait to get away." The dimpled cheeks were covered with a film of perspiration. "Golly, it's hot beside this thing. How can you bear it?" She stood up. "I haven't even got close to Sir William. If I can't shake his tiny paw, the entire evening shall have been a frightful waste. It's been charming talking with you. Have a lovely time in the mother country."

After she moved off, Edward stood up and tried to look animated. Julius Southwick, the subject of his current Bloomsbury research, would not have hung about in the corner at such a gathering. Julius would work the crowd, gossiping, telling outrageous jokes, even pinching a few bottoms here and there. Julius was a rogue. He was never bored. Edward sighed, took out a small notepad, and scribbled "It's such a strain" on it so as to remember for Persis. Then he left.

A young woman stood by the elevator. There was something about elevators, waiting for them, riding inside them, that produced a sepulchral silence. Edward wondered if people associated them with coffins. The shape was right.

Inside, Edward and the young woman sank about thirteen feet and lurched to a standstill. There was a heavy clanking sound, then nothing. Edward watched his companion. She stretched out a hand and punched the emergency bell. It set up a perpetual faraway ring. Edward thought the woman's fingers, short with unpainted nails, conflicted with the fur coat and glittery makeup.

"I hope I'm not going to have a claustrophobic fit and make a fool of myself," she said apologetically. Her voice was almost childish, it was so soft and light. "I've never been particularly fond of elevators. Lifts, I mean."

"It's all right, I'm American, too," Edward said.

"A-*ha!* It's a plot. Sabotage the Yanks."

"No doubt."

"Were you at the party?" she asked.

He nodded.

"I didn't see you there." She held out a hand. "I'm Karen Wells."

"Barbra Streisand of the eighties. I'm Edward Vaughn."

She gave him a gratified smile. "Hello, Edward." While Karen examined the panel for emergency instructions, Edward took a hard look at her. She was shorter than medium height, with a compact, athletic body. Her pale brown hair was straight and very thick, cropped like Buster Brown's in the old advertisements. She had intense blue eyes, dark lashes, and a wide mouth. When she pressed the bell again, a rhythmic thumping noise began far below. She shrugged off her coat and slid down into the corner. "May as well settle in," she said. "The Brits aren't so hot at fixing things."

Edward sat down and then tried to remove his topcoat. It was an awkward process since he was sitting on it. Karen watched a moment, then got up again and helped him. She folded the coat neatly and laid it down beside her.

"What would Edward Vaughn be doing at that blast in there?" she asked.

"Spying for my sister back in the States. She suffers from celebrity lust."

"And you don't?"

"I'm afraid I wouldn't know one if I trod on him. I gave up on movies when Jean Arthur retired."

"You knew who I was."

"Some stars shine through even my colossal ignorance."

Karen regarded him dubiously. "What do you do for a living?" She held up her hand. "No, wait, let me guess. You're an ace agent for William Morris." She giggled. "No, no, just kidding. Let's see. Tell you one thing, you're a hairy son of a gun."

"I play the lead guitar with a rock group called Hirsute."

She laughed. "You're a writer."

"Not so's you'd notice. Mainly, I teach," Edward said.

"Where and what?"

"Early twentieth-century literature at Columbia University. But I'm on sabbatical."

"But that's not strictly a vacation, is it?"

"No. I'm doing research for an article on a fellow named Julius

Southwick, a diarist from the Bloomsbury era. Virginia Woolf and so on."

"I thought you said you weren't a writer."

"Articles don't count. They merely keep you from getting fired."

"So why don't you do a book on this guy?"

"You sound like my sister," Edward said grimly.

"Sore subject?" she asked.

Edward smiled. "I guess perhaps it is," he admitted.

"So then tell me what's interesting about this Julius."

"He was a good gossip."

"Rona Barrett, eh?" She watched him. "Look at that, how terrific to meet somebody who never heard of Rona Barrett. Listen, Edward, I know you'd like to write that book. I can tell, but I promise not to harangue you about it. I feel the same way about poetry. God damn, I wish I could be a poet, but I don't have the depth. That's my excuse anyhow."

"Have you tried?"

"Yeah, but I've got this compulsion to rhyme everything. So I wound up writing lyrics instead."

"That's a kind of poetry."

"If you're Stephen Sondheim."

"Pretentious rot," Edward said.

"Hah! There's somebody else you've heard of."

"My sister's a poet," Edward said.

"She must be nice. You smile when you mention her."

"Is that so?" Edward thought it over. It was getting hot, even for him. The thumping had been joined by shouts far below.

"Do you suppose we could suffocate in here?" Karen asked.

But Edward was thinking about Persis. There was something in Karen Wells that reminded him of his sister. Physically, they could hardly have been more different. Persis was tall and rangy like him, her thick dark hair streaked with gray since her late twenties. Her austere good looks gave her authority, as if she should be running something, Hunter College, perhaps, or a consumer research group. But in actual fact, "absent-minded" did not go halfway to describing Persis. One night in January she made delicatessen history by getting herself locked inside Zabar's at closing time. They found her the next morning asleep among the giant coffee-bean bags. The manager sent her home with a smoked salmon, and the *Times* wrote her up in Metropolitan Briefs. She was always catapulting onto the wrong subway and telephoning Edward from someplace out in the hinterlands, like New Lots Avenue in Brooklyn. But for all her distractedness, she wrote poetry of power and originality.

Edward took a closer look at his fellow captive. Karen Wells would never get on the wrong subway, and yet there was something. Perhaps it was simply because he found himself interested in her, liking her. Persis was always telling him, ad nauseam, that he kept people at arm's length. "And look at the size of those arms," she would say.

"Edward, I'm boiling," Karen complained.

"If I'm not cold, it must be hot," he said.

Karen hummed a line as if setting his words to music.

"Is that how it's done?" he asked.

"Sometimes. But that one's no good."

"Why not?"

"Listen carefully." She hummed again.

"The man I love . . ." Edward warbled.

"Right. There's a group called Dried Fruit that just came out with a single. The composer must have been an Elvis fan because he's written 'Blue Suede Shoes' all over again. It can happen to anybody. You *have* heard of Elvis?"

"Of course," he answered with a certain amount of pride. "Why did you leave the party so early?" he asked her.

"I knew only one person there, and I'm shy," she said. Karen smiled at him. "I know, gimme a break. I used to watch those starlets tell Barbara Walters how they're really just shrinking violets. It made me laugh. But you know something, I walk into one of those parties and I'd just as soon hide behind the drapes."

"Isn't it merely another type of performance?"

"No, because I'm not singing. On stage, the music's something I can . . . wrap myself up in, like clothes."

"How extraordinary to be able to open your mouth and have beautiful sounds come out," Edward said. "When did you discover you could do that?"

"Oh, about eight, I guess, when my voice started to sound like something. But I was wild about music from the time I could speak. I knew how to operate the record player at fourteen months, and I played everything we had until the grooves were worn out. Let's see, we had Perry Como and *Peter and the Wolf* and some country stuff. My father finally broke *Great Romantic Compositions for the Piano* over the back of a chair."

"But they encouraged you, your parents?"

Perspiration had soaked the hair around her face, framing it in a dark oval. "Well, no, not exactly. Michael did, my brother, but not my parents. Mother has no music, she just . . . doesn't." Karen spoke with pity as if the woman were missing an eye or a leg. "Dad is gifted, but he doesn't think of it as anything special. Playing a banjo and singing is just part of living, like mucking out the barn and milking the cows. He could never figure out why it was such a big deal to me, why I had to have it, begging for piano lessons and all that. But he used to take us to concerts, my brother, Michael, and me, way back in the woods. People'd come from, oh, maybe two and three hundred miles, and these groups would jam, bluegrass, and half the audience wouldn't even be wearing shoes. We heard some pretty amazing stuff. Jim and Jesse and the Virginia Boys, Doc Watson, all the greats."

Edward was watching her and thinking of his own asphalt childhood. "I've never gone barefoot in my life," he said.

"My God," Karen whispered.

Edward laughed at the compassion on her face and began to undo his shoelaces.

"Nope," she said. "Doesn't count. It has to be outside. We'll go right down to Regents Park if they ever fix this thing. You have to promise."

"It's February."

"You'll like the frost. It crunches."

"All right." Edward grinned at her.

"Look how cute you are when you smile," Karen said.

Edward was trying to absorb the fact of his own cuteness when there was a crackling sound from the control panel. A distant voice sputtered, died, then erupted from the speaker. "Don't panic, mate, we'll get you down."

Karen signaled by tapping the floor with her foot. *Dot-dot-da-dot-dot. Dot. Dot.* "Know what?" she said. "I'm in no rush." Karen found that the evening had taken on a certain bite, a certain color, whereas before it had been soggy and gray like the flap of cardboard that stuck to her heel on her way to the car tonight. She studied Edward Vaughn. He did not look like anyone she had ever met. She was reminded of National Geographic television specials about water birds. Edward would walk that way, tentatively picking up a long leg and setting it down again with a slow bob of the head. A bearded flamingo with kind eyes. Deep and dark they were, with barely any white showing, and when he smiled, there was a startling wild quality that did something to the pit of her stomach. Tony's face popped into her mind. She blinked her eyes to erase him and he went away.

Karen had been observing herself in the movie of her life as far back as she could remember. By fifth grade she had become an expert commentator on the psychology of herself as the heroine. Even while she was in the midst of making a dumb mistake (in those days, spending all her Christmas money on a present for Dick Forrestal, who didn't even thank her; lately, sleeping with Moe Banda), she, as narrator, was instructing the audience that Karen Wells was, for instance, taking off her clothes for this man because there was a small part of her (very small, she hastened to mention) that asked for trouble. Looking back on it now, she realized she had been attempting a last desperate statement of independence from Tony. But certainly Moe Banda was a barracuda, and Karen explained in the voice-over that he would chew her up into Rice Chex-sized pieces if given the opportunity. On the other hand, he was an excellent lover. Not considerate or gentle, of course, but loaded with machismo, inventiveness, and stamina. The man was a stud, in other words, and what the hell.

In tonight's film clip, Karen watched herself realize that Edward Vaughn, for all his emaciated intellectuality, was reaching her on a visceral level. The heat didn't help, probably. Lord, it was hot, and there he sat, cool as Häagen Dazs. Karen was dripping. She plucked at the fabric of her blouse and it came away from her flesh with a sucking sound. Her mental camera zoomed in, straight down at the two occupants' heads, one tawny, one dark, with Edward's legs stretched out in front of him, his narrow feet askew at the ends as if they had been screwed on wrong. Christ, she was melting away.

"I figure Boston or New York," she told him, fanning her face with her hand.

"New York City, born and bred."

"I bet you went to Harvard."

He smiled. "Yes. How about you?"

"I'm a farm girl. Up near Ithaca."

"I assumed you were from California."

"I'm not that crazy."

"I guess it was that . . . fairy dust here." He reached out as if to touch her cheek. She felt the tiny breeze from his finger.

"Fairy dust," she echoed, smiling. "I have to do that kind of thing for the image, but at least it washes off. I had a manager once who wanted me to wear a safety pin in my right nostril. You married?"

"No."

"Gay?"

"No."

"Then why aren't you married? Forget I asked that."

"It's all right."

"Listen, once I started getting famous, people asked me the most incredible things. I had an interview with some lady in the States last month, wanted to know whether I ever masturbate. It's none of my business why you aren't married."

"I'd tell you if I had the answer." Edward thought for a moment. "I've never even come close."

"No long-term love affairs?"

He shook his head. "To my regret."

"You don't sound like you regret it."

"Don't I?" Edward looked at her sharply. He wondered if a musical ear intensified sensitivity to the nuances in human conversation.

"Maybe you don't like being crowded by anybody."

"I suppose I always assumed that someone would appear whom I'd wish to be crowded by."

"Maybe that's just bullshit," Karen said. "Propaganda by Hallmark cards."

"What about you? Is there anyone?" Edward asked. "Oh, sorry . . ."

She held up a hand. "Edward, I think I'd tell you anything you wanted to know. Don't ask me why, I've been interviewed to death lately. Actually, I do know why. You sit there looking sweet and curious, but you don't push. Oh, yeah, I've had some relationships . . ." She hunched her shoulders together as if she were being crushed in a vise.

The intercom popped, and suddenly a deep American voice buzzed out at them. "Karen? You up there?"

"Oh my God, it's Tony. My manager." Karen scrambled to her feet and talked into the receiver. "Yes, it's me."

"You okay?"

"Fine. Hot."

"I've been waiting down here for half an hour."

"Well, excuse me, I've been unavoidably detained."

"They went to get somebody who knows how to fix this thing. Hang in."

"Just have a six-pack waiting for us. We're frying."

"We?"

"For me and my friend."

There was a short silence, then the voice again, hurried. "Use the time to vocalize. You might be in there a while yet. Listen, get to bed as soon as you can. You need rest for tomorrow. Don't wait up. I've got to see some people. Bye." There was another burst of static and it was quiet again. Karen sat down with a sigh and smiled at Edward. "You want to be crowded by somebody, you just heard the world champion."

"I gather he's more than a manager." Edward spoke slowly, not really wishing to explore the subject.

"If Tony could find a way to walk around in my skin, he'd do it. He finds it so inconvenient dealing with my personality as a separate entity."

"Are you in love with him?"

"Oh. Love. There's only one human being I've ever really, truly loved, and that's my brother." She burst out laughing. "Well, that one just slipped right out, didn't it? I must be a real sick-o. Maybe I had some kind of perverse thing for him, or still do, even though he's been dead for thirteen years." She hesitated. "And since you don't ask, I'll tell you. He died in Vietnam."

"I'm sorry."

"They don't even know what happened to him. Jesus, Edward, I don't talk about this . . . We're just not going to get into it. I'm having too good a time. Oh, this heat. Three beads of sweat on your forehead and I'm dissolving like the Wicked Witch of the West."

They sat in comfortable silence for a moment.

"I like the farm," Karen said after a while. "I go back a few times a year."

"What about your parents?"

"Dad's pretty sick with arthritis. Mom's in charge now. She's really a pistol, but we're not exactly on the same wavelength." She stared off into space. Edward imagined that he could see blue sky and clouds floating across the surface of her eyes. "The horses never change," Karen continued. "I can be away a year and Jolie still recognizes me. I wish I could bring her down to Claremont Stables in the city, except she'd be miserable. That was the first thing I did when I made some money. I mean after I took care of some things for my folks. Got myself a beautiful mare. We ride in Central Park whenever I'm around. She's an urban animal, though. Disciplined. I don't think she could ever really let loose and fly like Jolie." She looked at Edward. "You remind me of Midler, you know. She's my New York horse. I think it must be the eyes."

It was somewhat unsettling. First he was cute, now he was equine.

"Tell me about your sister. What's she like?"

Edward forced himself to think of Persis. "She's immensely gifted and rather helpless."

"What does that mean?" Karen unbuttoned her blouse two notches. Edward caught a glimpse of tan line and felt an unaccustomed stirring.

"Helpless is inexact. Vague, perhaps."

"Give me a for-instance."

"All right." Edward paused. He had the teacher's habit of hesitating before he spoke so as to organize his sentences. "Last month my brother, Franklin, came into the city with his infant daughter. He had some business to attend to, so Persis volunteered to take charge of the baby. She pushed Delilah's carriage all the way down to the Public Library on Forty-second Street, ducked inside to borrow a book, depositing the baby at the side door with the guard. But she became enthralled with *The Late George Apley* and left by the front entrance, reading as she walked. She made it all the way to Sixty-eighth and Broadway before she remembered Delilah."

"Oh my God."

"It was Franklin's fault. He should have known better. Poor Persis went into a decline and couldn't write for days."

"Are you hung up on her?"

"On Persis?" Edward asked incredulously. He thought it over and found the notion preposterous, even hilarious. "I shouldn't think she's my type."

"Who is then?"

"That's not easy. Let's see. Dora Carrington."

"Who's that?"

"A Bloomsbury artist, long dead. Actually, she was fond of horses."

"You know why I'm asking."

"Yes," Edward said, "and I'm very flattered. But what would Karen Wells want with an old crate like me?"

"Damned if I know. I've always been partial to beautiful men."

"I was rather expecting you to protest the 'old crate' part."

"You're not insulted."

"No."

"Listen, I've got to take off my blouse. You won't be freaked out, will you?"

"No."

"I guess I've lost my youthful modesty. It happens when your changing room looks like Grand Central."

She slid the blouse off her shoulders and sat naked to the waist. "Take a good look and then you'll forget about it. Them."

Edward did as he was told. He had never been impressed with pendulous, bovine breasts. Karen's were small and perfectly round. He loosened his tie to keep her company.

Karen was grinning at him. *"I never knew abandon / Until I got abandoned / In a busted elevator / With you-oo-oo,"* she sang.

"Catchy," Edward commented, "but perhaps you'd sing a real one."

"I'll do you a dress rehearsal of my next concert."

"An undressed rehearsal," they said in unison and laughed.

She threw her head back against the wall, shut her eyes and hummed quietly to herself for a moment. Then she began to sing in a wistful soprano.

Where did the moon go
This morning?
Did the sunshine chase it
From the sky?
Who took away the magic
That lit the evening
With a million fireflies?
Look, the stars dried up and blew away,
The clouds are sad and bored
Just like your eyes.
I want to know:
Who stole the moon?
Who crept off with the stars?
Who stole your heart
And left an empty face behind?
Oh, last night we had the moonglow,
You touched me in the starlight,
The universe was endless, and so,
And so, you said, was like our love.
Forever was a whisper
Shimmering in the darkness;
I can't hear its echo

In the glare of morning.
Who had to turn forever into never?

The lilting sound built until longing, pure and potent, filled the elevator and seared Edward's insides like the thick fire from brandy on a cold night.

I want to know
Who stole the moon?
Who crept off with the stars?
Who stole your heart?
And left an empty face behind?

Edward sighed, thoroughly warmed at last. The song trailed off into a poignant coda. "*Who stole your heart and left an empty face behind . . .*"

Afterward, Karen kept her eyes closed for a while. When she opened them, Edward was staring at her. "That was lovely," he said.

"Thank you."

"You wrote that yourself?"

She nodded. "Corny."

"On the contrary. Poetic and moving."

The elevator lurched suddenly and Karen reached out for him. He caught her hand and held it.

"Sorry," buzzed the speaker. "We'll have you down in a jif."

"No hurry," Karen called.

"No," Edward said. His body was still tingling.

"That smile of yours makes you look unhinged," Karen said.

The elevator dropped with a squawk, then began to move slowly toward the lobby.

"Oh no!" Karen yelped. She grabbed for her blouse and stood up, but she was still buttoning when the doors slid open. Edward recoiled from the blinding, impenetrable assault of flashbulbs. "Come on!" Karen cried, clasping his hand. "Follow me! Barefoot in the park, remember?"

Faces and bodies materialized out of the spangled haze, but there were so many. He could hear Karen laughing. "You'll be an item, Edward! Edward!" But their fingers were forced apart and he lost her. She was surrounded by a mass of arms and legs that moved toward the exit in a single unit like some grotesque monster. A few stragglers remained behind to question Edward.

"Who're you, mate?" they wanted to know. One fellow held a microphone to Edward's mouth, but he was too preoccupied with trying to catch up with Karen. He reached the street just as she pulled away from the curb in a black limousine.

She waved frantically from the window. "Edward!" she called. "The Connaught, till Thursday!" Then she was gone.

"Dear Persis," Edward wrote. *"It's been an extraordinary evening . . ."* His handwriting, usually so precise and controlled, looked unfamiliar to him. It leapt and skidded across the blue air-mail stationery like the trail of a demented grasshopper that had fallen into a pot of ink. Edward ordinarily typed his correspondence, but somehow the prospect of the machine's metallic pecking seemed abrasive. He could still hear her voice—so pure and sad he could think only of Ophelia in the mad scene. He sighed, moved to the typewriter, and rolled the letter in. *"I met Karen Wells,"* he continued. What a sentence. It seemed the equivalent of "My first child was born today" or "Mother died in her sleep." *"I wish you were here right now,"* Edward wrote. In fact, he yearned for his sister. Persis, dear Persis, would drop into the faded red velvet armchair by the fire, wave her arms about like branches in a high wind, and analyze what had happened to him tonight.

"Smitten, Edward, that's what it is," she would gloat.

"But what do I do now?" he would demand.

"Enjoy yourself. For a change."

"She's involved with that manager of hers. He has a terrifying voice."

"She liked you, didn't she?"

"Yes. Christ, Persis, I'm not up to this."

"Of course you are." He was certain she would be in favor.

"I've never been infatuated in my life."

"What about Kelly O'Brien?"

"Don't be absurd. I was twelve years old."

"Adolescence was your finest hour," Persis would say. "When all the intensity wasn't intellectualized to death. You were rather heroic in unrequited love, hauling around that charm that fell off her bracelet in the cafeteria."

"I didn't know you knew about that," Edward would say. He wouldn't be surprised if she did. Persis knew just about everything.

It's no good, he decided, and flopped down on his bed to look up at the ceiling. Flaking paint, fourteen feet up, arranged itself into the shape of a face with wide eyes and a smiling mouth. There was such pain in her voice. She had mentioned a brother, a loss. Edward felt he would do anything to ease her sadness. If she were here, he would hold her, stroke her hair, put her to sleep in his bed and watch beside her all night in case she had a nightmare . . .

Oh, Persis, such excess, such intemperate balderdash from a man who is half a century old.

But Persis's image smirked at him from the corner.

He thought back to his last sexual encounter. Months ago, perhaps even six months it was now, with that professor of Victorian literature at the Boston conference. The woman had wanted it badly, and Edward had obliged, largely out of a sense of compassion. It was mildly enjoyable, rather like rice pudding on an upset stomach. Edward used to wonder if he lacked some essential male hormone. He would sit in the faculty room and listen to his cohorts discuss the comeliness of particular students. There was Mariah Cleary, who sat in the front row with her legs apart, *sans* panties. And Jennifer Kaplowitz, who contrived tearful conferences with her male teachers to confess her "abnormally intense drives."

"You were an invalid too long," Persis said not long ago. "Ardor makes your heart beat fast, and whenever you begin to feel anything, you put your hand to your chest and beg off."

"Are you talking about sex?" Edward asked.

"You know I am." She was crosslegged on his sofa in New York. Edward thought she looked like a praying mantis.

"Why are you beleaguering me?"

"Because I don't want you to miss anything."

"I like sex," Edward said. "It's like a fine meal, a hot bath . . ."

Persis was on her feet now. "Sex isn't any more stirring for you than taking a crap!"

"Sex isn't necessary," he answered calmly. "Bowel movements are."

"Christ, I feel sorry for any woman who gets involved with you."

"Fortunately, it's not likely," Edward said.

"Come off it," Persis said. "I've had at least half a dozen poor creatures come to me in despair during your wishy-washy lifetime. You must lead them on somehow or other."

"Nonsense."

Persis thrust her face an inch from his. "You have no passion, Edward. It's probably why you can't write a real book."

"And you have nothing but passion," Edward retorted, bridling at last. "No sense of perspective, no balance. You're the original primal scream."

Persis had retreated, stung, leaving Edward alone to analyze what he knew to be the truth.

He searched his mind for something with the power to arouse him. There was the Christopher Hogwood recording of the *Messiah,* certain paintings, poetry if it was very good, the ballet, and almost anything to do with Bloomsbury. So it wasn't as if he were without enthusiasms. But the insight struck him, one of those rare moments of clarity when it seems the wattage in the room has suddenly been increased. Excellence stirred him all right, but it was the excellence of the performance. There was nothing personal in the connection, no risk, not even a hint of possessiveness. Standing before Turner's *Whale Hunt,* his face would flush, his heartbeat quicken, but never did he experience the fantasy of plucking the masterpiece off the wall and carting it down the grand marble staircase under his arm. There was a kind of muted passion, he supposed, in his response to the execution of a perfect *jeté,* but again, where was the impulse to abduct Natalia Makarova and carry her off to his musty apartment? Perfection at a distance, that's what appealed to him. No intimacy. It seemed such a simple notion, he was astonished he had never thought of it before. But perhaps this was what Persis had been trying to tell him all along.

Still, he shrank from her extravagances. The outrageous love affairs always horrified him. There was the inevitable pattern of scenes beginning with the ecstacy of mutual discovery and winding up several months later with wrenching despair. Surely such embarrassing scenarios were not for Edward. Edward was a man of moderation.

And yet here in his bed beside the gas fire, Edward thought of Karen Wells and felt the thumping begin in his chest. The sensation was half terrifying, half exhilarating. He forced himself to recall her face, her breasts, her voice, while his heart bobbed about like Jonah in the great whale's belly. He closed his eyes and lay very still, arms stiff at his sides, and held on through the wild ride until finally, incredibly, he fell asleep.

Karen opened the window of the limousine and poked her face out, searching for Edward. There were too many faces on the crowded sidewalk. It seemed hopeless, but just in case, she shouted the name of her hotel. They pulled away, tires screeching.

"Where to, luv?" the driver asked.

"Take me for a ride, please, Jack. I don't care where, a park maybe. Then circle back here in a few minutes."

"Parks are closed."

"Anywhere, then. I just want to give them time to go away so I can find someone."

"Right you are."

They slid through the streets like a silent black fish. It was only ten o'clock but London had already shut down. Traffic was light and only a few strays hurried along, clutching their coats against the damp wind. With no heavy window gratings to screen their displays, the New Bond Street shops glittered festively. Karen began to sing to herself. *I never knew what it was all about . . .* Edward was homely, really. A prominent nose, a lumpy forehead to accommodate all those brains. And besides, men with beards were not to be trusted. What were they hiding behind all that hair, some repulsive carbuncle or perhaps a weak chin? Aesthetics had always swayed Karen. In childhood, it was the pretty Amanda Friar with the long russet braids who became her best friend. Michael had remonstrated with her. "Maryrose is a nice person. Intelligent," he said. "Why don't you spend more time with her?"

"She's so, well," Karen had hesitated to say it but the word hung between them. *Ugly.* "Her nose runs all the time. There's always that bubble sitting at the end." And she had a bad complexion and lifeless hair that dropped in strings.

"What's the difference what she looks like if she's got a first-rate brain? You can talk to her."

Karen had sighed. "But Mike, my eyes need something, too."

Karen leaned back against the plush seat. Past lovers paraded through her mind. She sorted them into two categories: handsome in the rugged, blond tradition, or sexually transfixing like Tony and Moe Banda. Edward Vaughn loitered at the edge of the lineup like a visiting professor who had strolled through the wrong door. He gazed at her with amusement. Those eyes behind the glasses were a lovely liquid brown. And when he grinned, she felt he was running his finger from her mouth all the way down to her crotch. Karen smiled, remembering the reporters' faces as she emerged from the elevator, still fussing with her blouse. Edward's grip had been strong on her arm. He had held her to the point of pain until they were wrenched apart by the crowd. She reached under her coat to touch her skin. Perhaps there would be a bruise.

"Here we are again, miss," Jack said.

The sidewalk was empty now. "Stop a second, will you, Jack?" But Edward was gone. She had no idea where he lived. Still, he had to have a telephone. She could track him down.

"Ready to go home?" Jack asked her.

"Yeah, okay, if you can take about half an hour getting there. It's such a pretty night." Karen did her best thinking in moving vehicles, cars, planes. Sitting still was not easy for her, but in the backseat of the limousine, there were simultaneously the comforting sensation of movement and the freedom to let her mind wander.

As far back as she could remember, she had been plagued with a kind of obscure yearning that felt almost physical. It lived in her chest, sometimes glowing quietly but now and then flaring up into a blaze that brought tears to her eyes. Michael would look at her and ask what was wrong, but she could only shake her head helplessly. Then he would fetch her guitar or escort her to the battered old upright piano. It helped to sing. The stinging fire would recede again and she could get on with life. For years, she had supposed that success as a performer would satisfy her need, and now, after Midem, it appeared that she might actually find out. There was great joy in the achievement of professional recognition. And yet, there was something almost impersonal about it. She and Michael had talked about love.

"Don't you want to fall in love?" she had asked him.

"Yeah, sure," he had said.

"No, but I mean urgently. Like it's an emergency."

He looked up from his sketchpad. "Quit bouncing around, will you? I can work up some urgency for sex. As for love, it'll wait until I'm ready to get married."

So for years, Karen poured out songs of love as if to a blurred photograph propped on a kind of altar in her mind. She had tried to fit specific faces into that picture frame: her sophomore history teacher, the guitar player in her first band, the manager who talked her into a brief stint with punk rock, even (or maybe especially) Tony Kahanian. The self-induced infatuations inspired her to write and perform songs so convincing she practically broke her own heart. And yet that mental portrait remained indistinct, and the lovers disappeared sooner or later, with little regret from Karen. She realized, through the ruthless lens of her autobiographical camera, that since songs never emerged without feelings, a kind of self-hypnosis was required to produce a creative emotional state. With the exception of her rebellion with Moe Banda, Tony had been the only man in her life for a very long time. He held enormous power over her, but it was difficult to convince herself that she had ever truly been in love with him or anyone else. When that happened, surely the man would be a fellow musician with a beautiful body and intense sexuality, a subtler, sensitive, thinking man's Bruce Springsteen.

And then tonight, the photograph had snapped into focus almost audibly, like a slap across the face. There it hung, stage center in her brain, and the face framed in neon suggested not Bruce Springsteen but the great-great-uncle in the photograph over her parents' fireplace, a solemn bearded gentleman in an odd black coat. No wonder she had never come close to this feeling before. It had happened so quickly, as if that elevator were some kind of magical box. Perhaps any two people stepping inside would be similarly stricken. What if Sir William MacIntyre had been her fellow captive? Or even Guy Burlingame? Enter unsuspecting on the tenth floor with a polite nod to the stranger beside you; stagger out at the lobby a besotted fool.

"I'm a pop singer," she murmured to herself, as if that explained it. Perhaps it was the music. She had written a few of those songs herself, instant romance, love at first glimpse. "Thunderbolt," for example, a hard-driving number with a relentless backbeat of drums. *You've taken me by storm, babe / Eyes like lightning / Voice like thunder / Yeah, electrified me, filled my nights with wonder* . . . Could it be that after all these years of singing the stuff, she had fallen for her own lyrics?

Edward Vaughn. Well, that was it, for whatever reason. It seemed as clear as the fact that she would sing until her vocal cords dried up and turned to dust. As the splendid Marble Arch drifted past the window, bathed in golden spotlights, Karen began to sing again. *I never knew what it was all about / Then you showed up and turned my life around / It's no use to cling to the familiar / Cause tonight familiar's standing upside down.*

Karen woke early. It took a few seconds to remember why she felt disoriented. Perhaps she had forgotten traveling on to yet another city, another hotel room. It had happened before. She would wake up thinking she was in Los Angeles when in fact she had returned to New York the night before. But no, there was the graceful Regency mirror hanging above the dresser. This was London. Still the sensation persisted; something critical had shifted in the night. Then she remembered. Edward. The memory of his face flooded her with such giddy joy that she began to laugh out loud. She glanced quickly at the other double bed. It was rumpled but empty. She plumped her pillows and sat up. Fragments of last night's delirious dreams murmured in her mind like pieces of songs begging to be written. But Edward had been torn away from her. How would she ever find him? She sprang out of bed and opened the drawer that held the bulky series of London telephone directories. There were several Vaughns, but no Edwards or even *E*'s. She would just have to wait for him to get in touch. After all, he knew where she was. Her alarm rang, and she reached out automatically to shut it off. In the meantime, there was her debut with *Britvideo,* the quaint and cumbersome relic of a television program that began as England's version of *American Bandstand* and was still regarded as a necessary step in the climb to international stardom.

After she had showered and dressed, she gave herself a quick inspection in the mirror. Her appearance was the subject of much dispute with Tony. Karen preferred light makeup and towel-dried hair, a look that Tony dubbed her Andy Warhol face. And this morning, she rationalized, the television studio would redo her own efforts anyway, so why bother? She bounced down the sedate wooden staircase into the Connaught's hushed lobby and out onto the streets of Mayfair. Karen had visited Great Britain once before, as the opening act for the forgettable Miles Delight. That tour took her to cities like Manchester, Liverpool, and Hull rather than London. Today she stood transfixed as taxis whizzed past like toy beetles on wheels. A policeman in his Bobby helmet ambled down the street, twirling a truncheon. The sight of such symbols was simultaneously thrilling and reassuring, as if England provided some atavistic sense of parental security.

The winter morning was unseasonably mild but thick with moisture. No wonder the English had such gorgeous skin, Karen thought, with all that water packed into the atmosphere, like a gigantic humidifier. She entered Hyde Park at Grosvenor Gate. Through far-off curls of ground fog, she could see a pair on horseback rising in and out of the mist like phantoms, soundless and ghostly astride two dark mounts, the man in a red waistcoat, the woman in black. They seemed like apparitions from another century, lovers who would dissolve into thin air when the sun dried out the morning.

Neat flower beds lined the footpaths. Karen imagined them blooming, disciplined and orderly, in the spring. Countless early-morning rides had given her an intimate connection with New York's Central Park. From Midler's sleek back she observed the arrival of spring with joy. But there the daffodils and narcissus were scattered chaotically beside the track and in the underbrush along the roadway, the brave blossoms forced to keep company with assorted debris—cellophane wrappers, stray gloves, bottle caps, and used condoms. Perhaps if America were permitted to accumulate another two hundred years of history, it might achieve a reverence for such things as public gardens and monuments unstained by graffiti.

The *Britvideo* studios were housed in an ugly concrete structure beyond Bayswater Road. It appeared that the English had not yet mastered the art of modern architecture. Karen found their twentieth-century buildings uniformly hideous.

Tony Kahanian paced outside the entrance. Cardboard coffee cup in hand, he tracked back and forth, glancing up every few seconds in search of Karen. Beneath the rumpled topcoat, he wore one of the new suits Karen had chosen for him, expensive wools that looked exquisite on the hanger. But as soon as they were persuaded onto Tony's lumbering body, they became creased and exhausted. The waistband of his trousers began the day at midtorso but soon enough worked its way down until cuffs bagged over shoes. His thick blue-black hair grew in wild cowlicks, and his heavy beard cast a perennial shadow across his face. But Tony used his appearance to advantage. People lowered their guard, presuming an interior sloppiness to match the exterior.

When Karen was first hired to sing at *Tony's* in the West Twenties, she, too, had supposed the proprietor to be a rather easygoing fellow. But she soon began to notice that if a waiter mistreated a customer (and Tony was the sole interpreter of such a breach), there were no second chances. Musicians were expected to behave, as was the audience. Drunks and hecklers were ejected, often by Tony personally, and were not allowed back. Karen had endured many bistros where the singer was considered prey to a mob of unruly cretins. She had been struck in the head by a beer bottle and once had her cheek burnt by a cigarette lobbed from a front table. (Karen was oblivious to the wound at first, so deeply immersed was she in her music. It was only afterward, when she put her hand to her swollen cheek, that the drummer told her what had happened.)

With its atmosphere of congenial order, *Tony's* soon became her favorite place to work. During her third engagement there, Tony showed up at Karen's cramped dressing room after the show and announced his intention of becoming her manager. "Like Pop always says," Tony had urged, quoting his Armenian patriarch, " 'if the shoe fits, lie in it.' " She was flabbergasted, but acting on instinct, she agreed. And here they were in London a mere five years later, fresh from triumph in Cannes.

Karen watched Tony pace as she came within range and realized with a kind of jolt that he did not yet know about Edward. She was accustomed to Tony's scrutinizing every detail of her life, including the brand of tampons she used. She stopped on the sidewalk, staring at him with a mixture of fear and defiance. Tony had found out about Moe Banda the day after she slept with him, God only knew how. There had been all hell to pay, with Tony ranting and threatening and sulking. But Tony knew Karen well and quickly came to understand that Moe Banda meant nothing to her. Edward was another matter entirely. Karen's heart beat with panic as she imagined Tony elbowing his way into this new and tender world she had accidentally stumbled upon. She had to find a way to keep him out.

Tony looked up to see her standing halfway down the street. "Jesus, girl! Are you coming or not?" he shouted, running to meet her. "They wanted you in makeup fifteen minutes ago! Why in hell didn't you use the driver?" He grabbed her under the elbow and propelled her into the building.

"Cream cheese for breakfast?" she asked him, her eyes on his lapel.

He scraped absently at the spot with his fingernail. "Director's got delusions of grandeur. Thinks he's choreographing the queen's fucking wedding. Christ, you're slow." She allowed herself to be dragged down a long hallway and into the brightly lit mirrored makeup room. Tony plopped her into a chair and watched critically as the makeup man began applying extra touches that would render her presentable for a taping.

"Pity to put anything on this face," the man said, dabbing at her forehead with cotton. "Fabulous skin, like my eight-month-old niece's little—"

"Watch that dark spot beside her nose," Tony interrupted. "And she needs highlighting on the right cheekbone. She's lopsided." Karen rolled her eyes at the makeup artist. His breath smelled pleasantly of wintergreen.

"Fancies himself Helena Rubinstein, does he, dearie?" he whispered. Karen smiled as he swung the chair around, presenting her for approval. "All done."

"More lip gloss," Tony said. The makeup man obliged. Karen climbed out of the chair as the director rushed in, clipboard in hand. He greeted Karen with his eyes on her dress.

"That'll strobe. Have you got something else?"

"Yes, as a matter of fact . . ." Karen reached into her pouch which contained an unpatterned blue dress.

Tony covered her hand. "It won't strobe," he said.

"It will."

"Tony, I can change in two seconds," Karen said.

The makeup department stood in silent fascination against the mirrors waiting to see what would happen. The director, a slim pouting man with fair hair, was used to getting his way.

Tony glowered at Karen. "You'll look like a frump in that blue rag. Besides, this one came across in the Cannes interview." He spoke directly to her, as if it were she alone who defied him. "You're not changing."

Karen understood at once that Tony was offering the director a chance to save face in front of his employees. "All right," she sighed. "Have it your way, you bully."

It was clear that Tony would not yield. The director deliberated, then decided to cut his losses. "Far be it from me," he said, "to insert myself into a domestic dispute. This way." He took Karen's elbow.

The studio was a vast barn of a room with wires and cables writhing from the shadowed corners and across the floor. Karen and the others picked their way carefully to a raised platform where disco lights flickered like confetti tossed against the darkness. The small audience of young people began to applaud when they saw Karen. She waved and made a little curtsy.

Suddenly the first bars of Karen's record blasted through the speakers. "Oh, Lord," she moaned to the director. "I can't bear to lip sync. Will it screw up the tape if I sing along?"

"Depends on how loud you are. Try it. If it doesn't work, they'll stop you."

Surreptitiously, in a ritual dating from her first talent contest, Karen crossed herself. It had begun as a kind of joke. She was not a Catholic, after all. In fact, her vague Protestantism consisted of the occasional attendance at midnight services on Christmas Eve. And yet, it began to seem that venturing forth on a stage without this gesture, this token invocation, only courted disaster. She had forgotten once, at a gig on the edge of Lake Ontario north of Rochester.

A drunken college student flung himself at Karen in midperformance, knocking her over in a spray of cheap beer and precipitating a brawl that involved the drunk's fraternity brothers and the members of the band. Every dollar of the group's fee went toward paying for repairs in the demolished bar. Secretly, Karen suspected the incident might have been avoided if she had remembered her good-luck gesture. Besides, other performers indulged in their own pre-performance rites. Denny Harper slipped a special pebble into his right shoe, never mind the discomfort. Marlena Caryatid refused to walk out onto a stage unless she had practically bathed in 4711 cologne. Performing was too scary to manage alone. One needed some kind of armor.

After a few false starts, the music began in earnest. Karen tried to look convincing. *Didn't I always tell you? / Didn't I? Didn't I?* The song had a relentless backbeat and energy that she liked, utilizing the anger that had exploded out of her first big blowup with Tony. She smiled, remembering the scene of their shouting match on the corner of Eighteenth Street and University Place. Tony had spent a week trying to persuade her to cut her hair.

"You look like an albino Shirley Temple and just about as sexy," he had complained.

"Leave me alone. I had my teeth done, didn't I? That ought to satisfy you. Besides, long hair's erotic."

"Not if it makes you look prepubescent."

So in the night, while she slept, he had attacked the disputed tresses with a pair of kitchen shears. The hatred she had felt for him was one of the purest emotions she had ever experienced. But she was forced to admit that the incident provoked her first real hit, not to mention a very becoming new haircut.

Karen tried not to cringe as the song continued toward the dreaded spot. Coming up in the next line was a B-flat that was not quite clean enough. The technicians in the recording studio had told her it was perfect, but Karen knew better. And now she would regret that note forever. *You said, you said I'd never leave / I told you so, I told you so.* Karen screwed up her face as if she were screaming with triumphant rage while nothing emerged from her mouth except a wisp of sound. The audience held their hands above their heads and clapped rhythmically. Karen began to feel dangerous hilarity gurgle deep in her throat. What a strange species we are, she thought, executing such ludicrous contortions to entertain ourselves. Music was supposed to be a direct form of communication, and here she stood in a mock performance, parodying herself for television. What would an interplanetary alien make of it? What would Edward Vaughn make of it? She imagined his quizzical, tolerant amusement. Laughter was inevitable. Here it came, what the hell. And then it was over. There was enthusiastic applause and cheering.

Tony was upon her. "What the fuck was that all about?" he wanted to know, sweeping her away from the crowd.

"I particularly liked the haunted laughter," the director puffed, trying to keep up. "Bitter mirth of an outraged lover. Very creative." Karen shot him a grateful look.

"Came off like a smirk to me," Tony muttered.

"Well?" Karen said, waiting for more.

"Other than that, it was all right."

"She was sensational," the director said, and gave her a peck on the cheek. "Really, darling, you're an original. Tell me, do you honestly and truly write all your own material?"

Karen glanced at Tony.

"Not any more, she doesn't," Tony said.

"Yes, I do," Karen said sweetly. "Writing the music is really what I enjoy most about this crazy business."

"Takes too goddamn long to churn them out," Tony complained. "We're going to let somebody else write the stuff, and she'll get out there and sing her heart out." He turned to Karen. "Could have used a little more body language. Like Pop says, 'If you're going to give 'em an inch, you may as well give 'em a mile.' "

Karen explained to the director. "Tony believes in focusing on the negative."

"Actually," the director said, hesitating, "there was one slight hitch . . ."

Karen sighed, waiting for the inevitable.

"We lost you on camera three. It'll be fine if we just shift your mark stage right. Once more ought to do it."

But of course, once more wasn't nearly enough. The sensitive electronic equipment snagged piece by piece, then Karen's makeup had to be redone, then the technicians had to break for tea. The process wound up taking four hours. Karen reminded herself that live television would have terrified her. At least taping the half-hour program permitted a certain level of perfection. During the delays, she perched on a stool and sipped coffee, chatting with members of the audience and signing autographs. Recording her album had taught her patience. In fact, if she had been in less of a rush then, that fuzzy B-flat could have been corrected.

Finally it was over. There were kisses and handshakes all around. Tony and the director might have been old buddies.

Outside in the pale sunshine, Tony handed her a slip of paper. "Here's Burlingame's address. I suppose you're going to walk it, but don't be late. I've got to see that Brit lawyer about the tour. Christ, another English meal." He rubbed his stomach protectively and fumbled at an open button. "Listen," he said, peering closely at her. "You feeling okay?"

"Sure, why?"

"Dunno. You look a little weird."

Karen knew he was trying to see inside her brain, where the image of Edward shimmered. She closed her eyes, hiding him. "I'm tired, that's all."

"Or maybe not tired enough. It's been almost a week." Karen ignored the reference, and Tony shrugged. "I can wait. You women get a hormone imbalance when you travel trans-Atlantic."

Karen, relieved at his complacency, allowed the outrageous remark to pass. "Was it really okay in there?"

"Yeah, you were fine. See you at the hotel, no later than six." He passed his hand behind her neck, gave her a bristly kiss on the cheek, and walked away.

"Aye-aye, your grandiosity," she called after him, trying to ignore the tingling sensation where his fingers had brushed her skin. "Like Pop says," she murmured, " 'Timeliness is next to cleanliness.' " She had asked Tony once, "If you and your father never speak, how come you're always quoting him?"

"Because he's a shrewd old bastard and he taught me everything I know about business. And I'm not always quoting him."

Tony's father ran a Middle Eastern restaurant in the East Twenties near where Tony grew up. Mr. Kahanian ruled like a despot over five sons, enlisting them in the restaurant as soon as they were old enough to push a broom. Tony, "the trouble-maker," was sandwiched in the middle. "I was too much like him," Tony told Karen. "The fights were so wild that sometimes the cops came. Once he flung a silver platter at me, you know, like a Frisbee. It sliced right into the wall behind my head and hung there vibrating, *whan-n-g*."

The final breach had occurred when Tony tried to focus his father's attention on the youngest boy. Stefan, terrified of his father and of the world in general, had sought refuge in drugs. Mr. Kahanian's icy rage had frightened even Tony. He listened helplessly as his father arranged with the local precinct to have Stefan locked up for three nights, "Just to put a scare under his behind." Tony moved out, and on the fourth morning, he removed Stefan from jail and took him to his new apartment on the West Side. But despite Tony's solicitude, Stefan eventually overdosed and died at the age of nineteen. Tony had not spoken with his father since.

I'm in London, Karen reminded herself. It was easy to forget that fact around Tony. The atmosphere surrounding him hummed with New York City. His gestures, his voice, even the aroma of his trenchcoat conjured up harried New Yorkers hurtling down congested sidewalks, cabs honking, vendors shouting. Karen's armpits grew damp whenever she was around him.

Last summer she had dragged Tony to a cousin's wedding out in wealthy King's Point. Although she had not seen Rosemary since they were both fifteen, Karen was curious about this branch of the family her father called the "Oil Well Wellses." But Karen had not realized that Tony, even more than she, was an anomaly in that world of tea sandwiches and slices of cucumber garnished with caviar. A discreet trio of strings played show tunes, but nobody danced. The women wore simple, expensive dresses, and despite the fact that the guests became quite drunk due to a minimal amount of food, the decibel level remained low. Tony prowled around like a grizzly at a cocktail party. Karen could pick out his gravelly voice no matter how far he strayed, and his wild hair poked up over the careful coiffures of the other guests. Finally, he sat on an eighteenth-century chair and one of the legs gave way, spilling him with a crash onto the polished floor.

"Fucking thing's made of toothpicks," he had complained to Karen.

Here, too, in this land of miniature automobiles and vine-covered buildings with the trusting ungated windows, Tony was incongruous.

She had not slept with him right away, resisting for fear of losing herself altogether to his powerful personality. She held her wardrobe sacrosanct as well. It pleased her to invent costumes for her performances, despite Tony's complaints that her choices were too tailored and mannish. He took to showing up at her dressing room with a gown tossed over his arm, or she would arrive to find something already draped across a chair or hanging behind the door. After several months of this subtle invasion, curiosity won out as Tony had known it would. Karen began to investigate the clothes, letting the soft fabrics caress her fingers, even surreptitiously trying things on. The effect startled her at first. Sometimes the necklines revealed a substantial portion of her lightly freckled breasts. "*You* are not a horseback-riding farmgirl," she would accuse the fragile reflection in the mirror. Eventually, confronted with an electric blue chiffon that made her eyes look like chips of sapphire, she succumbed. She strode wordlessly past Tony on her way to the stage. His only comment after the performance was that she had "sung sexy." Otherwise, he never mentioned his victory. Soon afterward, he took charge of her makeup, her dentist appointments, and her checking account. "How did I get these hiccups, Tony?" she would tease him. "Did you authorize these hiccups?"

The first time they made love was the night of her debut at the High Cloud Café in Greenwich Village. Word had crept out that Karen was someone to be heard, so augmenting the faithful from *Tony's* were a throng of uptown people and a smattering of Broadway denizens. The place was packed, and there were dozens herded at the door hoping to slip inside. Karen wore one of Tony's choices, a sheer paisley silk and underneath nothing but minuscule black panties. She performed for two and a half hours, but they refused to let her go. Finally, with her voice growing hoarse, she began to sing a torch-type composition she had never tried out in public. *You sought me, you bought me / You taught me how to cry* . . . She stood barefoot with her back arched, her damp dress clinging to her breasts. She was in a kind of sexual trance. She wanted to make love to the entire audience, to strip off her clothing and throw herself into that ecstatic crowd and be devoured by them. The song was over, the spotlight went black, and in the din of wild applause she moved offstage, and there was Tony looking down at her. He held out his arms and picked her up off the ground. She wrapped her legs around his waist and he carried her that way to her dressing room where they locked the door and made love on the floor to the sound of frantic pounding and yelling outside. She remembered later that he had murmured, "I love you, Christ, I love you. I'll never stop." But he had never said it again. From that night on, he usually came to her apartment and spent the night in her bed. There was no getting away from him.

Or at least that was how it had been until last week. Tony had taught her the power of sexual attraction. He was a tireless, inventive lover, and Karen had come to depend on the release that sex provided. A lot of performers took drugs to come down after an all-night gig. Karen wondered sometimes if sex wasn't her own form of cocaine. The thought frightened her.

When they arrived in London, Karen had insisted upon separate rooms, pleading a need for space. There had been a heated argument, with Tony finally making a great show of relenting to demonstrate his "flexibility." Nonetheless, he had managed to slip into her room every night to sleep in the other bed. He hadn't touched her.

Guy Burlingame plucked his handkerchief into three perfect points and arranged it carefully in his jacket pocket. He glanced at his watch. She was fifteen minutes late. Perhaps she had forgotten the appointment, or perhaps Tony Kahanian had neglected to give her his address. When the desk buzzer sounded, he started.

"Miss Wells," said the disembodied voice from the speaker.

"Show her in, please."

Guy went to the door, reminding himself not to grab her. He

would permit himself a tiny hug, but no more. Over the years, Karen had made it clear in her gentle fashion that she was uninterested in any sexual connection.

"Hi, Burlingame. Sorry I'm late." Her obvious delight at seeing him simultaneously warmed and dismayed him. There was no other woman on the face of the earth who held such power to rattle him, and Lord knew, he'd met hundreds of the most glamorous females extant.

"How's it going?" Karen asked. She strode to the window and looked down at the trees in Soho Square. Then she settled herself into a chair opposite his desk. "Nice office. I hope *Orbit* is treating you right. I miss having you in New York."

"It's been amusing so far. The Brits regard me as some sort of half-genius, half-freak."

"Listen, I was a little blasted on champagne at the party and forgot to ask. Are you okay? Last time I talked to you, there was this little thing on your cheek that was supposed to come off . . ."

"I'm fine. No more ultraviolet rays for Guy, however. So sad. I used to take such satisfaction in out-tanning George Hamilton. Now hush, darling. I'm supposed to be interviewing *you*."

After many hours of puzzling over his fascination with Karen, Guy had decided that one of the elements was her lack of ego. The world of show business reeked with narcissism. Guy's favorite incident along these lines was his interview with Valerie Gordon, which took place beside the pool at her palace in Beverly Hills. Valerie's slick peach lips had launched into a monologue about her various benefit performances and how such projects gave her "such a warm feeling, like, it makes you feel a part of the world community, you know?" when her housemaid showed up with two tall glasses of iced tea. Suddenly, as Guy reached for his, the tiny Mexican woman collapsed onto the flagstone and lay there like a pile of empty clothes. Guy was on his knees beside her in an instant, loosening her collar and propping her head to open a channel for air.

"Low blood sugar," Valerie remarked from her perch on a deck chair. "She'll be okay in a few minutes."

"How about calling a doctor?" Guy asked.

"I'm telling you, she'll come around." Valerie glanced at her Rolex with some impatience. "I've got an aerobics class in half an hour, so I'll just keep talking. Lord, I hope it doesn't take her too long this time. There're people coming for cocktails."

So Guy sat on the ground beside the unconscious woman while Valerie smoothed suntan oil on her face and rambled on about her latest film, how everybody on location had been "just like a family, everybody so, you know, simply darling," and how her latest marriage would, she hoped, yield half a dozen children whom she could barely wait to "nurture" because she was really an earth mother in disguise (this last remark accompanied by a tiny tinkling laugh).

As predicted, the maid recovered. She sat up, blinked, and began silently gathering pieces of shattered glass. When Guy asked if she was all right, she looked at him with surprise.

Then there was Karen Wells. When Guy's brief marriage began to break up, it was Karen who carved hours out of her demanding schedule to offer support and a willing ear. It wasn't that she was unconditionally sympathetic. Far from it. Karen expressed her firm opinion that Guy's obsessive-compulsive behavior was driving Christine away. "You have to make allowances for spilled nail polish on the bathroom tiles and pantyhose drying in the shower," Karen told him.

"But she uses my razor," Guy protested. "And she even leaves little tiny hair shavings in the sink."

"Keep Christine and get a better cleaning lady," Karen advised. When it was all over, she took him out to an expensive restaurant and held his hand while he got ludicrously drunk.

And here she sat today, focusing her attention on him without a thought for herself. The novelty of this particular quality of hers never failed to move him.

"How did it go at *Britvid?*" he asked.

"All right, they tell me. Lip sync is really so silly. I was tempted to mouth the lyrics of the 'Battle Hymn of the Republic.' "

"Well, think of poor Molly Martin. She can *only* lip sync. Put her in front of a live microphone and all you hear is a death rattle. How's the single doing?"

"Number twelve in *Billboard* and climbing."

"And the album?"

"The album is alive and well," Karen answered.

"Is that why you look so smug?"

"Do I?"

Guy narrowed his eyes. "What's going on between you and Tony these days?"

"Copacetic. You're acquiring an English accent."

"Don't be so slippery." There was something different about her today. She was practically setting off sparks. "Are you pregnant?"

Karen burst out laughing. "Sorry, dear. No, I'm not pregnant."

"There's something . . ." Guy felt the cool journalist take over. She was holding back. He glanced at the newspaper clipping on his desk. There was a photograph of Karen emerging from the elevator. Her head was turned toward the blurred bearded face behind her shoulder. The man's bespectacled eyes stared out owlishly. "Hey, Wells," he said suddenly. "Who was that person in the elevator?"

"You mean Edward."

"I mean Edward who?"

"Vaughn," Karen said.

Guy wrote the name on his pad and drew a rectangle around it. "Tell me about him."

"No."

"How come?"

"Not ready."

"You can't mean there's something going on *there*." Guy's voice was incredulous. Karen merely smiled at him. "Look, Karen, from what I saw, he's not exactly your type."

A grin burst its restraints and spread across her face. "Isn't it amazing?"

"Isn't *what* amazing? Jesus!" Guy inserted a cigarette into a mother-of-pearl holder and lit up.

"That Edward isn't my type," Karen explained.

"So there's nothing."

"I didn't say that."

"You're having a fine time, aren't you? So what is he, your shrink? Your grandfather? What?"

Karen shook her head. "I'm sorry. I'm in a state of great . . . weirdness today."

"I can see that. How long have you known him?"

"Long enough."

It looked to Guy as if she was trying to suppress more laughter. "Karen . . ."

Suddenly she began to bubble. It was like watching a pot boil over. Guy stared at her while his cigarette turned into a worm of gray dust. "Look," he said finally. "There's been a lot of pressure, Cannes, the album . . ."

Karen took one deep shuddering breath, then another. "It's only that I'm so happy," she whispered. "I'm not used to it. And confused. Oh, boy, am I confused."

"I never thought of you as being particularly *un*happy."

"Make that delirious. I'm delirious."

"I'd like a photo of you and this Edward character."

"I don't think he'd like that."

"Tell me about him. What does he do for a living?"

"He's a scholar."

"Ah, he's broke."

"I suppose so."

"How will you see him? You're not in the U.K. that often."

"He's American."

"Christ, I never would have guessed that." Guy took another look at the photograph. "Lithuanian, maybe."

"Don't be so bitchy. I think he's cute."

Guy smiled at her. "Okay, he's cute. But we're side-stepping a certain rather crucial issue here, aren't we?" Guy watched the glow disappear. She was like a television set when the picture fades from color to black-and-white.

"Tony," she said.

"Exactly."

"Oh, God. I tell myself the man's my manager. I'm not married to him. He's never, well, nothing's ever been said about any kind of formal commitment or anything."

"But?"

"But. Well, you know, everybody knows, we've been together in a way, more than a business way. Oh, shit." Her face pleaded with Guy. "What am I supposed to do? Here's this amazing situation, this incredible man I'm so drawn to, I don't know why. Am I supposed to just drop it and never find out what it all means? Look, I know it could come to nothing. I spent a couple of hours with him in an elevator. But Guy, he's already taken up residence inside my head. And then Tony . . . well, Tony's got this proprietary interest in me. But I'm not his wife, am I?"

"Oh, dear," Guy said.

"That's all? 'Oh, dear'?"

Guy lit up another cigarette. "You, of all people, are well aware of my complete incompetence in the field of human relationships."

"Tony's responsible for everything. The album, Midem, the tour coming up. He orchestrated it all. If it weren't for him, I'd still be back in some ratty little club."

"Quit breast-beating. Don't you think you've had a little something to do with your own success? It's *your* voice, not Tony's. God forbid."

"I wouldn't have known what to do with it." Karen's restless hands fussed with a memo on his desk, folding the corners into triangles. Finally she looked up at him with a sigh. "Tony's been the most important person in my life for such a long time. I've resented him terribly, the way he just took everything over until I couldn't blow my nose without his instructions. But I've depended on him and he's never let me down. And then there's the sex thing." She hesitated. "That's been pretty . . . powerful, although recently . . ."

Guy exhaled a billow of smoke. "What are you going to do, Wells?"

Karen put her hands to either side of her head. "My brain feels like that scene in *2001,* you know, where the pilot is catapulted into another dimension. Everything is rushing past the windows like some kind of crazy kaleidoscope. Lord, what a trip. Edward's probably forgotten all about me already. I haven't heard from him." She reached out and grasped his hand. "I promise, if anything significant happens, you'll always be the first to know about it."

And so she left. Guy sat at his desk for a long time, gazing down at the photograph of Karen and Edward. "Some interview," he murmured finally, and wadded the clipping into a tight little ball.

* * *

"Persis Vaughn! V-A-U-G-H-N! Somewhere on the West Side, I think!" Karen could barely hear the operator. "Yes, P. Vaughn, that'll do! Thanks!" she yelled, and took down the number.

The voice on the other end sounded sweet and breathy, not at all what she had expected from a sister of Edward. Tallulah Bankhead, perhaps, but not Mariel Hemingway.

"This is Karen Wells calling from London. I'm sorry to bother you, but I'm trying to track down your brother, Edward."

"Karen Wells," the voice echoed. "Not the singer."

"Well, yes. Could you give me Edward's London address and telephone number?"

There was a silence, then, "All right, I guess so. I hope somebody's going to explain . . ."

"We met at a party."

"The MacIntyre thing?"

"Yes."

The sound of Persis's laughter was all chopped up into pieces like confetti. "Good old Edward," she said. There was an awkward silence until they both said good-bye and hung up.

Karen and Tony were booked on the eleven A.M. flight to New York, so there was not much time. Karen tossed the last few things into her suitcase, slipped out of the hotel and hailed a taxi. The driver let her out on Cheyne Walk in Chelsea. She stood in the rain a moment, watching the cars speed along the Embankment, each one kicking up a fine mist of water that billowed out behind like a veil. Then, with stomach fluttering from anxiety and no breakfast, she turned to the building that presumably contained Edward. She climbed the steps and shook a shower of raindrops from her hair. The doorbell made a faraway clanging sound that seemed musical compared to the harsh American buzz.

After a moment, Edward appeared in the doorway wearing a wool flannel bathrobe. As he hooked the bows of his glasses behind his ears, Karen watched the transformation of his face, the expression resolving from perplexity into joy.

"I hope it's all right," she said.

"All right!" he laughed. "Come in." He ushered her through the first door on the right. "Here, by the fire."

There was a gas heater glowing in the fireplace. Edward drew two chairs up close, removed Karen's wet raincoat and hung it nearby. "I'll get some tea. And a biscuit?"

"Fine," Karen said.

She watched him prepare the tea on a two-burner stove. He was so thin that his shoulders under the robe seemed like the wires of a coat hanger. He needed feeding.

"What do you look like under that beard?" she asked.

"Gaunt."

"Have you always had it?"

"I was born with it." He brought her a cup of tea and a round tin of biscuits with chocolate icing. "I hope you're not going to catch cold. No umbrella?" He touched the top of her head.

"I like the rain," she answered, imagining the imprint of his fingers glistening on her wet hair. "Is this what you eat for breakfast?"

"And lunch, too, mostly. I'm partial to chocolate."

"You need to be looked after," Karen said. "Edward, I'm going back today."

His face fell.

"Why didn't you get in touch with me?"

"It was up to you, wasn't it?"

"Why?"

"You're the star."

"What does that have to do with it?"

"Something."

"How did you imagine I'd go about finding you?" she asked.

"Through the British Museum."

"I don't think you told me you work there."

"I didn't? I was certain I had."

"I called your sister."

Edward looked confused. "You called Persis? In New York?" Karen nodded. "Did you tell her who you were?"

"Yes."

Edward smiled. "I'm surprised she hasn't telephoned me already."

"What will you tell her if she calls?" Karen asked.

"I'll tell her to wait for my letter."

"I'd give anything to read it."

Edward was silent. Karen took another sip of tea. The brim of the teacup felt frail as an eggshell against her lips. "This is antique china, isn't it?"

"Yes. I like old things."

"Aren't you afraid you'll break it?"

"Well, then, I'll have had great pleasure from it. Sometimes I hold it in my hands and think of the generations who've enjoyed that particular teacup. Victorian dinner parties by candlelight, gentlemen with muttonchop whiskers and ladies in satin gowns."

Karen's spoon clinked delicately as she stirred. She thought about yesterday's performance at *Britvideo.* The world of electric guitars and synthesizers seemed so alien to this hushed room filled with bookshelves and battered antiquities.

"Is this where you write about Julius Southwick?"

"You have an excellent memory. But no, I'm not writing as yet. I'm still researching the diaries at the museum."

"How long will it take you?"

"I'm due back at Columbia next fall, which is plenty of time, actually. The article itself won't take long, but there are vast amounts of material to sort through, to organize. It's all so interesting I find it difficult to be selective."

Karen removed a book from the shelf beside the mantlepiece. *The Bloomsbury Phenomenon: A Literary Psychoanalysis,* by Edward R. Vaughn. "I thought you said . . ." Karen began.

"My sister compiled several years' worth of scribblings and had them bound as a Christmas gift. You're holding the only volume extant."

"How can you dare look embarrassed? My God, Edward, look at what you've done, all these words." She flipped through the pages. "This stuff is in the library, right? In the original periodicals?"

"Well, yes."

"People will be reading these after we're all dead and gone, your words, your thoughts. You're immortal."

"So are you," Edward said. "Preserved on record and videotape."

She laughed. "Yeah, yesterday's *Britvideo* tape will wind up in the Museum of Natural History. Anthropologists can study it in the year 3000 and wonder what the hell I was doing."

"Did you enjoy it?"

Karen thought this over. "Yes. Maybe not exactly the way I anticipated I would." She held her cup out for a refill. "Thanks. You brew a mean cup of tea. It's all very new to me, the big time, I mean. *Britvideo* counts as big time. So did Midem. These are things I've been working toward for such a long time, and I guess I figured once I got here there'd be a huge high." She hesitated.

"But there was none?"

"No, not really. There was more a sense of . . . integration. As if I was doing what I'm supposed to be doing. It was appropriate somehow, even if it was awfully silly."

"Are you denigrating yourself?"

"Well, look, Edward, it's not like writing."

"Why not?"

"Because what I do is the result of something I was born with, like having blonde hair. I didn't spend months compiling research and putting together one sentence after the next. I opened up my mouth and out came a sound that most other people don't have. It's just genes, or maybe God. I can't really claim it as an accomplishment, can I?"

"Yes. There are plenty of people with talent. But they never become known because they're not willing to work and grow and put themselves through the hard times. You can't expect me to believe the world just said, 'Oh, look, there's Karen Wells,' and handed you a record contract. Don't get caught up in some distorted notion about the elite intellectual."

"I'm pretty awed by literature."

"I can see that."

"But I'm still proud of what I do."

"That's all I meant to impart by that great long speech. You have to forgive me. I'm used to lecturing."

She grinned at him. "I love it. Hot damn, you're so cute I can barely stand it. Anyway, we all know you could write a wonderful huge, long book if you felt like it."

Edward laughed out loud and ate another biscuit. Suddenly he felt unaccustomed hunger. "I have no great literary ambitions," he said through the crumbs. "It's merely that I'm fascinated by a particular group of people the way others are attracted to celebrities nowadays. The Bloomsbury era is compelling in that most of the personalities kept diaries or daily correspondence. So if I were interested in, say, Duncan Grant, there's access to intimate opinions of a dozen of his peers. Ideas conflict, perhaps revealing more about the writer than about Grant, but eventually a multidimensional portrait emerges. I don't think there's been another time in history when a particular group of individuals wrote so voluminously about one another."

"Are you telling me that if members of *any* group were to write about one another, it would be just as fascinating?"

"Precisely."

"Say the top stars of day-time television, everybody from *Guiding Light* scribbling notes on one another and their fellow actors from *As the World Turns?*"

Edward nodded. "Given the same degree of literary craft, which I allow you they're not likely to possess. But it's the personalities and not the talent that magnetize researchers like me. Julius Southwick was a self-centered, vain dilettante. But he had insight and he was a good listener."

"I'm not informed enough to argue with you," Karen said. "But I'm going to work at it and give you a run for your money. Maybe after I write my musical."

"Are you writing a musical?"

"Oh, my God, I can't believe I said that. I've never told one person." She looked stunned.

"Why ever not?"

"Because it's ridiculous and pretentious, me thinking I could ever pull off such a thing."

"How do you know you can't do it?"

She waved her hand at him in dismissal. "Oh, come on, Edward. It's not like writing the lyrics to a three-minute song, is it?"

Edward was quiet for a moment. Then he said, "If we were mathematicians, we might observe regarding this conversation that a song is to a musical as an article is to a book."

It took a moment for her to absorb it, but soon she smiled at him. "Ah, Edward, you are a whiz at synthesis."

"Have you begun your musical?"

"I have a few notes," she confessed. "Tony would kill me dead if he ever caught me at it."

"I don't understand."

"He would be so pissed, I can't begin to tell you. It's bad enough that I keep insisting on writing my own songs. He considers it a colossal waste of effort." They were both silent, thinking of Tony. Then Karen spoke slowly. "I'm sorry I brought him up. I was having such a good time."

"Then let's not talk about him," Edward said.

"I haven't been with him, I mean, *with* him, since I met you."

"You don't have to tell me . . ." Edward began.

"You mean you don't want me to. All right, Edward, I won't crowd you. I know exactly how that feels. What's the *R* for?" Karen pointed at the spine of the book of collected articles.

"Rabican."

"What's that, an old family name?"

Edward smiled. "I was born when my father was immersed in Carolingian legend. Rabican was a fleet-footed horse who fed only on air."

"I knew there was something!"

Edward looked baffled.

"Horses. I told you about my horses in the elevator. Why didn't you mention your middle name?"

He laughed.

"All right, you think it's dumb. But there's a connection. Rabican, how pretty." She traced the *R* with her finger. "Edward, did you want to see me again?"

His eyes flickered to the bureau. Taped to a corner of the mirror was a newspaper photograph of the two of them emerging from the elevator. The caption shrieked, RISING POP STAR KAREN WELLS GETS NO LIFT FROM LIFT.

Karen reached into her bag, unfolded the identical clipping and flapped it at him. "You're much better-looking than this," she told him.

"Actually, I thought it rather flattering," he said. "It's marvelous of you. If one could wear out a photograph by staring at it, there'd be nothing left but a smudge."

Karen got up. There was an early-model stereo in the corner and a shelf full of records. She flipped through them: Brahms, Vivaldi, Bach. "I don't know anything about this stuff. And books, too. I've pretty much neglected the classics in favor of *People* magazine."

"You have a treat in store."

"It'll be a treat if you teach me."

"But you're going away."

"I'll be back. Give me a reading list."

"Where would you like to start?"

"I want to write better lyrics. It drives me crazy, not having proper access to the English language."

"People with limited vocabularies don't ordinarily know what 'hirsute' means. Or were you bluffing in the elevator?"

"No, that's crossword puzzles. I'm an addict. But vocabulary isn't enough."

"All right, then, let's begin at the beginning." He rose, took a slim leather-bound book from the shelf, and handed it to her.

She read the title: *Beowulf*. "That's a rock group!"

"Well, now you'll learn the derivation."

The book felt soft in her hand. She sniffed it, and the scent made her think of something delicious to eat, lightly smoked and chewy. "You sure you don't mind my taking this?"

"You have to return it because it's valuable. It's a bribe, you see."

"You don't need a bribe." She glanced at her watch. "Damn, I've got to go. I've had a lot of lovers, Edward."

"I don't care."

"I know you don't. What in the world is going on with us?" Edward shook his head, his hands opened in a gesture of helplessness. Karen took them in her fingers and held on tight. "I think I've been struck by lightning," she said.

"Me, too, darling. It explains the conspicuous aroma of ozone around here the past few days."

"Will you see it through, whatever it is, or are you going to chicken out on me?"

"There's a sense of unreality about it all, Karen."

"You think it's absurd, our being together."

"Yes."

She tried to move away but he held her fast. His thin arms were remarkably strong.

"I'll make you change your mind," Karen said finally.

He bent down and gave her a long deep kiss. Then she grabbed her steaming raincoat from beside the fireplace and bolted, leaving him standing in the doorway.

As soon as Karen had left the flat, the telephone began to ring. Edward, in his dazed state, did not hear it at first. Finally he answered, half-expecting to hear Karen's voice.

"Edward Vaughn?"

"Yes."

"This is Guy Burlingame, *Orbit* magazine."

"Oh, dear," Edward said.

"I'd like to talk with you about Karen Wells."

"He's not in," Edward said.

"I thought you said you were Edward Vaughn."

"I was mistaken. He's not in. I'm terribly sorry."

Edward hung up, and the telephone began to ring again. It went on all day and into the following afternoon. At last, it stopped. Edward supposed the cutoff time for the magazine's next issue had passed and that he was safe. But there were many moments in the past thirty-six hours when he had been tempted to pick up the receiver and say, "Yes, it's true." The very notion produced beads of sweat on his forehead.

He watched the newsstands anxiously. On Monday evening, *Orbit* magazine appeared with a photograph of David Bowie on the cover. There was a bright red blurb to the left of Bowie's pale cheekbone that read KAREN WELLS IN LOVE. Edward stood on a busy corner of the Kings Road and read it straight through. "Wells, never one to follow the pop traditions, is patently besotted with a brainy American scholar who shall remain nameless for now but who is reported to be fifty-five years old and a respected biographer of Virginia Woolf . . ." Edward moaned. That's what he got for not speaking up on the telephone. "Wells and her mystery man have not yet set a date, but leave it to Karen Wells to surprise us all with a most intriguing symbiosis of the pop world and the literary scene. One must surmise that this event signals the end of the talented singer's stormy relationship with manager Tony Kahanian."

Edward bought two more copies, one for Persis and one for Karen. Fifty-five years old. The impudence of the man. But he laughed his way across Sloane Square.

Soon afterward, Edward received Karen's record album in the mail. He unwrapped the flat square package and hunted for a note. But there was none, merely the face of Karen Wells smiling at him through cellophane. She looked unfamiliar, but perhaps it was the elaborate hairdo and bright lipstick. The album title screamed at him: *Karen Wells: Told You So!* Intimidating, he thought, and turned it over and over in his long fingers.

On the back was a list of acknowledgments: to the executive producer, to the members of the band, to publishing companies, to the record manufacturing company. Such a complex career compared to the isolated life of the academic. He thought of Karen surrounded by the seething mob of reporters outside the elevator in Mayfair. There was a short paragraph, presumably written by Karen herself, in which she thanked her manager, Tony Kahanian, "to whom I owe my success." Perhaps the "stormy relationship" would resume once Karen was separated from Edward by three thousand miles of cold Atlantic sea water.

He had memorized every item of small print on the jacket by the time he put it on the turntable, replacing Vivaldi's *Four Seasons.* He sat down and waited, wondering what would happen to his feelings for her if the music turned out to be truly ghastly.

First came the patter of drumbeats like a pair of boots falling down the stairs. PA-ta-ta PA-ta-ta PA-ta-ta BOOM. And then Karen's voice, angry and pounding: *Didn't I tell you?* Unrecognizable, this was raw and mean. He didn't understand it and he didn't like it. He had lost her already. But no, he would try. After all, think of how he had despised *The*

Firebird Suite. "I resent dissonance," he had told Persis. But she had persuaded him to listen to her recording again and again, talking him through it until ultimately his ear began to anticipate and enjoy the intelligence, even the genius, of Stravinsky. So now Edward rose from his chair with a sigh and set the needle back at the beginning.

Sure enough, this time through, he detected how the repetition of the percussion motif (Patata Patata Patata Boom) beneath the vocal expanded into intricate almost fugal combinations. And on the third go-round, Karen's voice mimicked the drums. *Didn't I / Didn't I / Tell you I'd go?* It was the same rhythm, relentless and hypnotic. Interested now, and relieved, Edward let the needle slide on into the silent groove. "Who Stole the Moon?" followed, but Edward preferred the simple *a capella* version she had sung in the elevator. This one was clubbed to death with violins. Next was a mischievous, sexy number called "Look Over Your Shoulder (I'm Following You)," and by this time, Edward was too excited to pick up the needle and listen to it again. He was hungry to absorb her in all of her moods, to learn about her through the quivering maze of sound.

Karen's voice began the last song, which seemed to be aimed directly at him. It was called "Wings," and though it was very melodic, almost old-fashioned, there was a soaring urgency to it that gripped him. *You can stay on the ground, / But babe, look around / And you'll see it's the sky / Where you really want to be. / Feel them sprouting! / Feel like shouting! / Freedom, babe, that's what it means. / Say good-bye, spread your wings, / And Fly! Fly away!* The message seemed so personal that prickles began low at his spine and climbed with the sound of her voice, ascending like tiny black notes scaling his vertebrae until the back of his head was creeping, every hair vibrating. His shoulder blades began to itch where he imagined the little knobs would begin to grow in response to Karen's challenge. He sat still for a long time without opening his eyes. Then he sent a silent telegram to Persis: *Perhaps I'm alive after all.*

Ordinarily, Julius Southwick dominated Edward's thoughts from the moment he stepped off the bus at the museum, as if the living man himself were pacing impatiently inside the sprawling marble edifice, brimming with acerbic *joie de vivre* to share with Edward. But this morning, Edward strolled into Russell Square and gazed up at the pale blue sky and at the tourists milling about in search of inexpensive cashmere. I'd like to bring Karen here, Edward thought. I'd like to walk along the street with her on my arm. I'd like to let them think she's my daughter. I'd like to sit on a bench and kiss her.

A harrassed-looking couple with two small children approached. The woman, who had a deep vertical pucker between pencil-thin eyebrows, reconnoitered Edward while her husband, a soft, short man, tried to pry the children apart.

"Scott, you're going to make her do pee-pee right here on the sidewalk," the husband said in a reasonable tone of voice. Edward, meanwhile, had evidently passed inspection because the woman appeared at his elbow.

"Pardon me, can I ask you something?" she said. The midbrow crease, like a conductor's baton, bobbed up and down with every syllable.

Edward nodded.

"Is there a bathroom, I mean a toilet, around here? Shoot, Marty, can't you control those kids?" She swatted behind her, catching the little boy on the back of the head. He began to howl.

"Now, Marge . . ." Marty said.

"Right across the square," Edward directed. "There's a public convenience."

"Shoot, Marty, he's American." The upper portion of her face was fairly dancing. Edward thought of punctuation marks frolicking across a blank page.

"Lookit, Marge, let's go. Bettylou's going to do pee-pee any second," Marty said.

"I have a trillion questions," said Marge, plucking at Edward's arm. "We have a resource here."

"Margaret!" the husband bellowed, reasonable tone no longer in evidence. Marge snapped to attention, as did the children. She gave Edward a cowed nod of thanks, and the family trooped off toward the public toilets. Edward watched after them affectionately. He supposed they knew who Karen Wells was. *Wait up, Marge,* he wanted to say. *I kissed Karen Wells. I held her and kissed her and the rain was thick in her hair and she smelled so clean and I feel young. I never felt so young.*

Julius Southwick's diaries were scratched out in barely decipherable longhand. Each word began legibly enough, with one or two letters quite clearly formed, but thereafter the pen grew restless and disposed of the words with hasty strokes that were often mere horizontal lines. "L— ev——," Edward knew, meant "Last evening." "Af——d– c——," was "affaire de coeur," "V&D" referred to Vanessa Bell and Duncan Grant. Decoding became easier with time and with the sense that Edward had somehow hooked into the dead man's unconscious. It made Edward's scalp creep sometimes when a few seemingly random marks on the aging paper arranged themselves into words and sentences. But there were days when Edward spent many hours puzzling over one phrase. "The Woolves held court," Edward read in early December. He plunged ahead eagerly since Southwick's observations regarding Virginia and Leonard Woolf were inevitably entertaining. "V looking positively daunting in p—— j———." Perennial jonquils? Edward wondered. Obviously out of the question. Pigskin jacket? Paisley jerkin? Patterned jumper? Edward was forced to discard them all, but he became obsessed, his dreams filled with visions of Virginia in all manner of outlandish costumes. He became giddy in his little corner of the museum and started muttering aloud: profitable junket, papaya juice, preposterous jabberwocky, pickled jellyfish. Finally, he gave up and pushed on, hoping that time and perhaps some subconscious detective work would provide the answer. Then, one afternoon during the past week, Edward had been perusing a letter Southwick had written to his favorite cousin. "I would kill for a pair of Virginia's purple jodhpurs," Julius wrote. Edward had to restrain himself from letting out a whoop.

Today he reminded himself of that moment, of the thrills that awaited him within the battered red notebooks Julius preferred for his daily jottings. Yet for all Edward's newfound resolve, concentration evaded him. At each rustle, he looked up curiously with the wild hope that Karen had flown back across the Atlantic to surprise him. He forced himself to open the manuscript. He had left off with Julius at a dinner party at Ham Spray, the home of Dora Carrington and Lytton Strachey. After half an hour, Edward was able to make out the sentence: "Carrington is bewitching with her yellow hair cropped like a haystack and her eyes the color of forget-me-nots." *Karen,* Edward thought, and drifted away into the blurred living room of Ham Spray where the literary elite sat cross-legged at Karen's feet while she sang to them by the fire. "Rapt, they were," Julius would write. "Alix with her knees drawn up to her chin, bones sharp as letter openers, Vanessa with eyes heavy-drooping, her body swaying slightly with the music. Even Lytton forgot his sardonic pose and with liquid eyes admired the nightingale." It was no use, Edward realized. Karen had invaded even the sanctum sanctorum of the British Museum. Edward leaned back in his chair and summoned up the image of Julius Southwick. "Come on, inspire me, you reprobate," Edward said. Dutifully, Julius Southwick, dressed in the rakish attire of Edward's favorite photograph, shimmered against the backdrop of Edward's closed eyelids. He smirked at Edward in the cocky manner that was both endearing and maddening. *"You can stay on the ground,"* Julius sang in an awful melodramatic baritone, *"But babe, look around / And you'll see it's the sky / Where you really want to be."*

"Spare me," Edward said.

"Spread your wings and fly!" Julius sang on, mocking.

"I'll open my eyes and send you packing," Edward threatened.

"My dear fellow," Julius went on, "what do you suppose it is she's trying to tell you? Why is it you're unable to concentrate? You know perfectly well that it's not mere sexual distraction troubling you today. Listen to the woman."

Edward's heart began to pound. "I don't believe I'm prepared to hear this."

"You are indeed. Our Miss Wells has made sure of that."

Edward took off his glasses and rubbed his eyes with his fists. "I know what you're going to say."

Julius sat down on the corner of the desk and folded his arms. "Then suppose you carry on."

Edward felt his body tremble from far inside. "How did I imagine I could do justice to you, the great Julius Southwick, in a simple article?"

"Go on," Julius said.

"What we're talking about here is a book," Edward said. "The definitive biography."

"Now was that so terribly difficult to articulate?"

"You bet," said Edward. "Now go away. I'd like to have my heart attack in peace."

"Freedom, babe, that's what it means," Julius sang, fading fast.

"I think I'd better go home now," Edward muttered. Shakily, he set the diaries aside and left the museum.

There was an air-mail letter waiting, from the States, in unfamiliar handwriting. Inside there was no letter, only a newspaper photograph of Henry and Nancy Kissinger. Baffled, Edward tucked the clipping into another corner of his mirror. The following day brought a picture, torn from *TV Guide,* of Tony Randall and Jack Klugman. Edward began to get the point. Soon his mirror was fringed with photographs: Sophia Loren and Carlo Ponti; an advertisement from *La Cage aux Folles;* even a Bronx Zoo elephant being nuzzled with heavy-lashed adoration by a llama. His sensitivity raised now, Edward began to notice such twosomes everywhere. His research, of course, was full of them. Bloomsbury could boast of barely a single conventional marriage. He began to stare at people on the street. In Sloane Square was a punk girl, hair in alarming chartreuse spikes, clutching the hand of a gray-suited man with a briefcase. On the bus, a frowsy middle-aged woman cuddled possessively beside an olive-skinned youth who shot her glances of blatant lust. Edward even found himself staring thoughtfully at photographs of Queen Elizabeth and Prince Philip. In a tattered magazine at the dentist's office, he spotted a photograph of diminutive comic Dudley Moore stalking down Piccadilly with a blonde Amazon of a woman. He ripped it out, scrawled a note across the front: "Arriving New York April 22. Call me at 555–6221. E." and sent it to Karen.

As if she were astride Midler rather than on the aisle of a Boeing 727, Karen felt the floor rise and fall beneath her feet, six miles up in the black sky between Denver and Atlanta. It pleased her to be awake while the other passengers slept, scattered like bundles of rumpled laundry among the seats. Growing up on the farm, while the town kids were still groggy in their beds, Karen and Michael rose early, before daybreak, to help with the chores. Far from resenting the ritual, Karen welcomed each morning with curiosity, even suspense, wondering how the dark would melt into dawn on this particular day. Michael usually needed prodding, but eventually Karen would coax him out of sleep and into the morning.

In June they would open the screen door behind the kitchen and step out into the rich, sweet odor of foliage. Michael suffered with hay fever and invariably began sneezing, but Karen stood sucking in deep breaths, convinced that if she stood still, soon she would become a new genus of the lush vegetation, with leafy arms and tiny flowers blooming at her fingertips. In October the air was sharp enough to make the eyes water and carried a welcoming scent of ripe pumpkin and rotting leaves. But the winter months required bravery. Sometimes the temperature at five A.M. dropped to twenty degrees below zero. Yet snow was like the sea, always different, always compelling and beautiful. It could be light as dust and froth up around their ankles in a fine cloud, or it could be heavy and thick, retaining precisely the shape of the treads on their boots. The drifts shifted into fabulous patterns of curve and shadow across the back meadow. She and Michael would stand and gaze, unwilling to break the intensity of the silence with their voices or desecrate the incandescent surface with their footsteps.

So every morning, by the time they arrived at school, they had put in half a day already. They felt sorry for the others, wasting time in oblivion beneath the covers when Karen and Michael had been meddling in the business of life for hours.

Tonight, Karen listened to the sounds of sleep above the throbbing jet engines and felt the sharp pain of missing her brother. She forced her mind away from his sweet, round face and tried to reflect on the tour.

It had been a real coup, opening for Denny Harper on his multicity extravaganza. With his pleasant, ingratiating manner and soothing voice, Denny attracted enormous audiences. On the tour's opening night in Los Angeles, Karen arrived at the auditorium with sweaty palms and stomach cramps to find her dressing room bursting with flowers. The note read, "You're the best. Love, Denny." The trouble was, Karen had created a sensation at each stop. Her energy and fire contrasted cruelly with Denny's monochromatic style—so much so that, in some cities there were boos and catcalls when he made his entrance. Karen and Denny's comfortable camaraderie began to fray more with each performance. Denny's entourage flew first class, while Karen was booked in tourist. Denny enjoyed the hotel's most luxurious hospitality and was squired everywhere by limousine, and yet the tour belonged to Karen. She tried to concentrate on the music and ignore the sick pity she was beginning to feel for the star. When Tony referred to him as the King of Bland, Karen had grabbed his arm and hissed, "Don't. If you pick on him, I'll deck you. I swear it."

Then, in Denver, there had been audible shouts after Denny's first number. *We want Karen! We want Karen!*

"Did you plant those cretins?" Karen accused Tony afterward.

"Of course not. But why should they settle for vanilla pudding when they can have zabaglione?"

When she couldn't think of what else to do, Karen had apologized to Denny for the behavior of her fans. The apology rankled, and by now, Denny was no longer speaking to her.

Two rows back in the plane, Nicky Stein, Karen's drummer, lay curled in a knot with her head against the window. Nicky's long, thick ringlets stood out as if she existed in zero gravity. Sometimes, watching Nicky's body gyrate as she slammed the double-headed toms, Karen imagined the girl rocketing up into the snarled cables of the stage and through the roof, leaving nothing behind but a puff of blue smoke. Nicky had graduated from Brooklyn College magna cum laude, with a degree in English literature. Fleeing her Orthodox Jewish family, she had established herself as the best female drummer in the business. And she possessed a gift for drama. It was Nicky who suggested the effective thematic flirtation that transpired on stage among Karen and two of the men in the band. Nicky constructed the performance so that a subtle sensual conflict gradually intensified until, in the final set, the two musicians, guitarist and keyboard, engaged in a wild musical duel with Karen as the prize. Karen also discovered that Nicky liked to distract herself by jotting clever verses, often satiric doggerel aimed at members of the music business. Karen had tried to enlist Nicky's interest in writing lyrics. Nicky had declined.

Karen took an unsteady stroll as the plane pitched. Tony was asleep beside Ferris Pauling, the keyboard player. Ferris shaved his head and wore black leather jumpsuits. He was a homosexual and a drug addict. Tony worried that the groupie Ferris had picked up in Phoenix was supplying him with something more potent than Quaaludes. His young men were invariably angelic-looking, with huge china-blue eyes. They drove Nicky Stein frantic with frustrated lust.

The plane gave a violent jolt. Karen nearly landed in the lap of John Garver, her guitarist. She clung to the back of his seat so that she could watch him while he slept. He was the band's only black man, and Karen found him quite beautiful. John was the son of Jumpin' John Garver, the Rhythm and Blues man. Unlike his ebullient father, John Junior was so soft-spoken and dignified that it was sometimes difficult to get him physically into the music. Karen worried that on stage his stolid presence might blunt the audience's enthusiasm, but she liked his lean grace and natural elegance. He stirred in his sleep, opened his eyes, smiled at her and reached out to squeeze her hand. Then he drifted off again.

Across from John lay Billy Lundgren, whose sneakered feet protruded over the arm of his seat into the aisle. Billy was only eighteen, but the boy was an electronic wizard with the synthesizer, bass guitar, and any other piece of equipment, including Karen's hair dryer. Last week, after takeoff from Kansas City, the pilot, claiming "minor technical problems," announced that the plane would return to the airport. Karen's entire retinue had called out in unison, "Let Billy fix it!" He was the only person who could make John Garver laugh, but if you asked John what was funny, he would only smile and say, "You had to be there."

Atlanta stood at the end of a grueling ordeal characterized by chronic lack of sleep and inevitable snags—fouled-up hotel accommodations, erratic stage equipment, inedible food (dangerous food, Nicky Stein declared: in Detroit she had discovered a used Band-Aid in her health food salad), and even, in the outdoor arena in Miami, a thick cloud of grasshoppers that clogged the instruments and set their hair in motion with tangled insect bodies. The band had endured it all with sardonic good humor. Surveying them now in their various postures of sleep, Karen felt her throat grow tight with affection and gratitude.

A flight attendant appeared beside her. "There's some turbulence, Miss Wells. I think you ought to find your seat and buckle up."

"Okay," Karen said, and dutifully sat. The movement wakened Nicky, who stared at Karen solemnly.

"What's the matter, honey?" Nicky asked. "Can't sleep?"

Karen shook her head.

"Me, either."

"On the contrary," Karen said. "You've been totally sacked out since five minutes after takeoff."

"Have I? I feel like I've been driving a huge truck over mountain roads. Right on the edge." Like a child, she rubbed her eyes with the heel of her hands.

"You were dreaming."

"What are you doing for sex?" Nicky asked drowsily.

Karen laughed. "Must've been some sexy truck in that dream."

"You haven't been doing it with Tony lately." Nicky's eyes, a pale, clear green, were beautiful and a little spooky.

"How can you know that?"

"First of all, he looks like a man in a cage. Second, he made a slight pass at me and then backed off like *I* was the one who did it. He surprised himself."

"You could have encouraged him if you wanted to. It's no problem for me."

"It is for him. That was just massive testosterone buildup making him slide his hand down my ass. Tony himself is otherwise engaged. Hopelessly, and you know it."

Karen sighed.

"Look," Nicky persisted. "This Edward brain trust is four thousand miles away. Meanwhile, you're just as horny as Tony. I recognize all the signs, believe me. The ridge between the eyebrows, the tension around the mouth . . ."

"Why are you hassling me on this particular subject?"

"Because deprivation is not healthy for a highly sexed person, which you are. I don't want you showing up five years from now with breast cancer."

"Good God, Nick, it's only been a few weeks. Oh, I know it. I can't deny he gets to me in a certain primitive way. Whenever I'm with him lately, I've been making sure there's always a third party present. Look, if I sleep with Tony, he's going to think we're back at square one. Besides, what about all those nuns? Most of them live to a ripe old age."

"First of all, how do we know what goes on in those convents, and second, when God made you, he left out the chastity molecules. Have you said anything to Tony about Edward?"

"No. He hasn't asked and I don't feel like telling him."

"How come?"

"Because I don't know what it's all about. I can't get the man out of my mind, but here I am at the brink of making a big splash in the business, or so they say . . . oh, hell. It's confusing."

"So what are you going to do for sex?"

Karen gave Nicky's wild hair a swipe. "Talk about horny. Go back to sleep. I'll figure it out."

"Yeah." Nicky curled up in a ball again and closed her eyes. "Let me know."

By now, it was three A.M. and Karen was exhausted. But when she closed her eyes, the lids flickered and twitched and her brain felt crowded. Images and thoughts shoved and bullied one another behind her forehead. She held her hands to her ears and pressed hard, trying to restore order, but it was like closing subway doors against the rush-hour mobs. She resigned herself to wakefulness, determining to make periodic stops along the dark track of her consciousness. If she discharged a few passengers, perhaps her head might not explode.

First, of course, was Edward. She had been hard put on this hectic trip to carve out private time to gloat over him. Absurdly, in every city they visited, she found herself hunting for him. In the audience, in the hotel lobbies, everywhere, her eyes sought a tall, bearded fellow with a cracked smile. Nonsense, she told herself. Edward was in England. And yet, if he *really* wanted to find her, he could do it. The tour was well publicized. Yet in London, it had been Karen who did the pursuing. Edward had held back, waiting for Karen, the star, to make the first move. She wondered if he would always leave everything to her.

She squirmed in her seat and tried to shut the doors against him. She reminded herself that this tour was the reward for many years of hard work and disappointment, for the single-minded journey from the Sprague's Hollow Hotel bar in Upstate New York to the Midem festival in Southern France. No husband, no sleeping children, no loved ones grasping at her, demanding attention, distracting her from the goals of a lifetime. There had only been Tony, who, far from an impediment, often provided fuel when she felt too worn out or discouraged to carry on. Suddenly, the brass ring was within reach. A few more cycles on the carousel, a little more stretching, a little more reaching, and she'd have it in her hand. But the memory of Edward's face made her feel like dropping her arm, sliding off the horse and hitching the next flight to London. How could she miss so intensely a person she'd only just met? And now Nicky had raised the sexual issue, which had lately begun to disturb her more than she cared admit. It had been several weeks now since her last sexual episode with Tony. She was accustomed to regular doses of exciting sex. There had been moments when she had stood beside him gazing at the shape of his hand or remembering the texture of his hair and thought, Oh, what the hell, it's just bodies, where's the harm? And then she would anticipate how she might feel two minutes afterward and how Tony would feel and what he would make of it. So she had dodged the issue by dodging Tony. But Nicky was right. Tony stared at Karen like a starving dog. And between Karen's legs burned a sensation of greed and loss.

Agitated, she twisted under the restraints of her seat belt. She and Michael had devised a method to deal with such moments. They called it the Soothing Game, to be employed during times of stress. Michael used it to cope with his extreme shyness. For Karen, it was mostly utilized after an argument with her mother. The trick was to relax the body, take deep breaths, and bring to mind a beautiful scenic image, the West Hills beyond the meadow, the creek where the willow tree dipped its branches in the shallow water. Karen closed her eyes, let her hands go limp and thought of Colorado, now far behind her. Colorado—primitive and clean.

Yesterday, on her day off, she had rented a car and driven up into the high country west of Denver. At a roadside restaurant, the local sheriff had ambled in, wearing pointed cowboy boots, a braided leather holster, and a tin star. Karen had almost laughed out loud, but when she checked the other patrons for a reaction, no one seemed at all startled. Evidently, this was no actor straying from a nearby movie set. The sheriff's boots creaked as he crossed the room. When he passed close by, Karen caught his clean scent and felt suffused in mythology. This was the American West in all its macho beauty. She had watched him leave and peered through the window, half expecting to see a palomino hitched to a post. But instead there were only jeeps, pickup trucks, and a Chevrolet painted official for the sheriff. Karen flattened out her paper napkin and began to write down phrases. *Riding tall behind the wheel / Whinny's just the horn of an automobile / Thundering hooves now squealing tires / Windswept mane's transmission wires / Once so noble, wild and clean / Stinks of rancid gasoline* . . . She stuffed the napkin in her pocket. Might be catchy, she thought, as real corny Country Western or maybe even Bluegrass with lots of banjo riffs. Colorado was open and wild. Your eyes could escape the high-rise claustrophobia of the cities. She missed the farm, the trees, the smell of horses and mown hay. She was not an urban creature.

Her eyelids began to relax. Something clinked rhythmically in the gallery behind her where the flight attendants stood gossiping. The sound evoked the delicate china cup Edward had handed her as she warmed herself by the gas fire in his flat. The porcelain was old. Edward, she supposed, was old, too, and here she was thinking of him again. Her eyelids felt heavy now, as if the lashes were weighted. For Karen, the word *old* resonated with negative connotations. *Old* meant worn and faded, like the shabby sofa in her parents' living room, decrepit and musty-smelling like her grandfather. It meant grimy, dated, or useless, lines in the face and sore joints. Karen had never understood Nicky Stein's obsession with flea markets. But Edward had called her attention to the cup, encouraging her to acknowledge its beauty, provoking her curiosity about its past. It was a small moment that had dimmed without notice until just now. But Karen felt enriched. She remembered trekking through the Metropolitan Museum to gape unmoved at ancient pottery. She would like to make another visit. With Edward as a guide, history would breathe behind the silent display cabinets.

Drowsily, she imagined herself moving along a hushed wainscotted corridor. Her jeans and pullover seemed to disintegrate into the shadows. As she disappeared around the corner, her elegant velvet gown swept the floor with a sigh.

There is a song here somewhere, she thought. But she fell asleep instead.

Tony propped her up and trotted her through the vast maze of the Atlanta airport. Half dreaming still, Karen imagined the computer-generated voice, ever reasonable, echoing along the tiled corridors: *Attention all passengers. Please be informed that the world is coming to an end. Place all litter in the proper receptacles. Thank you and have a nice day.*

Finally, ensconced in her suite at the Hyatt, she crawled into bed for two delicious hours. The telephone woke her at noon, its shrill ring like a hot finger poking at her ear. Numbly, she grappled with the receiver, dropping it next to the bed and finally retrieving it with groans of sleepy frustration.

"Jesus, Karen," Tony said.

"I'm up, I'm up."

"We've got a meeting with Manfred Warm in twenty minutes."

"Right."

"Leave the door open. I'll clean up the living room while you take a shower. Jesus, Karen."

When she emerged from the bathroom, Tony was fussing with three chairs at a glass table. He tried one configuration, stood back to appraise the situation, then rearranged them. Karen watched for a while.

"Why don't you put one *under* the table," she suggested. "I'll sit in that one."

Tony went to her at once. "Fix your hair," he said, licking his fingers and trying vainly to plaster down a cowlick in her bangs.

"Leave it. It's my concession to punk," Karen said. His familiar obsession with her appearance was a relief. She had been alarmed at the prospect of their intimate isolation in this room. "And quit prowling," she went on. "Everything looks fine. If you want to do something constructive, go fix *your* hair."

Tony glanced at himself in the mirror and grunted. "I look okay."

Karen laughed. The man could spot a pimple on her chin from four hundred yards, but when it came to the square inch of whiskers that his razor had missed or the tie whose rear flap hung down half an inch behind, extreme myopia set in. "Tony, why do you wear suits all the time? Nobody else does."

"This business can use all the class it can get," he replied.

"Oh," Karen said.

"Listen, don't be flip with this guy. He produced a great video for Denny Harper, and if we can snag him for you, we'll be on our way."

"I thought we already were. On our way."

"That's what I mean," Tony said. "Don't be such a wiseass." He moved an ashtray two inches to the right, then shoved it back again.

"I just want to write my stuff and sing. I leave the rest of it to you." She perched on the sofa and crossed her legs under her.

"We won't get into that." He scrutinized her carefully. "Hey, Wells, where's all that famous passion? Stand on your tippy-toes and you can reach the Big Time this very day."

"It's a career, not a holy quest." She traced the piping on the arm of the sofa. "But you're right. Manfred Warm would be a coup. Maybe I'm just nervous. And I can tell you one thing for sure. I'm tired."

"Yeah, I know, it's the tour. Fucking exhausting," Tony agreed. "You haven't been yourself for weeks. But just try to hang in there a couple more hours and don't screw things up with Warm."

Manfred Warm and their lunch arrived simultaneously. While the hotel staff unloaded trays, Tony greeted the producer with his double-handed Ronald Reagan handshake, which was reserved for only the most important contacts.

"This is our girl, Karen Wells," Tony said, making an oddly formal bow in her direction.

Karen hopped off the couch and joined them. "You did a fabulous job on the Harper video. Congratulations."

"Congratulations yourself," Warm said. His voice was very nasal, like Willie Nelson's without the melody. "I hear you've been blowing Denny out of the water all across the U.S. of A." Karen winced. Warm glanced at Tony with amusement. "It's a cruel world. Listen, can we talk while we eat? I'm peckish."

Tony looked startled. "It's okay," Karen explained. "He's not talking about his anatomy, he's just hungry."

Warm grinned at her and settled down at the table. He was slim and sinewy and very tan, with a head like a wrinkled leather ball. He wore jeans and a suede vest and smelled of pipe tobacco. There was a haunted quality in his face that Karen had seen in only two categories of people, marathon runners or those who had endured some private tragedy. She sensed that Warm's covert pathos did not emerge from putting in fifteen miles a day in Nikes.

"Are you a jogger?" she asked.

"Christ, no," Warm said.

Karen speculated silently about the man's past and nibbled on a carrot stick. Meanwhile, Warm, with a few intermissions for gulping water, swallowed a mound of liver paté smeared on French bread, a quarter pound of brie, a platter of cold meats, a tomato and mushroom salad, two pumpernickel-raisin rolls, and an immense slice of chocolate cake. All of this was accomplished in near silence while Tony and Karen gaped at one another. Finally, Warm leaned back, lit his pipe and said, "Okay, let's figure this thing out." His stomach protruded like a compact pumpkin beneath the vest. "The way I see it," he continued, "you have to introduce yourself. People need to know what you look like; God knows they've heard you by now. I've listened to your album a few dozen times and I want you to tell me who it is you're trying to reach here."

"Everybody, I guess," Karen replied.

Warm just sucked his pipe and watched her.

"Whoever goes for Barbra Streisand," she suggested. "Plus some teeny-boppers, if possible."

"Okay," Warm said, "then we're going to take the best track, which is *Who Stole the Moon?,* and do a concert video."

Karen looked at Tony.

"We were hoping maybe something a little more imaginative," Tony said. The fingers started mowing the hair back to front.

"Look, they don't know her out there yet," Warm said. "You've got to give people a face, let the voice reach them. Then you can start with the fancy footwork and the animated effects and all that. But don't get tricky first time out or you'll just wind up one more novelty toy."

Tony's heel was pumping soundlessly on the carpet. "You'd shoot it with the rest of the band?"

"Noop. Karen alone, up front. Band way in the background. No distractions."

"Can we think it over?" Karen asked.

"Noop again. I've got the studio lined up starting a week from Monday, and if it's not you people, I've got something else waiting in the wings."

Karen looked at Tony. "Well?"

"We'll do it," Tony said, but held out only one hand this time for Warm to shake.

"We'll work out the rest of the bullshit in New York," Warm

said. "Your lawyers and my lawyers and all that crapola. But ballpark like we said over the phone."

"Right," Tony said. They all stood up.

"Gotta run," Warm said, but not before popping a last chunk of cake into his mouth. "It's been a pleasure. Thanks for lunch." He gave Karen a kiss on the cheek with his leathery mouth. "You've got a much nicer nose than Barbra and a set of pipes like I never heard. We're gonna have a good time."

When the door shut, Karen began to giggle. "I want to do a video of him eating lunch. Some metabolism."

"Congratulations. He's ours." Tony took a step toward her, but she slid over to the table and picked up a stalk of celery. "I'm not very thrilled. Are you?" she asked.

"Well, look, he's the best. We've got to figure he knows what he's doing. Like Pop says, 'You gotta grab the bull by the balls.' "

Karen went to the telephone and dialed her apartment in New York. The cleaning lady came on Fridays, and Karen always called in to check her messages.

"Hi, Fiona, what's new?"

"Nothing much, Miss Mmm . . ." When Fiona first came to work two years ago, Karen had asked that the older woman call her by her first name. Despite Tony's accusations of misguided liberalism, Karen persevered. In fact, when her internist had introduced himself by holding out his hand and saying, "Hello, Karen, I'm Doctor Sterling," she had startled him by giving him a firm handshake and saying, "Hello, Phil." The same policy pertained, she figured, to Fiona. But Fiona had difficulty complying. Even now, the woman avoided calling Karen by name, or else the "Miss" slipped out to be trailed by a garbled assortment of syllables that bore no resemblance to either "Karen" or "Wells." Tony gloated over such moments and gave Karen I-told-you-so looks.

"There's a letter from your father. Something that looks like an invitation maybe, and a letter from, uh, London, England."

"What? Open it, Fiona, please."

Karen imagined the brown fingers slitting the envelope. What color was the stationery? Was it typewritten or longhand? Pen? Felt-tip marker?

"It's a picture from a magazine and some writing."

"Read it, please."

Tony, responding to the urgency in her voice, stopped reading the newspaper and watched her.

"Well, Miss . . . uh . . . it says under the picture, 'Dudley Moore and Susan Anton strolling on Oxford Street.' " She pronounced *strolling* with a short *o*. "Then there's writing across the bottom. It's scribbly, but I think it says, 'Arriving New York April two-two. Call me at 555–6221. R.' "

" 'R'? Are you sure it's not an *E*?"

"That's right, it's an *E*."

"What was the number again, Fiona?" Tony's eyes narrowed as she wrote. She turned away from him and faced the window. "Tell me about the envelope, Fiona. What color is it?"

"White."

"Is it typed or handwritten?"

"Typed on the envelope. But the insides is pen."

"Blue or black?"

"Red."

"Red!" Karen exclaimed. It delighted her that Edward should have written to her in red ink. She wanted to ask if the handwriting was printed or script, but Tony was upon her. "Thanks, Fiona, my darling. I'll be back Sunday night. Can you come Monday to help out with the laundry?"

"Sure. It'll be nice to have you home again."

"I can't wait," Karen said and hung up.

"What was that all about?" Tony asked, examining the telephone number on the pad.

"Just the mail," Karen said. "Listen, I've got some things to do before the show."

Tony stood very close and looked down into her face. He did that with others, too, Karen noticed. Sometimes she thought people on the opposite side of a deal gave in just so he would quit looming over them with his black eyes lit up like the headlights of an oncoming train in a tunnel. She stared at the shoulder of his suit. Underneath the layers of cloth were powerful muscles that would flex as his arm reached out for her. She took a step backward into the table.

"Ouch," she protested, rubbing the small of her back.

Tony sighed heavily and turned away. "Get some rest. Last performance better be a doozie."

"You think Denny'll give me a few minutes for a reasonable sound check tonight?"

"Not likely. He saw that item about you in *People* magazine, and he's pretty pissed. It was also impressed upon me that you get one encore tonight, period."

"Poor Denny."

"He's a schmuck. If he had half a brain he'd be kissing our asses. Next year this time, he'll be lucky to open for *us*."

Karen's eyes flickered toward the telephone. She shifted her weight from one foot to the other like a child who has to get to the bathroom.

"Okay, I'm leaving," Tony said.

Edward's New York apartment was small but charming. Persis had "chintzed up" the place, as Edward put it, pressing needlepoint pillows into the corners of the overstuffed sofa and lining the walls with antique prints of Dickens characters. Ordinarily, Edward found the place cheerful and soothing, but today he sat at his desk and tapped a pencil against *Webster's Third Unabridged*. He stared balefully at the telephone. *She hasn't called,* he wanted to write on the blank piece of stationery before him. To Persis, to the provost of the university. *She hasn't called.* To the landlord of the building, to a student from the University of California, to the ghost of Julius Southwick in particular: *She hasn't called.* There were dozens of explanations, of course. She was probably out of town. What if he had to leave New York before she came back? He doodled on the stationery and astonished himself by having drawn a heart with an arrow through it. "Good God," he murmured out loud, and scribbled it out with heavy black lines. When the telephone rang, he leapt up out of the chair and stood staring at it foolishly. After the third ring, he lunged.

"It's me," she said, and Edward forgot to correct her.

Backstage, Denny Harper was chasing around in a foul temper. Throughout the tour, he had allowed Karen the use of his string section to beef up her small core of performers. But suddenly, on this all-important night, Denny had proclaimed that the strings were "stressed out" and off limits to Karen. She would have to make do without them.

"Let me talk to him," Karen pleaded with Tony, who stood glowering in her dressing room doorway. They could hear Denny's voice retreating down the narrow hallway making lists for the entourage that clattered along behind him. "And I want . . . and I want . . . and I want . . ." the voice said, trailing off out of earshot.

"You will *not* talk to him. I'll talk to his fucking lawyer," Tony said.

Karen laid her chin in her hands and stared at the mirror. There was a crack in the glass that split her in half, lengthwise. She smiled, and her mouth performed on two independent levels.

"What's the matter with you?" Tony growled. "Aren't you even upset?"

"Sure," Karen said. "It's sabotage, pure and simple. But kind of pathetic, don't you think? The guy's having some kind of midlife crisis."

"It's because of the coverage in *People* and now *Rolling Stone*. They should've kept the damn thing from him until tomorrow."

"Well, look, there's nothing we can do about it now. Anyway, we'll manage. I've sung without strings before."

"You'll sound like Uncle Jodie's Jug Band."

"Tony, I've sung with nothing but keyboard."

"Yeah, in a club, not in a fucking mausoleum like this. Look. Let Billy fix it. He's got a string patch on the synth that'll come off like the New York Philharmonic."

"I don't want to get into that. Leave it."

He stared at her. "Have you been popping Valium?"

"Why should I have a stroke when you're doing it for me?"

Tony waved his arms helplessly and stormed off. Karen picked up Edward's *Beowulf* and began to read. "Hrothgar, protector of the Scyldings, spoke: 'Do not ask about pleasure! The sorrow of the Danish people is renewed. . . .' " After a few moments, Nicky Stein poked her head in. She had doused her hair with spangles. The effect was like squinting at the stars through a bramble bush.

"You reading that crap again?" Nicky asked.

"Is it crap?"

"It ain't relevant, babe."

But when Tony went thundering past the doorway, Nicky winked at Karen. "There goes Grendel," she said.

"Don't change," Tony told Karen after her performance. "You're to hang around until Denny's finished. In the VIP section."

"What for?" Karen asked. Her blue jeans hung invitingly on the back of the dressing room door.

"One of life's great mysteries," Tony said. "But you'd better do it. There's a couple of seats in the second row on the aisle."

"Okay," Karen said, baffled. But it was agreeable to sit on the opposite side of the footlights for once and stare up at Denny. He was a pleasant-looking man with features that appeared to be in the process of melting off his face. Another decade, Karen thought, and there would be nothing left but a smooth flesh-colored surface with a small hole for a mouth. In an attempt to heat up his image, he had frizzed his hair. But he looked fluffy rather than frizzy, evoking dandelions gone to seed. One stiff blast with the hair dryer, and all of it could go sailing away on the wind. He had a good, clean voice, however; Karen found it soothing to listen to somebody who could hit a note straight on. But there was no grit in it. Denny tried to build emotional impact by climbing up the ladder of transpositions, reprising the punchlines in ever-higher keys. He and his orchestra grew steadily louder, but no more intense. Karen used to think that the capacity for interpreting the emotional content of a song had something to do with being black. That was the mythology: either you had "soul" or you didn't, and rarely did a white performer tap into the reservoir of love, sexuality, and pain. But by the time Karen was playing in Tony's club, her audience had begun to include blacks. Reporters from *Ebony* magazine asked for interviews. She knew she had crossed the line in a way that Denny Harper never could.

She listened to each number and began to squirm as she imagined how the song should work—a delay in the melody line here, a catch in the voice there—but Denny marched on as if he had a metronome ticking in his head. Still, the audience was enthusiastic and insisted upon two encores.

Finally, Denny held up his hands for quiet and said, "Ladies and gentlemen, ladies and gentlemen, this is the last stop of a very special tour for me. It's not often that we discover an exceptional new talent, and to have the opportunity to launch the career of someone as gifted as the young lady who opened this show was a rare privilege. I'll always be grateful for the chance to boost her into the stardom she so justly deserves. Ladies and gentlemen," he held his arms out toward Karen and gestured to her to join him. "The sensational . . . Karen Wells!"

Up on stage, Denny kissed her on both cheeks and held her by the shoulders as the audience went berserk. They were standing now, stamping their feet, clapping and yelling. Denny, with face scarlet and frizzed hair wilted, stepped aside and bowed to Karen, then made a gesture with his index finger and the curtain came down. It was as if the curtain fell across his face as well. The beaming goodwill and generosity slid off his features in an instant. He turned away from her wordlessly, as if she were nothing more than a stage prop.

"What was that all about?" Karen asked Tony as she stared at Denny's receding white-satin back.

"His publicist convinced him to cash in on some of your electricity," Tony explained. "This way he comes off like your founding father."

"I liked the bit about launching my career. That's a hot one."

"I should've known something was up when they gave us more than three seconds for a sound check. I wish I could figure out a way to sue the bastard," Tony mused. "Come on. I've got a couple of splits in the suite. Let's celebrate the end of this fucking thing."

"Thanks, but I think I'll just crawl into the sack. I'm beat."

Tony rested his hand on a microphone and leaned close. "You always hit bottom after an important gig. You'd better have company."

"I'm not the least bit depressed," Karen said firmly. "Just tired. Very tired. See you tomorrow. Oh, and Tony? Thanks for masterminding the tour. You were a brick through it all." Then she turned and walked off the stage.

At three A.M., Karen sat bolt upright with a scream in the back of her throat.

"Shh," Tony said, and sat down beside her. "It's just me."

Karen snatched at the sheet to cover her naked body. "How did you get in here?" she whispered.

"I have a key."

She shivered as his hand drifted along the curve of her arm. "I want to go back to sleep, Tony."

He cupped her chin and kissed her lightly. She twisted her head, but his fingers gripped harder and his mouth held hers. Nobody kissed like Tony. He could keep his lips motionless against hers for what seemed forever while his hands did other things, slowly, coaxing her.

"I've left you alone for weeks, haven't I?" he murmured. "But I miss you. Please." He pressed her down into the pillows. "You've just been all screwed up from the tour." He kissed her neck and shoulders with more and more ferocity. Karen felt her body begin to pulsate like the lower registers of a bass viol. Maybe it was a dream. There had been vivid ones lately, sometimes like this. She should try to wake herself up. She pushed against him, resisting, but he pinned her wrists down to either side of her head. His hands knew where to go, how to touch, to please. He pulled the sheet away from her, and with her back arched, her bare nipples brushed against his T-shirt. "Oh, God," she moaned. "No good."

"Yes, good," Tony murmured. "So good. Your skin's on fire. My hot girl."

"Don't," she said. Her voice was a whisper but her body was screaming, sobbing, wild.

He slid slowly down her body, kissing and nipping gently, until his mouth was between her legs. Karen was frantic now, and her arms, freed, could only grasp at his thick hair and pull him closer against her. She reached orgasm immediately, but it wasn't enough.

"Come inside," she begged.

He did, but so slowly, entering her just a little way and withdrawing, teasing her to reach for him with her hips, until finally he, too, was lost and thrust himself into her again and again, both of them taking the desperate journey, she to be filled, he to possess.

When they were finished, Karen lay silent with the sweat turning cold and damp on her body. "That wasn't fair," she said finally.

He lay beside her, naked also, though she couldn't remember how he got that way. "I've missed you."

"You woke me up. My defenses were down."

"This was the real Karen, not that cold bitch you've been masquerading as since Midem."

"I hate myself and I hate you."

He propped himself up on one elbow and looked down into her face. Her eyes were dark and dead like sockets with the bulbs removed. "How can you hate yourself for being natural and real?"

"I'm at the mercy of my cunt," she said bitterly.

"Listen, you owe me . . ."

"I owe you?" she interrupted. "Thirty percent of the gross and a hundred percent of the body?"

He sat up now with head drooping. "Oh, shit, Karen." He took her hand but the fingers were cold and unresponsive. "An explanation is what you owe me," he went on. "That's all. You've never thrown me out of bed before."

"You've never jumped on me in the middle of the night before. Anyhow, I thought that part was over."

"Nobody ever said so."

"It's been a long time since we've been together."

"That's a fact, not an explanation," Tony said. "And for your information, it's been exactly six weeks and three days. Remember that mattress in Cannes with the lump that turned out to be the last guest's vibrator?" Karen didn't answer. Tony's slouched body formed the shadow of an old man. "Things have been different for a long time but I didn't want to get into it with you. I was afraid of what you might tell me. My God, we haven't even had a fight in a month."

Karen sat up against the headboard and covered herself with the sheet. She was resisting the impulse to reach out. She had never heard Tony admit to being afraid of anything. But if she gave way to sympathy, where would it end? "I know things have changed. I've changed. I don't understand it myself. Not yet. I need time. I need space. Oh, listen to this psychobabble."

"You need *me,*" Tony said.

"Yes."

"And I need you, too." It was the closest thing to a whisper Karen had ever heard from him. She could think of no response, so she just kept quiet. "The first time I saw you I knew there was something," he went on meditatively, as if he were speaking to himself. "Not just the talent. Oh, I knew you were . . . phosphorescent; you just glowed up there like a whole galaxy. And I knew you didn't really give much of a shit about the money, even the fame. You just wanted to sing your head off. But I cared about the other stuff, and I knew we'd make some unbeatable combination. And we have, even though I drive you crazy. You need me to push you." He was not looking at her; his eyes seemed fixed on some point beyond the wall. "I just wasn't prepared for the other. The incredible . . . love . . ." The word seemed to strangle him. "That I have for you. God, Karen. Maybe it's because of Stefan and Michael, both of us losing brothers. We're neither of us close to our families, sort of like orphans, maybe. I don't know what it is. I wish to Christ I did because then maybe I could get rid of it."

She made a small sound of pity, and he turned to her angrily. "It's the same for you. I'm not going to let you sneak away from me. I can be patient. I know you don't think so, but I can. I'm not giving you up just because of some wimp in London."

Karen was silent still. He shook his finger at her. "We'll be here again." He jabbed at the mattress. "And you'll be loving it the way you did just now." He stood up, but slowly, as if it caused him pain to move. It seemed a long time before the outer door clicked shut. Finally, when she was relaxed enough to slide under the covers, it was impossible to shake the memory of Tony lying on top of her, as if a giant tree had fallen to pin her helpless beneath its limbs. It was so easy for him to obliterate her. She felt like a thing, not a person, something lost under his physical and psychic bulk. She held her fists to her chest, trying to quell the panic.

And then she thought of Edward. His voice on the telephone, full of pleasure and warmth, yet so calm. The thumping in her heart began to quiet. Edward would never crush her, never crowd her. She fell asleep into a dream where she and Midler were trotting around the bridle path in Central Park. There were men jogging nearby, laboring and sweating with weights on their ankles and in their hands. At first, Karen was amused, lighthearted. These urban men should spend a few weeks on a farm and then they wouldn't have to go to such absurd lengths to exercise their bodies. But the piles of dead leaves beneath Midler's hooves began to thicken until she could barely struggle through them. There was some great menace closing in behind. Midler began to gallop; leaves flew everywhere, but so slowly, turning and floating in a leisurely ballet behind Midler's hooves. Karen urged her up, up, and finally over the top of a tall chain fence, across a stretch of water where gulls circled below, slowly like the leaves, and into the sky where Midler turned to fire, first her tail in a blazing streak of red, then all of her, until Karen was riding a great shimmering animal into the blue-black night.

She woke up panting and soaked in sweat. She rolled over to reach for the notepad beside her bed, and scribbling in the dark, wrote the word *video* and then *horse of fire*. After that, she lay in bed and watched the room grow light.

Sunday morning, Edward woke with a bellyache. Well deserved, he thought, clutching his throbbing abdomen. Soon after hanging up from Karen's telephone call, he found himself standing at the full-length mirror behind his bedroom door making a survey of his body. It wasn't that he was misshapen; in general, the outline pleased him. But oh, the midsection from neck to hips. Every bone stood up to be counted. Karen might be tempted to recruit him as a xylophone for her band. So from Saturday afternoon until well past midnight, Edward had consumed as much bread and ice cream as he could stuff down his throat. The probable futility of such a binge was not lost on him, but perhaps even a few generous fat cells here and there might make a difference, in which event indigestion would not have been in vain.

But Edward's stomach declared breakfast out of the question. He took a long shower and then inspected his apartment. Karen was due at seven, allowing him the entire day to make neat piles from the chaos of *Atlantic Monthlys* and *New Yorkers*. He sent a grateful nod to Persis a few blocks away. If not for his sister, the place would be just another of the spartan cells Edward had always used to call home before he settled here.

At four o'clock, after finally eating half a pint of Steve's chocolate ice cream and pretending to read the Sunday *Times,* he sprang up out of his chair with the sudden realization that flowers were imperative. He prodded the elevator button obsessively, cursing himself for such an obvious omission. Out on Broadway, shuddering without his hat and gloves, he chose a healthy-looking bouquet from the Korean greengrocer and dashed home only to discover that he had no vase. Out he went again, still clutching the flowers, to scour the neighborhood. Finally, exasperated, he ducked into a little Spanish groceria and bought an ornate white vase that said "Enamorado" on it.

"Haven't you got one that says 'Demencia'?" Edward asked. The patient clerk looked quite beautiful with a plastic rose pinned in her hair.

He spent the next hour perusing the Sunday magazine section devoted to men's fashions. Ordinarily, he would have dropped it onto the "toss" pile without opening it, but now he examined it thoroughly. Youthful models glared at him, challenge in their square-jawed faces. Surely Karen Wells was surrounded by such men. Perhaps Edward had fabricated the entire encounter out of some befuddled middle-aged fantasy. Perhaps this quite unnecessary trip home would prove futile after all. The telephone squatted like a shiny black beetle on his desk. It was no dream that Karen's voice had emerged from that machine. She was certainly coming, and soon. His stomach turned over, rendering impossible any further attempt to accumulate fat cells.

At ten minutes to seven, the buzzer rang. Edward spoke into his intercom, listened to the vibrations that passed for human communication, and pushed the button to open the door downstairs. Then he rushed back into the bathroom to wash away the tiny clippings of beard from the last of several trimmings. The elevator doors opened down the hall. He heard her footsteps. Panic pounded in his ears. There was still time to seek refuge in the bedroom and hide there until she grew discouraged and left. Life would go on as before. Teaching, writing, serene, a little boring. By God, it was madness to open that door. At the first ring, he turned to stone. They would find him some day, he figured, a statue in the front hall, gray as granite and just as cold. He imagined Karen on the other side of that inch-thick wooden barrier that separated them, her open face trusting, brave, ready for anything life had to offer. Edward leapt to the door in terror that she might have gone away.

Karen's face was full of entreaty: *Do you still want me?* it said. He reached for her, slid his hands under the coat and kissed her. She responded warmly. Soon her fingers were tangled in his beard. It seemed to Edward that his entire body was flushed. In his feverish condition, he could imagine Julius Southwick smirking at him from the shadows.

Suddenly Karen broke away and stood back. Her eyes looked damp and her voice trembled. "Edward, do you think . . . do you have . . . I'd like to use the bathroom."

"Of course," he said, and taking her elbow, led her through his bedroom. She slipped inside the bathroom and closed the door.

There was an old-fashioned tub with claw feet, and though the toilet was modern, the old tank and chain mechanism had not been removed from the wall. Karen put the seat cover down and sat, still in her coat. Her heart was pounding, her face was hot and she felt on the verge of tears.

"What am I, some kind of slut?" she said to herself. Two nights ago, she had twisted and writhed under Tony Kahanian in Atlanta, and here she was in another man's arms, more than ready, more than eager. Granted, the lovemaking in Atlanta had evolved from a kind of conspiracy between Tony and her anatomy. They had teamed up in the dark and clobbered her while she was still half asleep. Nonetheless, she had wanted it, and now she wanted Edward. What did this mean? Tony had said she owed him. But *what* did she owe him? She stood up and stared at herself in the ancient medicine chest mirror. Even without the black spots where the glass had worn away, she knew the image would not reflect clearly. Where am I? she wondered, staring. She leaned against the door and thought of Edward's face. He had stood in the entranceway just now like a tall question mark: Do you want to be here? Do you feel anything? Shall we pursue this crazy thing? And Karen had wanted to shout in the affirmative.

So why hold back? I'm afraid, she thought. He's going to complicate my life. I don't know what to do about Tony. My sexuality scares me half to death. But still, she could picture Edward waiting outside the bedroom. She had forgotten the warmth of his eyes. They penetrated so far inside and accepted what they found. He was kind and tender, and if she backed off from him now, she would never know. He wanted her. She wanted him. Suddenly it seemed very simple.

She stripped off all her clothes, and put her coat back on. Then, barefoot, she crept out of the bathroom and went to him. As he turned to look at her, his face lit up and she felt his familiarity, the comfort in having somehow known him forever. She went into his arms and when his hands touched her bare skin, he said her name softly.

"I had kind of figured we'd go slow," Karen whispered.

"I don't think I can," Edward said.

They made love on his single bed with the fur coat heaped on the floor beside them like a friendly watchdog.

"So that's lust," Edward said. A strand of golden hair had caught in his beard. He wound it around his finger like a ring.

"Definitely," Karen said. She raised herself up to study his face. Without his glasses, he seemed vulnerable and young. She shook her head.

"What?" Edward asked, stroking her cheek with his finger.

"It's nuts."

"Beyond improbable," he agreed.

"You scared?"

"Beyond scared. I can't imagine what will happen next."

"You know what they say in the vernacular, Edward."

"What's that?"

"Go with the flow."

He smiled. "All right. But you'll have to be patient with me. If I had tried to predict what would transpire during the second half-century of my life, lying here in bed next to you would be as likely as my sprouting wings and flying into the sun."

"Icarus," she mused. "I had this peculiar dream, but very beautiful."

"Are you going to tell me?" Edward's myopia gave her face the textured look of soft fabric.

"Not yet. It's cooking in there, and I don't want to open the oven door until it's ready."

"Is it going to be a song?"

"Maybe." She took a finger and traced the outline of his ribs, counting. "One, two, three . . . Edward, we have to fatten you up."

He smiled. "I've been trying."

"You've been failing." She crawled over him, grabbed his hands and pulled him out of bed. He groped for his glasses. "And another thing. We've got to get you a decent-sized bed. This time we were both so crazed it didn't matter, but wouldn't it be nice to have a little more room to roll around in?"

Edward, standing stark naked in the middle of the rag rug, wore a stunned look on his face.

"I'm scaring you, aren't I?" She stood unself-conscious in her nudity, hand on one cocked hip. "Michael calls it my bully tendencies. I get awfully pushy sometimes. No new bed, then, but food for you, that's for absolutely." She regarded him in silence for a moment, then grinned. "I know what it is, it's those paintings of Jesus Christ in the Prado. But you ruin it when you put on your specs."

He slid his glasses down his nose and peered at her with arms straight out at the shoulders.

"Sick. You hang right there and I'll go out to fetch us something to eat."

Edward watched her dress. It seemed to take no longer than ten seconds from bare to fully clothed. She was quick and graceful, with no wasted motion. When she came to wrap her arms around his waist, the coat felt silky against his skin. It was as if the pelts were Karen's own fur, that she was a wild creature fresh from the woods.

She felt him caressing her and leaned back in his arms. "Shall I get you one of these? Think how chic you'd look."

"It would most certainly create a sensation in the faculty room."

"I don't really approve of furs, but it was tough showing up at galas in my down coat, looking like some kind of hand grenade. I called the Sierra Club for advice and they told me that mink's the thing. They chloroform the little bastards. Every other kind of animal is tortured, and don't believe anybody who tells you otherwise."

"I won't," Edward promised fervently.

"Really, they tell you raccoons are gassed or put to sleep with a fabulous Quaalude shot, but they trap them in awful metal jaws. I won't buy you raccoon." She kissed him, disengaged herself reluctantly, and left.

After the door had closed, Edward stared at it remembering that merely an hour ago he had agonized over whether to let her in. A single hour, and it was apparent that, indeed, life had changed irrevocably. It seemed peculiar and illogical that out of a lifetime of fifty years, a tiny pinprick of time could change everything. But, of course, that was true of earthquakes and winning the lottery and all sorts of events. A few seconds and *wham,* if one permitted oneself to stoop to onomatopoeia, nothing was ever the same. *Wham,* Julius Southwick, take *that.* It suddenly occurred to Edward that he was standing totally unclothed in the drafty hallway and he was not even cold.

"They want me to do this video," she said, slicing herself a chunk of brie. The table in the dining alcove was littered with plastic wrap and containers.

"You'll have to explain," Edward said. "I'm woefully ignorant about anything electronic."

She looked around the room for a television set. "Is it broken or are you truly the only person in America without a TV?"

"Not the only person, surely."

She shook her head. "I may begin to break out in a cold sweat at any moment. I've never been without one."

"You'll adjust."

"Well, I was going to show you what a video looks like. They're on MTV, VH-1—oh, you don't know what I'm talking about. It's like a tiny movie that record companies finance. Now that my album is doing so well, they want to push it along even more by making one. And actually, sometimes these things can be pretty imaginative, either with a story or maybe some kind of mood piece. They've got this red-hot producer, I met him in Atlanta and I like him, he reminds me of this leather doll I had when I was a kid. Edward, the only reason I'm talking so much is to provide cabaret while you eat. No, slop more butter on that bagel. So I said I'd do this thing, which is just a straight concert video, me standing there by the microphone with my tonsils showing for two-and-a-half minutes. Essence of tedium. But I didn't give much of a damn at the time because I was worn out and just wanted to get home. And then I had this dream." She paused to pour Edward another glass of milk. "Drink this." He rolled his eyes and obeyed. "The dream I wasn't going to tell you about." She explained about the horse.

"It's a startling image," Edward said.

"My manager's having a fit because we're supposed to start taping next week. He's arranged a meeting for tomorrow at the record company, and they'll all try to beat me down."

"What are you going to do?"

"I don't know. I'm scared to death. But it's what the album is all about, escape and flying and freedom and sex. And defiance."

"And moonlight," Edward said. She smiled at him. "Don't let them intimidate you." He set his napkin down firmly next to his plate. But she slid a box of chocolate-chip cookies in front of him. He ignored them.

"What about screwing up my career?"

"You can charm them into it."

"Oh, my dear, you have a lot more faith in my charm than I do. These people are not susceptible to charm. They don't have a creative notion in their heads. They'll hear 'fiery horse' and they'll say, 'Balls, think of all that lighter fluid!' Everything is dollars and cents to them. And Tony's having a stroke. Not that I haven't squeezed past that on other occasions. He went nuts when I decided not to use the synthesizer in concert any more, but I finally got my way. If you refuse to eat the cookies, at least don't neglect the avocado."

"You're a persistent sort, aren't you?"

"Yeah."

"Remember that in your meeting."

She was quiet for a moment.

"Listen to me," he went on. "You're the important piece of equipment in all this. They can't do anything without you. They're fully aware of your special gifts and ultimately they have to please you. Don't compromise your dream. In my opinion."

"Your humble opinion."

"Yes. And Tony will get over it."

"You don't know him."

"Do I want to?"

"Probably not. I wouldn't say he's exactly your type."

Edward peered at her.

"It's a very old story," she said, "and becoming more anachronistic every day."

"All right." He looked at her almost shyly. "I want you to meet my sister."

"And I want you to meet my horse," Karen blurted. They both laughed.

"Seems a fair exchange."

"And I want you to tell me about *Beowulf.* I read it."

"We have a lot to do."

"I'll say. Oh, all right, you can quit eating, you look plumper already. You mean to tell me, Edward, that you've never had a really good roll in the hay?"

"Speaking of horses?"

"Yeah."

"Did I say that?" he asked.

"You implied it."

"Well, it's certainly never been, I mean to say . . . actually . . . Good God, is sex going to render me inarticulate?"

"Nothing could render you inarticulate."

"Will you believe me if I tell you that in the past, I participated in it mainly out of a sense of duty?"

She thought this over. "You're pretty damn expert at your duty."

"No. This was close to rape."

She considered his face, owlish with wire-rimmed spectacles, and grinned. "They'd never convict you, Edward."

"I could do it again right now," he said incredulously, looking down at his lap.

"Oh, no, you don't. Not until those calories have a chance to settle on your ribs." She got up and headed for the stereo. Her album was on the turntable, its empty jacket propped alongside. "Did you bring this all the way from London?"

"No, I bought another one here."

"Ubiquitous me."

"Spoken like a true punk lexicologist."

She smiled. "Oh, I went through the 'like, wow' stage, but it got so I couldn't write any more. Brainless garbage kept seeping into my lyrics. '*Baby, like, okay, I want ya,*' that kind of crap. Not that it doesn't sell, but I wasn't happy. So I went on an emergency word binge and started doing crossword puzzles with a vengeance. Whew, let me tell you, it was a year before I could finish the Friday *Times*. Those buggers get worse as the week rolls on. And I made myself use one new word a day in conversation. Sometimes it got pretty funny. You'd get all these showbiz types who don't understand words more than four letters long. They think you're putting them on or showing off or maybe you're from a foreign country. I told this record promo guy I thought his tour coverage was cursory and he figured I was accusing him of bad language. You know, this place looks a lot like your flat in Chelsea. It smells like you, too."

"Oh, dear," Edward said.

"No, it's lovely. Like wet wool, only milder. It's your body, I found out." The curtains were a rich beige-and-wine stripe. "Your sister choose these?"

"Yes."

"When do I meet her?"

"Whenever you say. She's eager."

"She knows we've been together?"

"Of course."

Karen frowned.

"You don't approve?" he asked.

She thought a moment. "I do and I don't. I'm glad I'm important enough to you that you'd want to tell her. On the other hand, I'm nervous. We're having a good time, Edward. I don't want to screw it up by introducing foreign elements."

"Then let's wait a while."

"And besides . . ."

"Besides what?"

"She scares me. She's a poet."

"So are you, my darling," Edward said.

"Don't be ridiculous."

"I've listened to your record."

Karen stared at him. "I don't think there's anything you could say that would give me more pleasure," she murmured finally.

"Come here." She went to him and sat on his lap. He studied her face. The skin around her mouth was faintly pink, irritated from his beard. "Everything I want to say to you is a dreadful cliché," he said.

"I don't care."

"It's difficult for me to use such language."

"You can show me instead."

He kissed her.

"That's good. Are you ready for dessert?"

"Absolutely." He lifted her off his lap and led her to the bedroom.

"You want to piss it all away?" Tony asked. He kept peering out the window of her twenty-fifth-floor bedroom.

"Looking for snipers?"

"You just be as smart-ass as you feel like and let the world come to an end."

"You're making me more nervous than I am already. I thought we were going to meet over there." Piles of discarded clothing lay on her bed. At the moment, she wore a black knit dress. She made a face at herself in the mirror. "Funereal," she muttered and began to undo the zipper at the back. Suddenly she stopped and glanced at Tony. "Excuse me a minute, will you? I want to change into something else."

" 'Excuse me'? What is this?"

Over the years, Karen had become inured to removing her clothes in Tony's presence. But this morning, her nakedness seemed like a gift for Edward only. "Just wait outside the door. It'll take a second." Another time, she might have given him a playful shove, but she was afraid to touch him now. The hotel bedroom in Atlanta had reminded her all too graphically of Tony's sexual power over her.

He yelled through the crack in the door. "You might as well dress for a funeral, if you ask me! Listen, I don't want to go into that meeting without knowing exactly what you're going to say!"

"I can hear you, you don't have to shout. I don't know what I'm going to say."

"Wonderful."

"It's a good idea, Tony. And it's not even going to be expensive."

"You don't understand," Tony said. "It's not that it's a bad idea, it's that it's not *their* idea. If they want you to black your teeth and sing 'Clementine,' you'd better damn well do it. Hurry up; it's going to take a while to find a cab."

She emerged from the bedroom in a navy blue suit with a patterned silk blouse. "What did you do with the limo?"

"I want you to remember what it's like to live in poverty." He fingered her lapel. "What the hell is this anyway?"

"It's my authority suit," she explained.

"You look like a fucking stewardess," he complained.

"Flight attendant. I wish I had a hat."

"Why don't you wear your riding helmet?"

"Wrong color. Hey, listen, Tony, aren't you supposed to be my champion through thick and thin?"

"Thick and thin is one thing, stupidity is another."

"The fact is, I'm scared to death. Help me out, okay?"

"Oh, Christ."

When they got in the cab, Tony gave a deep sigh. "I feel like a drowning man, watching my life pass before my eyes. My youth on the streets of Manhattan, stickball, fistfights, my father with that belt when I got caught playing hooky, all of us kids in one bedroom, my mother in her faded housedresses, finally getting a job and taking all that shit from the owner . . ."

"Look, Tony, you're a self-made man. You should be proud of yourself."

"Don't blow it for me, Karen."

She looked out the window. The trees in the park along Fifth Avenue were covered with tiny green buds. The sun bounced off them, making them gleam like emerald dewdrops. She was afraid, but fear was a familiar companion. Every time she stepped out onto the stage and stared at that mass of people, she was afraid. The feeling was something she had come to expect, like the sensation of hunger in the pit of her stomach when she awoke in the morning.

But guilt, that was something else again. Tony was fond of saying that he had "created Karen Wells," as if she were a blob of plastic he had molded to his own specifications. In a way, he was right. It was Tony who had badgered, cajoled, and pleaded with pivotal representatives of the media. He once rented a stretch limousine he could ill afford and drove to Montauk in pursuit of a record producer. He tracked the executive to the beach and stood in the surf while his cuffs filled with wet sand. "Just listen to her," Tony had begged the astonished man. "If she stinks, okay, but give her a chance." He once closed the club to everyone except music people and provided free imported champagne. The crowd consumed ten thousand dollars' worth of Dom Perignon, but Karen's voice was heard.

"Damn it," she whispered to herself. "Damnation."

"You okay?" Tony asked.

"When God created guilt, he overdid it."

The building that housed American Voice Records was a tall, sleek skyscraper that from the outside appeared windowless, like a grim, secretive monolith. Or perhaps a giant gravestone, Karen thought, marking the end of her career. As if stepping out onto a stage, she crossed herself before entering the lobby.

In the elevator, two young women carried steaming paper cups of coffee. The taller of the two, who wore a spiked hairdo, said, "So they call me down for this commercial and there's all these people sitting in a row staring at me and one of them, this broad in a seven-hundred-dollar suit, says, 'So what do you think of our product, Miss Jenko?' and I says, 'Nodust is my most favorite product in the whole world! In fact, before I came down here, I sprayed Nodust all over my entire body!' Well, they laughed their asses off, but 'a course I didn't get the job. I don't know what come over me." Karen, cheered, glanced at Tony, but he was staring straight ahead.

She counted six people in the conference room. Her hand was shaken in order of executive rank. First, the president of American Voice Records, then the vice-president, who was the only other woman present, then Manfred Warm, who introduced her to the director he had hired, then the head of the video department, and finally the president's assistant, a young man who gave Karen a wide grin. Everybody was dressed informally except for Karen—and Tony in his inevitable mangled suit. But Karen noticed that nobody sat until the president did. Comfortable armchairs were arranged so that Karen faced a semicircle of expressions ranging from receptive (the president's assistant) to hostile (the vice-president). Karen thought about the girl in the elevator and felt a sudden urge to burst into song, perhaps a spirited ditty about household cleaner. *Gimme yer grit / Gimme yer guck / Gimme yer turbid greasy yuck.*

"Well, Karen, I understand we have a difference of opinion concerning your video," said the president. He had a facial tic that pulled his lips back spasmodically into what resembled a smile.

"Yes, sir, I guess we do," Karen said. The president's eyes blinked. No recording artist had ever called him "sir" before, except with heavy sarcasm. He searched her face for irony and found none. "I'm sorry the notion didn't occur to me before we met with Mr. Warm in Atlanta. The timing was unfortunate."

"That's not the only thing that's unfortunate," the video head chimed in. The president held up his hand.

"Suppose you describe to us exactly what you had in mind," said the president. These creative types were mostly babies, but one had to make allowances.

Karen did as she was told, carefully including cost projections and a detailed description of how to execute the concept. "Nicky Stein, my drummer, figured out most of the logistics." Tony looked stunned at this revelation. "It ought to come in well under the forty-thousand-dollar figure."

"I thought you were in philosophical agreement with me," Warm said. His leathery face had faded to a taupe color, perhaps in response to New York City.

"That was before I fell asleep that night," Karen said. The director and the head of the video department exchanged looks.

The president sighed. "Karen, first I want to make it absolutely clear that we are delighted with the album and with your commitment to us. We think you're headed straight up. We want to make you happy. But you're inexperienced. In this matter, we feel that wiser heads should prevail." The tic twitched once.

The video head shifted in his seat as if there were tacks beneath his posterior. "Okay, who's going to fall for this horse thing? You're supposed to be a pop singer, not Willie Shoemaker. And there's not one single song on this album that has anything to do with horses."

" 'Wings' does absolutely," Karen said. "All the feelings are there. What it's like to ride a horse. And this would be a very special ride, visually. There's something else. I'd be naked."

"Oh, give me a break!" the vice-president cried.

"It would be subtle, of course," Karen went on. "There'd be so much light it would be like looking at the glowing form more than a nude. And no saddle, just me and the animal." Her voice had taken on considerable passion. The room was silent. Karen glanced at the president's assistant, who had leaned forward eagerly, watching her with interest.

"Hell, look, there's room for compromise here," the president said. "We have Manfred and Dil all ready to go. Let's try a run-through of the concert thing, and if you don't like it, we'll talk. How about that?"

Karen shook her head. "I don't think so, no. I'm really committed to this."

"For somebody who's just had one fucking album . . ." the video head began, but the president snapped his head around to glare at him.

"Karen," Tony said. "Maybe we ought to have a private conversation in the other room."

"Don't, Tony, please," Karen said quietly.

The president laced his hands together and cracked his knuckles. "You've put us in quite a position here, Karen. You're a new artist and we're taking a flyer on you. Setting up the tour with Harper, that was quite a risk. We've showed good faith, don't you agree?"

"Yes, I'm grateful and I hope I didn't let you down," Karen said. Here was the crux again: debt, obligation, gratitude. She felt herself begin to waver. After all, she was such a novice, and look how they had all demonstrated their confidence in her. But then she heard Edward's voice, calm and assured, reminding her that this was *her* career, *her* choice. They would threaten her next, she supposed. So what the hell, she'd get the jump on them. "Perhaps we should just forget the video this time around. I hope I'll be doing many albums with you and next time we'll all agree and can work together without anyone feeling disappointed."

The video head made a grunting sound. The president stared at Karen for a long time. She held his eyes, mustering every shred of self-control not to watch his teeth as they appeared and disappeared behind the twitching lips.

Finally the president turned to the director, who until now had remained impassive. "What about it, Dil? Think you could pull off this horse thing without covering us in manure?"

"Yes."

Karen smiled at the man. She could see that he was excited by the idea.

"Nobody's ever done a nude video before," said the vice-president. Her voice squeaked with outrage.

"It'll be tasteful," Dil said.

"Tell that to VH-1," said the video head. "They won't play it."

"They'll be falling all over each other to play it," Manfred Warm said. Karen knew she had won.

"We can get a flesh-colored body suit," Tony suggested.

"No," Karen said. "I'll be naked."

"There's a party Saturday night at Hot Tomato," the president said. He had stopped smiling or twitching, whichever it was. Karen was comforted. "It's a welcome-back-from-triumphant-tour party. I expect you to be there."

"I'll be there," Karen said. He could throw his weight around all he liked as far as she was concerned.

But Tony did not speak to her in the elevator, and he stalked away down Fifth Avenue without a word.

Karen padded barefoot back and forth across Edward's living room. He sat in the armchair trying to read, but every now and then he peered at her over the rim of his glasses, his head zigzagging back and forth as if he were watching a tennis match.

"Maybe she won't come," Karen said. "Maybe she got lost on the subway and went to the Bronx instead."

Edward smiled. "It's a five-block walk. No subway."

"I shouldn't have worn this. It's too showbiz." Karen's sweatshirt was mottled with colorful handprints.

"Come here," Edward said, laying aside his book.

She sat on his lap and put her arms around his neck.

"Were you this nervous before the meeting yesterday?"

"No," she said.

He cocked his head at her.

"But that was business," she protested. "This is your sister."

"Ah, it was merely your career on the line."

"It's too soon. We should have waited."

"Until you and I know one another better?" Edward suggested.

"Oh, hell, it's true," Karen sighed. "We've known each other a hundred years at least." She glanced at her watch. "Maybe she's going to stand us up?"

Edward laughed at the blatant hope in her voice. "Persis is always late. She'll be here."

The buzzer sounded.

"I have to go to the bathroom," Karen said.

Edward went to open the door while Karen fled. She locked herself in the bathroom and slid down against the door. This is ridiculous, she told herself. What am I, three years old? *I'm three / I'm three / That's all I'll ever be.* She covered her ears but the childish tune played over and over in her head. There was a low vibration of voices from the living room. "She's not the pope," Karen said to herself. "She's just another human being who sweats and farts and wakes up with bad breath. Get a grip on yourself." She stood up, took a look at her face in the mirror, smoothed her hair, and stepped out into the living room. Persis was sitting in the corner of the couch nearest Edward's chair. She leaned toward him in earnest conversation. When she saw Karen, she stopped abruptly. Karen came to stand in front of them like a child summoned by her parents. Edward rose. "Karen, this is Persis. Persis, Karen Wells." Persis reluctantly unwound her long limbs to stand beside Edward. Karen, dwarfed by the two lean figures, held out her hand and craned her neck up at Edward's sister. Then Persis sat down again, leaving Karen to perch on the far end of the couch.

Persis peered at Karen. "We've been enjoying your album."

"Thank you." Karen supposed the "we" was meant to include Edward. "I've been enjoying your poetry."

"Oh? Were you actually able to find a copy in a bookstore?"

"Well, um, Edward let me borrow his." Karen felt obscurely guilty, as if, what a piker, she should have bought her own.

"Of course," Persis said. She was what Karen would call a handsome woman, with a face photographers would like. Lots of bones, deepset eyes, and dark hair with dramatic streaks of gray. There was a long silence. Karen glanced at Edward, but he looked merely amused.

Karen wanted to say, "I love your brother." Instead, she asked, "Do you have an apartment near here?"

"Not too far," Persis answered, but did not elaborate.

Karen shot an accusatory look at Edward. He had told her that

Persis was a celebrity hound. Where was all that reputed fan mentality now? The woman just sat there squinting at her.

"Persis," Edward said. "What's the matter with your eyes? You look subversive."

"I lost a lens this morning," Persis admitted. She gave him a little smile and Karen got a hint of what might be a strong resemblance to Edward.

"What's that, number four hundred twenty-three?" Edward got up and retrieved a pair of glasses from his desk drawer. Persis put them on and blinked at Karen, who was resisting the impulse to giggle. If one were to paste a false beard on the woman, she and Edward might be identical twins.

"Persis brought the Macy's Parade to a standstill one Thanksgiving by losing a lens under, who was it, Minnie Mouse?"

"Snoopy," Persis muttered. "They were damned uncivil about it, as if I would do such a thing on purpose."

"Well, you held the thing up for a full twenty minutes."

"You exaggerate." Persis swung around to Karen, who jumped. "Are you going on tour?"

"I've just been," Karen answered.

"I told you that," Edward said to Persis.

"Oh, yes, I guess you did."

"How did it turn out with the bound galleys?" he asked his sister. "Are they going to fix the margins?"

"Oh, Christ, there's a huge hassle," Persis said. "They claim the margins are fine and that changing them would put me well over my allotted ten percent. So Maynard has gone to battle and we'll just have to see."

Edward explained to Karen. "Persis's next volume is in the final stages of production. She found some things wrong, but if what she wants to alter uses up more than a certain percentage of the composition costs, she has to pay for the excess herself."

"That doesn't seem fair," Karen said. "Not if it doesn't look right."

"It's in my contract," Persis said.

"And Maynard is her agent," Edward said.

"So what do you plan to do?" Karen asked. But Persis directed her reply to Edward. "I'll make them fix it. The stanzas look so isolated and strange this way. I can't think what's the matter with those people."

Soon Edward and Persis were deeply ensconced in a discussion about the bastardization of the craft of typesetting since the arrival of computers. Karen tried to look absorbed as well, but the vocabulary was totally unfamiliar. She began to amuse herself by making up songs with stray words that appealed to her ear: *What'm I gonna do with these here cursive fonts? / My ellipsis lost its grips, 'n' baby, whaddaya think he wants? / He's in the dark in lightface and he says he's feeling blue . . .*

"Karen?" Edward looked at her as if he had been calling her for a while.

"Oh, sorry. Off in a dream, I guess. Sorry."

"You were going to take us to meet Midler," Edward reminded her.

Karen imagined what a peculiar sight they must make walking up West End Avenue, the spindly, towering Vaughns and Karen bobbing along between, two giraffes and a chimpanzee. If we just keep heading north, Karen thought, we'll wind up at the Bronx Zoo.

Rounding the corner onto Eighty-ninth Street, she could see the dingy sign for the Claremont Riding Academy. Suddenly she wished she had not brought them here. Why was she in such a hurry to introduce this hostile woman to a dear old friend?

She wanted to erase Persis's image from the sidewalk, "disappear" her the way she and Michael had "disappeared" their despised Aunt Barbara when she came waddling up the long dirt drive, laden with questions about their teachers and whether they ever touched the children in a nasty way when nobody was looking. It had become possible eventually for Michael and Karen to ignore the woman so totally that despite her immense bulk she almost ceased to exist for them. Once when Karen was alone, Aunt Barbara had grabbed her by the arm, holding her so tightly that bruises appeared on the young skin. "What about your brother?" Aunt Barbara had hissed. "Does he ever, you know, put his hands in places they have no business being?" Karen had closed her eyes and concentrated. She is not here,

Karen had thought. If I try hard enough, her fat body will just turn into mist and evaporate. "It's naughty, you know," Aunt Barbara whispered, holding Karen very close to her enormous breasts. "Tell me what he did. You'll feel much better. I'll keep it a secret, just between you and me." It's not working, Karen thought with rising panic. Her eyes were still clamped tight shut. But suddenly the iron grip loosened on her arm and Aunt Barbara gave a sigh that sounded like steam escaping into the air. Karen had walked carefully to the kitchen door and did not start to run until she was safely down the back steps into the yard.

Soon enough, Karen and Michael learned that the disappearing game had its limitations. No amount of concentration erased the teacher who accused Michael of stealing or the little girl who spent an entire year unaccountably taunting Karen with scatalogical name-calling ("Cowpie Karen," "Weewee Wells"). It became apparent that other means would have to be summoned to deal with such unpleasant people. So as much as Karen would prefer to eliminate Persis Vaughn from the scene, the woman was, after all, Edward's sister, and Karen would have to figure out a way to cope with her.

Karen led Persis and Edward up the steep ramp to the right of the riding circle. At the top they stepped through a doorway into a large expanse filled with narrow stables. Each booth was labeled with the horse's name and feeding instructions.

"This isn't humane," Persis said. "They're jammed in here like sardines."

"Not really," Karen said. "These are city horses. They're not used to running wild. Actually, the police department keeps some of its mounts here."

"Hm," Persis said, as if this fact merely confirmed the iniquity.

Karen looked for Edward, but he had fallen behind to stare up at the ceiling. It was festooned with spider webs.

"Extraordinary," he said. "Persis, look at this."

She followed his gaze and caught her breath. "That's quite beautiful," she murmured. "How many years hard labor for the spiders, I wonder."

"It's a comfortable symbiotic relationship," Karen said. "The spiders feed on the insects that annoy the horses."

She led them through the labyrinth of narrow corridors and stopped in front of a booth that said, "Midler: Savory Pellets." At the sound of Karen's voice, the mare began to stomp restlessly and toss her head. Karen unlocked the stable door and went inside. "Hello, darling," she crooned, and laid her head against Midler's shiny brown neck. "Patrick'll be by for a ride later on, but I wanted you to meet my friends."

Despite herself, Persis was staring at Midler in fascination. "What a beautiful creature. Are you sure it's not crowded in there?"

"She's fine. I don't let her get stir crazy. If I can't be here, I hire a student friend to ride her." Karen took some peppermints out of her pocket and held them to Midler's mouth. The horse gobbled them up with her lips.

"May I do that?" Persis asked.

"Sure." Karen passed the candy to Persis. The woman held out her index finger with a mint poised delicately on the end. Midler lapped it up.

"It's very soft. I guess I assumed its mouth would be tough and prickly."

"Have you ever been on horseback?" Karen asked, stroking Midler's back.

"No."

"Yes, you have," Edward corrected her. "Remember when Mother concluded we lacked contact with the natural elements? She took us to the botanical gardens and made us smell everything and on Sundays it was the Central Park Zoo for pony rides."

Persis laughed. "Oh, yes, and we listened to incessant quotations . . ."

" 'The noblest conquest man had ever made,' " Edward said, with a nod toward Midler.

"George Louis Leclerc de Buffon," Persis said. "Midler fits the bill, too, but those pathetic nags in the zoo—well."

" 'All in green went my love riding / On a great horse of gold / into the silver dawn,' " Persis said.

"That's nice," Karen said, thinking of her dream. "Who wrote that?"

"e. e. cummings," Edward said. " 'O! for a horse with wings!' "

"Shakespeare," Persis said. "How about 'Now the wild white horses play, / Champ and chafe and toss in the spray.' "

"Hmm," Edward said. "Matthew Arnold."

"Clever boy," Persis said and they both laughed.

Karen caressed Midler absently while gazing at Persis with a mixture of awe and dismay. Edward came to stand beside Karen and drape an arm across her shoulder. "e. e. cummings would appreciate your video, don't you think?"

"Sounds like he got there before I did."

"You won't be all in green," Edward reminded her.

"Not unless I'm deathly ill." She shook her head with a tiny movement, hoping that Edward would not elaborate. She was not ready to share with Persis the intimate offspring of her creativity. At that moment, a young man on horseback rounded the corner and clipclopped past. The horse loomed over them and was as shiny black as a polished ebony piano.

"Hello, Jim," Karen said.

"Wells," the man answered with a smile.

Persis stared after them, open-mouthed.

"Would you like to ride with me sometime?" Karen asked her.

"I wouldn't know what to do on a horse."

"I'll teach you."

Edward smiled. "You don't know with whom you are dealing, Karen. You'll wind up chasing her down Fifth Avenue."

"You have no faith in my innate athletic ability," Persis protested.

Edward explained to Karen. "You're in the presence of the only person extant who nearly committed suicide with a tennis racket." Persis glared at him. "She was racing to reach a return," Edward went on, "and sliced at the ball. Only the racket whipped around and smacked her in the head. Knocked her out cold. They thought she'd had a heart attack."

"There were webbing marks on my cheek for days," Persis said. "Anyway, that has nothing to do with riding a horse. All you have to do is sit there."

"Well, more or less," Karen said. She gave Midler a farewell kiss on the nose and closed the stable door. "Back tomorrow, darling. We'll take a long ride, I promise."

At the corner of Broadway and Eighty-ninth Street, Persis and Karen said their stiff pleased-to-meet-you's, and Persis set off for her apartment. Karen and Edward walked in silence for a moment. Then, under her breath, Karen muttered, "Does she have to be so damn smart?"

"There's smart and there's sense," Edward said.

"Look how you two quote all that stuff."

"It was how we were brought up. Even at meals, we each sat at the table with a book beside the plate."

Karen sighed. "I was shoveling horseshit while you were memorizing *Macbeth*."

"When I was memorizing *Macbeth,* you weren't even born."

"I'll never catch up," Karen said.

"If you start feeling inadequate about your intellect, I'm going to start feeling inadequate about my musical ability. You'll have to listen to me sing. Incessantly. 'My ship has sails . . .' " he began in his wavery tenor.

"All right, I get the point. But it's not just measuring myself against you and Persis. I want to learn it all for me."

"I understand that. We'll work on it."

"She didn't like me."

"How can you know that?"

Karen rolled her eyes at him.

"She'll come around."

"She thinks I'm . . . trivial."

"It doesn't matter what she thinks," Edward assured her.

"Oh, but it does. She's *the* most important person in your life."

"Was," Edward corrected her, and paused. "Oh yes. That's a problem I hadn't given any thought to."

"She's pretty close to hating my guts," Karen said. "If I were some gigantic brain trust, maybe I'd be acceptable. But as it is . . ."

"I'm not so sure you're right. It's better that you're not about to invade her territory. She doesn't have to worry about your spouting lines of Chaucer. In any event, she'll just have to get used to you."

"Thank you, Edward." She tugged on his arm until he stopped. "Let's postpone dinner for a while and just go back to bed."

He kissed her forlorn mouth and took her home.

* * *

"You weren't what I would call warm," Edward complained.

Persis was folded into the far corner of the couch that Karen had occupied the day before. "I arrived here totally unprejudiced," she said. "But Edward, really."

Edward stood up and began pacing. "You're the one who's been after me ad nauseam to 'fling myself into the emotional pit of life.' "

"I said emotional pit, not armpit."

"That's uncalled for."

Persis gave a great sigh. "I'm sorry. But darling, talk about inappropriate. How are you going to feel dragging her to faculty dinners?"

"As a matter of fact, you may be interested to know that I have an appointment with my department head tomorrow to discuss the possibility of turning Julius into a full-fledged book."

Persis stared at him. After a moment, she said, "I'm supposed to conclude that Karen Wells talked you into making that commitment."

"I haven't made it yet, nor have I mentioned it to Karen. But surely there's a connection."

"I suggest you take her along to the meeting . . ."

"Persis," Edward interrupted. "You've spent a few hours with her. You can't pretend to know anything about her. She has so much to offer, vitality, sensitivity, a special kind of wisdom. I'm making myself sick here. There's no reason for me to be defending her to you."

"Are you going to get married or something?"

"I never thought about it."

"I think you should consult Doctor Myers."

"I should consult a psychiatrist because I'm seeing someone of whom you disapprove? Christ, Persis, think back to some of *your* choices. At least Karen's not pathological, nor does she have any difficulty remembering which sex with which to identify."

"We're not talking about me. Perhaps I'm a lost cause in the romance department, but there's no excuse for you to follow my sordid example."

Edward took off his glasses and rubbed his eyes. "You're my sister and my best friend. I can't tell you how much I dislike being at odds with you. I couldn't sleep last night for making speeches to you, all about trust and loyalty and tolerance. You're the poet. You're supposed to be receptive to life's vagaries. Here's one. Don't be so quick to dismiss it."

Persis was silent. Edward knew he was beginning to get through because she was winding strands of hair around her fingers. He sat down next to her on the couch and took her hand. He could not remember ever having touched her. Her skin seemed dry and papery, the texture of Kleenex. "Persis, all these years you've been right about me. I was a dead man. She's bringing me to life. Can't you be pleased for me?"

Persis closed her eyes, held Edward's fingers to her cheek and nodded her head.

Hot Tomato had been converted from a deserted printing warehouse on Hudson Street into the newest of the chic discotheques. Suddenly stretch limousines appeared in the neighborhood against the backdrop of graffiti and street litter. Now and then a five-hundred-dollar satin slipper was forced to step over the ragpile of a derelict to reach the entrance to this fashionable glitter palace, but such forgettable brushes with poverty were considered a small price to pay for a chance to breathe the same air as the world's most celebrated personalities.

Tonight that air smelled like a warm mist of sweat and Obsession, Karen thought, as she stood gyrating on the dance floor, crushed by bodies in motion on all sides. She could no longer guess who her partner was. Men grabbed her by the shoulders and spun her around to plant damp kisses on her face and neck. *"Mazel tov!"* they shouted. "Super job!" The faces and snatches of sentences swirled past her like the flickering lights pulsating from the ceiling and walls. The shattering howl of the band and the exotic manic flashing against flying bodies confused her sense of equilibrium. She staggered, fell against the nearest broad back, and clung to it tightly. It was Tony.

"What's the story?" he shouted.

"Air!" she begged. He drew her laboriously through the crowd to the edge of the dance floor. Even here, the place was packed, but at least people were standing still, drinking, watching, and trying to converse. Karen clutched desperately at her ears. "I can't get them to stop buzzing! Christ, can't they lower the decibels?"

"You know they like it this way!" Tony yelled. "Keeps the party alive! Hey, there's Bill Wexler! I'll go get us some press!"

"Don't leave me!" Karen cried after him. But as soon as he disappeared into the seething mass of shadows, two men jostled her, one on each side.

"Good show, Karen Wells!" one of them shouted. He wore a sequined cowboy hat. Karen watched the lights leap off it and remembered how Michael, as a little boy, had called sequins "sinkweeds."

"Do I know you?" she yelled.

"Frank Asquith! And this is Joe Minard!" It was impossible to discern their features in this crazy light. Karen kept her eyes on the hat and Joe Minard's collar and cuffs, which glowed in fluorescent splendor. She felt as if she were flanked by invisible men whose existence was evinced only by these random spots of illumination.

"We think you could use some guidance!" Frank yelled.

"What?" Karen heard it as "some spiders" and knew that was wrong.

"Guidance!" Joe screamed. "Your career! It's time you traded up! We're with I.T.!"

Karen caught on. International Talent was an immense agency that handled the careers of top-flight artists around the world, Denny Harper's included.

"I've got a manager!"

"We'll work it out with Tony!"

They pressed against her, both shouting at once. She began edging toward the dance floor, but they moved right along beside her. She wriggled her shoulders, trying to shrug them off, but still they clung. She wedged herself into the foot-stomping throng and tried to scrape them off, but they adhered, shrieking at her about percentages and record deals. Finally, she let her body go completely limp. She slid to the floor between them and quickly crawled away beneath the tangle of legs. She got clipped on the side of the head by a pair of fine-tooled leather boots and once looked up to find that the young lady dancing above wore no underpants beneath her tiny ultrasuede skirt. When Karen finally crept out, she was on the far side of the dance floor, hundreds of bodies away from the persistent agents. She scrambled for the exit and stumbled out into the street. It was damp and chilly with a fine misty rain falling. She stood gasping, sucking in gulps of darkness and silence. Then she hailed a cab and headed uptown.

By the time she arrived at Edward's apartment, it was past midnight. Her heart was still pounding and she kept having to remind herself to breathe. Every time she closed her eyes, she could see the lights spinning around and felt the crush of bodies pressed against her. When Edward opened the door, she practically fell through it.

"Karen. Darling. What is it?" He drew her into the living room when she stood blinking. The room glowed softly in the light from Edward's reading lamp. His book lay open beside his chair and the radio played with the muted sounds of the classical music station WQXR. Edward urged her into a corner of the sofa and, still holding her hands, sat opposite her in his chair. She looked up at him, his eyes so full of concern, but patient, not pressing her, and she fell on her knees and buried her face in his lap. "I can't do it," she cried into the soft wool of his robe. "I can't do it any more." He stroked her hair, and after a while she sat back on the Oriental rug and looked up at him. Her eyes moved over his face, then around the room, along the rows of bookshelves and the Edwardian prints, past the needlepoint pillows and the china figures on his desk. She gave a deep sigh. "It's very quiet here," she said at last.

Despite her concern that he was far too thin, Karen enjoyed tracing the outline of Edward's ribs. In the near total darkness of his bedroom, it seemed very intimate to be almost touching his bones beneath the spare covering of flesh. Edward was not buried deep inside layers of muscle and flesh, but close to the surface, accessible.

" 'She walks in beauty like the night / Of starless skies and cloudless climes,' " Edward said, smiling at her. "Wordsworth was a corny old bastard."

"I'm glad you feel moved to quote corny."

"What time is it, do you suppose?"

"About three."

"I never slept all night with a woman. Until this past week."

"Shame on you."

He could hear the delight in her voice in the darkness. "What's more, I've never gone to bed without brushing my teeth."

"I'm glad I'm having such a positive influence on your routine."

"My darling, you have turned my life on its ear. I sit by the hour listening to your record while I should be down at the Public Library. Absolutely ludicrous for a man of my age."

"Fifty is not Methuseleh."

"I was a mental Methuseleh."

She crooned in his ear. *"He was a mental Methuseleh / and she sang a teenybopper song. / She tried to grab at his you-know-what / But his beard was much too long . . ."* Edward laughed appreciatively. "Edward, what do you think about when we make love?"

"I wasn't aware that I think at all."

"You can't be a total blank. Don't you have fantasies?"

He was silent for a moment. "Oh, well, I suppose there are certain images."

"Like what images?"

"Well . . ."

"You don't want to tell me."

"They seem rather sordid in the afterthought."

"All right, I'll tell you mine. Then you can tell me yours, but only if you feel like it. And be impressed, Edward, because I've never told anybody this before in my life."

"Are you sure you want to?"

"Yes."

"Why?"

"Because I can feel your ribs. I want you to feel mine."

He thought it over. "I see," he said. "Tell me."

She lay back and talked up at the ceiling. "There are almost always two other people, usually men but sometimes one is a woman. One of them is active and one passive. There are different scenarios, but I'm always being persuaded to have sex against my will. But not really. *They* know I want it. Sometimes it begins with oral sex, but by the end there's always penetration. I'll say, 'No-no-no' and struggle, but the passive one holds me down while the other one performs whatever he wants, and pretty soon I'm begging him to keep going." She stopped for a moment.

"Where does it happen?" Edward asked.

"Different places. Sometimes my own apartment. Sometimes on the deck of a sailboat floating in the middle of the sea and everything is bright, shiny blue. Sometimes on stage in front of a huge audience. But not so often any more. I guess maybe I exorcise that one by performing."

"Where was it tonight?"

"Funny, that's what made me think of it. I can't remember it happening before, but there was no fantasy at all. I was just with you."

He leaned over and kissed her gently on the mouth. "Karen," he said.

"What?"

"Nothing. Just 'Karen.' "

"I like macho types in my fantasies," she said. "Delivery men, superintendents, maintenance men, the window washer. I imagine them putting things inside me, these great huge gleaming tools."

"Oh dear," Edward said.

"Don't be intimidated. I did sleep with a very good-looking plumber once. It was one of life's major disappointments. So much better to keep it in fantasyland. Now you."

"Well . . ."

"You keep saying that."

"Well . . ." he said again and they both laughed. He took a deep breath and she could feel his chest shudder a little. "I am on a platform tied hand and foot to a tall post. The rope is tight and it hurts my wrists. I'm naked under a brown robe, I suppose something like what monks of a certain order would wear. There are many women milling around below, angrily. They seem fierce. Then one climbs up and snatches the robe away so that I'm exposed to the crowd. And she . . . well . . ." Karen waited. "She puts her mouth on my penis," he continued. "She's quite rough, but I become very . . . agitated."

"You mean excited."

"Yes. When I'm really rather frantic, they cut the ropes away and

I don't run. I stay to take the woman while the others jeer and call out."

"Edward," Karen said.

"What is it?"

"This conversation is turning me on."

"You have to give me some time, darling. Things don't spring to life as quickly as they once did."

"Are you okay?"

"Certainly. I think another twenty minutes or so . . ."

"No, I mean talking about this stuff. You're not upset?"

"No." He paused. "I trust you completely."

She was silent for a long time. Finally he heard her sniff and realized she must be crying. He cupped her damp cheek with his hand. "Sometimes the gods are kind," he murmured. She threw her arms around his neck and kissed him again and again, digging her fingers into his hair, his beard. After a while, he said, "Well, perhaps not quite twenty minutes."

Karen woke early the next morning. She climbed over Edward and went to fix coffee. When she came back into the bedroom with two steaming mugs, he was propped up against the headboard staring myopically into space. Karen laughed, handed him his coffee and sat cross-legged on the bed.

"Where are my glasses?" he asked.

"You can't have them."

"Why not?"

"Because I look better in the morning without them."

He blinked at her. "Ah," he said finally. "You don't really mind what you look like, not with me."

"No," she said. "They're under the bed right beside you."

He reached for them. "Well, good morning," he said with a big grin.

"Good morning yourself. I want you to promise me something."

"I'll try," he said.

"Don't give your telephone number to anybody."

He looked puzzled.

"They'll be after me. Tony's very clever at tracking me down."

"All right." He took a long sip of coffee. "But you'll have to be found eventually."

"Will I?"

"What are you saying?"

She made pleats in the blanket between her fingers. "I don't know."

"Don't you have another tour coming up after the video?"

"Yes," she sighed. "I dread it."

"Was this one so hateful?"

"I didn't think so at the time, I guess. But when I imagine going through it again . . . Oh, it was exciting in the beginning, my very first tour. Especially because it was such a success right from the start. But people are nuts on the road, Edward. You get all cranked up into this incredible performance mentality where you're existing on a strange high-frequency level . . ." She paused to make the tinny hum of a mosquito. "Then it's over and the audiences, these huge masses of faces, are all screaming with their mouths wide open and their eyes popping and they want you, you, more, more, and finally you go back to your hotel room and sit there with your heart pounding, wondering how on earth you'll ever get to sleep even though it's three A.M. And the rest of the band is off doing dope to try and calm themselves down. It's gotten so Ferris can't make it for more than a couple of hours without coke, so he's doing it everywhere, even in the john on the plane. I kept trying to find little quiet holes where I could hover over your *Beowulf* so I wouldn't feel so insane myself. It's catching. How long can you get off on applause anyhow? You drive yourself like a lunatic so you can hear a whole bunch of people smack their palms together in the middle of the night. Don't you think that's a little bizarre?"

"Isn't it what sustains most performers? The roar of the crowd?"

"I'll tell you what's sustaining this one. Making that video. The preliminary stuff is almost done now, and, God, it's a gas, working with Manfred and especially with Nicky. She's really blossoming with this, it's so exciting to watch, and they all thought I was nuts dumping my drummer into the pot. But she's so bright and she's got such a great sense of what works visually. She's the one who thought up the background for the flight section when nobody else could get it right. It'll be a cartoon, really, with the chain-link fence and the trees and birds all moving but growing smaller and smaller in the distance. It's going to look great." She sighed heavily. "Ah, what's the matter with me anyway? I've got no right to bitch and moan. Most singers would kill for what I've got going right now. It's what I've worked for all these years." She paused. "But I didn't know *you* all these years."

"I don't ever want to draw you away from your work."

"Edward, it's not even you exactly, it's what you *mean.*" She shook her head. "Screw it, I want to write songs and I suppose I'll have to keep on performing to pay for the privilege."

"And what about the musical?" Edward asked.

"Self-delusion on a monumental scale."

"I'm getting angry," Edward declared in amazement.

Karen, alarmed, sat up in a hurry, crossed her legs Indian style and reached for Edward's hand. "Why?"

"I'm a fine one to lecture you about self-expansion, courage, testing one's limits, and so on. Neither am I an expert on modern popular music. But it seems to me that your song-writing is basically theatrical. It's vivid, dramatic, it could be effective in a visual medium. I wish you would try." He hesitated. "There's something I haven't told you." Karen looked frightened. Edward smiled and took her hand. "No, don't be alarmed. It's merely that I spoke with someone at the university about doing a biography on Julius Southwick. It would mean a leave of absence, but they seem quite receptive. There's been no major work on him to date, and I think they'd like to feel associated with such a project."

Karen stared at him, stunned. Then she broke into a grin. "God damn it, Edward, you're an inspiration."

He held up his hands. "I haven't settled anything yet. At this point, it's simply a thought."

"Well, I'm dazzled," she said. "All right, Edward. Since you're so brave and since I refuse to let you get the better of me . . ." She paused and took a deep breath. "I'm going to call a man about the musical."

"That's my girl," Edward said, giving her a kiss.

"But Edward, if you do the book, it means you'd be in England for months and months."

Edward nodded.

"Do you ever think . . . I mean, do you have any notions about us, well, being together more?"

Edward blinked. Sometimes he appeared myopic even with his glasses on. "I don't know specifically if I've given it much thought except that certainly I miss you when you're not here and I look forward to your arrival more than I can say."

"Not very forward-thinking, are you, Edward?"

"I suppose that's true."

"Don't you look at me and think," Karen did her best imitation of Sylvester Stallone, "that woman, that's what I want, gimme that woman."

Edward laughed. "Certainly not."

Karen's smile was a little wan. "I know you don't."

"What is this all about, Karen?"

"I wish we could live together," she answered.

"But that's not possible."

"If we want something enough we can *make* it possible."

He shook his head. "I don't quite see . . ."

"Ah, Edward. Now you're the one who's imposing limitations. The first thing to decide is whether or not you want me with you. There's three weeks left before you go. That's plenty of time."

"But the tour. Wherever would we live?"

Karen waved her hand impatiently. "Forget all that. Let's deal with the basic issue first." She watched him lying wide-eyed and stiff against his pillow. "Edward, you look like you were just run over by a truck. It's just an idea, that's all."

"I've been a bachelor for a long time."

"I'm not asking you to marry me."

"But to live together, that's what you mean, I believe."

"I'm not sure. I'm just interested in investigating the possibilities with all due freedom of self-expansion. Don't look so terrified."

"I'm sorry. It all seems too fantastic to be real. Here I am committed to do this book. And I'm completely unaccustomed to thinking about anyone else. You're so very young, our lives couldn't be more opposed. I'm afraid I'm not the impulsive type."

"I'll say. Well, that's quite a list. Is there anything on the positive side?" Her voice was beginning to lose its humor.

Suddenly Edward's body relaxed. He reached out to take her face between his hands. "Yes," he said softly.

"And what's that?"

"Oh, my."

" 'Oh, my'?"

"I love you," he said.

"Goodness," Karen said, and then fell speechless at last.

Edward smiled at her. "You are dazzling, my darling. I'm not used to such incandescence."

Karen, recovered now, climbed on top of him with a leg to either side. "I'll buy you some dark glasses. And I won't rush you, I promise." She gave him a long kiss. "And since you're going to be very brave and consider taking on a young floozy, I'll be equally brave and tell you what I did this morning before you woke up. Ready?"

He nodded. After a moment, she began to sing softly.

Rumpled sheets in a narrow bed,
Battered pillow where we lay our heads,
Sun sniffs at the window with a golden snout,
Snap shut the curtain! Keep the morning out!

Do not disturb!
Can't you read the sign?
We're much too busy loving
To be bothered with the time.
Don't tell us to climb out of bed
And face the light of day,
'Cause we're much too busy loving,
Keep your nosy sun away.

She paused. "Then this part is repeated, the 'Do not disturb!' which is the chorus. That's all I'm sure I know the music for, that section." She looked at him shyly. "So?"

"There's a poem you must hear," Edward said. He got out of bed, went into the living room and reappeared with a volume of poetry by John Donne. He flipped through it, then began, " 'Busy old fool, unruly sun / Why dost thou thus, / Through windows and through curtains call on us? / Must to thy motions lovers' seasons run? . . .' " Karen sat transfixed. As Edward read Donne's stanzas, the poet's warm and tousled seventeenth-century bed seemed as real as the one she was sitting on. " 'Shine here to us, and thou art everywhere,' " Edward read. " 'This bed thy centre is, these walls thy sphere.' "

"Whew," Karen said. "Makes a person feel pretty inadequate."

"You needn't. I read it to you because I think the old preacher would have been pleased with your song."

"That's a preacher?"

Edward nodded. "He had his secular side."

"No kidding." She glanced at the bureau where a small antique silver clock ticked quietly. "I'd like to pick that thing up and fling it out the window."

"You have to go."

She nodded and began retrieving articles of clothing that were strewn around the apartment. She called to him from the bathroom. "I've got a question!"

"Fire away," he said, slipping into his robe.

"Don't come in here. I don't want to see your face when I ask it."

He stopped in the doorway and put his hands over his glasses.

"That's no help, you silly man. I want you to come home with me next weekend. I mean to my parents. Will you?"

He gaped at her.

"See? I knew you'd be horrified."

"Am I horrified?"

"Yes."

He thought it over. "Certainly I'll come."

"I said you were a brave man, Edward Vaughn."

"Don't tell me that. I may back out."

"Nope, only your death or mine can stand in the way now. You're committed."

"Perhaps I should consider murdering you and then leaping out the window." He put his fingers around her throat and squeezed gently. She extracted herself and slipped under his arm into the living room. "Where's my coat? Oh, I didn't bring one, did I, escaping the way I did. Tony must have rescued it." She did a pirouette in her spangled red dress with the spaghetti straps. "What a reputation you'll have, with this disco dolly emerging from your parlor on a Sunday morning."

"It'll lend me an air of mystery."

"Or lechery." She hugged him. "Ugh, I hate leaving. It rips layers off my insides." She flung herself at the door and tapped off down the hall on her skinny high heels. She turned to shake a finger at him before disappearing into the elevator. "Don't you dare forget breakfast!"

Edward padded aimlessly around the apartment. Everything seemed unfamiliar. He stared at objects: the stereo, the armchair with its neighboring floorlamp peering curiously over its shoulder, the manuscript scattered across his desk. Trying to orient himself, he picked up the porcelain elephant Persis had bought for his fortieth birthday and flopped down on the sofa. The ceiling still needed a paint job. One panel of the curtains still bagged at the top. Familiar, and yet he was shaken by the sense of never having been in this room before.

"She's too young for me," he protested. "Too vital, too free, too physical, not urbane, not intellectual, too short." He turned the elephant over in his fingers. "I don't need anyone. I don't want anyone. I didn't ask for this." The apartment was very quiet as usual, yet now the silence vibrated as if a hundred brass instruments had just blared out a triumphal march and suddenly stopped. She was here, echoing in the stillness.

He bolted up off the couch and went into his bedroom to dress. He would escape to the coffee shop and read the Sunday papers over breakfast.

It was warm and sunny out on the street. The West Side was wide awake and bustling with families, dogs, joggers, bicyclists, and a group of young boys doing a sidewalk slalom on skateboards, with soda cans as their markers. Edward felt buoyant and fit enough to take a turn himself. He went into the coffee shop and sat down at the counter.

"Toasted corn and black coffee, no sugar?" asked the counterman.

"Not this morning, Nick. I think I'm hungrier than that. I'll take scrambled eggs with rye toast. And bacon, crisp, and a large juice."

"You training for the marathon or what?" Nick asked, then commented to the waitress, "Guy's been coming in here ten years, always orders a corn muffin. You never know."

Edward ate every scrap. But while he was spreading jelly on his toast, he felt Karen's clear eyes on him, smiling approvingly. He glanced out the front window. He looked over his shoulder at the tables in the rear. She was not there. But she was there. It was no use.

He remembered a conversation with his brother Franklin, just a month after Delilah was born. Franklin and Molly had married late and both were over forty when Delilah arrived. At first, there had been elation, pride, relief, and total absorption. But finally Molly was persuaded to leave the baby with a sitter. The new parents went out to eat, then stopped by at Edward's apartment for a late drink. Edward could not forget the sight of them crumpled exhausted into the corners of the sofa.

"Extraordinary," Franklin had said. "One would think that once out the door, everything would revert to the old days when we were just a twosome: Molly and Franklin out on the town, situation normal." He shook his head forlornly. "Not the case. That child was with us through every nibble of *ravioli langoustine,* every sip of *potage du jour*. If we weren't talking about her, we were thinking of her and trying not to telephone the babysitter."

Molly had given a soft little moan from the far corner. "It'll never be the same, Edward. We're forever trapped."

Nick came to clear away Edward's plate. "You look great, man. You got a new lady or what?"

"Or she's got me," Edward said.

When he arrived home, Persis was sitting cross-legged on the threshold reading the Arts and Leisure section of the Sunday *Times*. She looked up at him without making any motion to rise. "If I have to read one more sentence about Aaron Copland, I think I'll break my recording of *Appalachian Spring*."

"You can skip that article."

"There's always the vain hope that somebody will say something incisive or maybe let slip a juicy piece of gossip." Her legs straightened under her and suddenly she was standing. "You going to have a cup of tea?"

"Of course."

As soon as they stepped inside, Persis hesitated. "It smells funny in here."

"It does?"

"It's like, hmm, I don't know, sweet sweat." She followed Edward into the tiny cubicle that served as a kitchen and began poking through the refrigerator. "Avocado? You've got two avocados in here!"

"Yes," Edward said.

"You never ate an avocado in your life."

"You err. I consumed one just the other day. They are exceedingly high in calories."

"California," Persis muttered.

"I'm being fattened."

"For the kill?"

Edward looked at his sister.

"Sorry," she said. "Let's go in the living room while we're waiting for that to boil."

"All right." Edward could hear that he was about to be lectured. But he felt light on his feet, springy, full of energy. He could take her on. He sat down in his chair but Persis paced back and forth.

"If you're going to stand, I shall, too," Edward said. "Otherwise you have an unfair advantage."

Persis sat, but on the very edge of the cushions. Some of the silver threads in her hair had kinked and zigzagged so that they stood up like antennae. They were quivering.

"I'm concerned," she began. "We're all concerned."

"We?"

"The family."

"Do you care to be specific?"

"Well, Franklin, Molly . . ."

"What about Mother?"

"Oh, Mother," Persis said with a shrug. "You're having a midlife crisis."

Edward laughed.

"Don't be evasive."

"I'm not being evasive. I'm just laughing."

"That's a defense."

"Against what?"

"Against this foolishness with Karen Wells."

"It certainly is that."

"Certainly what?" Persis asked, disconcerted.

"Foolishness."

"And destructive."

"Don't push your advantage. I only concede to foolishness. What's more, I just polished off a gigantic breakfast the likes of which I haven't eaten since I was an adolescent. I've never felt better in my life."

"It's all a part of this . . . extremism."

"Oh, Persis!" Edward whooped. "What is it you've been nagging at me about all these years? 'Passion, Edward! Commit yourself! Live!' "

"Well, Christ, you didn't have to go do it with some punk rocker."

Edward stared at her and she dropped her eyes. The teapot had begun to whistle, but they both ignored it.

"What kind of life can you have with her?" Persis asked. "Have you thought about the future?"

"I'm pretty much taking it one day at a time. However, I'll be going upstate to meet her family next weekend."

Persis stood up again. "Is it her celebrity?"

"You know it isn't."

"Her youth?"

"She's as old as I am in some respects."

Persis was looking at him with such open love and frustration that he softened. "Persis, I know how peculiar this entire thing appears. We met, something happened, and we're living it out. I don't pretend to know what's ahead."

"Are you in love with her?"

"You care to explain exactly what you mean by that?"

By this time, the teakettle was furious. Persis waved her arms up and down. Edward thought she looked like a very handsome crane trying to take off, and he could not resist a smile.

"Read my poems," Persis said. "That's the closest I ever get to an explanation. Just how do you think she'd fit in at Mother's?

Everybody spouting philosophy and obscure literary quotations. She's going to pick up a guitar and play us a tune?"

"Don't be flip about her, Persis. I won't have it."

Persis went to the window and looked out. She said something muffled into the curtains.

"I didn't hear that," Edward said.

She spun around. "I said I'm jealous. And I'm sorry. I won't be flip, it's just that I feel shut out for the first time in my life. Look at all those years I tried to persuade you to write a book and she comes along and in a couple of weeks you've practically got a contract . . ."

Edward stood up and approached her. He took her hand and began to pat it awkwardly. "Dear," he said. "I'm sorry."

Persis sniffed at him through her tears. "You've found something I never had, probably never will have. I can see that, I'm not blind. Look at you, you're flourishing. Probably all that sex. Christ, Edward, I thought you'd always be there for me. No sharing my big brother with anybody, especially not some pretty little thing who sings like an angel and is famous on top of everything else."

Edward put his arm around her shoulder. She was bony. He wondered if he felt like this to Karen. "Come, let's go calm that kettle down before it explodes. I'll pour you some tea."

"How do you think you'd feel," Persis said, blowing her nose between words, "if you knew you'd never see her again?"

"Is this a test?" Edward asked.

Persis nodded.

Edward considered. He thought of his inability to rid himself of her this morning, this unfamiliar sensation of being crowded, intruded upon. Then he imagined her face and her body against his, and her eagerness to absorb whatever was in his head so that it got churned around inside hers and often as not came spilling out, transformed into music. Her kisses were like a baby's exploring a toy with its mouth, curious, loving, and soft. "If I were never to see her again," he said, "I guess it would break my heart."

Persis sighed and walked into the kitchen. "Well, maybe she'll teach me how to ride."

Karen picked Edward up early Friday morning. He was standing on the curb with a dilapidated suitcase at his feet.

"You look like a little boy who's being sent off to military school," she said. "Dump that thing in the back and hop in."

He settled back into the leather seat. "Isn't this a Jaguar?"

She nodded. "Yup, it's not mine; I rented it. But I figure, why not go in style?"

She drove expertly and very fast, weaving in and out of the northbound traffic on the West Side Highway and up across the George Washington Bridge onto the Palisades Parkway.

Edward took a deep breath. "It even smells green. Rather makes you wonder why anyone submits to life in that ungodly pile of concrete and stone."

"There can be no reasonable explanation." She accelerated and swerved into the left lane.

"Don't you worry about the police?" Edward asked.

"This car won't go slow. It's like Jolie." She looked over at him with a smile. "You're going to meet her."

"Not to mention your parents."

"You're not nervous, are you?"

"Not exactly. It just seems inappropriate somehow. They're certainly not much older than I."

"My mother's sixty-two and Dad's seventy. You're just a baby compared to them."

"I'm more of their generation than yours."

"Then you'll have a lot to talk about, won't you?"

"What are they like?"

"Dad's sweet but pussywhipped."

"What was that?" Edward asked.

"Pussywhipped. Henpecked. Dominated. A weak Nelly. Mother's tough, a hard-working farm woman. It wasn't always that way, though. When we were growing up, she was sort of, I don't know, feeble. I never took her very seriously. But then when Dad got sick, this iron woman emerged. She's had the best time learning to be an autocrat. Now she does everything, hires the help and snaps the whip."

"The pussywhip?" Edward asked.

"Yeah. See how I'm enlarging your vocabulary?"

"I'm afraid of her already."

"She doesn't like me much," Karen remarked.

"I don't hear any regret."

Karen shrugged. "I'm not crazy about her either. We've never had anything to talk about."

They drove a while in silence. Every now and then Karen would look over at Edward and smile. He wore a thick tan-colored sweater. Seeing him in the sweater, with his curly hair and beard, she longed to pet him as if he were some gentle, llama-like creature. She amused herself by imagining a llama in Edward's spectacles. Soon they rounded the circle that ended the parkway and pulled up a long, steep hill toward the northwest. "Look, Edward!" she cried, startling him. "A doe! And two fawns, look by the roadside." The animals stood watching quietly as she slowed onto the shoulder and stopped the car. In a moment, the deer began grazing again, unperturbed. "God, I wish I could do that sometimes," Karen said.

"Eat grass?"

She gave him a little punch. "Blend into the background. They're barely visible."

"I don't believe I've ever seen a deer outside of the zoo. Extraordinary."

"You have been deprived, my darling."

"I'd like to see one with antlers."

"We'll see what we can do." She pulled back onto the road and began to sing softly. Edward leaned against the headrest and soon fell asleep. The Catskills rose soft and smoky in the distance and a pair of hawks circled in the updraft away overhead. Karen wondered if she had ever been this happy.

And then she remembered Michael.

For the first time since his death, more than a day had passed without a thought of him, perhaps even several days. She struggled to think back. But her mind had been so full of Edward and Persis. She tried to focus on memories of her brother's face: sitting at the table in the kitchen with that half-grin of suppressed mirth over some idiotic remark of their mother's; the quick anger over some obscure injustice; the intensity of concentration as he listened to Karen sing; his three-quarter profile as he turned back to wave that last time before disappearing into the bus. It had never been difficult to conjure him up. In fact, there had been so many times when Karen had squeezed her fists against her eyes in the attempt to blot him out. But this morning she could remember only disparate pieces of him, the olive skin, the shiny black hair that hung straight across his forehead, the gray eyes, the wide mouth like hers, only punctuated by a single dimple above the left-hand corner. Pieces of a jigsaw, magnetically charged to repel one another. Her hands began to sweat on the steering wheel. I'm losing him, she thought, and then shook her head hard. He was already gone, of course. But grief had kept him close to her, sharp and real, for thirteen sad years. This morning's unaccountable sense of his loosening, fading, breaking apart in her mind, sent her into a panic. She pulled off the road and parked near a diner. The car jolted to a halt, waking Edward.

"What is it, more deer?" he asked sleepily.

She could only shake her head.

"Karen." He unsnapped his seat belt and reached for her.

"I'm missing my brother," she said, the words muffled in his sweater.

He stroked her hair. "It's because you're going home."

"It's because of you," she said, and sat back.

"I don't understand."

"You're chasing him away."

"No, darling, I can't do that. No one can do that."

She rubbed her forehead. "It's confusing. You're such a comfort. I don't know whether I'm miserable or elated. Some of each, maybe. I'm just feeling so much . . . *something*. Poor Michael."

Edward cupped her face with his hands and kissed her very gently.

"You dear man," she whispered against his mouth. "The only reasonable thing I can think of to do is eat. Come on, this place doesn't look too bad. Let's have lunch."

The diner was crowded with patrons, most of whom appeared to weigh upwards of two hundred pounds. Karen found a booth in a remote corner and shoved in beside Edward rather than taking a seat opposite.

"Why do you suppose they're so fat?" Edward whispered. "Is there an obesity spa nearby, one of those Catskill resorts?"

"You're just used to Manhattan. Real Americans are immense. We eat breakfast at Wendy's, lunch at McDonald's and dinner at Kentucky Fried Chicken. Furthermore, by the time I'm finished with you, you're going to look just like that fellow over there." She indicated a middle-aged man whose chair was in danger of being swallowed up by his billowing posterior.

"Extraordinary," Edward said.

Suddenly the jukebox, which had been churning out Country Western classics, bellowed with Karen's voice. She watched Edward for his reaction. *"Where did the moon go this morning? / Did the sunshine chase it from the sky?"* His eyes snapped onto her face and she began to mime the words with exaggerated drama.

"You're blushing!" she cried.

"My God," Edward said, looking around the restaurant suspiciously.

"Don't worry, nobody's going to mob us. They have no idea who I am."

"Who stole your heart and left an empty face behind?" sang the voice. Edward squirmed.

"It'll be over soon," Karen reassured him. "You know, I don't think you'd do well at the Palladium." Edward looked blank. "That's a discotheque, darling."

"No, I don't suppose so. It's a wonderful song," he said apologetically.

She laughed. "If you were Tony, you'd be on your feet pointing me out to the crowd and organizing an autograph session."

"How about you?" Edward asked, munching on his grilled cheese. "Aren't you supposed to enjoy all that?"

"I know I'm supposed to. It's one of the things I appreciate most about you. You really don't give a damn about my career."

"That's untrue."

"No, I don't mean it that way. I know you care, but about the important stuff, the writing, the creative end of it. You're just not impressed with hype."

"I think 'terrified of it' might be more accurate."

She nodded. "Yes. Your face outside that elevator when those reporters closed in, like a man facing the firing squad. You're a private fella, Edward Vaughn. I love climbing into that quiet place with you and shutting out the rest of the world. Eat your fries."

"I should think it would be a rather heady feeling for you, hearing your own voice in a public place like this." The song had died away, and Edward sat back against the seat, relaxed.

"It used to be a tremendous kick. The first time, in a taxi from the airport, on WPIX, I thought I'd faint from the thrill. I told the driver, 'That's me, I'm Karen Wells!' And he took my autograph for his kids and his mother and God knows who all." She shook her head. "Everything is fun the first time: the first tour, the first *Rolling Stone* interview, the first Midem. But then I think, well, okay, I did that, it was nice, but I don't really need to do it again. So far, there's only one part of it where the novelty doesn't seem to wear off, and that's messing with lyrics or sitting at the piano picking out melodies." She smiled at him. "That was quite a speech. Bottom line is, I don't know if I'm cut out for the big time."

"Even if it means relinquishing hearing yourself on the radio?"

"If I could do it all and still somehow isolate myself from the madness. But there's this sensation of being on a gigantic, streaking locomotive, pounding along full throttle. Karen Wells is not just me anymore, it's this . . . *thing*. I don't know how to slow it down, much less think about getting off at the next station." She stared out into space for a moment and then suddenly looked down at the table. "You didn't drink your malted. How am I going to turn you into a tubby if you don't cooperate?"

"Quit pussywhipping me," Edward said.

She burst out laughing, removed his glasses, and put them on the end of her nose. "Extraordinary," she said.

"I suppose I deserved that," Edward said.

It was midafternoon when they turned north out of the Catskills into the long rolling hills of upstate New York. Little towns, many whose names ended with *-kill,* Dutch for "stream," dotted the valleys with village greens and white-spired churches. Buds had sprouted on the black branches of the trees, softening them with a fine yellow-green fuzz. Here and there forsythia bloomed in dazzling golden bushes beside the farmhouses. Finally, Karen turned off onto a narrow road that wound uphill. A creek bubbled and churned alongside, filled with melting snow and rainwater. At the top of the ridge, she turned left onto a dirt driveway and stopped the car. Edward looked at her with alarm.

"The worst thing that can happen is you'll all hate each other," Karen said, and tugged on his beard.

"That wouldn't disturb you?"

"Not a lot," she admitted.

The front door slammed and a woman came out onto the porch wiping her fingers on a dish towel. She was stocky, with faded blonde hair and deep pink arms and hands. She took a look at Edward, then swiveled her head around to Karen with a face full of shock.

"Hello, Mom," Karen said. She hesitated, then gave the woman a quick kiss on the cheek.

"Did you have a good trip?" Eunice Wells asked, ignoring Edward.

"Yes. Mother, this is Edward Vaughn."

With reluctant eyes, Eunice looked at Edward and held out her hand. "Excuse the flour," she said. "I've been up since five o'clock baking."

"I told you not to go to any trouble," Karen admonished her.

"No trouble," the woman answered and moved up the steps. "Somebody has to feed people, you know."

Karen glanced at Edward and rolled her eyes.

Eunice held the screen door open. "Just put the screens on this past weekend and wouldn't you know we had a freak snow Monday morning? It never fails. Your father's in the living room."

Karen took Edward by the hand and led him down an uncarpeted hallway and through an archway to the right. It was a curious room, narrow and running most of the length of the structure. There was a fireplace at the far end but no space for a couch in front of it. Instead, the sofa sat lengthwise, facing out a row of windows. Edward caught his breath at the view. There was a long stretch of lawn giving way to a plowed field that disappeared over the edge of the hill, and in the distance, the next ridge rose high with farms made miniature in the patchwork squares of pale green. The clouds were streaks, applied hurriedly with a light touch. Edward wrenched his eyes away to greet the man who had risen from the single chair by the fireplace. He walked, or rather shuffled, toward them, carrying his head forward as if searching for some lost object underfoot. Karen hugged him, but gently. He held out a hand to Edward. The fingers were swollen and twisted. Karen's father, too, seemed surprised and glanced at his daughter briefly. But then he smiled at Edward, and the old man's face was open and sweet.

"Welcome to the boondocks," Carter Wells said.

"It's very beautiful," Edward replied, with a gesture toward the windows.

"Yes, I've often wished I was a painter so's I could do justice to that. I've tried with my Kodak but it's all flattened out and sapped of its grandeur. Come have some coffee."

The kitchen seemed to Edward like the movie set from some early American film about the Midwest. There was an ancient white enamel gas stove and open pantry shelves displayed jars of flour, brown and white sugar, rice, and various types of beans. Biscuits in cast-iron muffin tins cooled on the counter. Eunice tapped them onto a platter and brought them to the table with butter and a jar of thick honey.

"Sit down, Mother," Karen said. "You don't have to wait on us."

"All right, you pour the coffee. I just have some things to see to in the guest room; then maybe I'll sit a minute."

"Not likely," Carter remarked at her receding back. "The woman never stops, especially now I'm so useless with this damn arthritis."

"You provide moral support, Daddy," Karen said. "Besides, she loves it." The old man made a gesture of frustration. "You've got enough help now anyway," Karen continued.

"Oh, sure, with the farm, but she won't hear of anybody lending a hand in the house. Says they get underfoot and trip her up. Like me." They could hear his wife's quick sharp footsteps overhead as she moved about. "Uh, tell me," Carter went on. "How did the two of you connect up?"

Karen smiled. "You tell him."

Edward explained about the elevator in London.

"It wasn't even a very good party," Karen said. "And look what I found there. Edward's writing a book."

"Well—" Edward began.

"He's got half a proposal and almost a publisher."

"It's rather vague, as you can hear," Edward said quietly.

Sensing Edward's discomfort, Carter shifted his attention to his daughter. "You a spoiled brat yet?" he asked her.

"Daddy's convinced I'm going to turn into a jet set type who's too big for her britches," Karen said.

"What's that car, a Jaguar?" her father accused.

"Oh, don't freak out, it's only a rental."

"Hmm," he grunted.

"You want me to buy you one, Daddy?"

"I'd just as soon have a Ferrari," he said, and the others laughed. The man's eyes were hazel, not blue like Karen's, but there was similar mischief there, a tiny laser beam of light that assured he could be trouble if he felt like it.

Eunice came down the stairs. Edward watched Karen and her father turn toward the doorway with a hint of apprehension.

"Your rooms are ready if you want to get settled in," she announced.

"Great. Thanks, Mom, we'll take our stuff up." Before they had quite left the room, Eunice exhaled a deep sigh of exhaustion.

Karen led Edward up the narrow stairway. There were small rooms off in every direction from the hall.

"Here's mine," Karen said and led him by the hand into a bright neat square with garret windows. Edward promptly banged his head on a low eave.

"Good thing you never acquired full adult stature," he grumbled, rubbing the bump on his forehead. "Listen, Karen, you didn't give your parents any preparation for me, did you?"

"What kind of preparation? I said I was bringing a guy."

"A guy! Do I look like a guy to you?"

"Oh, a man, then." She picked up a china figurine from the bedside table and examined it. "What's the difference?"

"I think they expected somebody in a black leather jacket on a motorcycle."

She put her hands on her hips and studied him. "I'll bet you never rode a motorcycle in your life."

"As a matter of fact, I'm delighted to disabuse you," he said. "One of my graduate students gave me a lift to the garage when my car broke down. I enjoyed the experience enormously."

"I'll bet it was extraordinary."

He grimaced at her. "I wouldn't mind owning a Harley-Davidson just to get around the neighborhood." He surveyed the room. Practically every inch of wall space was covered with photographs and posters, but the theme was equine rather than musical. There were blue ribbons from local fairs, snapshots of Karen posing beside one horse or another, a theatrical advertisement for the play *Equus* with its dramatic twisted metal sculptures of horses' heads, 4-H awards for horsemanship, and many rather amateurish drawings of the animals. "Did you do these?" Edward asked, pointing to one in blue pencil.

"Michael did. They're pretty good, don't you think?"

"Yes," Edward lied.

"I used to make him draw all the time. He got so sick of it."

"Why isn't there more from your musical life here?"

"Well, I left home before it really got started. Besides, what would I keep?"

"Oh, I don't know. Programs, posters from places you appeared, photographs. Local-girl-makes-good kind of thing."

"Here's a picture from *People* magazine. Me and Denny Harper. But I don't know how it got here. Daddy must have cut it out and taped it up."

"You're an odd one." He put his arms around her and gave her a kiss.

"Come on, let's get you settled in. You must have to pee."

"I'm all right."

She took him into a nearby room that appeared to be a kind of study. "You've got a bladder like a camel. Do camels have huge bladders, actually, or is it just that . . . That's funny, the couch isn't made up." She walked slowly across the hall to stand in another doorway. Inside, Edward could see a twin bed covered with a patchwork quilt and a set of towels on top. Karen was standing very still.

"This was Michael's room," Edward guessed.

She nodded. It was very sunny. There was a small desk in one corner on which paperback books sat in piles. Squinting, Edward could make out a few of the titles: *Catch-22;* Tolkein's *Lord of the Rings; Catcher in the Rye.* There was a publicity photo of Karen hanging alongside pictures of Humphrey Bogart, James Dean, Montgomery Clift.

"He could never seem to find any modern-day heroes. He used to say America died with Gary Cooper."

"I can sleep in the other room," Edward said.

"It's all right."

He looked at her carefully. "I don't think so."

Her face was pale and shadowed. She waved her hand in the air in a gesture of futility. "I always figure it'll be easier the next time I come in here, but there's always this jolt as if I'd almost forgotten he was gone and have to get used to it all over again. Maybe it's because I haven't been home enough without him. He's all over the place here. I keep expecting to hear his voice. And all this after freaking out back there on the road because I thought he'd slipped my mind. Oh, hell, Edward, you have to sleep in this room. The place is a goddamn shrine."

Edward put his arms around her. "I'll do as you ask. But understand that I don't mind for a moment staying in the room across the hall."

"No." She picked up his suitcase and set it on the bed. "You go wash up. The bathroom's just outside to your right. Meet you downstairs in a minute." She pulled free and left.

Edward unpacked some things and spent a few moments staring

out the window, this one with a view of a large gray barn with a stand of trees behind it, mostly maples. After a while, Karen came and sat down beside him, put her head on his shoulder and said, "I'm so tired."

"Coming home," Edward murmured, as if giving the day a title.

"Do you mind if I leave you alone for a little bit?" she asked.

"Of course not," he answered.

"I think I'll take Jolie out for a ride before dinner. You'll meet her later on, okay?"

"Certainly."

Edward stood at the window and watched for her. At first, she walked purposefully down the dirt road toward the barn, but soon she began to run. She had a natural exuberant stride, more like a child going full tilt than a grown woman. She disappeared inside the gaping doorway and remained out of sight for a long time. Then she emerged mounted on what Edward imagined to be a palomino horse, pale gold with white boots. The horse carried no saddle, merely a head harness and reins. Karen bent forward to hug the animal around the neck and they trotted for a moment in an embrace. Then she sat up again, easy and straight, and as horse and rider disappeared into the tall grass with the sun low before them, Edward's eyes imagined them as one complete creature, a mythological beast of nobility and grace.

Dinner was memorable for Edward because of a remark made by Karen's mother. They sat around the table eating pot roast while Eunice leapt up and down, each time making a harsh scraping sound with her chair. She seemed incapable of taking more than three bites without interruption. She would stand, offer more drinks, a fresh napkin, second helpings from the stove. If her invitation was rejected, the deep crease between her eyes deepened with resentment. If, indeed, someone responded positively, she barely repressed a martyred sigh. But over coffee, she sat down for a long stretch and joined the conversation, which had consisted mainly of Karen's narration of the Denny Harper tour.

Carter glanced at his wife with pride. "Well, Eunice, did you ever think we'd have such a famous person as a daughter?"

She responded with the closest thing Edward had yet seen to a smile, which was a tight little twitch of the upper lip. "You know I always had my doubts she was really ours. And now, you see? She's wound up a movie star."

"I'm not a movie star," Karen said.

"Well, whatever," Eunice said. She turned to Edward with a look of confidentiality. "Even in the hospital, I would stare down at her, she was just a little bit of a thing, and think she surely wasn't mine. There was something even then, a differentness. I couldn't find a trace of Hazelton—that's my family—or Wells either. I made them show me her records in the nursery, the footprints, birth certificate, everything."

Edward, chilled with horror, looked at Karen, ready to whisk her into the car and snatch her away from this terrible woman. But Karen appeared unperturbed.

"Then it turned out she was musical like her daddy," Carter was saying. "So we claimed her as our own."

"Oh, applesauce," Karen's mother exclaimed. "Your music."

"Daddy could have been a real musician if he'd had a chance to develop. Even in the Grand Ole Opry, there wasn't anybody who could play mandolin—"

"You exaggerate," Carter interrupted her. "I could work up a passable banjo, passable mandolin, before my hands got ruined. But it's just something like eating or sleeping or mucking out the barn. It's what you do to pass the time." He looked at Edward. "But for her, it was something else again. If she couldn't sing, she might as well be dead."

"She was always strange," Eunice continued dreamily. "Not like any of the other little girls . . . off by herself or with her brother, making up tunes, listening to those tired old records hour after hour. Didn't give a hang about clothes or any of that. She just kept company with her brother and her horse. Now Michael, there was a Hazelton."

"Eunice," Carter said. "I'd like another cup of coffee and some more of those cookies. I expect the young people would enjoy a walk on such a fine evening."

"Come on, young person," Karen said, pulling Edward out of his chair.

"He's younger than I am," Carter said, "and that's plenty young to me."

Outside, Karen walked him down the driveway toward the barn. "She's pretty incredible, isn't she?"

"Yes," Edward said.

"I always wish she'd be more talkative, and then when she says something, I'm sorry she ever opened her mouth."

"You're your father's daughter," Edward said. "You even look like him."

Karen smiled. "You're worried about that orphan business. Don't. I've heard it all my life. She thinks some gypsy dropped me off in her kid's bassinet at the Avoryville Central Hospital." She regarded Edward carefully. "You look like you're going to cry. Now, listen, how terrible would it be *really* not to be related to her? Don't think I didn't have the same fantasy she does. And there was my dad."

"It's rather horrible to hear."

"Yes, but she makes great cookies."

"True." Not baked with love, however, Edward thought, imagining the woman standing over her mixing bowl stirring rancor and irritability into the batter. He stopped and leaned against her.

"What are you doing?" she asked.

"Taking off my shoes."

She laughed. "You're so brave. Think of the manure."

"It's getting dark. I won't see it."

"All right, then. Me, too." She stepped out of her moccasins and grabbed hold of his hand. He hobbled along the road as if it was full of hot coals. "Not here. On the lawn."

"Ahh," he sighed as he sank half an inch into the soft grass of the lawn. Peace seemed to creep up his body through the soles of his feet.

"Nice, huh?"

"Better than nice. One ought to concoct out of it some kind of treatment for the psyche, like est or psychodrama."

"I'm sure they've got it in California. Turf therapy. There's got to be some guru out in L.A. with very dirty feet."

Edward stopped. The sky was the deep purple-blue of the stained glass windows in St. Thomas Church on Fifth Avenue. The evening star clung to a tiny wisp of cloud like a jewel he could reach up and pluck off its bed of cotton.

"Karen," he said quietly. "I've always resisted sentiment." She drew her arm through his and leaned against him. "I've had my head buried in print for decades. Oh, I've marveled at the technique of a clever writer who describes the twilight so that I can almost see it myself. But I never did see it myself, not until I met you. Do you understand me? It's as if there's a child in me who's been locked in a dark airless closet all these years. You've opened the door and let it free." They embraced for a long time, until their bare feet turned cold in the soft spring grass.

Karen crouched on a stool milking an immense black-and-white Holstein cow. "It's done by machine these days, of course," she told Edward, "but I still enjoy it this way." Her forehead pressed up against the soft belly of the animal as she worked. Edward took a deep breath. He liked the sharp smells of cow dung and moist hay that filled the barn.

"Do you suppose it derives any sort of sexual gratification from that?" Edward asked.

"Well, how does she look?"

Edward studied the cow's face. It chewed its cud and returned Edward's gaze with bored eyes. "I believe you're fulfilling its most lurid fantasies."

Karen laughed. "They aren't very dynamic, cows, but I'm partial to the calves. I had a pet one once."

"Is it all grown up here somewhere?"

"No, Charlie came to a tragic end." She straightened up, grabbed the pail and led him to a large vat into which she poured the milk. "Lord, I haven't thought about that little guy for ages. He was small and weak from a tough birth, and Dad said he wasn't likely to make it. Well, naturally that was all Michael and I had to hear. He was mostly white but had this marking on his forehead like a baby's footprint, just as if a toddler had stepped into a puddle of ink and pressed his foot against him right here." She placed the heel of her palm against her forehead. "We called him Charlie after Charles Bronson because we figured the name might give him strength and make him fierce. And he did get stronger. We bottle-fed him at first because he was too weak to nurse, and once when he got sick with colic, Michael and I took turns sleeping in the barn with him. And by the end of the summer, Charlie was still small, but feisty, and he had the most expressive face. When he'd see us coming, you'd swear he was smiling. I've seen dogs do weird things with their mouths, they really grin at you, but I never saw a calf do it." They stood leaning against the stainless steel tub while the milk churned around in a whirlpool. "One day I came home from school," Karen continued. "I don't remember where Mike was, some kind of sports thing. I grabbed some cookies for me and Charlie and went out to the pasture to hunt for him, but he wasn't anywhere." Her voice slowed. "I looked all over. Nothing. And then way over on the far end of the field I heard him calling. It was so sad, this pathetic bleating. And then I found him all tangled up in a combine. I don't know how it happened, he must have been leaping around doing one of his crazy dances and not looking where he was going, and there he was, fur all mixed up in these awful metal jaws and I could see he was suffering terribly. Let me tell you, Edward, farm accidents are the worst. Nobody tells you that in all those romantic articles about returning to the earth." She stopped to take a breath. "So I came home to get Dad and he wasn't anywhere. I just took the rifle and went back out there and shot him."

"My God," Edward said. "How old were you?"

"Oh, about ten, I guess. Maybe nine. It was harder than losing my grandmother."

"You didn't have to shoot your grandmother."

"Well, maybe somebody should have. She didn't have such an easy time of it either." Karen shuddered. "Anyway, if I'm ever suffering and there's no hope for me, I would want the same." She put her finger to her temple and cocked her thumb. "Quick and merciful."

"I never heard you call your brother 'Mike.' "

"Oh, did I?" she smiled. "I must be listening to his ghost. He always liked 'Mike' more than 'Michael.' But I always thought he was more of a Michael, really. Come, let's go for a walk."

Saturday night was so cold that Karen put a fire in the fireplace. Carter sat in his chair with Karen at his feet playing the banjo. The old man watched her fingers wistfully. *"Goin' up Cripple Creek, going in a run,"* they sang. Their duet arched and dove together in close harmony. *"Goin' up Cripple Creek to have a little fun . . ."*

Edward listened from the couch as for nearly two hours the music lifted out of the warm glow of the firelight resting comfortably atop the metallic sound of the banjo. *"Bile them cabbage down, down / Bake that hoecake brown, brown / The only song that I can sing is bile them cabbage down."*

What am I doing here? Edward wondered, not for the first time this weekend feeling as if he had traveled to the farthest outreaches of civilization. The world was totally black outside the window beyond Eunice's knitting needles, not a streetlamp, not an all-night deli, not a siren screaming down Broadway, the only noise the winding river of sound that struck his ears as totally foreign, totally enchanting.

Sometime in the early-morning hours, Karen slipped into bed beside him. Her body was warm and soft, and even coming up out of the haze of sleep he knew it was Karen, but for a moment he could not remember where he was. They could be adrift on this small bed anywhere in the deep darkness beyond the earth, suspended like motes in the vast universe.

"Edward," she whispered, anchoring him to Michael's little room.

"Won't you freeze? You don't have a stitch on," he murmured. Despite the total blackness, he tried to find his spectacles. He could never seem to think properly without them.

Karen ran her hand down his body across the sensitive skin of his stomach where she knew she would elicit a shudder of pleasure, and then down between his legs. "I want to love you in this room." There was a catch in her voice. Edward kissed her gently. She arched her back and drew his hand down to her breasts. Her body had been warm moments ago, but now her skin seemed to sear his fingers. They rocked together, clinging, and after a while, fell back next to one another exhausted.

"I'm sorry," he said.

"Don't be silly," she answered, but she sounded wounded.

"Perhaps it's this room. I can't seem to forget your brother."

"Yes."

"Are you all right?" he asked.

"Fine. A little horny."

"I can correct that." There was a question in his voice.

"You don't need my permission," she said.

He put his fingers between her legs and soon her body trembled. Her exhalation seemed a sigh of sadness and resignation. While they lay side by side holding hands, the window that faced east turned to a dim gray rectangle.

"Edward."

"What is it, dearest?"

"You know that I'm in love with you."

"Yes."

"But you're also such a friend to me. You know how I can tell?"

"No."

"Because when I'm with you, I'm never ashamed."

He kissed her forehead. "Sometimes you say things that make my heart . . . Oh, Karen, honestly, it's no good being an academic. Everything I'm feeling is such a dreadful cliché. Someone ought to invent a new language for such occasions."

"Minra hatha brewganit."

"Bux flurpling merganser philoppash," he answered.

"*Merganser*'s a word," she protested.

"It is?"

"Sure, it's a kind of duck."

"Those damnable crossword puzzles."

"I wish we didn't ever have to go back to New York," she said. "Except we'd have to get rid of my parents. Just you and me and Jolie and the cows. What bliss."

Edward was silent for a long moment. When he spoke, he sounded helpless, even frightened. "I wasn't expecting this," he said.

"I'm sorry, Edward. But tell the truth, since you met me you've gained weight, correct?"

"Six pounds," he admitted.

"And you've learned to appreciate another avenue of musical expression?"

"This is true. I even know who Cyndi Lauper is."

"And you're going to write a great biography."

"The mere mention of the subject fills me with terror, and I consider it your fault entirely."

"Thanks, I accept full credit. And let's not forget sex. Tonight was merely an aberration. Admit it, you've never had such a great time in the sack."

"There's no denying that. The last blaze of glory for a tired old man."

"Oh, shut up, Edward, you're not old and you're far from tired."

The room was gradually taking form like images emerging onto a photograph in the darkroom tray. "It's really getting light out there," Edward remarked. His momentary attack of panic was receding with the darkness.

"The help will be showing up soon. By five, the place'll be in full swing."

"I should have made an abominable farmer. How will your mother react when she meets you running down the hall stark naked?"

"She'll just look a little more pained and a little more convinced that I couldn't have descended from the Hazelton line. Anyway, she's used to my interest in sex."

"Tell me about your first seduction."

"Edward, sometimes you're so archaic. Let's see, I fooled around a lot, you know, groping hands in the backseat, that sort of thing. But the first time I really *did* it was in the barn with one of the hired guys. I was fifteen at the time, but extremely mature."

"I'll wager you were. Was it a positive experience?"

"It was terrific. I don't know, the girls in 4-H Club told me all these horror stories about how much it would hurt. Maybe it was all those years of riding horses, but I thought I'd died and gone to heaven. First of all, the guy was pretty wonderful. Considerate and gentle and very grateful and fabulously good-looking, a kind of blue-collar Cary Grant with one of those things in his chin. He was here one whole summer and we had quite a time of it up in the hayloft until we got caught."

"By whom?"

"Mother." She could not resist a giggle. "Oh, my, Edward, you think she looks grim *now*. She made Daddy fire him, but it was okay because harvest was over anyway."

"How did the others react, your father, Michael?"

"Daddy just looked sort of . . . confused. That side of his life has never held much allure for him, I think. I'm sure he's never cheated on my mother, and God knows they don't do it much."

"You can't tell. They might be in there this minute, he with a whip and she in a black garter belt."

She stifled her laughter against the pillow. "And Michael just rolled his eyes. I was the only sexy one in this group. It just wasn't dished out properly, no equal distribution. All of it got dumped into this little body."

"I'm eternally grateful."

"Me, too, now, but in those days, I sometimes felt like a freak. Now it's your turn. I want every sordid detail."

"I was a late bloomer," Edward said solemnly, to her laughter. "Nineteen, I think."

"That's not so late. I thought you were going to say thirty-five."

"Every other male had been doing it for years."

"That's what they told you."

"No, I was different. There was a great deal of anguish in the teenage years about unbridled erections. My brother, for instance, would dread being called upon in class for fear he'd have one when he stood up. The lingerie pages in the Montgomery Ward catalog would send him into a frenzy. I, on the other hand, had romantic crushes, but my fantasies were more along the lines of Arthurian legend rather than naked women. Come to think of it, I suppose I felt rather freakish myself."

"But you finally managed to get it all together."

"In college, yes. There was a girl I saw, I suppose you could say we dated. In my philosophy class. She was very intelligent, a nice person, but rather, well, unattractive."

"You mean she was a dog."

"I suppose so. But she had remarkable breasts. She never wore underwear and they stood straight out. It was extraordinary. They seemed to defy all the laws of physics." He was silent a moment, remembering. "We used to study together and I would find them so distracting. And sweaters, she wore revealing sweaters."

"Naturally."

"She would put her arms up over her head and stretch . . ."

"She had the hots for you, Edward."

"And one time we were in my room, and I found myself unbuttoning her cardigan, and that was it. But the experience didn't become addictive, though there was a short fling with a faculty member's wife. But with her as well, the earth decidedly did not move. My relationships with women were primarily intellectual, until I met you. Darling, there's a car in the driveway."

"That's the Johnson truck. Oh damn, I hate to leave you." She sat up on the edge of the bed. In the dim light, her vertebrae made a perfect track from the base of her spine to her neck. She sighed and got out of bed. "Try to sleep a little more. We've got a long trip today."

"Karen," he said. Without his glasses, she was a soft blur against the doorway. "I do . . . love you."

She was very still. Then he heard her whisper, "I know," and she left.

At ten o'clock, Eunice called to Karen, who was still in bed, to answer the telephone. Edward heard her groping down the stairs.

When she appeared at his door, he sat up and put on his glasses. She looked pale. "What's the matter?" he asked.

"That was Tony. He's booked me on the Bob Sterling show."

"Congratulations. Here, come sit. You look as if you might faint." She did as he said.

"Do you know who Bob Sterling is?"

He smiled. "Of course I do." He smoothed Karen's hair where she hadn't yet brushed it smooth. "When will this happen?"

"Next week."

"So soon."

"Yup."

"You sound singularly unimpressed with yourself."

"I know it. I should be impressed, shouldn't I?"

"You'll sing?"

"Yes, and then sit there for an amiable chat with the great man. At least he gets a desk to hide behind."

"It sounds intimidating."

"Yeah, well, the worst that can happen is I make an ass of myself in front of a few million people." She got up and went to look out the window. With her bare legs and oversized man's shirt, she looked like a child. "Oh, I'll do it. The Sterling show sells records, and that's what I'm trying to do, isn't it?"

"I presume so."

"Edward, there's this guy called Sam Dawkins who I'm sure you *haven't* heard of. He's a rockabilly type, really a very fine songwriter. But he lives on a boat off the Texas Gulf Coast and only surfaces when he's broke. Then he cuts a record, hits the top ten for a few weeks and goes back to the boat."

Edward was silent, waiting.

"I think if you're going to be a real performer," she went on, "you've got to have tunnel vision. It's got to be what you eat, sleep, and inhale every hour of the day. Some people thrive on it, it's what defines them. But there's not really room for anything else, except for the occasional lover here and there and a visit to the folks at Christmas if you're not doing a gig somewhere."

"I've thrown a wrench into your life, haven't I?" Edward said.

"Yes, you have, my darling. God, I was a real creep on the phone just now, not screaming with joy. It's not just for me, you understand. This kind of thing is terrific for the band. What's good for me is good for them, and I'm not just me, I'm this thing that gives *them* what they need. Creatively, financially, professionally. Tony was so proud of himself, pulling off such a coup. I can tell he also thinks it'll help . . ." She hesitated.

"We haven't talked about that," Edward said slowly. He hated to use the word *Tony*.

"I know, I know." She put her hands to her ears, pressed hard and then dropped them helplessly at her sides. She turned away from the window. "I hate leaving these hills. It's like being torn from some beloved person. I visualize myself belonging in this pastoral painting." She gestured to form an imaginary frame around herself. "I'm in the middle of the meadow, sometimes on horseback, sometimes lying there looking up at a lovely pale blue sky. I can smell fresh-mown grass—corn smells like that when you snap it off at the stalk. It's where I belong, and when I'm not in that picture, there's this ugly gray smudge where I've been scraped off the canvas. And I'm left wandering around without my frame like a ghost. Hell, Edward, I don't belong in New York or L.A. or on the Bob Sterling show."

"Where do you belong, my dearest?"

She was standing beside the bed. "With you."

"In London?"

She threw her arms out in frustration. "Don't you think so? Damn, *damn,* what a peculiar reaction to good news. Maybe I'm just petrified. Come have some breakfast. Mother made gorgeous muffins with blueberries and blood stains."

"From working her fingers to the bone?" Edward asked.

She grinned at him. "Yes, you clever man."

12

On foot, Karen and Persis led their horses across Central Park West and onto the bridle path. The earth smelled thick and dark with yesterday's rain.

"This thing keeps taking nibbles of my arm," Persis complained.

"Give him a lump of sugar and try to keep beside his shoulder," Karen advised. "He's gentle, honestly."

"He's also very oral. Here, Mandrake."

"Fine, go ahead there, right beside that tree and hold him." Karen hung back and watched Persis maneuver the jet-colored animal. They made a handsome couple, the tall, slim woman and the shining horse.

Tony had been outraged this morning when Karen walked out on a meeting to take Persis's telephone call.

"Who the hell is Persis Vaughn?" he demanded.

"A friend," Karen had said, slipping on her jacket.

"Where the hell are you going? You've got people in there . . ." He gestured at the conference room that was full of record company representatives.

"You can handle the nitty-gritty stuff. Just tell them I had an emergency."

He took a deep breath and made the supreme effort at a reasonable tone of voice. He almost succeeded, though his face was deep red. "Well, where are you going?" he repeated, raking his fingers through his hair.

"Tell you later."

He followed closely behind, making pronouncements about commitment and follow-through. But finally the elevator doors slid shut and she was left alone. She would not tell him later. There was no way he could understand the importance of Persis's call. The woman was reaching out, and Karen was not about to let the opportunity slip past while she sat listening to arguments about tour support and packaging deductions.

"What do I do now?" Persis asked.

"You mount."

"Oh, Jesus," Persis muttered.

"Here. Watch me." Karen placed her foot in the stirrup and flipped neatly onto Midler's back. Then she dismounted and went to help Persis. It took some jostling to force her running shoe into the stirrup, but they managed, and eventually Persis sat atop her horse, flushed with triumph and terror. Karen was rewarded with a tiny smile of appreciation.

"All right," Karen said, and remounted Midler. "Let's go." She kept close to Mandrake, giving Persis quiet instructions and encouragement. "That's right, hold the reins just a little looser, you don't have to pull so hard. Fine, relax, you're doing fine. You're sitting very well. No, try not to hold onto the saddle. Let him do the work. Okay, great. How do you feel?"

"Fine," Persis said tersely with her head stiff. She reminded Karen of Nicky Stein, whose fear of flying in the early days made it impossible for her to leave her seat. Any movement to one side or the other might tip the plane over.

"All right," Karen went on. "We're just going to have a nice easy walk along here. Mandrake's done it a thousand times. Pretty from up here, isn't it?"

Persis stared straight ahead. "Uh. Yes." Her eyes in her immobilized face shifted from east to west. "Lovely. Yes. Trees in bloom. Actually, this is rather pleasant, I must say."

Karen smiled. Sometimes Persis sounded so much like Edward. After one very slow circle around the bridle path, Persis began to look more relaxed. She risked turning her head to talk to Karen. "This is a civilized horse. Very kind."

"You're doing great. Want to take another turn around?"

"Certainly. It's not so difficult after all. Did you ever see the film *Fantasia?* There's a section with centaurs, Beethoven's *Pastoral,* I believe. You might as well be a part of that horse. Extraordinary."

A compliment, Karen thought, gratified. Maybe the woman was actually beginning to unbend a little. She let Persis move on ahead. The woman really had potential if she could learn to relax. Perhaps if they came out a few times a week. But suddenly something happened. Persis had begun to tilt to the left in her saddle. Silently, inexorably, she rotated, back and neck perfectly straight, like a stiff doll. Karen held out her hands from yards away in a reflexive attempt to help, but Persis hit the ground, left foot still jammed in the stirrup. Mandrake, confused now, began to turn, slowly at first, and then with Persis hopping beside him, faster and faster until he was circling at a brisk pace. Under a nearby tree, a young man with a suitcase-sized radio stood watching. A rock station blared out, *Dance, baby, dance! You know how to do it!* The young man, inspired by Persis and Mandrake's wild choreography, began to leap about in time with the music.

"Whoa!" Karen yelped, dismounting. She tried to grasp Mandrake's reins, but he shook his head violently as if to say, No, this is fun, leave me alone. *That's it, honey, stomp those feet!* blasted the radio. *You know how to shake it sweet!* Persis, who was bobbing up and down in a frantic effort to avert having her foot snapped off at the ankle, had been rendered even more helpless by convulsive laughter.

"Oh! Oh!" she howled. "Help! Oh!"

Karen was finally able to grab Mandrake's reins, pulling him firmly to a halt. Then, still gripping the leather straps, she extracted Persis's foot, at which point Persis collapsed on the ground in a heap of laughter, tears streaming. Karen tried to talk, but she, too, was overwhelmed with relief and comic appreciation.

"You . . . you . . ." Karen gasped. Persis was sitting up now, trying to gain control over her hysteria, but she kept exploding into new outbursts. It took several minutes for them to settle down. Meanwhile, the horses and the young man gazed at them with perfect equanimity. The radio's disk jockey shouted today's weather forecast, a paragraph jammed into one long word of barely discernible syllables. Karen examined Persis's ankle. "It looks all right. How does it feel?"

"Fine."

"It's a good thing you're fast on your feet," Karen said, and that set them off again. Finally, they managed to remount the horses and return to the stable. On their way out, the stablemaster said, "So, Wells, how'd it go with your new student?"

"Oh, fine, thanks, Bill. Uneventful."

Persis shot Karen a surreptitious glance of gratitude. Out on Eighty-ninth Street, Persis said, "My legs feel most peculiar."

"Yes, it's a little like taking off your roller skates. The ground seems so unyielding."

"I wouldn't know," Persis said. "I've never been on roller skates." As if recognizing the harshness of her tone, Persis went on, "I'm very grateful for your patience with my clumsiness. Please let me take you to lunch."

"That would be very nice," Karen said, wondering just how nice it could be if the woman kept retreating into stony superiority. But this was a campaign, Karen reminded herself, this was Edward's beloved sister. She must persevere.

They started down Columbus Avenue. Persis stopped in front of each prospective restaurant, considered, and rejected.

"No, too trendy . . . No, this one loads the food with MSG . . . There's a jukebox in here. Deafening . . ." She paused by a storefront with a sign that said "Tarot Cards and Palms Read by Christine." "Have you ever done this?" she asked Karen.

"I had my palm read in a restaurant when I was a kid. The lady told me I'd be a forest ranger."

"What do you think it costs?"

Karen started through the door. "What the hell, let's find out."

As they entered, a bell rang out, and an attractive dark-skinned woman appeared from behind a beaded curtain.

"How much to have our fortunes told?" Persis asked.

"I don't tell fortunes," the woman said with a smile. "I can read the cards for you. It's fifty dollars."

"Good heavens," Persis said.

"But for five dollars, I'll answer two questions."

"What do you think?" Persis asked Karen.

"I'm going to do it," Karen said, and followed Christine toward the back of the room. The woman held up her hand to halt Persis.

"No, one at a time."

Christine parted the curtain for Karen who followed her to a nook so intimate that their knees nearly collided when they sat down. Christine's face was smooth and kind, with dark eyes that kept flickering to a spot two inches above Karen's head.

"Now," she said in a melancholy voice. "What can I do for you?"

"Um, let's see," Karen said, suddenly unnerved by the sad tranquility of the woman, who was probably no older than she. "I wonder . . . what about my love life?"

"I must explain to you that I always tell the truth," Christine said. "Think and then tell me. Do you wish to know the truth?"

Karen hesitated. Chills began a slow crawl up her spine. "How can I back off now? Sure, fire away."

Christine nodded. "You will marry an invalid," she said.

"But I'm not getting married," Karen blurted.

Christine shrugged. "It's very clear."

"Is it someone I know right now?"

"Do you want this to be your second question?" Christine asked.

"Yes."

"It is someone you know now," the woman answered. She stood up and held out her hand. Karen placed a five-dollar bill in it. "You may send your friend in," Christine said.

Karen sat down in the chair warmed by Persis's body. The whole thing was nonsense, of course, but it was difficult not to react with a case of the creeps. After all, clairvoyance had become respectable enough to be used by the police to help solve crimes, so there must be something in it. There was only one person Karen would consider marrying. Well, she would simply not marry Edward, she would never marry Edward. They would beat the fates, and save him from becoming an invalid.

Suddenly there was a burst of laughter, and in a moment, Persis emerged. Christine trailed behind looking perplexed and a little annoyed.

"Come back again, ladies, and we'll do a fuller reading," she said, giving Persis a dubious glance.

"Thank you, perhaps we shall," Persis said.

They settled into a booth at the coffee shop two doors down. Persis appeared to be at war between intense amusement and sullen reserve. Her eyes kept flickering at Karen above the menu, first twinkling, then resentful. Karen waited curiously for a resolution. Amusement won out.

"Christine has a definite gift," Persis said, setting down her menu. Her lips were twitching at the corners.

"Why do you say that?" Karen asked, careful not to appear too eager.

"I asked her about the man in my life," Persis explained. "Christine said, 'You have had a terrible argument with him. A violent fight. He threw you to the ground.' When I asked what he looked like, this mysterious frightening man, she said, 'He has shiny black hair and very thin legs.' "

"That's Mandrake!" Karen said, laughing.

Persis's customary pale complexion was replaced with a healthy flush from exercise and laughter. "What did you ask?" she said, "if you don't mind . . ."

"Not at all," Karen answered. "About the man in my life."

"Oh, dear. Are we all so obsessed with men? I thought surely you'd want to know about your professional future."

"Didn't occur to me to ask about it. I'm hoping Christine is off the mark with this one because she told me I was going to marry an invalid. I got the most awful creepy feeling. She kept staring at a spot somewhere over my head as if there was an evil spirit hovering around up there."

"She was checking out your aura," Persis explained.

"What's that?"

"It's a kind of psychic cloud that's supposed to surround you. They can tell all kinds of things by its color and intensity."

Karen peered above Persis's head. "I don't see a thing."

"It's not visible to us ordinary mortals."

There was a pause while they ordered their lunch. The mousy middle-aged waitress had wispy hair and a neck discolored with what appeared to be bruises. After scribbling their orders, the woman turned and bellowed in a *basso profundo* to the chef in the kitchen. Persis and Karen both studied her.

"Wonder what the story is there," Persis murmured. "Some voice."

"Some neck," Karen said, pleased that Persis shared her curiosity.

Their tea arrived. Persis squeezed a lemon quarter into her cup and two seeds shot out like bullets, narrowly missing a patron in the next booth. Karen grinned, but Persis was oblivious, sipping her tea and looking preoccupied.

"Uh," Persis said, shifting uncomfortably against the back of her seat. "There's something I wish to say." Karen kept silent and waited while Persis struggled. "I don't know if Edward has told you," she went on stiffly, "but I have been urging him for many years to write a book. He never paid the slightest attention to me. I believe this Julius Southwick project is directly related to his meeting you. I felt I should tell you how grateful I am. The biography will be a great achievement for him and will most certainly benefit those of us in the literary community."

Until this moment, Karen had not realized the depth of Persis's jealousy. When Karen worked in the studio preparing songs for her album, the complex taping equipment allowed for a highly selective listening process. One could play back several tracks simultaneously—say, the strings, the drums, the vocal—or just one. Karen chose to hear Persis's little speech in a similar fashion. Snuffing out the pomposity, the envy, and the intellectual snobbishness, she opened her ears only to the generosity. Karen understood that it cost Persis plenty to credit her with Edward's project. But she wasn't about to diminish herself either.

"I was afraid of the water when I was a kid," Karen said. "I was fine unless I had to put my head under. But finally the time came to learn how to dive. My father spent an entire morning with me at the edge of the local pool explaining the procedure, demonstrating for me, and describing how the water felt. He was very patient, but hours passed and still I stood paralyzed with my toes curled over the edge. Then I took a deep breath, bent my knees, and at that moment, my brother came along and gave me the tiniest shove and I made my first dive. I was ready, but I maybe needed that little extra push."

Persis looked at her quietly and said, "You are an intelligent and gracious person."

"Thank you," Karen said, and quickly changed the subject. "What do you suppose Edward would have asked Christine?"

"Like every man, about his work."

Karen smiled. "You're right. Boy, I ought to go right back in there with some questions about mine. I'm really not paying enough attention."

"I think it would be divine to be able to sing," Persis said. The tension had left her voice. Karen thought the change in the older woman's face was dramatic as well. As Persis's mood softened, she became quite lovely.

"I can't really imagine not being able to," Karen said. "I've always felt sorry for people with little tiny voices. For speaking, even. Not strong ones like yours or that waitress's. I had laryngitis once and I was actually frightened, as if I were . . . I guess *impotent* is the only word to describe the feeling. I sing all the time, all by myself, partly for the fun of it, but I think for reassurance, too, to show myself it's still there."

"I think I can imagine that," Persis said. "It's a little like what writing poetry is for me. Almost as if it's a gift somebody just randomly dumped on me and there's no particular reason why whoever doled it out shouldn't just as randomly take it away."

"Exactly," Karen said.

Their sandwiches came, but they sat talking long after they finished eating, until the waitress took to sighing each time she passed their booth. They left a large tip.

Karen's suitcase sat in the middle of Edward's living room rug like a forlorn pet waiting to be let out while Karen and Edward lingered over the remains of their breakfast. Edward watched her closely. She had not spoken for several minutes.

Finally, she looked up at him. "I hate to leave you," she said.

"But that's not all." She didn't answer. "You're not merely sad," Edward went on. "You're depressed."

Her smile was half-hearted. "How come you know me so well?"

He just took her hand and examined the sturdy, rounded fingers.

"I haven't had time to write," she explained. "It's getting me down." The words came out sounding like a question.

Edward shook his head. "No, there's more."

She sighed. "Yesterday was Michael's birthday."

"Why didn't you say?"

"Because I forgot."

"Oh," Edward said. "I see."

"How could I?"

"It's just a date, a blot on the calendar."

"I could have tipped my hat to him," she said. "I don't want to stop missing him."

"You're remembering him every minute of every day, even if you're not conscious of it. But you don't have to suffer to pay tribute."

"I'm sorry to put you through this stuff again," Karen said.

"You're not putting me through anything. Life is fluid. Too much mourning will make you stagnant. Move on and take him with you. Otherwise you're merely celebrating death."

She was silent, thinking it over. "You know what," she said finally. "I wish I could figure out how to turn everything you say into a song." She came around the table to sit on his lap. His thighs were more padded now with the extra pounds. "I have to go," she whispered into his neck. His beard, smelling of wood, prickled the side of her face.

"We'll watch you on Persis's television," he promised.

"I don't know if that's good or bad."

"Are you very nervous?"

"Not yet."

"My girl," he murmured, and kissed her good-bye.

She had been gone for more than an hour when the lobby buzzer sounded. Puzzled, Edward went to the intercom. Persis was taking her riding lesson in the park and Karen was surely at the airport by now. A deep, unintelligible rumble emerged from the speaker. But Edward was able to discern the words "Karen Wells." He pushed the button to release the front door and waited curiously in his hallway. When he heard the elevator open, he squinted out the peephole to see a large dark-haired man in a rumpled linen suit lumbering toward his apartment. *Tony,* Edward thought. His heart began to pound. This visit was not likely to be pleasant, and Edward disliked unpleasantness. He waited a moment after the bell rang to calm himself.

"Tony Kahanian," the man said, and extended a huge paw. Edward took it and pulled himself up to his full height. He had about two inches on Tony; it seemed prudent to take advantage of any edge.

"Hate to barge in like this," Tony said, "but I thought we better talk." He found the table in the dining area and sat down, with Edward following along behind as if he were the intruder.

"Would you like something? Coffee?"

Tony shook his head. "Have a seat," he said.

"Thank you." The touch of irony in Edward's voice was lost on Tony.

"Karen's got this thing for you," Tony said as if he were describing her contraction of a fatal disease.

Edward smiled. "I don't understand it either."

"It's fucking up her career."

Edward waited.

"She's just at the brink. Things could go either way for her. This business doesn't tolerate a lot of screwing around any more. You've got to be committed. You've got to show up. She was single-minded about it until you came into the picture."

Edward did not respond. His silence seemed to irritate Tony. He got up and began to pace. "Does she talk about it?"

"About what?"

"The music, the performing."

"Yes."

"What does she say?"

"Why don't you discuss it with her?"

Tony stared at Edward as if he were an exhibit at the zoo. "What does it mean? What does it mean?" he said, but he seemed to be addressing himself rather than Edward. The hem of his shirt had worked itself free of his pants and hung over his belt buckle. He shoved it back in distractedly. "Look, Eddie, I need your help."

Edward laughed.

"That wasn't meant to be a joke," Tony said.

Edward shook his head. "How can I help?"

"I want to enlist your support. To get her back in the groove. She's not concentrating. She's going to destroy her chances. These people . . . the business end . . . only have so much patience."

Edward was struck with the aptness of Tony's desire to get Karen "back in the groove." "I should think with her talent, she could do rather as she pleased. She tells me there's this fellow who lives on a boat somewhere, Sam Dawkins, I believe she said . . ."

Tony recoiled in horror. "Christ! Oh, my God, Eddie, the man's a recluse!"

Edward laughed again. This time Tony's face flushed ominously. "Sorry," Edward said. "It's just nerves."

"So will you?" Tony asked. He hunched over the table, resting on his palms. Edward figured he must weigh upwards of two hundred pounds.

"I'm not sure I understand exactly what it is you're asking."

"Tell her. She's got to get a grip on herself. It's not just her own life she's messing with. Not just mine either. Lay the guilt on her. She responds to that."

"Wouldn't you agree that in the end it's her decision?" Edward asked. His neck was getting stiff from craning up at Tony. He stood, and the two men faced each other over the debris from this morning's breakfast. Edward felt Karen's presence as an ally in her empty coffee cup and half-eaten toast.

"That voice of hers means she doesn't have the right to her own decision."

"I beg your pardon?"

"It's like royalty. You think the fucking queen of England likes being the queen, or those poor kids of hers, just regular ordinary kids with funny ears growing up to be princes and kings and can't take a piss without the world knowing it and writing a review? It's just tough luck. They were born into it and there's no choice. The world won't let them have a choice. Same with Karen."

"I think that's absurd, frankly."

Tony raised his arms in exasperation. Edward backed off for fear of being accidentally swiped at by one of those powerful arms.

"I've known her a lot longer than you have, Ed," Tony said. "She'll come around. She just gets these notions into her head, the creative temperament, you know? She'll get over it."

"She'll get over me, you mean," Edward added.

Tony shrugged. "She can burn through a man pretty quick. She likes what she does. She likes the glory, the whole bit. She may pretend otherwise, but she's as much of a fame junkie as any of the others."

"She despises that part of it."

"Bullshit. She loves it, *loves it*. I knew her when she was singing in filthy clubs downtown and making no money. And now the world's open to her. For Christ's sake, if she wants to be all by her little self, she can shut the door and turn off the phone."

"Perhaps she will. I've never known anyone who needs freedom as profoundly as does Karen."

"All right," Tony said with a sigh. "Can't say I didn't try. But it's okay, it'll work out." Again, he seemed to be talking to himself. Edward, being uncooperative, no longer counted. Tony had already started for the door, doubtless off to wage the next battle. On the way down the hall, he stooped to pick up an object that was glittering against the doorframe. He examined it and when he looked up at Edward his face was full of pain. "I gave her this," he said. He put the earring in his pocket and left.

Persis volunteered to screen Karen Wells's appearance on the Bob Sterling show. "I'm inviting you all for dinner," she told the skeptical Edward. "You, Mother, Franklin, and Molly. It'll be a painless way to introduce Karen, and besides, we haven't all been together in months."

"There's a reason for that," Edward said.

"Oh, we get along better than most," Persis protested. "Come at eight-thirty. The show's not till eleven."

"Fine. That'll give you and Franklin plenty of time to argue about the dissection of aborted fetuses."

"You're just nervous about Karen's debut. Stop for wine on your way over, would you, two bottles of white. We must pickle Mother, she's so divine when she's drunk."

* * *

Edward walked up Broadway toward the liquor store and tried to remember the last time the family had assembled. While Oscar Vaughn was still alive, they managed to gather several times a year. But since his death, the fabric of family unity had somehow begun to fray. Not that historically the Vaughn dinner table wasn't fraught with disputation. Edward had long ago determined the pattern. First, the family was called to the table. As ritualized as evening grace, the meal began with Oscar Vaughn's description of his day as head librarian at New York University. Oscar possessed a rich, deep voice and a delivery so theatrical that even the most banal narration took on a dramatic flavor. "This particular student, a freshman," (*freshman* intoned as if the term contained all the wonder of youth newly emerging into a vast and magical world) "asked *me*" ("How delightful that he should choose me, of *all* people!") "to suggest a work of fiction which allowed the reader to select an ending." ("Have you ever heard of such a thrilling prospect as to direct the finale of a novel oneself? Omniscience! Omnipotence!") "Evidently, there are scores of such books about in paperback" (the deep sense of horror referring to the existence of any literary work not properly bound in hard cover) "having to do with medieval adventures."

At this point, Persis would interject, "What about *The French Lieutenant's Woman?*"

"Exactly!" Oscar would exclaim, his thin, pale face coloring with delight. "I had very nearly forgotten it entirely!" ("What a travesty, and I a librarian! But how very brilliant you are, my daughter, to think of it.")

This discourse continued for perhaps ten minutes until soup or salad disappeared. With the first forkful of the main course, Edward would wait for his mother's opening remark. She rarely failed him. Quietly, she would drop a casual comment—perhaps about Marxism, Ezra Pound, the value of tobacco, or in the early days, topics that engaged the children, such as playground morality or single-sex schools—that would bait the hook for either Franklin or Persis. Her son the scientist and her daughter the mystic could be relied upon to disagree, and soon the words would buzz and sting across the table like a swarm of wasps swooping over opposite sides of the fence. The arguments raged while the instigator calmly consumed her meal and Edward felt his stomach churn and tremble in revolt against the turmoil.

Oscar tolerated the battles for a while, showing increasing signs of discomfort until suddenly he would begin quoting the stanzas of a great poet—Spenser, perhaps, or Alexander Pope. Eventually, the low rumble of Oscar's voice penetrated the fractious atmosphere of his offspring's dispute to pacify and heal. However, it occasionally happened that Franklin and Persis had plunged too far into warfare for such an easy truce. At such times, while Persis howled imprecations at her brother about his cold-blooded pursuit of scientific truth ("Truth! What's truth anyway? Surely not a blob of your precious DNA, you arrogant dope!") and Franklin, with neck veins popping, took exception to Persis's methods of investigation ("You sure as hell won't discover it by holding a crystal in your lap and making noises like a deranged hummingbird!"), Oscar, his more temperate efforts ignored, would rise at his place and bellow stanzas from Milton's *Paradise Lost*. The argument would cease as if Persis and Franklin's vocal cords had been suddenly snatched from their throats. Every family has its hierarchy of sins, and for the Vaughns, inattention to the blind old Puritan's genius represented the ultimate evil.

In the liquor store, Edward selected two bottles of inexpensive white wine. He stood holding them beside the pile of wooden crates near the cash register. It had been a long time since he had thought of his father, now dead, what was it, seven years already? Edward felt a sudden pang of nostalgic affection for the man whose generous, optimistic nature had probably held the disparate personalities of his family together more effectively than any of them had realized. Edward suddenly noticed the refrigerator with its front row of champagne on display. Thinking of his father, and of Karen, he slipped the white wine back into its rack and left with two bottles of imported champagne.

Persis's apartment had six small square rooms exactly the same size, three off to each side of the hall. The bedroom held a bed and a wardrobe, the dining room a small round table with six chairs, the living room a couch and television set. But what the rooms lacked in horizontal space, they made up for in the vertical. With its fourteen-foot ceilings, the place seemed like a series of shoeboxes stood on end. But Persis, perhaps because of her stature, felt comfortable there and had called upon her considerable talents for design to paint the ceilings and walls contrasting colors for either accentuating or minimizing the architecture.

When Edward arrived, his mother was already there, perched on the single kitchen stool, watching Persis steam vegetables for the pasta. Caroline Vaughn was a small woman who had diminished in her eighty-five years to somewhere just above five feet tall. She weighed one hundred pounds and still had shapely, trim legs that she showed off with short skirts and dark-hued stockings. Her hair was a fine, soft frizz of white. Persis maintained her mother enjoyed standing at the sink in the ladies room at Tavern on the Green, opening her little beaded handbag, and removing a gigantic "Afro" comb, with which she poked and prodded her soft cloud of a hairdo.

"Mother, you look wonderful," Edward said, and for the first time he could ever remember, he gave her a kiss on the cheek. He half expected her to recoil with embarrassment or shock, but to his surprise, she looked pleased, even touched.

"I could say the same of you. What have you got there, not champagne?"

"Whoa!" Persis exclaimed, and took the bottles from her brother.

"We were engaging in a little girl talk," Caroline said. Her bright green eyes surveyed Edward from head to toe, missing nothing.

"Don't let me interrupt," Edward said.

Persis poured a potful of steamed broccoli into a colander to drain. "Mother was just saying that she used to pretend disinterest in sex because of us, but that she was actually a nymphomaniac."

"Persis Vaughn, I said nothing of the sort!" Caroline exclaimed with unconvincing horror.

"Thinking back to our youth, I can't recall the subject ever arising," Edward said, with a wink at Persis, "unless the context was strictly literary."

"All that time father was quoting from 'Leda and the Swan,' and little did we know the two of them were mixing it up like horny old Olympians under our very noses."

"Persis, you were always prone to hyperbole," Caroline remarked. "I don't see any reason why we should wait to open one of those bottles, do you, Edward?"

Persis reached into the refrigerator and began twisting at the top, but Edward took the bottle from her. "Remember the last time, dear. You nearly castrated your boyfriend and drowned me."

Caroline held out her glass. "I was merely pointing out to my lurid-minded daughter," she went on, "that sexual activity becomes somewhat dispirited in the advanced years and that I bemoan my prior restraint. I find one seldom regrets what one *has* done, merely what one has *not*. Not that I wasn't perfectly competent at such activities, but I wish I had placed a higher priority on it. Now, of course, I'm mainly reduced to denture kisses, which are hardly romantic."

"Do you take out your teeth for those?" Persis asked, fascinated enough to tear her attention away from the stove and stare at her mother.

"No, no. It's merely that nobody my age has teeth that fit properly, and they rattle. It's distracting to hear myself clicking every time some brave soul attempts to make me 'immortal with a kiss.' "

Edward and Persis smiled at one another.

"What I think Mother's trying to tell us, Edward, is *carpe diem*."

"You know what they say about 'this same flower that smiles today.' " Caroline tried to sound somber, but her eyes were twinkling.

Edward and Persis responded in unison, " 'Tomorrow will be dying.' " Persis shook her dish towel impatiently. "Mother, you have no intention of dying, tomorrow or ever. There's the bell. Go let them in, will you, Edward?"

He went to the front door and opened it to Franklin and Molly Vaughn.

"I'm so glad to see you," Edward said, with such fervor that the couple looked a little stunned. The brothers had never been particularly close, and Edward found Molly to be a rather humorless person. His delight in their attendance surprised even himself. "Come in. Mother's holding forth in the kitchen."

Edward let the others precede him to the kitchen doorway.

"Hi," Persis said. Her eyes made a token stop at Molly's face, then moved quickly on to Franklin and stuck. "It always amazes me how sort of adorable you are," she said to Franklin.

"Thank you, I suppose," Franklin said. Though he was also tall and slender, the youngest of the Vaughn siblings did not have the gaunt, sculptured features of the other two. His face was rounder, his hair fine and shiny black, and he wore tortoise-shell glasses over green eyes that were a muted version of his mother's.

"It's the nose," Edward decided, scrutinizing Franklin's face for adorability.

"Yes, Edward and Persis got mine," Caroline chimed in, well into her second glass of champagne. Her nose was her strongest feature. It was prominent and shapely, just slightly too large for her face. "My nose is why I never suffered from penis envy."

"I think Mother's been dipping into Masters and Johnson," Persis explained to her younger brother. "Edward, where are you? Let's take the champagne into the dining room where we can breathe. Dinner's ready whenever we feel like eating."

Persis had set the table with a mixture of colored paper napkins folded in an attractive fan pattern; in the center was a shallow bowl filled with flowers. Her dinner plates were an eclectic assortment of pottery garnered from flea markets and thrift shops. The effect was festive and attractive. When everyone had been seated according to Persis's instructions, she lifted her champagne glass, tilted it at Edward, and said, "Hurray for Hollywood."

Molly, her face wrinkled in perplexity, whispered to Franklin. "I don't get the reference."

"She means Karen Wells. That's why we're here, after all."

"To family assemblies, whatever the excuse," Edward said.

"Now tell us about her, Edward," Caroline said. "We need preparation. What sort of young woman is she?"

"Young and gorgeous," Franklin said. Molly continued her systematic consumption of mixed-green salad, but the muscles in her jaw rippled ominously. Molly wore her fine pale hair in barrettes like a young girl. She was earnest and sober, with an adolescent awkwardness that Edward found poignant.

"Karen Wells is gifted and generous and down to earth," Persis said with a kind of possessive pride that caused Edward to suppress a smile. He knew better than to let Persis see his pleasure.

"But can she think?" Caroline asked Edward. "That's always the critical issue."

"She's very bright," Persis said. "It's rather difficult to determine at first since she's shy and self-effacing, but there's real intelligence there."

"Intelligence is no asset in her business, Persis," Franklin said. "In fact, it's probably a liability."

"Intelligence is always an asset," Caroline said.

"Not if you're surrounded by idiots. Molly has a friend who writes screenplays out in Los Angeles. The prevailing mentality rises to somewhere below moronic. But then perhaps Karen Wells isn't sensitive to such cretinism."

Persis and Edward exchanged glances. Their brother had earned the caption of "Prove it!" under his high school yearbook photograph. The epithet still applied.

Molly was the first to dispose of her salad. She sat back and folded her hands in her lap. "Franklin got promoted," she announced. She gazed at her husband with the fierce intensity of hero worship.

"How marvelous," Caroline said. "I'm quite sure I wouldn't understand *from* what *to* what. My ancient brain hasn't the capacity to absorb computer technology."

"It really isn't all that obscure," Molly murmured.

"I'd like to hear about it," Edward lied, knowing full well that the explanation would elude him as surely as it would his mother. He was rewarded with a look of deep gratitude from his younger brother. While Persis and Molly cleared the salad plates, Franklin set his professional triumphs before Edward like a small boy removing treasures from his pocket. Edward tried to look as if he understood.

"I guess it's been a big month for the Vaughn men," Franklin said finally, with a surreptitious glance at his mother. "Edward connecting with Karen Wells and me with my meteoric rise up the corporate ladder."

"You can't really compare the two events," Molly said, arriving with an immense Mexican bowl filled with pasta and vegetables.

Edward felt a familiar twinge of guilt. In their mother's eyes, Franklin's accomplishments had never seemed to measure up to Edward's. There was always the subtle expectation that good old Franklin, the scientific grind, would achieve. In a family where inspiration was held sacrosanct, Franklin's plodding intellect got short shrift. Molly was quite correct, Edward thought. Where was the credit in an accidental meeting with Karen Wells?

"I'm quite overcome with pride," Caroline said, smiling broadly at her sons, and Edward relaxed. Perhaps it was unrealistic to expect his mother to have equal regard for each of her children. After all, it was Edward who had spent so many days home from school, suffering with assorted respiratory ailments and a sensitive digestive tract. He and his mother had filled the hours with imaginative games, reading aloud to one another and catching up with Edward's homework together. Edward remembered that in first grade he had missed an entire month due to a severe bout of gastroenteritis. Caroline had picked up the early-reader books from his teacher, but since Edward was already consuming sophisticated storybooks and poetry, he and his mother experimented with reading the Dick-and-Janes backward or by inserting silly words into each sentence.

"Just *how* did Dick run?" Caroline would ask, sitting on the edge of Edward's bed. "Pigeon-toed? Knock-kneed? And what was his mood, do you suppose?"

"Goofy," Edward would say. "Nutty, loony, and drunk."

Caroline encouraged Edward to invent bloodcurdling stories about the Dick-Jane-Baby Sally family, of how the older children trained their delectable little sister to beg and steal and how the parents were always in and out of jail for extortion or tax evasion. There was always a great deal of laughter emanating from Edward's sick room. Even now, it was obvious that Franklin envied his older brother's special access to their mother.

"How's my favorite niece?" Persis asked Franklin.

"She's your only niece," Molly remarked.

"I could have twenty nieces, and Delilah would still be my favorite," Persis said. She wound several strands of spaghetti around her fork and sighed as they slipped off onto her plate before they reached her mouth.

"She's fine," Molly replied. Her smile transfigured her face entirely, smoothing away all the hard edges.

"She's strange," Franklin said.

"What is she now, three?" Edward asked. "I barely know her."

Persis leaned forward eagerly. "You're missing something, Edward. She's a special little person, a poet already."

"Oh, I don't know about poet," Molly said.

"We can't figure it out," Franklin said. "Sometimes I think she needs therapy."

"Therapy!" Caroline exclaimed.

"She has this new little ritual. She picks lint off her blanket or off her sweater and plants it on her eyelashes. I can't imagine how she can see, especially if it's a dark color—from her navy-blue cardigan, for instance."

"We've noticed that if she really takes a liking to someone, she puts some on that person's eyelashes."

The others laughed. "How charming!" Caroline said.

"Well, you may think so," Molly said, "but we were concerned enough to speak with the pediatrician."

"What did he say?" Persis asked, making an effort to keep her eyes averted from Edward's.

"He laughed," Franklin said.

"He did not," Molly objected. "Well, maybe at the beginning. Then he said we should keep an eye on it."

"So to speak," Persis said. "Listen, you two, I would be honored to wear blue lint on my eyelashes. In fact, I'm prepared to be insulted if Delilah doesn't give me any."

"Oh, she will," Molly said with weary resignation. Then she turned to Edward and said almost shyly, "Perhaps you'll come see her before you go back to England. She's so beautiful."

"I shall certainly try."

There was a moment's silence while everyone enjoyed Persis's meal. Then Caroline, without looking up from her plate, said, "Franklin, I suppose you'll be voting Republican again this fall."

It was a quiet little comment, but Edward knew it would have the effect of dropping a small nuclear device onto the dinner table.

"Probably," Franklin answered.

Persis, already anticipating her brother's reply, had set her fork down and was glaring at him. "You can mention that child, your precious posterity, in the same breath that you speak of a Republican?"

"Yes," Franklin said.

"*Republican* doesn't necessarily translate as fascist," Molly said.

"Of course it does," Persis snapped. Her cheeks had begun to color. "You obviously don't give one damn about the environment, about the mess you'll saddle poor Delilah with . . ."

Suddenly, Edward stood up and over the rising decibels of his sister's voice, began to recite in a loud voice:

Me miserable! which way shall I fly
Infinite wrath, and infinite despair?
Which way I fly is hell; myself am hell;
And in the lowest deep a lower deep
Still threat'ning to devour me, opens wide,
To which the hell I suffer seems a heaven.

At first, there was silence. Then everyone burst into laughter. Caroline applauded, Edward made a deep bow and sat down.

"All right, all right, I get the point," Persis said, waving her hands in surrender. "No more politics. Okay, Franklin?"

"Fine with me," Franklin said. "I was just minding my own business."

"Mother," Persis said, "why do you *do* that? You're a regular provocateur."

"Shouldn't it be 'provocateuse'?" Caroline asked.

"Don't try to wriggle out of it," Persis said. "You set me up."

"I was just gardening," Caroline said. "That's what your father used to call it."

"Rabble-rousing's more like it," Edward said.

"I always wanted my children to think. If I managed to encourage a nice, stimulating argument, I could leave the table satisfied. A good, healthy dispute is the most effective way to sharpen one's wits. That was fine Milton, Edward. Your father would have been proud."

"I'm beginning to think we were all at your mercy, Father included," Persis said. "Now somebody finish off that last little smidgen. I'm anxious to see how dessert came out."

At five minutes to eleven, Persis herded everyone into the living room. Molly and Persis sat on the floor so that Caroline could perch on the couch, her tiny figure like a doll propped between her two lanky sons. The television set was small, but the picture had good quality. In a moment, the theme music for *The Bob Sterling Show* blasted out, full of brass and cymbals.

"Gracious," Caroline said.

"Edward, I'm getting nervous already."

"Karen Wells is a professional," Franklin said. "She won't be nervous."

Edward imagined Karen crossing herself backstage. The talk-show host, silver-haired and smiling, began his monologue. The audience laughed harder at his reaction to their nonreaction than they did at any of his jokes.

"Curious," Edward said.

"His charm is lost on me," Molly said.

The first guest was Mops Lanigan, the tiny comic whose aging cheeks drooped despite the face lifts and whose eyes held the hard glitter of the chronic alcoholic. His feet, with their built-up heels, barely touched the floor. He sat next to Bob Sterling's desk and made jokes about his inability to find work. "I tried to get a job as a derelict in New York City, but Mayor Koch told me I didn't have enough class." The audience seemed to find him funny, but no one in Persis's living room smiled.

"This man is an embarrassment," Molly muttered.

After what seemed an endless stream of commercials, Mops Lanigan appeared seated once removed from the dais, and Sterling began his introduction of Karen.

"Uh-oh," Persis said.

"Yes," Edward murmured. He found himself instinctively pressing his body into the upholstery.

". . . American singing sensation, Miss . . . Karen . . . Wells!"

The curtain parted, and out she came, smiling, poised, in a midnight-blue dress that clung to her compact body and showed off her legs. She wore very high heels, and her lips glistened with shiny lipstick.

"Jesus Christ, Edward," Franklin said, staring at his brother across the top of Caroline's head. Perhaps an explanation for the relationship could be found somewhere in that familiar bearded face. But the music had started, and Franklin turned back to the television screen. Karen sang "Wings" with a brassy accompaniment from the band that seemed tinny and false. When it was over, Karen bowed to enthusiastic applause and whistles. She clutched the bodice of her dress close to her chest as she bent over.

Edward looked at Persis in dismay. "It's not Karen, is it?"

Persis shook her head. "Just electronic impulses or some such nonsense."

"Shh," Franklin said.

Karen had settled into the seat formerly occupied by Mops Lanigan.

"I've been looking forward to meeting you," Bob Sterling was saying in his extra-sincere voice. "You have a reputation in the business as being an original, really sort of poetic and sensitive."

"Oh, dear, I guess I should try to come up with something poetic . . ." Karen began.

But Mops Lanigan interrupted. "I can see she's *real* sensitive by the cut of that dress." He leered at Karen's chest while the audience tittered. Edward felt himself begin to sweat, and Caroline clicked her tongue.

Sterling glanced down at his desk for a moment and then up at Karen. "I understand we have a rather controversial video to look at. There's been a lot of advance publicity about this one. We're going to show a little clip of it tonight, first time, folks. Fellas?" He looked out at the camera crew and soon Karen's video snapped onto the screen. Karen, naked against a black sky, was riding a horse that slowly turned to fire.

"No wonder he looks so well," Caroline whispered.

"Lady Godiva of MTV," Mops Lanigan commented in a harsh voice.

"What a schmuck," Persis said.

The video flickered off. Bob Sterling made one of his wide-eyed stares at the audience, indicating he was overcome with the audacity of Karen's sexual charms. There was laughter and more applause.

"Tell me," Bob Sterling said, with another ingenuous look. "The question we all want to know the answer to is . . ." He dragged it out, each time getting laughs. "Were you really . . . well, in the buff?"

"This girl's got *talent,*" Lanigan interjected loudly.

"It's supposed to look realistic," Karen replied to Sterling, ignoring the comedian. "I'm not going to give away any technical secrets, but let's just say the imagination of the viewer is enlisted to assist the visual effects."

Lanigan leaned over to her and grinned. "If I set fire to my tushie, will you ride me too?"

Karen waited a moment into an awkward silence, then smiled sweetly at him and said, "Mr. Lanigan, you would play a horse's hindquarters with great authority."

The audience howled and cheered, Bob Sterling broke up, and Persis whooped.

"That's my girl," Edward said smugly.

During the commercial break, all eyes turned to Edward. There were congratulations from everyone except Franklin.

"These things are surely not spontaneous," Franklin said. "They must rehearse beforehand."

"Don't be absurd," Persis said.

"Well, Edward," Caroline said. "I, for one, am impressed. The girl's got a head on her very pretty shoulders and plenty of sex appeal besides. It's about time."

When the show returned, both Mops Lanigan and Karen had disappeared from the dais. Persis got up and shut off the television.

"That man ought to be whipped in the public square," Molly remarked. "Outrageous."

"I'd say Karen did the job pretty neatly," Persis said. The telephone rang and Persis reached for it. "Hello? . . . Karen, you were wonderful, skewered him, the idiot . . . Yes, he's right here." She handed the phone to Edward who was blushing with pleasure.

"So, whadya think?" Her voice sounded so close it startled him.

"You were marvelous."

"I didn't get a chance to say anything intelligent. That jerk kept interrupting me. How was the song?"

"Lovely. My family's here with me."

"What? Oh, Christ, Edward, who all . . ."

"My mother, Franklin, and Molly. And Persis, of course."

"Well, I'm glad I didn't know that before. Did I look like a flat-chested Barbie Doll? Edward, don't make me pump you. Volunteer a little."

"You looked very pretty, but not like you. I don't think I enjoy seeing you on the screen like that. You're too flat."

"My boobs felt like they were falling out of my dress."

"You know what kind of flat."

"Yes, darling, I know, I'm just wired. We taped hours ago and I've been going nuts waiting for the show to hit the East Coast. I knew you'd be watching now, but Jesus, your whole family. Whew, I wouldn't want to make a career of this."

"You'd better not tell that to Tony."

"No." Something in his voice made her hesitate. "What do you mean?"

Edward suddenly looked up to see everyone's attention trained on him as if the telephone conversation was merely a continuation of *The Bob Sterling Show*. "Excuse me a second, darling." He was enjoying himself enough to relish exhibiting his use of the endearment, particularly, he thought with a pang of self-reproach, in front of Franklin. Edward put his hand over the mouthpiece. "May I use the kitchen extension, Persis?"

"Oh, uh, of course," Persis said, snapping out of her dazed state. She got up and held the telephone while Edward crossed the hall into the kitchen.

"He was here," Edward said.

"*Tony* was there?"

"Yes—I mean, of course, at my apartment, before he flew out to Los Angeles. Is he with you right now?"

"No, they tell me he's having a fight with Mops Lanigan in the Beverly Hills Hotel parking lot."

"He kept calling me 'Eddie.' "

Karen laughed. "Oh, my God. Fast Eddie, that's you. What did he want?"

"To persuade me to persuade you to commit yourself."

"To an institution? Oh, I know what you mean. I'm just freaked out. My career, the long haul, etcetera, etcetera, etcetera, to quote Yul Brynner. Oh, Christ, he's back. You know what? I'll call you at your house later. Did the video shock everybody? God, your little old Victorian mother."

Edward laughed. "My little old mother hasn't stopped talking about sex all night. The video was stunning."

She was silent a moment. Then she said, "Thank you. I love you," and hung up.

He stood outside the living room door for a moment listening to the conversation.

"It's perfectly obvious that you're jealous," Persis was saying to Franklin.

"Are you?" Molly asked. She touched her hair, smoothing it behind her ears.

"It just seems like science fiction," Franklin said. "We all think Edward's terrific, but that dazzling young thing . . ."

Edward decided it was not likely to get better, so he entered the room with a clatter. "I couldn't agree with you more," he told Franklin. "I don't know about anyone else," he went on, glancing at his watch, "but I'm thoroughly exhausted. I have to go to bed. Persis, dinner was wonderful. Molly, Franklin, it was a treat to see you. Mother, let me find you a cab?"

Downstairs on the street, Caroline put her old clawlike hand on his arm. Edward could feel it tremble.

"How long will you be in London this time?" she asked. There was a sadness in the question Edward had never heard before. He was astonished to feel his eyes sting.

"I don't know, dear, but I'll be back and forth. We'll see one another." When the cab came, he ushered his mother carefully into the backseat, and leaned in to peer at the driver's nameplate. "Mr. Ramirez," Edward said, "I want you to take very good care of this lady."

13

"The Sterling show is a complete farce," Karen said into the darkness over Edward's bed.

"Why do you say that?" Edward asked.

"It's totally artificial. First, some talent coordinator calls you and does this pre-interview over the phone to find out if you're a moron or halfway interesting. They make a list of the things you say that they think Sterling will like, and then you get on the show and do this fake thing. It's almost like a script."

"Your interview didn't appear to be rehearsed."

"Well, that was because Lanigan was out of control. But it's a kind of machine. The staff is very calm, very efficient, they've been pulling this thing off for so many years now. It's creepy. And the band plays so loud even I can't stand it."

"It didn't seem that way over the television, just rather a superfluity of trumpets."

"No, I mean during commercial breaks. They do it to keep the energy level up, the excitement, so that the audience feels like there's this big deal going on. But there's no real contact. Not with Sterling, not with the audience . . . it's just more of the same bullshit unreality." The window shade flapped against the frame like a pair of listless hands applauding in the dark. "But Edward, guess what I did while I was out there. I called Manfred Warm about the musical."

Edward, responding to the sudden excitement in her voice, turned on his pillow to peer at her through the darkness. "And?"

"Well, the video's been such a success and everybody knows it was my idea. Apparently, I've got what's known as 'credibility.' Manfred and Dil, that's the director who did the video, seem to think they can stir the record company up to provide some seed money, enough to work out a backers' audition once I've got songs . . . and, well, I'm trying not to get too worked up about it, but they really want me to put some stuff on paper. Yikes. So really, now, who wants to do this thirty-five-city marathon when I could be playing around with my new baby?"

"I'm so proud," Edward said.

"Well, you oughta be. You provoked me into this thing."

"It's funny . . ." he began, then broke off.

"Don't do that to me," Karen said.

"Well, I'm rather embarrassed, actually. I was thinking that if you become totally entranced with the musical, you won't much feel like visiting London."

"What, I can't think on the other side of the Atlantic? They have no pencils there, no pianos? Of course I'll come to London. What better place to write a hit musical?" She waited. "I heard that smile."

"How can you hear a smile?" Edward asked.

"It has a sort of little crackle to it, lips against teeth, I guess."

"Perhaps you'll surprise yourself and find you enjoy the tour without me around to distract you."

"You're what keeps me from going totally nuts," she protested. "Oyoyoy, Ferris Pauling with his druggie groupies. Did I tell you he tattooed his head? The Statue of Liberty in a black garter belt, and instead of a torch she's extending her middle finger."

"Charming."

"He says he's going to grow some hair around it to represent the grass on Liberty Island. He's promised me he'll put himself back in Smithers, the drug rehab place, but not until after the tour. I'm terrified something awful will happen to him. The tour's enough to turn anyone into an addict . . . Edward?"

"Yes."

"Are you still attracted to me?"

"Of course. Can't you tell?"

"Well, I know we did it and everything, but I just thought . . . there was something."

"Don't forget, I'm an old man."

"Yeah, sure, Rip Van Winkle."

"Rip 'Fast Eddie' Van Winkle," he corrected her.

"How'm I going to get through tomorrow, saying good-bye?"

"I'm not looking forward to it myself."

"What asshole said, 'Parting is such sweet sorrow'?"

"Shakespeare."

"Oh. Well, there's nothing sweet about it. It's so bizarre, because obviously I was getting along in this world before I met you and now I can't conceive of being away from you for more than a day. You've got my insides packed in that damn suitcase." She was silent a moment. "Do you think you'll miss me or will it be a relief?"

"How can you ask that?"

"Well, you're not always so forthcoming, and I'm curious."

He thought a moment. "I'm not fond of the separations. It's rather as if, well, let me see, it's as if the electricity has been turned off. The lights just won't go on."

She kissed him and wound her fingers through the curls in his beard. "Can you think of a way to make it easier?"

He was quiet.

"How come you don't say, 'By promising you'll visit me in London'?"

"You know I would never ask that."

"And you know your not pressuring me only makes me love you more."

"I can't help that."

"Should I come to the airport with you?"

"No, I shouldn't think so."

"Okay, but let me put you in a cab. Otherwise, I'll know you're still in the city and it'll make me crazy."

He draped an arm and a leg across her body. "Always so warm," he murmured.

"You know something? You're getting positively pudgy." She squeezed the flesh on his forearm. "I'll bet you've hit one-sixty-five.

And that was not a complete sentence, 'Always so warm.' That means you're ninety percent asleep."

"Mm."

She let him drift away, but her eyes remained wide open. They glistened in the darkness like a pair of teardrops on the pillow.

Karen hunched over the microphone in the middle of the studio. Except for John Garver, the other band members lolled about the room, occupying themselves until needed.

"B-flat, honey," John said, plucking the note for her on his guitar. "E-flat's the next measure."

"Damn it, John. Maybe this shouldn't be a blues after all."

"It's a blues, it's a blues."

Karen looked up at the technician's face watching them through the window of the control room. "Gonna take a break, okay, Pete?" She glanced at the huge white clock on the wall. "We might as well have lunch."

Pete nodded. His disembodied voice poured into the room. "Sam'll pick up the usual."

Karen nodded.

"Incidentally, you're getting ahead on the sixteenths."

"Yup," Karen said. "At least I'm getting ahead on something."

John set his guitar down and began to massage the back of Karen's neck. "Girl, you got knots in here bigger than Billy's big feet."

"Oh God, oh God, somebody sent you from heaven." She looked around the room at the others. Nicky Stein sat in the lotus position, a hand on each knee, index fingers and thumbs touching. Billy Lundgren was sprawled out on his stomach staring fixedly at a small chunk of machinery between his fingers. Ferris slumped against the shingled fake-Swiss-chalet wall in a drugged sleep. From the top of his bald head, the Statue of Liberty gave them the finger. "How come nobody ever sits in chairs around here?" Karen asked, plunking down near Nicky. "Oh, sorry, Nick, I didn't mean to screw up your mantra."

Nicky blinked up at her. "I'm done. Is food coming?"

"Any minute."

"Good food?" Nicky asked John.

"Of course it's not good food," Karen said. But John nodded at Nicky.

Suddenly the studio door burst open and in strode Tony. Attached to his arm was a young blonde woman in a very short skirt.

"Hi, band," he said. He did not look at Karen. "I wanted you to know we've got final travel arrangements. Friday morning, Kennedy at seven A.M. sharp, no screwups, right? Ferris? Somebody tell Ferris when he wakes up. Your gear's going out Thursday night. Everybody got that?" There were nods. Then Tony stared at Karen. "You all set?"

"Yup," Karen said.

"This is Marylou. Marylou, Karen Wells."

Karen reached out to shake hands. The girl's fingers were chilled and sweating.

"Okay, just so's we're clear," Tony said. "See you there."

On their way out, Marylou clung so tightly to Tony that she lost her balance trying to keep up. He put his arm around her protectively and glanced back at Karen. When the door slammed shut, Nicky began to laugh.

"Well, that was some display," she said.

Karen looked stunned.

"He brought her here just for you," Nicky said. "All of that business about the airport, he could have just called us."

"Oh, yes, I guess so," Karen said. "She was so young."

"Poor Tony," Nicky said.

"Poor Marylou," John said.

The door opened again, this time admitting Sam, the small wheezing youth who was Pete's assistant and whom Karen suspected of supplying Ferris with pills. He began unloading plastic containers and soda cans. At Karen's feet he set a Diet Coke and a tuna on rye. Karen thought he looked shiftier than usual, making quick surreptitious glances over his shoulder at the studio entrance.

Nicky went over to Ferris and bent down to give his legs a shake. "Hey, wake up. Lunch. Come on, Fer, put something nontoxic in your stomach."

Ferris reached out a hand and Nicky pulled him to his feet. He was a slight man with a beautiful lean body. His gentle sleepy smile contrasted ludicrously with the tattoo on his head. "Oh, yeah, is it time for the par . . . ?" he began. Nicky gave him a sharp kick and his eyeballs snapped into focus. They sat in a circle on the floor, all cross-legged except John, who stretched out on his side, elegant as a cat.

"So's everybody looking forward to the tour?" Karen asked. She ate the crust off her sandwich first, indulging a childhood habit.

"Something to do," Billy said.

"I'm not sure we'll be ready with this number," John said. "It's rough in the turnaround."

"There's something wrong with the lyrics, that's why," Nicky said.

"There is?" Karen asked. "Can you fix it, Nick?"

"Try it like this." She hummed in a tiny soprano. "*Don't you tell me how I feel.* Accents on the *you* and *I.*"

"Right," John said. "That'll work."

"See, John?" Karen said. "Shouldn't she be writing? I keep trying to tell her."

"Don't start," Nicky said.

"It would be fun, though. We could work together. What if we started messing around with a musical? Just for instance. Look how great you were with the video. You've got a real instinct for visual stuff, and with your facility with words . . ."

"Will you give me a break?" Nicky said. "I just want to play the drums."

Ferris looked up from his beer. "I don't believe that."

"Well, who asked you anyway?" Nicky gave Ferris a friendly swipe. He grabbed her hand and kissed her fingers.

"Ych," Nicky said, but she grinned at him.

"Do you guys ever wonder . . ." Karen began, then stopped herself.

"What?" Billy said. He had already finished one sandwich and had begun the second. The studio was accustomed to Billy's adolescent appetite and always provided extra for him.

"Oh, I don't know," Karen went on hesitantly. "What you'd do if you didn't do this?"

John and Nicky glanced at one another.

"You mean if the group broke up?" John asked.

Karen nodded.

"I'd survive," John said.

"But what would you do?" Karen prodded.

"Kick around for a while and then hook up with another group. I don't want to sell insurance."

"You got some plans we don't know about?" Ferris asked.

"Not really," Karen said. "I just think sometimes it might be, well, that I could take a rest, a leave of absence."

Billy stared at her with fearful eyes. John reached out a hand and touched him on the shoulder. "You're a hot commodity, Billy. You'd have another job in ten minutes."

"I don't want another job."

"I shouldn't have said anything . . ." Karen began.

At that moment, Pete's face appeared in the control-room window again. He tapped quietly on the glass. Nicky nodded at him and he disappeared, but Karen was too busy staring at her soda can to notice. The studio door opened, and in came Pete carrying a huge round cake, candles blazing. John grabbed his guitar, and they all began to serenade Karen with a rock version of "Happy Birthday to You."

At first, all the color drained out of her face; then she flushed deep red. At the end of the song, which Nicky punctuated with a roll on the cymbals, Karen squeezed her eyes shut and blew out all the candles. Then she sat back and looked at everyone smiling at her.

"Thirty," she said. "I'm thirty. It seems like such a big deal."

"Makes a person think about the future, doesn't it?" Nicky asked.

"Thirty is *mature,* man," Billy added. "You gonna cut that cake or you want me to do it?"

Karen handed him the knife. "You do it. I'm too mature."

Suddenly she felt the tears coming. She hung her head, but she could not control her trembling chin.

"What is it, babe?" John asked.

Karen looked up at them, her faced streaked. "Oh, you guys . . . it's just . . . I love you guys."

Karen sat at the edge of her sectional sofa with a mug of coffee in her hand. From the twenty-fifth floor she faced east, affording her a breath-catching view of the river. The planes rising up out of La Guardia Airport reminded her of the models Michael used to make, with their sharp scent of glue and paint that Karen had found so mysterious and masculine. Tony had ensconced her in this place last year when it became apparent that she was on the way up. He felt it crucial that she shed the sordid trappings of her hole-in-the-wall in the East Village. So she signed the lease and found a decorator who whipped the place into livable condition within a month. Karen thought the contemporary furniture, chiefly mauve and gray, looked squat and bloated. What's more, one of the silver sculptures, a free-form oval with a hole through the middle, suggested a toilet seat. But she hadn't really minded since she spent so little time here. But she was trapped for the next several days, resting in anticipation of the tour. Here it was, a balmy early June morning, breezy and fine, or so they said on the radio. But her windows were sealed. Used air billowed up behind the living room curtains, creating a fraudulent breeze. She began to break out in a sweat and felt a sudden impulse to fling her coffee mug through the window, to shatter that blank wall of glass and take a bath in some real sky. But of course there were people scurrying along below; the consequences were unthinkable.

She got up and went to the piano, an old, battered upright that was the only piece of furniture imported from her downtown apartment. Tony had flailed his arms, the decorator sneered, but Karen held her ground. She slid onto the bench and began to pick out a tune. She was not proficient at the keyboard, but could manage basic chords. The more complex structures resonated in her head and she was able to work them out painstakingly, note by note, beginning from the lowest tone and working her way up. *"I got the highrise blues,"* she hummed, and jabbed at the keys with her index finger. *"I got the closed in, stale room, lowdown highrise blues . . ."* She experimented with the notion for about half an hour, took a sip of her cold coffee, then got up and went to the telephone.

"What are you doing?" she asked Persis.

"Pretending to work."

"Want to go for a ride?"

"Sure."

"I'll meet you at the stables in an hour."

Karen had outfitted Persis at an equestrian shop on Twenty-fourth Street. They had ridden twice together since then, and Karen saw that the woman combined two opposite qualities: a natural athletic ability and a predilection for catastrophic klutziness. It was a bewildering mix. But this morning their two hours in the park passed by uneventfully.

In Persis's apartment, the scent of horses clung to them and filled the rooms with a friendly mustiness. While Persis opened a can of tunafish in the kitchen, Karen padded around in her bare feet. She stopped in front of a framed silhouette of a dog that hung in the hallway. At the bottom of the picture were strange markings: *Sun in Scorpio; Moon in Sagittarius.*

"What is this?" Karen called.

Persis poked her head out of the kitchen. "That's our dog Lochinvar's astrological chart. My father had it done."

"He must have been quite a character."

"Oh, yes, except he had a penchant for antique needlepoint. He chewed up a fabulous pillow my mother got from her aunt as a wedding present."

Karen giggled. "I meant your father."

Persis appeared with a plateful of sandwiches, which she took into the dining room. "Oh, no, Father never touched tapestry, just chintz." As always, the table was brightened with a vase of fresh flowers. "I'm famished beyond words," Persis admitted.

"It's the riding. You don't realize how much energy you're expending."

"I realize it, and so does my rear end. It's so bruised I think I'd better invest in one of those hemorrhoid cushions."

"That'll improve over time."

"I hope I'm not going to acquire calluses on my posterior," Persis said. "I'm having enough trouble with my sex life as it is."

"Anybody special?" Karen asked, warmed that Persis felt free enough for such a confidence.

Persis sighed. "There's always somebody. Ask Edward, he's been listening to me carry on for decades. I fall wildly in love, enjoy the Era of Bliss that lasts anywhere from one night to a few weeks, then disillusion, or rather reality, sets in, and we begin the long slide down. Which is sometimes a gradual descent and sometimes like being pushed out of an airplane window."

"Where are you in the cycle with this guy?"

"At the edge of bliss. The far side."

"Is it going to be a freefall from thirty thousand feet?"

"Don't know yet. Christ, I need another sandwich. Maybe it's from hanging out with you. Edward is getting positively obese."

"How did you meet your new man?"

"In the library. We were competing for a volume of the *Lyrical Ballads* that's not published in the U.S. An incredible coincidence, I thought."

"Or fate."

"That's what he decided. At the time, however, he nearly punched me. We had this loud scrap at the checkout desk over who needed the book most, he for his doctoral research or I for inspiration. The librarian finally settled it by persuading him to check it out and share it with me. She's a lascivious type who's always trying to match people up, you know, a big D. H. Lawrence fan with scarlet lipstick an inch thick and fluorescent eye makeup." Persis poured them each a cup of coffee and sliced into a lemon pound cake. "He's very clever. I always go for the clever ones. But they have enlarged brains and shrunken hearts."

"Edward doesn't." Karen stared down at her coffee. "I wonder how long it's going to take him to finish this book."

"Well, he was amazed at how much material he'd compiled," Persis said. "He may actually begin writing in a couple of months."

"How long does that part take?"

"We won't know till it's over. Could be two years, could be ten. How long does it take to write a song?"

"Could be two minutes, could be two months," Karen replied. "If I can just get this wretched tour over with. Oh, hell, I suppose I'll always feel this way until opening night. Then the adrenaline starts pumping and it's like living through a wild, psychedelic dream. Right now, I just want to hang out with Edward and work on the musical."

When Persis's attention was totally engaged, her entire body became taut in what Edward called her "cobra response." Now she pushed her plate aside, clasped her hands together in a tense knot on the table and stared at Karen with burning eyes. "I don't remember hearing anything about a musical."

"I just told you my most profound secret," Karen said, alarmed.

"Why would you want to keep it secret? It sounds thrilling to me."

"I feel a little as though I were hiding an illegitimate child somewhere—you know, my joy and my shame."

"Are you actually working on this illegitimate child?"

"I have the basic idea. It's a pretty lunatic notion, very Country Western. Once I've got some of it written, a few songs, some scenes—oh, Lord, my heart—then these people in California seem to think we can raise some money. I'm trying not to get too freaked out—they like it this week; they may hate it next Monday."

"You're dying to do it," Persis declared. She unwound her fingers and stretched luxuriously.

"I'd really have to leave the band," Karen said. "At least for a while. In the studio the other day, I raised the issue of a break, kind of figuring they'd start screaming about loyalty or something."

"No such luck?"

"They seem to think they'd survive. God, maybe this is the identity crisis I should have had at eighteen. It'd be like walking away from my family."

"Maybe a little like growing up."

"Oh, dear."

"I'm a sanctimonious shit," Persis said. "Sorry. Maybe we ought to go ask Christine what you should do."

"Yeah," Karen said. "Wouldn't it be nice to have all the answers?"

In Boston, which was a giant exclamation point at the end of the tour, Tony finally challenged her. He showed up at her dressing room and stood in the corner with arms folded while the visiting notables offered their congratulations. Finally, after they had all left, Karen removed her makeup and turned to see Tony watching her. He had not appeared so haggard and thin the last time she looked at him.

"Something?" she asked.

"You tell me."

"It went fine, don't you think?"

"As far as anyone else is concerned."

"But not in your opinion."

"This whole tour's been a long way from fine."

"Tony, I know it's not . . . we're not . . ."

He shook his head. "I'm not talking about us. It's you, your performances. I didn't push it until now because I was actually afraid you might take a walk on me in the middle of the tour. I don't trust your professionalism anymore, and that's really scary. What the hell is the matter with you anyway?" His voice had been carefully calm, but she could hear it thickening. Her scalp began to prickle with fear and excitement. She was out of the habit of fighting with him.

"Those crowds were ready to eat me up," she protested. She stared at his hand propped against the door frame. Those expert fingers had traveled everywhere on her body. She turned away from him and fussed at the mirror. Perhaps it was the olive wallpaper he was standing against, but his face seemed sickly gray.

"The fact is, you don't give a shit anymore."

There was a long silence.

"Maybe you're right," she said.

"It's fraud, Karen. How long do you think you can bullshit the public?"

"I signed a contract to do this thing. I didn't tell them I'd love it."

"Your job is to be the best you can be. It's just not happening."

"I need time . . ."

"You need a kick in the ass."

"You'd make a great psychiatrist, Tony. Ever think of getting a degree? So subtle, so sensitive."

"Oh, yeah, and I've heard about this musical crap. Give me a fucking break. It'd be laughable if it weren't for the fact that you've got so many people depending on you. You wanted this and they got it for you. *I* got it for you. You can't just slide through. Sooner or later, the message will make itself clear."

"Am I obligated to be a superstar?"

"Yes."

"Why?"

"Because you spent the last ten years of your life going for it. And my life, too. Once it's here, you can't shit on it." He closed in and loomed over her. She stood up and began backing away until she was halted by the floor-length mirror. She had the sudden fantasy that she could press herself through it and on the other side would be Edward's little flat in Chelsea. Tony's face was two inches away from hers. She could stop him, if she only tilted her face up to his and kissed his mouth. His kisses were deep and hot and sometimes seemed to go on forever, as if she would never draw breath again, as if he could kill her with his mouth and she would die willingly.

"Things happen," she whispered. "Life is unpredictable."

"Oh, now we're talking about your professor with the hairy face. Jesus, Karen, what's the mystery there? Is he hiding something in his pants that doesn't show?" He grasped her wrists and pinned them up above her head. His chest pressed against her breasts. His knee dug between her legs, parting them.

Karen told her body that it did not want him any more, that the wild clattering of her heart and the heat between her legs were obsolete. "You think the only thing that interests me in a man is the size of his—"

"Correct," Tony murmured against her neck. "That's exactly right."

Karen squirmed free and sat down in her chair. She clutched her knees with her arms and rocked back and forth. For a while there was silence except for the sound of Tony's heavy breathing, and hers. Finally, Tony turned toward her with his body slumped against the wall. "You can't deny what happens between us." His voice sounded tired.

"I don't deny it," Karen said.

"I turn you on, don't I?"

"Yes."

"How can you give it up?"

"There are other things."

"You're really hooked on him."

She nodded.

"Does he touch you the way I do? Does he know exactly when to come inside you? Does he know when you're so hot you're ready to . . ."

"I don't have to listen to this," Karen said quietly. "Look, I need a vacation."

"And just what am I supposed to tell the band? And the people at American Voice? Production on the new album begins in two weeks."

"I know. It stinks. I don't feel great about it, but I can't go on doing this without . . . without the joy. You said so yourself. It's not there. I don't know if it's ever coming back. I'm sorry about all the people who count on me. I've talked to the band, and I know it'll be hard, but they'll be okay. As for American Voice, tell them whatever you like, that I'm having a breakdown, an abortion, a nose job. I've got to get out of it for a while, to gain a little perspective maybe, or maybe I'll even have to quit. I don't have any answers. I wish I did." She threw her arms out helplessly.

"Jesus, Karen," Tony said. He looked deflated. She could see that his belt had been cinched one hole tighter, leaving a ridge where the old notch had been. His shirt seemed loose at the collar. Suddenly she had the wild notion that whatever weight Edward had put on came directly from Tony's body.

"That Marylou you brought to the studio was very pretty," Karen said. "I understand she has talent, too, a really nice voice."

"Oh, please," Tony said with wave of his hand like a flyswatter, dismissing the notion of Marylou as if she were a tiny whining insect. "I suppose I know where you're going," he said.

She didn't answer.

He walked out of the room and slammed the door.

There was a row of telephone booths near the newsstand in the hotel lobby. When Karen stopped to buy a copy of the *Boston Globe* on the way to her room, she did not notice Tony closeted behind one of the glass doors.

"Manfred?" Tony said into the phone. "Look, this is a real sticky situation for me, but I decided since I'd feel like a shit either way, I might as well feel like an honest shit. Karen's got a problem. I know you've spoken with her about developing a musical, but I thought you should be aware of the fact that she's been doing dope pretty heavily." He turned his back against the phonebooth door as Nicky Stein walked past. "Yeah, hard stuff. She was into it years ago, but I cleaned her up. Maybe the stress from the tour, I don't know, but I figured I'd better alert you before you get in too deep. I've convinced her to take a leave of absence and try to get herself back on track. But do me a favor and don't say anything to her about this. You can understand that. There's part of me that feels like a rat . . . Yeah, I know, we all hope so. You're welcome. Speak to you soon." Tony opened the door but sat in the booth for a long time watching the lobby with vacant eyes.

14

It took Edward five rings to answer the telephone.

"Hi!" Karen shouted. "It's the reluctant starlet! How're you?"

"Fine," Edward answered. "Tour's over?"

"Yeah, a triumph. I hated every minute. God, this is a lousy connection. How's the research coming?"

"All right."

"Edward, you're not talking."

"I have a little cold."

"I thought it was the phone. You sound awful."

"I'm better now."

"Then you must have been half dead. I'm coming over."

"No, I'm all right, truly. You don't have to."

"I was coming anyway. That's why I called, to warn you, so you could scare all those English broads out of your flat before I get there."

"English frogs?"

"Broads!" she yelled. "Wenches!"

"Ah." He began to cough.

"Christ, you must have T.B. I'll be there in the morning, day after tomorrow. Hang up the phone, Edward, and make yourself a cup of tea. Promise."

"All right." It sounded as if he said "love," but she couldn't be sure.

She telephoned her travel agent, then Persis, and finally Tony. Mercifully, she got his answering machine and left a message that she would call him from London. Then she pulled on her riding boots and hopped into a cab for the West Side. If only it were tomorrow already. If only there weren't that damn ocean between them. If only she could stay atop Midler for the hours remaining until her flight, then perhaps the anxiety would be manageable. If only the horse could truly fly, they would spring up into the atmosphere and streak across the sky from West Eighty-ninth Street to the Embankment in Chelsea. He had sounded so terribly ill.

"Oh, Edward," she said when he came to the door to let her in.

He gave her a shamefaced smile and croaked, "Hello, darling."

She hugged him, but gently, for fear of bruising the bones that once again seemed too close to the surface. Then she led him away from the door and sat him down in the armchair by the fire. She drew the footstool up at his feet and held his hands. "How did this happen?"

"I caught a cold."

"But, Edward, this is worse. Have you seen a doctor?"

"I don't know any doctors here."

"For a bright person, you can behave like a world-class dolt." She got up and put the kettle on the stove. Then she looked in the refrigerator and the cupboards. "There's nothing here," she accused him.

"I don't seem to have much appetite, and besides, I just couldn't summon the energy to go out shopping." From the effort of speaking, he began to cough; the sound was hoarse and painful. After the spasm was over, he said, "I was going to see to this, honestly."

"If you weren't so sick, I'd pluck out your beard," Karen muttered, bringing him a steaming cup of tea. "I want you to load this stuff with honey, two teaspoonfuls at least."

"Teaspoonsful," he said.

"Oh, don't give me any of your erudite lip. And lemon. I'm going out this minute. Where's the closest grocery store?"

"The Kings Road," he said meekly.

She held his face in her hands, kissed him, murmured something about his glasses being dirty, and let herself out.

She cooked him a dinner of broiled fish, baked potato, and carrots with butter and brown sugar. Then she watched him eat, her eyes following every forkful from plate to mouth. "We're starting light, because I don't know if you can digest anything too rich. Eat the carrots, Edward. Cooked carrots prevent cancer."

He raised an eyebrow at her. It took him nearly an hour, but he managed to clean his plate.

"You're going to have three full meals a day and snacks in between. All that lovely weight, all gone . . ."

"I'm sorry."

"All right. Now I'll quit nagging you for a minute and you can tell me about the research."

"I came down with this plague just as I arrived at a critical section in the diaries. I was very lucky in that they allowed me to remove some of the material to work on at home, quite a coup, actually. Oh, that tea is lovely." He took two long swallows. "I'm now so accustomed to Southwick's handwriting so that I can read it almost as quickly as I could anyone else's. He spent two weeks in Charleston and developed a terrific crush on Vanessa Bell. He seemed particularly fixated on what he called her 'noble breasts,' so he bitterly regretted missing the party in London when she danced naked to the waist." His face suddenly went pale. "My goodness, I haven't talked so much in weeks." Karen stood at once, helped him to bed, and propped him up on pillows.

"Tomorrow I'll buy a vaporizer," she told him. "But for tonight, we'll keep the kettle going to steam the place up a little."

"But you have to rest," he said. He was very nearly asleep already.

"I'll be fine."

She dozed off and on in the chair by the fire, waking to refill the kettle and to arrange Edward's blankets. He was restless and coughed in his sleep, but did not fully awaken until morning. When he opened his eyes, she was curled in the chair smiling at him.

"Good morning," she said softly. "How do you feel?"

"Fine," he said with a cough as punctuation. "That's the first night I've slept straight through."

"You talked in your sleep."

"Nothing pejorative, I trust."

"You said, 'Hair so flaxen in the soft convergence of her thighs.' "

"I didn't."

She waved a piece of paper at him. "You said it twice. It's a damn good thing I've got blonde pubic hair."

"I must be recovering." He sat up and swung his legs over the edge of the bed, testing. "Much better, Karen. Yesterday, I tried this and fell right out onto the floor."

She went to sit next to him. He put his arm around her. "It's making me well just to have you here with me." A look of worry passed his face.

"What is it?" she asked.

"I'm reluctant to be grateful for fear you'll feel you can't leave when you wish."

"I'm here because it's where I want to be. Go ahead and be grateful if you like, it won't change my plans one way or the other."

Over the next three weeks, with Karen monitoring his meals and his rest, Edward regained strength, though his weight remained stubbornly low. Karen urged him to see a doctor.

"You remember, of course, the inimitable words of Baron Gottfried Wilhelm von Leibnitz," Edward said. Karen raised her eyebrows at him. " 'I often say a great doctor kills more people than a great general.' "

"You made that up." Karen rarely sensed even the slightest irritation in Edward's response to her. She was not eager to press him into anger, so she backed off. Each morning, she ate breakfast with him, prepared lunch, and left for the day so that he could work in peace. Sometimes she was gone overnight, but Edward never asked where she had been. One evening, she arrived at seven with a glowing face.

"What's going on?" he asked her with a smile.

"I found you a house."

"I beg your pardon?"

"What did you imagine I was doing these past weeks, going off to some romantic tryst, or what?"

"I felt you would tell me if you wished."

She tugged at his beard. "It would never occur to you to ask, would it?"

"No. What house? What is this all about?"

She handed him a Polaroid photograph of a square building with a long drive and several trees to either side. "It has a wonderful porch in the back that goes the whole length of the house. It's in Yorkshire, Edward, near Helmsley."

"Yorkshire!"

She pushed him to the table, sat him down in the chair and made him wait while she fixed two mugs of hot chocolate. Then she sat facing him. Her words came out in a rush. "You're nearly finished with the research, isn't that true? You'll only need the museum every now and then, and maybe I could even dash into London for you if it wasn't anything too complicated. You need to get out into the country, Edward, where it's clean and healthy. You could write totally undisturbed. It's so beautiful, like the farm, only nicer. We can sign a lease for just a year. I've got tons of money. Please say you'll do it."

"It seems terribly radical, Karen. I'm such an urban creature."

"Promise you'll think about it."

"Good Lord." He stared at her and at the photograph face-up between them on the table. "All right," he said finally, and took her hand. "Is this what you've been doing then, trekking all over Yorkshire looking for a house?"

"And Berkshire and Sussex and Hertfordshire. Yorkshire seemed awfully far away, but once I saw the house, it was no contest. You were wonderful to let me keep it a surprise."

"It's horse country, isn't it?"

She grinned at him.

"There's something we're assuming here, darling," he said slowly.

"I know, I know, but I need a break from all that tumult. I can afford to take a few months off."

"What does . . . your manager . . . have to say about that?" Edward still disliked saying Tony's name.

"I haven't told him yet." She got up and began pacing. "I can't go back, not now. It's not just that I don't want to leave you."

"What will it mean to your career?"

"It won't be helpful, that's certain. Not in the short run. But I'm burned out. The thought of facing another tour, another recording session in the studio . . ." Her voice trailed off.

"I'd like to take the house, darling," Edward said, "but there are conditions. First, everything will be in both our names. You're not going into this all by yourself. Also, the very instant you feel you want to perform, you must agree that you'll pick up and leave."

"All right," Karen said.

"There's more. You must promise me that you'll write, too. Preferably the musical, but songs, if you like. I won't have you playing nursemaid to me while your creativity rots away."

"Nothing will rot."

"I am rather excited," Edward admitted.

"I can see that. Your eyebrows are quivering."

"Is that how you can tell?"

"With you, it's the only hint I know of."

"Tony must have been berserk," Edward said. He strolled beside Karen in Battersea Park. On a fine Saturday morning, the walkways were a parade of families.

"I think that would have been easier than the quiet wounded response. He made me feel like I was letting God down along with everybody else."

"How did you leave it with him?"

"That I'd take an indefinite sabbatical. He should feel free to hook up with someone else. He denies it, but I happen to know for a fact that he's been doing very well with Marylou Cadillac. Nicky, John, and Billy Lundgren are working with her, and I bet when Ferris cleans out, he'll wind up with her, too."

"Any regrets about not performing?"

"Some." She stopped and looked up at him. "But not significant enough to make me change my mind. Look how the English put their children in harnesses and walk them just like their dogs."

"Keeps the little creatures in line," Edward said. "Actually, I've been entertaining the notion of buying one for you."

"And you'll be my favorite fire hydrant," Karen said.

They sat down on a bench that faced the Thames. A flat-bottomed barge with a striped awning slid past filled with tourists. The surface of the water flickered with brilliant pinpricks of color like waves of sequins.

"We've been invited to a party," Edward said.

"Oh? How nice," Karen murmured, mesmerized by the shifting hues of the river and the sky. "When's that?"

"Tonight," Edward answered.

Karen stared at him. "Tonight!"

"Why? Is there something else going on tonight?"

"No, but Edward, I need a little notice. What shall I wear? I didn't bring a thing with me."

He glanced down at her slacks and light cotton sweater. "What's the matter with that?"

"Oh, Edward."

"Don't forget, these are literary people, not show folks. Though I must admit that I'd enjoy the spectacle of Malcolm Dinnert's face were you to arrive in that red spangled dress of yours."

"Maybe you'd like me to go all punked out. Turquoise hair with black streaks," she said.

"I'll do it if you'll do it."

"A daunting concept," she said absently.

Edward took her arm. "What is it?"

"I think I'm a little nervous."

"Whatever for?"

"They're your friends. I've never met your friends. Remember what Persis was like?"

"They're a bunch of moth-eaten old dears, not alarming in the slightest."

They had come to a pond where children were feeding bread to a demanding congregation of geese. A mother stuffed a crust into her two-year-old's fist and pushed him toward one of the birds. The animal, easily as tall as the child, stretched out its beak and hissed menacingly. The little boy ran with a terrified shriek back to his mother. "Don't be such a silly. The nice birdie won't hurt you," the woman said. "Watch Mummy." She extracted the mangled crust from the little fingers and headed for the goose.

"I hope it bites her," Karen muttered.

The woman stretched out her hand, and again, the bird gave out with a sound like air escaping from a rubber raft. The hand was quickly withdrawn. "Mummy thinks the goosie isn't hungry just now, darling," she said to the child.

"Perhaps there is some justice," Edward commented.

"I'll bite her myself," Karen said.

"Now listen here," he said, taking her by the shoulders. "These people tonight regard you as a star. They'll be thrilled to meet you, and if anybody's intimidated, it'll be them."

"Shit."

Karen spent the afternoon in Harrod's and finally came home with a simple navy-blue shirtwaist and a pair of espadrilles. She bathed and dressed and squinted at herself in Edward's pockmarked mirror. Her hair had grown and hung straight and thick to her shoulders. With no makeup she looked ordinary enough.

"Very pretty," Edward declared.

"Very dowdy."

"Well, then, you'll fit right in. Come, we're going to take a taxi. My treat."

"I thought we agreed to leave the extravagances to me. This place is halfway to Oxford." She picked up her handbag and a bottle of wine wrapped in last December's Christmas paper.

"We ought to be circumspect with your money. It'll run out soon enough." He closed the great heavy door behind them and locked it.

"Why do I get the feeling there's a message in that remark? Did Tony call again?"

"Yes. While you were out shopping."

"Why didn't you tell me?"

"Slipped my mind. He didn't bother with a lecture this time, just hung up when I told him you were out. There's a cab." He ushered her into the backseat and slid in beside her. "West Allersham, please. It's off the M-forty. I'll direct you when we get there."

"That'll be twenty quid, mate."

"It's all right. She's a star."

Karen giggled. "Listen you'd better prepare me for this thing. Give me the lowdown on the cast of characters."

"Well, let's see, the hostess is Lady Mariah Feddlescombe."

"You're kidding, right?"

"She's a patron of the arts, a very generous one, actually. Lady Mariah has bailed out more than one insolvent writer in her day."

"Where's Lord Fed . . . fid . . . fiddledeedee?"

"In an urn on the mantlepiece in the library. She keeps him beside the humidor because he could never be without his cigars."

"I see. And the guests?"

"I won't know them all. But Vincent Lipton-Smith is the Roger Fry expert, wrote the definitive biography."

"I thought you said Virginia Woolf did that."

"She left out a few things. Fry's affair with her sister, for instance."

Karen laughed.

"Lipton-Smith is married to Millicent Compton Lipton-Smith—"

"Oh, dear."

"Milly is Vincent's researcher and never gets credit. He plays bridge at his club all day while she slogs through documents at the British Museum. He's very bright, however, and writes elegant prose from her notes."

The city was beginning to disintegrate into neighborhoods with low, semidetached stone houses and gas stations on the corners.

"Malcolm Dinnert is the editor of *Chapman's Review,* which is the most prestigious literary magazine in England, perhaps in the world. He also writes detective stories of an extremely salacious nature under the pen-name of Dick Slade."

"His paperbacks are all over the airports."

"Yes. Malcolm's on his third wife, I believe. Perhaps fourth. I can't recall her name. The last one was Emily."

"Don't tell me. Now I'm sure to call this one Emily."

"It doesn't matter, everyone else does. We only just get accustomed to the next wife and he divorces her. There'll be art people.

Vincent is a collector. I'm told Andrew MacGregor will be there. I've not met him, but he's rather a legend in British publishing."

"How about if he publishes Julius for you in the U.K.?"

"The thought had entered my mind," Edward admitted.

"Well, you corner him right away and tell him what you're up to."

"No, I don't believe I'll do that."

"Why not?"

"I'm sure he's aware of the project. MacGregor doesn't miss much."

"But you have to go after him," Karen pressed.

"That's not the way things are done here," Edward said.

"That's the way things are done everywhere," Karen said.

"Are you pussywhipping me?" Edward asked.

"Yes, definitely." Karen stared out the window contentedly. They had left the city behind now, and the pale evening light of summer gave everything a dreamy quality, as if a soft veil had been draped across the meadows and walnut groves. She began to sing softly. Edward leaned his head back against the seat and listened.

"Did Cole Porter write that?" he asked when the last notes of "In the Still of the Night" had faded to a whisper.

"Yeah. I thought I'd better get into the proper time frame."

Edward directed the driver through a little town and beyond into low wooded hills. Finally, they turned up a circular drive. The wheels crunched on the gravel as they approached the entrance of an eighteenth-century manor house.

"Holy cow, Edward," Karen said.

"Tidy little cottage, isn't it?"

The driver whistled. "Wouldn't like to pay the heating bills in January."

"Nobody bothers," Edward explained. "It's arctic in there from November to May."

When they got out, the air smelled thick and sweet with something Karen could not identify, perhaps a distant relative of honeysuckle.

"Edward, remember," she whispered. "You get that MacGregor guy."

"Shh," Edward said. An elderly butler opened the door. Though the evening was warm, he wore a wool vest under his black velvet jacket. Before he could usher them inside, a tall woman came swooping down the hall in a floor-length taffeta gown, crying "Ed-*ward!* Ed-*ward!*" She had shocking pink-red hair and a long narrow face. When she smiled, she revealed a mouthful of crooked yellow teeth. But the smile was generous, and she gave Edward a warm hug.

He handed her the wine bottle. "Hello, Mariah. Merry Christmas in July. Lady Mariah Feddlescombe, this is Karen Wells."

Karen was struck with momentary panic, having neglected to ask Edward how one greets a titled person. Finally, she decided to be American and thrust out her hand. Lady Mariah took it and covered it with her own jeweled fingers.

"Edward, she's lovely. How did you manage to snag her, you old reprobate?" Rainbows bounced off her head from the metallic glint of hairspray. She gave Edward a closer inspection. "You're too thin. Come in and see everybody. We're working up the courage for charades, but nobody's drunk enough yet." She swept them along a marble hall and into a living room with ceilings Karen estimated at twenty-five feet. The curtains hung in dingy folds beside the windows and the sofas and chairs had worn through at the arms to reveal the stuffing. The crystal chandelier was missing several bulbs. Edward followed Karen's eyes, and as Lady Mariah glided away to fetch them drinks, he explained.

"Mariah doles most of her money out to support talented writers and painters. She can't bear to waste any of it on the decor."

Lady Mariah reappeared with two glasses of wine and a middle-aged couple in tow. Edward leaned over to kiss the woman, then shook the man's hand. Lady Mariah went off with a whoosh. The air seemed to hum in the vacuum she left behind.

"Karen, I'd like you to meet Milly and Vincent Lipton-Smith," Edward said.

Karen, remembering Edward's sketch in the taxi, looked at them with interest. Milly appeared to be in her fifties. She had a pleasant face except for two deep lines, like parentheses around her mouth. She had thin gray hair that hung in strings. But her eyes were friendly and direct. Her husband was round and solid, his round head sitting on his round body like one perfectly constructed circle atop another. Looking at him, Karen recalled a toy she had had as a child, a clown shaped just like Vincent. If you pushed it with your finger, it bobbed back upright again.

"I've enjoyed your album so much," Milly said. "I'm particularly intrigued with the guitar riffs in 'Told You So.' There's a real Eddie Van Halen quality to them, don't you think?"

Karen was speechless.

"Milly's got quite a collection," Vincent informed them. "Thank God they invented CDs or we'd have to find another flat."

"I'm afraid I'm a bit of an addict," Milly confessed. "Come sit over here with me," she urged Karen, settling on a nearby sofa. "You won't mind if I . . . what is it you Americans say? . . . pick your brains for a little?" Karen followed obediently and sat down. "Now, were you aware that the reprise in Jennifer Moore's new single sounds suspiciously like 'Look Over Your Shoulder'?"

Karen chatted with Milly while snatches of other conversations swirled around them:

". . . new exhibit is absolutely appalling. Her sculpture looks as if it has acne."

"I thought those were barnacles."

"Whatever does John think he's putting over? Did you *see* that play? It's the cult of noncommunication, where the actors stand and gape at one another without saying anything."

"No dialogue whatever."

"Simply appalling."

A half hour passed during which Karen developed a profound respect for Milly Lipton-Smith's encyclopedic knowledge of rock music. Suddenly, she felt a body sitting down beside her, squeezing between Karen's backside and the arm of the sofa. Milly produced a wry smile for the intruder.

"Hello, Malcolm."

Karen turned to see a small monkey-faced man grinning at her. He handed her a full glass of wine.

"Here, Karen Wells, have some rot gut. I can't imagine where Mariah got this stuff, it's worse than usual."

"She has an arrangement with Selfridge's," Milly said. "They sell her the bottles nobody else will buy."

"Well, permit me to propose a toast in Afghanistan rosé or whatever it is. To Karen Wells with the golden vocal cords." He glanced defensively at Milly who had not lost her sardonic smile. "I *have* heard her, you know."

"Oh? Where?" Karen asked curiously.

"In a lift in New York City. You Americans do insist on entertaining one even if one isn't in the mood. However, your selection was bracing. Quite perky, really."

"Thanks," Karen said, while Milly gave her a wink. What had Edward said about the man? Ah, yes, half prestigious editor, half sleaze hack. Karen had, in fact, picked up one of his detective stories once. She had made it partway through, but the pseudonymous Dick Slade seemed to have an obsession with sadomasochism, especially for people being lashed on their bare bottoms with a wide range of devices. It got boring after a while.

"Tell me," Dinnert said. His voice was percussive, each syllable exploding like a kernel of popcorn. Karen watched his lips, fascinated. "Do you write any of your own lyrics?"

"All of them," Karen replied.

"Do they arrive in a flash of inspiration or must you slog away at it for weeks on end?"

"A little of both. You're a writer, how do you get your ideas?"

"Oh, pure inspiration," he said. She could not detect even a speck of irony. "I wait a few months between opuses," he went on, "and then suddenly, I'm struck by the bolt. I write in a frenzy for several weeks. It simply pours out of me as if I'm being purged of a demon. I believe Dostoyevski used to write in that manner."

Karen glanced at Milly for her response to this, but she had left. Immediately, a horse-faced woman sat in her place and began to talk across Karen, grilling Dinnert about a review in last month's *Chapman's Review* magazine. Dinnert kept glancing at Karen wistfully, but she slid out from between them and went to hunt for Edward. She could see his head poking up above the others away across the room. The gentleman with whom he spoke kept shaking his head affably while Edward talked. Karen smiled, knowing the topic must be Bloomsbury. Edward could never look so absorbed about anything else. Perhaps the man was Andrew MacGregor and Edward had sought him out as instructed.

Karen worked her way to the edge of the room. As she passed an open window, suddenly a hand at the end of a long arm was stuck out directly in her path. It came from the garden outside. A deep voice with a trace of a Scottish burr boomed at her through the window pane.

"Karen Wells, isn't it." It was not a query.

Karen peered through the glass at the tall shape. The hand was still extended, so she shook it. "You are . . . ?" she asked, raising her voice due to the thick antique glass that separated them.

"Andrew MacGregor."

"The publisher," Karen said.

"A publisher," he corrected her, then took a long look at her face. He appeared wavy due to imperfections in the window, so she supposed she must seem somewhat distorted as well. "When you're eighty-five and are ready to write your memoirs, I'd like you to come to me," MacGregor said finally. "Do you approve of memoirs?"

"Yes. As a matter of fact, I'm reading Virginia Woolf's diaries at the moment."

"Not at the moment. At the moment, you are talking with me. Have you read *Moments of Being?*"

"No, what's that?" Karen asked.

"Virginia at her best. I'll send you a copy. Care of Mr. Vaughn, isn't it." Again, this was not a question.

"Will you come meet him, I mean Edward? You'll be interested in the work he's been doing."

"Southwick. I'm delighted." He raised the window and climbed through.

Karen headed for the far end of the room with MacGregor loping along beside her.

"Edward, this is Andrew MacGregor. Mr. MacGregor, Edward Vaughn."

"Andrew," boomed MacGregor. He had a beautiful complexion, rosy cheeks like a boy's and no whiskers. "You're turning your woman into a Bloomsbury fanatic, Vaughn. Next thing you know, we'll have pop songs about Leonard Woolf. Julius Southwick a fellow interesting enough to publish a book about?"

Karen crept away, not wishing to distract the men from establishing a camaraderie. On her way to hunt down the bathroom, she ran into Guy Burlingame.

"Good Lord, Guy!" she exclaimed. "What on earth are you doing here?"

"Hanging out with the literati, darling. Give me credit for some breadth. My, my, no makeup and such a simple little frock."

Karen pirouetted. "The real me."

"Frankly, you look quite ravishing. Where's the boyfriend?" She gestured in Edward's direction. "Ah, I see he's finally hooked up with Andrew."

"What do you mean?" Karen asked.

"Not a thing. You'll introduce me to Edward later on?"

"MacGregor already knew about Edward's work. You put the bug in his ear, didn't you?"

"I hardly remember," he said. "Come sit down and talk to me." He drew her to a nearby loveseat.

"Thank you, Guy," Karen said, kissing him on the cheek. "Edward is not the sort of person who pushes himself forward. Things have to sort of fall in his lap."

"Just like our old friend Tony Kahanian," Guy said.

"Oh, right," Karen said. "God, it's so good to see you. Got any gossip for me?"

"Well, let's see," Guy said, fussing with the blue silk handkerchief in his vest pocket. "There's a wonderful fracas going on. Fruit and Nuts and Soup to Nuts are stealing each other's lead singers. What do you suppose they'll do with their names? Fruit Soup and the Nuts?"

Karen laughed. "Have you heard anything about my band?"

"Nicky's suffering with Marylou, says she's got the vocal range of a castrated mosquito, and they put Ferris in a detox hospital."

"Oh, Lord, poor thing. Smithers?"

"No, the place David Crosby was in. I don't remember the name."

"I'll find out and write to him."

"Aren't you going to ask about Tony?"

"Uh, sure."

"As far as I know, he's just sticking with Marylou for the moment. Probably waiting for you to recover from your temporary insanity."

"It's not temporary."

"But you don't deny the insanity."

"Love is always a little insane, I suppose."

He studied her carefully for a long moment, then shook his head. "I think we may have lost you, Wells."

"What makes you say that?"

"Your hands. They used to be so fidgety, flying around all over the place, doodling and drumming. Look at them now."

Karen stared down at her lap where her hands lay folded neatly.

"Portrait of serenity," Guy said. "Unless he's got you on Quaaludes. Listen to me. Don't you worry about dealing with Tony. You ever run out of money and need a quick gig, call me up. I can arrange something, London, New York, wherever."

"You take good care of me," Karen said. She captured his hand in both of hers and held it to her breast. Guy's pale face reddened and he got up. "Now I'm going to mix, darling," he said. "Mariah likes me to romance the 'dowdies,' as she calls them. She thinks they get a thrill from consorting with a notorious representative of yellow journalism."

"You're not the least bit yellow," Karen said. She watched him thread his way into the crowd. Later on, when she hunted for him to meet Edward, she discovered he had left.

Karen found the bathroom, an old-fashioned version with a pull-chain toilet. When she emerged into the hallway outside, sinewy fingers pulled her around the corner into the library. It was Malcolm Dinnert. He pressed her to the wall and leaned close with an arm to either side of her body.

"God Almighty, but you're lovely," he said.

Karen did not reply. He was very drunk.

"Just plain folks, as they say in the U.S. of A. Isn't that what they say in the U.S. of A.? You're not at all showbiz, darling, and by God, you have a lovely shape."

Karen tried to disengage herself, but he pushed his face into hers and kissed her with whiskey-filmed lips. Suddenly her eye caught sight of a large Chinese urn on the mantlepiece at the far side of the room. Lord Feddlescombe, she thought, and began to giggle. Dinnert, looking for the source of her laughter, turned away for a moment and Karen struggled free. As she left the room, she could hear him muttering, "Oh, do be generous, dear heart. I know what goes on in the record business."

Fleeing in the general direction of Edward, she overheard a snippet of conversation beside the liquor table.

"I can't comprehend what that formidable intellect is doing with that little songbird," said a woman wearing an ostrich feather pinned behind one ear. "She can't have a brain in her head."

"She doesn't need a brain, darling," replied an effeminate man with an ascot.

Karen passed as close to them as possible and gave them a dazzling smile. Suddenly a gong sounded. Edward caught up with Karen as everyone began filing out of the room.

"What's that, a fire drill?" she asked.

"No, food. The gong is a hint of what Mariah's dinner sounds like as it hits your stomach."

"Dear me. What did you think of Andrew MacGregor?"

"I like him. He's a bit of an eccentric."

"I'll say. Guy Burlingame talked to him about you."

"Yes, I wanted to thank him." Edward looked around. "What does he look like?"

"I think he left. He gets embarrassed when he does favors for people. Is MacGregor going to publish Julius?"

"Maybe. He wants to look at the manuscript as I'm writing it." He grinned down at her. "He says he doesn't want me to spoil your 'childlike spontaneity' with too much literature. 'If she must read,' he said, 'she must do it in the bath.' "

"No wonder you hang out with this crowd," Karen said. "They must seem just like home."

"Are you having a good time?"

"Smashing, with a few minor exceptions."

"Oh?"

She shook her head. "Come." The table in the dining room was set up as a buffet, and now, as the guests formed into an orderly queue, Karen saw that there were fewer people than she had originally thought. She speared a number of unidentifiable objects and followed Edward back into the living room. It was pleasant to sit beside him with the rough wool of his jacket brushing her arm. She could survey the room and pick out a few faces to regard with the beginnings of affection.

After what was indeed a barely digestible meal, Lady Mariah announced that there would be charades, a proclamation that was greeted with a mixture of moans and applause. Edward looked at Karen with the blank expression that she knew signaled covert amusement.

"Authors only, no titles tonight. Here, Malcolm, you're first."

Dinnert stood, none too steadily. His wife, whose name nobody could remember, held out her hand to take his wineglass. She was a rather pretty woman, a good ten years younger than Dinnert. She had prominent teeth, which gave her smile a goofy aspect Karen liked. Dinnert began springing around the living room with arms dangling. He scratched his armpits and his thick head of hair.

"Gibbon! *Decline and Fall of the Roman Empire!*" Milly Lipton-Smith called out.

Dinnert looked crestfallen as everyone booed.

"A modicum of obscurity, if you please, ladies and gentlemen," Lady Mariah protested as Dinnert skulked back to his wineglass.

Karen had never heard of most of the authors thereafter enacted, though she enjoyed Edward's rendition of Anonymous which included using a dinner napkin to create a wimple for "nun" and standing terrified on a chair for "mouse." He came to drape an arm around her and watch the next offering being performed by the woman with the ostrich feather in her hair. She kept grasping her earlobes and looking worried, touching her neck and fingers, then hunting for something behind a vase or on the floor.

"Lost earrings . . . lost!" Milly shouted, but the woman shook her head.

"Jewels," Vincent yelled.

She nodded and gestured at him to expand.

Karen tugged on Edward's arm. "Jewel-less," she whispered. "Julius. It's Julius."

"Say it," Edward urged.

"Julius Southwick!" Karen called. The woman raised her arms in assent. Amid tumultuous applause, Karen gave her a thumbs-up sign. "Should've made it the middle finger," Karen murmured.

"What's that, darling?" Edward asked.

"Nothing," she said cheerily. "What do you think? Should we leave on a note of triumph?"

"Absolutely. Let me just go line us up a cab."

Edward nearly fell asleep in the back of the taxi. He did manage to ask her what the minor exceptions had been to her good time.

"I was kissed by the vile Malcolm Dinnert. He had a hard-on the size of a piano leg."

Edward laughed.

"Please at least have the grace to be jealous."

"I'm sorry," Edward said. "It must have been dreadful."

"Still, I'm really glad we came. I liked Milly and Andrew MacGregor and Lady Mariah. I survived, didn't I? It makes me think I might actually live through an evening with your family."

"You did more than survive. You charmed everyone, and they're not easily won over."

"Mm," she said, thinking of the ostrich feather. But she sank back against him and they dozed most of the way back to the city.

In bed, Karen let her hand fall between his legs. It had been over a week since they had made love, and besides, Karen was eager to erase the memory of Malcolm Dinnert's mouth. Edward kissed her, but the gesture was perfunctory. His hands on her naked skin felt somehow dutiful rather than eager. She backed off and looked at him in the dim light. "Not in the mood?"

"I'm sorry. Too much to drink, I expect."

But it had happened three times since she came to London. And once in New York, come to think of it. "Yes, that must be it," Karen said in a hollow voice.

"Karen."

She didn't answer, just lay next to him like a stone.

"You must remember I'm older than you are, by a great deal."

"Age doesn't mean a thing. I've had men in their seventies make passes at me. Look at Dinnert, he's no spring chicken."

"It isn't that I'm not attracted to you, honestly. It's just that something seems to be happening to my urges. They're not so . . . urgent," he finished up lamely. "In fact, it's rather odd because I feel that I have an erection and then when push comes to shove, it's merely a phantom."

She thought this over in silence. "I think you ought to see someone. That doesn't sound kosher to me."

"It doesn't sound kosher because you're young. It's impossible for you to consider the decrepitude of the human body."

"Don't patronize me. Besides, it's happened too quickly. A mere month ago, you were jumping on my bones like any stud."

"Poor Malcolm Dinnert. He would divorce his current wife for the chance to be lying here next to you."

"You're evading me. Why have you got such a thing against doctors?"

"Look, if I take my penis to the medical profession, they'll stick things up it and perform all manner of unspeakable acts. Give a man some credit for natural reticence."

"All right, then, don't go. But what do you propose we do? I'll get hornier and hornier and you'll just go on having phantom erections . . ."

They lay in silence for a while. Then Edward reached out to stroke her hair. "Don't be hurt. I want so desperately to please you. I promise I'll see someone before we leave for Yorkshire."

"Thank you."

He kissed her in the dark. "Are you all right?" he asked.

"Of course I'm all right. I'm a tough broad." She returned his kiss and shoved him back onto his pillow. "Now good night. You're exhausted."

He sighed deeply. "What a wonder you are," he murmured. Soon he was asleep, but Karen lay wide awake for a long time, feeling his breath on her hair like a soft whisper.

15

The first letter Karen received at the Yorkshire house was an apologetic note from Manfred Warm. "Dear Karen," it read. "Sorry to have been so slow about getting this off to you. It turns out that the musical idea has been shelved for the indefinite future. Seems the current climate on Broadway is so dismal that the prospects of making such a project fly are dicey at best. I know you've got plenty of other things going for you, so hope you aren't too disappointed. Look me up when you're Stateside. Much love, Manfred."

"You're going to write it anyway," Edward said. "Aren't you?"

"Well, shit," Karen said. "I might cry soon."

Edward put his arms out, and she did indeed weep for a few moments, then sniffed, dried her eyes, and went back to opening cartons in the kitchen.

She was amazed at the deep attachment she felt for the house. It seemed like a person to her, a welcoming, rambling, gentle soul with odd, whimsical notions that manifested themselves in a hexagonal window in the study, an unreachable window seat halfway up the living room wall, and a sound underfoot on the third tread of the main staircase that said "ribbit" like a friendly frog. This house cared little for appearances and yet managed to retain its dignity and fundamental beauty. Karen spent many mornings off in the neighboring villages on a quest for antique picture frames, linens, and crockery, which she felt were in keeping with the special character of the place. But on exceptionally fine days, she and Edward had worked out a routine that particularly pleased them both.

Edward sat at his table on the back porch, alternately typing his manuscript and watching Karen dig in the garden. The mid-September sun poured down on the scarlet geraniums, the roses, the salvias, the tall stalks of purple delphiniums. With Karen's patient coaching, Edward was now able to identify all of the species in their garden.

Karen was hunched over the flowerbed, weeding expertly. As usual, she had shed the floppy straw hat Edward had bought to protect her as she worked. Her head bobbed up and down among the blossoms, her hair and even the tips of her eyelashes sunbleached pale yellow. Edward knew she was singing to herself because every now and then the breeze blew the sound of her voice toward the porch. It blended pleasantly with the hum of insects and the birdsongs. She was like a mockingbird, he thought, with a vast, lilting repertoire.

He sighed happily and stared down at the typewriter. Oh, Julius, he thought. She has filled my garden and my very soul with flowers.

Julius Southwick's voice, cultivated and lightly sardonic, seemed to lift off the coiled page. *Ah yes,* it said. *But you are ignoring an important issue, are you not, my dear biographer? You made her a promise which you have failed to fulfill. Not gallant. In fact, if you don't mind my saying so, rather shabby.*

But she's not complaining, Edward protested.

The manuscript paper rattled in the wind. With irritation, Edward imagined. *She's not the complaining sort,* Julius went on. *How do you suppose she feels, lying next to you every night with all that youthful sap flowing in her veins and you with your chaste kisses and that dried husk you call a penis? You were to see a doctor before you came to Yorkshire.*

I know, I know, Edward thought. But moving turned out to be so complicated, and there were those multitudinous last-minute details at the museum . . .

Tut-tut-tut-tut-tut, Julius interrupted impatiently. *Sheer rationalization. You know full well it can't be avoided forever; you'll have to consult a physician. In the meantime, speak with Karen about moving into another bedroom.*

How could I possibly? Edward answered. She'd be crestfallen.

Karen's a lusty wench, Edward. For a woman like that, a lonely bed is preferable to a frustrating one. No doubt she's trying to find a way to wriggle out of yours without hurting your feelings. Broach the subject. You're a diplomatic fellow. Then get yourself down to Harley Street for a full examination of that useless organ. I realize you regard me as something of a dilettante, but when it comes to women, I know whereof I speak.

Oh, dammit, I suppose you're right, Edward thought, and vowed to bring the subject up at lunch.

Karen hummed quietly to herself as the sun burned the backs of her shoulders. A song called "Bliss" kept making fragmented noises in the corners of her brain, but the lyrics seemed saccharine. Perhaps she could try some offbeat tonal leaps to set off the sugary words. Such a song would work nicely at the end of the first act in the musical, before the romance began to go awry. The young girl would sing it, the character Karen thought of as BethAnn. Perhaps her lover, Tommy, would overhear, but BethAnn, unaware, would not see him standing off at stage right with his arm around the treacherous Madeline. Karen shook her head. So many of her thoughts these days centered around the musical, which seemed more than ever an elusive dream. She sometimes felt as if she were with child in a pregnancy that would last for years or perhaps forever. In the past, writing a song provided almost instant gratification. She wrote it, she sang it, the process felt like a complete circle. But this musical, this thrashing fetus, had gone way beyond full term.

Aching, she sat back on her heels and gazed over the flowerbed at Edward, who sat typing sporadically on his portable Olivetti. His legs were stretched out straight and crossed at the ankles, his feet bare as usual. For a man who had spent half a century devoted to shoes and socks, he had made a remarkable turnabout. His arms, though thin in the short-sleeved shirt, had browned in the late Yorkshire summer. Karen could see the muscles and tendons rippling as he tapped at the typewriter keys.

She was famished after a long morning's stint in the garden, but felt reluctant to interrupt Edward's concentration. She would wait.

One of their greatest pleasures was lunch together by the garden. So as the pages were piling up beside Edward's elbow, the weeds mounted at Karen's.

When at last she looked up again, it was nearly two o'clock and he was watching her. She stood, joints creaking painfully, waved her trowel at him, and limped over. Both feet were asleep.

"It's past two," Edward said.

"I know. I could eat a dozen nasturtiums."

"I didn't want to disturb you, you seemed so involved," Edward said.

"I was waiting for *you*."

Edward laughed. "I thought I would surely faint soon."

"Quick. Let's set up out here."

They went into the kitchen together and sliced sandwiches from the bread Karen had baked yesterday. Blackberries were heaped into bowls and covered with thick cream. Edward poured glasses of cider, and they trooped out into the yard where they sat munching and staring up at the hills that rose purple with heather in the distance.

"Productive morning, Li'l Abner?" Karen asked, poking at his bare toes with her own under the table.

Edward nodded. "It seems to be almost writing itself. It's almost fraudulent, as if I don't deserve the credit."

"Tonight do I get to hear what you've done?"

"We'll see. I thought perhaps some more Tennyson."

"I'd rather listen to your disciplined prose. I'm afraid my latest song is beginning to sound like 'The Lady of Shalott.' " She brushed away a honeybee that hovered over her blackberries.

"Is it a BethAnn song?"

"Yes."

"Why don't you try it out on Milly and Vincent this weekend?"

"It's not ready for public consumption. They'll have to endure the same stuff they listened to last time they were up. Hey, if they're coming tomorrow, today must already be the thirtieth."

"Heavens, I don't know. I keep losing track. Why?"

"We have to say 'rabbit-rabbit' at midnight."

"I beg your pardon," Edward said.

"When the month changes. Or when you're driving and the mileage goes into the next thousand. You say 'rabbit-rabbit' when you see the zeroes appear on the odometer."

"You're talking as if I should have some idea what this is about."

"It's for good luck," Karen explained. "Didn't you ever say 'rabbit-rabbit'? Oh, Edward, you did have a deprived childhood."

"What happens if you forget?"

"Nothing," she said.

They munched their sandwiches in silence for a while. Then Edward peered at her over the top of his glasses. "Er, Karen . . ." he began. "Julius was rather talkative this morning."

"Oh, and what's he been expounding upon today?"

"Actually, he brought up something we should discuss." Edward seemed so serious that Karen stared at him in alarm. She set down her glass. "No, no, don't be frightened," he reassured her, taking her hand. "It's about the sexual thing. I'm concerned about you, about your being . . . unfulfilled."

"I've never been so fulfilled in my life. You sound like Helen Gurley Brown."

"But I've not been a lover to you lately."

Karen looked down at her plate. It was the one she customarily chose at lunchtime, with lambs and shepherdesses marching around the rim.

"I worry that sleeping side by side causes you pain," Edward continued. She looked up at him and he could see that the words struck home. "This is true, isn't it?"

"Not always. Sometimes it's enough, and really very comforting just to be cozy."

"We have two extra bedrooms. Why don't you use one of them until I get straightened out?" The sentence hung in the air. Then they both laughed.

"A felicitous turn of phrase," Karen observed.

"I should have the first couple of chapters ready to show Andrew MacGregor in a few weeks. I'll make an appointment with someone in London and we'll see what's what. In the meantime, I won't feel abandoned if you'd prefer to have a bed of your own."

"You're sure?"

"Absolutely."

"I hope you'll miss me a little."

"I shall, I promise."

"If you get too lonely, you'll come crawl in with me?"

"Yes. And the same applies to you, all right?"

"Agreed."

Karen got up and went to sit on his lap. They kissed one another and then sat in a comfortable embrace. "Mmm," Edward said. "I could fall asleep. What with you and this sunshine . . ."

"Oh, no," she interrupted him. "I'm taking you for a walk after lunch. I found a wonderful new footpath in the hills, right along the edge. You can see all across the Vale of York. And there were two gliders up there, hanging in the sky like mobiles. The wind is extraordinary."

Edward smiled at her use of the word. Then suddenly he sat up straight. "What was that?" he asked her.

"I didn't hear anything. What?"

But then she, too, heard knocking at the front door.

"Out back!" she called, and climbed off Edward's lap to investigate. She had only taken a few steps off the porch and onto the lawn when a large figure in a suit materialized from behind the shrubbery that nestled against the house.

"Tony!" Karen exclaimed.

Edward stood up as well. Tony stopped in his tracks and stared at them. He was gaunt and unshaven.

"Is something wrong? What's happened? My parents?" Karen stammered.

"You ought to have a fucking telephone that functions," Tony said. "What's the matter with this country anyway? Everybody's always on goddamn strike, nothing works . . . Christ, you're a mess. How long since you washed your face?"

"She's been working in the garden," Edward said, and gestured proudly at the wild array of blossoms.

Tony gave Edward a careful inspection, letting his eyes linger on the bare feet. Then he turned to Karen in disgust. "I have to talk to you."

"Talk," she said, but she looked pale under the streaks of grime on her cheeks.

"Privately."

"No," Karen said. Edward took a step closer to her. "Would you like something to drink?"

Tony ignored the offer. "You think this is some kind of game? Playing with people's futures?"

"No. I never felt that," Karen said.

"You put the entire world on hold. You think it's going to be waiting for you when you decide to honor us with your presence?"

"I didn't put you on hold, Tony. I told you not to count on me, to find something else, somebody else. The others, too. You're all working with Marylou, except Ferris . . ."

"Oh, yeah, look what you did for him."

"Come on, Tony, you can't blame that on me. He was strung out long before I . . . retired."

"Is that what you've done, then, retired? Christ, you're such a coward."

"I'm only being honest," she protested.

"You have no right . . ." he began, shouting now.

"It's my voice, my music," she interrupted him.

Edward took another step, this time toward the patch of ground that stood between Karen and Tony. "Don't bully her," Edward said in a voice so full of menace that both Tony and Karen stared at him with astonishment.

Then Tony, a little wary now, turned his attention back to Karen. "You behave like a selfish, spoiled little bitch."

"All right, that's quite enough," Edward said, looming over Tony. "This is our home. Control yourself or I'll be forced to deck you."

Tony backed away. His voice shook with misery and defeat. "Are you coming back?" he asked Karen.

She shook her head. "I can't."

"Ever?"

"I don't know," she murmured.

Tony nodded his head toward Edward. "Will you be staying here . . . with him?"

"Yes," Karen said. "As long as he'll have me."

Suddenly the strong muscular features of Tony's face seemed to sag. His shoulders shuddered, water poured from his eyes, and his breath came out in short percussive sobs. He held his arms out to Karen soundlessly and mouthed the word *please*.

"Oh, Tony," Karen said. But she stood still.

Finally, Tony spun around and stumbled off toward the front of the house. They could hear the car reverse up the drive and roar off down the narrow country lane. Edward put his arms around Karen and held her for a long time.

"Where did that come from, Edward?" Karen finally asked, her voice muffled against his chest. " 'Control yourself or I'll be forced to deck you.' "

"It was in one of Malcolm Dinnert's detective stories. I quite liked the phrase, but I must admit I never imagined using it myself."

"Your heart's beating so fast."

"Yes."

"You were wonderful," Karen said. "Thank you."

After supper, he read to her by the fire. She sat on the floor and stared distractedly into the flames.

"A hand that can be clasped no more— / Behold me, for I cannot sleep," Edward read. *"And like a guilty thing I creep / At earliest morning to the door."* He stopped but she did not stir. "Karen, this is not exactly cheering you up."

She turned to look at him and made an attempt at a smile. He winced. "Don't do that, darling. Just go ahead and be miserable."

Karen laid her head against his knee. "It was his face," she said.

"I know."

"It's not that there's any conflict whatsoever."

"I sometimes wonder about that."

"Edward, I get more pleasure out of singing for our friends right here in the living room than I would at Madison Square Garden. Of course, it's not quite as lucrative."

"I wasn't thinking entirely of the singing."

"You mean me and Tony?"

"Yes."

She turned her face up to him. The flames from the hearth swam in her eyes like liquid evidence of a soul on fire. "That part of my life is over, Edward. He wasn't good for me."

* * *

Karen lay in the bed she had made up for herself in the spare room. Finally, she drifted off, but her sleep was interrupted by dreams about Tony, hot, wild dreams filled with deep kisses and greedy, tangled limbs. She woke many times, always mindful of Edward lying in the room nearby and of her body's need of him. The irony of it all, she thought, was that she should feel such incessant and potent desire for a man who could not respond.

At dawn when she woke to take a walk on the moor, she found a note taped to her door. It said, "Midnight, September 30. Rabbit-rabbit. Love, Edward."

16

Persis agreed to spend the Christmas holiday with them in Yorkshire.

"Mother's got the others anyway," Persis said over the telephone that was finally operating properly.

Karen drove into York to meet Persis's train, but Persis did not show up. Karen immediately phoned Edward.

"Don't worry," Edward said. "She'll arrive eventually. She's probably on her way to Land's End."

But Persis emerged from the very next London train. "Oh, my God," she said after giving Karen a hug. "I'm sorry, but my luggage got switched at the airport and there was all hell to pay. The suitcases were absolutely identical, and if it weren't for customs, I'd have lost my page proofs to the crook who was trying to smuggle in one of those miniature TVs. Let me tell you, I was surprised when they unzipped what I thought was my bag and there were all these jockey shorts. They were actually going to arrest me until I pointed out that really I'm not the jockey shorts type and perhaps they'd better find the sap who walked off with my bag. And the worst of it was, I didn't have one second to call you or I'd have missed this train as well."

"Welcome to the Motherland," Karen said.

After a two-hour tour of the walled city, they drove north toward Helmsley. "I hope it doesn't snow," Karen said. "We have so many lovely walks for you."

"You look wonderful," Persis commented.

Karen beamed at her. "I am. Wait until you see your brother."

Persis gave Edward a shy kiss and regarded him critically. "You are indeed flourishing. Even your beard is shiny instead of all dried up like a Brillo pad. I like your house."

"Karen did it all. The place was nothing but mouse droppings and peeling wallpaper."

Persis followed them down the hallway and into the living room. There was a fire in the fireplace and a tall Christmas tree in one corner. Karen had decorated it with shiny bulbs shaped like pieces of fruit: pears, peaches, apples, and bunches of cherries. "Edward did the top half," Karen admitted as they stood admiring it. The room had the fresh smell of pine.

"I know these are electric bulbs," Persis said, "but it really feels like candlelight in here, almost like another century."

"Come, let's feed you," Karen said. "You must be jet-lagged."

They sat in the kitchen with its bright yellow wooden cabinets and ate the roast beef hash Edward quickly heated on the top of the stove. There were plump biscuits with butter and hot homemade applesauce.

"How's Mother?" Edward asked his sister.

"She's got a boyfriend," Persis answered with a grin. "She met him in Lamston's. He was buying balloons, so she asked him if they were for his grandchildren, and he said, No, they were for himself, that when he gets to feeling gloomy, he blows them up and bats them around his apartment."

"Sounds just the match for Mother," Edward said.

"She's loonier than ever, but not a twitch senile."

"Will they live together?" Karen asked.

"Mother refuses. She says she likes her independence. But there have been some all-nighters. I made Wilhelm give me his telephone number because at her age I want to know she's in the sack with him and not having a stroke at home."

"Wilhelm," Edward said.

Persis laughed. "She calls him The Kaiser."

"Never too late," Edward said, with a smile for Karen.

" 'From your mouth to God's ears,' as they say," Persis mumbled through a mouthful of biscuit. "Actually, they insisted on coming to the airport to see me off, can you imagine? It was an excursion, and besides, Wilhelm wanted to do something special to celebrate his new hearing aid. Mother's getting pretty deaf too, by the way."

"They must make quite a pair," Edward commented.

"I said to him," Persis went on, " 'Wilhelm, Mother tells me you've got a new hearing aid. Congratulations.' " She gave Karen a wink. "And you know what he said to me? He said, 'What!?' " Over their laughter, she muttered, "Anyhow, I hope they're not still sitting in a taxi on the Grand Central Parkway."

There was a cold rain, and in the morning they woke to a dazzling world of ice. The trees were coated down to the tiniest twig. The willow outside the kitchen drooped under the weight of frozen droplets like a bride stooped by the opulence of her veil. Karen threw on her jacket and stepped outside. When the wind blew, there was a brittle tinkling sound, like an aeolian harp. Gently, she touched a bough of the ilex tree, fearful that it might snap. In the distance, the moors shimmered with snow. With each breath, she felt she could rise off the frosted ground, so exhilarated was she by the cold and the glistening purity of her world. She turned to look into the kitchen window where Persis and Edward sat over their coffee cups. They were deep in conversation, heads bent close across the table. Karen thought that if Edward shaved off his beard, their profiles would be like reverse sides of a paper doll cutting.

On the way down to the village, Karen concentrated on keeping the car from skidding while Persis exclaimed over the beauty of the landscape. "I don't know, I may never go home again. Oh, Jesus, of course I don't mean that. I'd drive you both insane within a month. Who would have thought England could be so majestic? He looks very happy."

Karen smiled. She enjoyed being carried along Persis's mental byways, though keeping up sometimes presented a challenge. "I think he is. The book is going extremely well. He seems to edit everything in his head before it comes out on paper. He rarely changes anything afterwards." They bounced into a hollow and up again. "In the summer, there's a little stream here that flows right across the road. I wonder if it'll even be passable in the spring."

The village consisted of a main street lined with gray stone buildings, a sixteenth-century church, and a small square with a hitching post, where two horses stood stamping their feet and breathing clouds of steam. The post office doubled as the grocery store, and there was a tiny café.

"Come, let's get warm," Karen said, and led Persis inside. The windows were so steamy it was impossible to look out. The proprietress-waitress, who spoke in a language barely identifiable as English, brought them a plate of scones and mugs of hot chocolate.

"Are you able to ride here?" Persis asked.

"Not often. There's a stable that lets me rent out a sweet little palomino, but it's not close by. And I find I'm so busy." She smiled. "A housewife's work is never done."

Persis shook her head. "Don't you miss your old life?"

"An occasional minor twinge. I'm writing. Pretty silly, really, a musical that will never get produced, but your brother nags me about the learning process. He's right."

"I hope he appreciates you."

"He's the most gentle and considerate soul. The strange thing is, now I can't imagine what life must have been like before. Very scattered and empty, I guess. A house without a kitchen."

"There's a song for you."

"I was just thinking that," Karen said.

"Or maybe a poem."

"Go ahead. I'd be curious to see what you make of it. Tell me what's happening with you. Any wonderful new romance on the horizon?"

"It's new, but far from wonderful. He's mean and interesting."

"Oh, are you into sadomasochism these days?" Karen asked.

"Not very seriously, but we do have a good time with mutual torment. We make dates and stand each other up. We say awful things about each other's work." Persis buttered another scone and took a bite. "There's nobody crustier than a failed playwright. So it's a nice break from the sweet but boring types. However, I think we're coming to the finale. He's met a new woman, an orthopedic surgeon. There's no way I can compete with her for nastiness."

"Maybe you ought to try that elevator where I met Edward."

"With my luck, I'd wind up with a psychopathic killer or a homosexual. And what's more, fall madly in love with him. How come you two haven't gotten married?"

"What for?" Karen asked.

"Well, people do, you know."

"I guess it's never occurred to us."

"What about children?"

"Actually, that idea has crossed my mind on occasion," Karen said.

"Has it crossed Edward's?"

"We talked about it when we first moved up here. Edward is concerned about being an elderly father. Besides, things have sort of changed . . . in that department."

"I couldn't help but notice the separate bedrooms," Persis said.

"Nothing is ever perfect, as my mother always used to say. Actually, *she* went so far as to suggest that nothing is ever halfway decent." Persis waited, unwilling to prod her, and after a moment, Karen went on. "I'm not sure what happened. In the beginning, the sex was wonderful. He behaved like a teenager. But now . . . well, the fact is, he can't seem to get an erection." The proprietress looked up from cleaning her coffee pot so Karen lowered her voice. "He saw a doctor in London several weeks ago, but there wasn't anything physical, not that they could find anyway. So they suggested he see a shrink."

"Did he?"

"No. We talked about it, but neither of us believe he has an emotional problem. It's a mystery."

"And meanwhile, you're left without sex. You're too young for that."

Karen sighed. "Ah, God was merciless, making me such a horny little thing. Edward did get one once, but we were at the movies in York, and by the time we got all the way back here, it had died and refused to be resuscitated. Edward has actually suggested . . . well, he knows I'm a pretty sexual person. He thinks I ought to seek relief elsewhere."

"Will you?"

Karen shook her head. "The ironic thing is, I really only want him. And yet sometimes this incredible wave comes over me when I could rape the mailman, and you should see the mailman."

"If there's an opposite of sacrificial virgin, you're it."

"A sacrificial slut?" Karen asked.

At that moment, the proprietress, looking grim, appeared at their table with the bill. Karen paid, and they left giggling.

Christmas Eve had been declared a night of gala entertainment in the best Bloomsbury tradition. Each person was obliged to prepare in secret some musical contribution. So after an immense and convivial dinner of roast beef and Yorkshire pudding, they crept into the living room, sleepy and overfed.

"Who's first?" Karen asked.

"You are," Persis and Edward chorused.

"What is this, a conspiracy?"

"We have to get the pros off the stage first crack," Persis said. "Union rules."

"Oh, all right. Then I can relax and watch the two of you make fools of yourselves."

" 'Give me the young man who has brains enough to make a fool of himself!' " Edward quoted.

"R. L. Stevenson," Persis said. She pointed at Edward. " 'This fellow's wise enough to play the fool.' "

"Uh, *Midsummer Night's Dream,*" Edward guessed.

"Hah! Gotcha!" Persis cried. "It's *Twelfth Night.*"

Karen stood watching them with hands on hips. "You guys going to play Stump the Sibling all night, or you want to see a show?"

"Merely trying to elevate the proceedings," Edward said.

"I dare you to get more elevated than mine," Karen protested, and flounced out of the room. In a few moments, she was back, wearing a pale blue blanket around her shoulders and a white pillowcase draped around her face. The blanket bulged out over hidden pillows in a convincing simulation of pregnancy.

"Blarmy," Edward said. "It's the holy mother."

"You've got it, mate," Karen said, then lifted plaintive eyes heavenward and sang with hands on her swollen belly.

Joe says my explanation makes him look a perfect fool;
When someone laughs he decks 'em with his carpentering tool;
And now we gotta split this town and flee to Bethlehem
'Cuz these freakin' angels tell me that I gotta hark to them.
Joe, he says he'll whop me when it finally comes to pass,
And meanwhile it's no picnic riding sideways on this ass.
Oh, Joe, I didn't do it!
Honest Injun, don't be cruel!
It's God what done me dirty
And despoiled me precious jewel.
If he was gonna do me in the middle of the night,
He shoulda used his magic wand and done the job up right.
Instead there's just this flash of light and next thing I'm with child;
I heard a girl should get some jollies when that girl's defiled.
Oh, Joe, I didn't do it!
Honest Injun, don't be cruel!
It's God what done me dirty
And despoiled me precious jewel!

The last chorus was delivered with extreme distress, complete with catch in the throat. There was wild applause. Karen grabbed Persis by the hand. "Come on, you're next."

"Oh, dear, I have to follow that?" But she stood by the window with her arms at her sides and in a thin soprano half sang, half spoke her song.

When will I make the best-seller list?
When will I be rich?
When will a multimillion-dollar contract for me
Come off without a hitch?
Why don't they read poetry,
Not "On Love's Fierce Tide"?
Don't they want their brains provoked
Instead of stupefied?

When will I be courted by Knopf
And dined at La Côte Basque?

When will the royalties never stopf?
It's not so much to ask.
When will I be picked to run
For president of PEN?
All I ask is glory, wealth,
And lunch at Twenty-One.
Oh, why don't they read poetry?
It ain't so hard to swallow.
I'm not in such a fearful rush,
Just let it be, let it be, let it be tomorrow.

She made a stiff bow while Edward stamped his feet and Karen put her fingers in her mouth and let out an earsplitting whistle. Then both women turned to Edward with pointed stares. He got up, excused himself and they sat waiting and giggling.

"He's chickened out," Karen said.

"Let's go get him," Persis said, but just then Edward appeared in a doorway covered top-of-the-head to ankles in a blanket. He shuffled over to the stereo, put a record on the turntable and whirled around with a great flourish, letting the blanket fall to the floor. He had tied bright red bows in his hair and beard and somehow managed to cram his frame into Karen's red sequined dress. It came more than halfway up his thighs, revealing thin and hairy legs. He lifted his bare foot up and rotated it to display scarlet toenails. Then undulating and gesturing seductively, he mimed Tina Turner singing "Private Dancer," which Karen had played ad nauseam when they first moved to Yorkshire. Persis and Karen howled and stamped their feet, begging for more when it was over.

"No, no, darlings," Edward protested. "I have to go get my legs waxed."

He disappeared through the doorway to raucous applause. When he came back, they congratulated one another on their performances.

"You lip-sync better than I do," Karen said to Edward.

"I practiced," he admitted. "Nearly got caught at it this afternoon, too." He sat down between the two women. "Now, Persis, isn't your new volume selling?"

"Oh, the usual three or four copies. I got a nice review in the *Times*."

"You didn't send it," Karen complained.

"I brought it with me." She took a frayed paper out of the back pocket of her jeans and handed it to Edward. He read silently for a moment, then quoted aloud. " 'At forty-four, Persis Vaughn has written some of this decade's finest poetry. It is clear that she is embarked upon an adventure in quest of the answers to our most perplexing emotional dilemmas: love versus loss; intellect versus sensibility' . . . so on and so on . . . 'her unparalleled ability to floodlight conflict' . . . etcetera etcetera . . ."

"Wow," Karen said. "Let me see."

Edward finished reading and handed the review to Karen. "Your best ever, isn't it?"

"Doesn't pay the rent," Persis said, then waved her hand in apology. "Oh, I don't mean to grouse. That kind of attention is lovely. But in a way it makes the lack of sales even harder to bear. If nobody wants to read the stuff when it merits a review like that, then where am I?"

"You wait," Karen said. "After all, it's only just hit the stores."

"Maybe I ought to do a video," Persis suggested. "How do you think I'd look riding naked on the back of a horse?"

"Absurd," Edward said.

"Splendid," Karen said. "I bet it would work, too. If only you had an extra forty grand lying around."

"Is that what it costs? Good Lord," Persis said. "Perhaps I'd better try a home movie of me astride the family dog."

"Kinky," Karen remarked, poured them all another glass of champagne, and settled on the floor beside Edward's chair. He rested his hand on her head, twisting tendrils of her hair gently between his long fingers.

Persis had stretched out on the couch. "What do you wish for the New Year, Edward?" she asked.

"Health."

Karen craned her neck to look up at him. "Why, is something the matter?"

"No, I'm just an old codger, so I think of such things. And I'd like to finish Julius before the year is done."

"Heavens," Persis said. "That would be record time for a biography."

"It would indeed," Edward said.

Karen got up to put another log on the fire. The sap crackled and spit as she sat down again.

"What about you, Karen?" Persis asked.

Karen thought a moment, then spoke slowly. "All my life, I've wanted certain things with all my heart. I had this terrific yearning. I guess I figured I wanted to be famous and rich . . . no, forget the rich, I was never much interested in money. But to stand in front of thousands of people and sing my head off, that was the ultimate." She glanced up at Edward for a moment. "That yearning's gone. I want to live here, write, learn, and figure out how to grow corn in Northern England. Your turn, Persis."

"That's easy." Persis looked at the two of them in comfortable intimacy by the fire. "I just want what you've got."

On Christmas morning, Karen woke at six-thirty as usual, despite the champagne. She was surprised to hear noises coming from the kitchen. On her way back from the bathroom, Persis appeared at her bedroom door.

"You can't come down yet," she commanded.

"What's going on?"

"You have to go back to bed and don't show your face until I call you."

"But what about breakfast?"

"Everything's under control."

"How could everything be under control with you two in my kitchen?" Karen asked, but she crawled obediently back under the covers.

Somehow she drifted off again, and it was nearly eight o'clock when she heard Persis calling her. She brushed her teeth, pulled on a pair of jeans and a warm sweater and hurtled down the narrow stairway. Edward and Persis met her in the kitchen. They were standing side by side in front of the stove looking very stern, like a self-conscious parody of Grant Wood's farmers.

"Coffee," Karen begged. "Quick."

"No coffee. Not yet." Edward handed her a jacket and they ushered her outside and down past the garden.

"Where are we going?" Karen demanded.

But they were silent. When they came to the edge of the meadow, they stopped. Hitched to the split-rail fence was a butterscotch mare with cream-colored forelocks. "Merry Christmas," Edward said.

Karen stared at the horse, then at Edward, in wonderment.

"She's yours," Persis said. "Edward bought her for you."

Karen couldn't speak. She touched the mare's soft nose, then flung her arms around Edward and buried her face in his chest.

Edward had arranged to keep Belle at a nearby farmhouse until the small stable could be finished beyond the garden. Karen rode her nearly every morning. "She's perfect for the moors," Karen said. "A wild, nimble little spirit, like the wind across the heather. Sometimes I can barely hold her back."

In April the days had begun to lengthen again and it was just warm enough for them to begin sitting outside at lunchtime. Edward wore a thick woolen sweater, but Karen was comfortable in shirt-sleeves in the pale spring sunshine. She had finished her sandwich, but Edward was still working on his, a thick slab of Double Gloucester cheese between slices of brown bread. Meanwhile, Karen sorted through the mail, discarding most of the envelopes without opening them. But she slit open the last with her knife.

"It's from Nicky Stein," she said, reading eagerly. Then she sucked in her breath.

"What's the matter?" Edward asked.

Karen read aloud in a shaking voice.

"Dear Karen,

I happened to run across Manfred Warm when we were in L.A. with Marylou. We were shooting the shit about this and that, and he asked me about you in this weird tone of voice, as if maybe you'd been buried alive. I told him I thought you were perfectly happy except you were disappointed about the musical. I saw there was some subtext I wasn't quite connecting with, and it turns out that way back last year Tony told Manfred you were having a serious drug problem and *that's* the *real* reason the musical didn't go down. I explained to Manfred that Tony was super-peeved you took off and would have made up any kind of fable to screw you up. I don't know what you want to do about this situation, but I somehow felt it should be in writing, not over the telephone, more substantial, if you know what I mean, and maybe some day these lines will be used in a court of law to nail Anthony to the outhouse wall. We're on tour, and you know what *that* means, but I'll call you when we get to Detroit. I didn't know whether you'd want me to say anything to Tony, so I haven't opened my mouth as yet. I just glare at him a lot and stick my foot out to trip him if I can get away with it. I'm sure you'll be pleased to hear that he went sprawling face down in the first-class aisle somewhere between Seattle and Minneapolis.

Much love, Nick.

Karen set the letter down on the table and smoothed it with her hand as if she could erase the words.

"I don't know what to say." Edward's half-eaten sandwich lay untouched on his plate.

"He probably figured I'd never find out," Karen said.

"You almost didn't." Edward picked up the letter and read it to himself while Karen sat lost in thought. "What are you going to do about this?" he asked finally.

She shook her head. "Boy, I'm having a lot of trouble absorbing it. I guess it means there's hope for the musical after all. Is that possible?"

"Absolutely," Edward said. "I think you should get in touch with Manfred Warm and set him straight."

"I don't like leaving you."

"You'll see him in person?"

"It's Tony I need to see in person."

Edward took her hand. "He's a pretty wild fellow and desperately in love with you. I'd rather you weren't alone when you talk with him."

Karen absently rubbed his fingers across her lips. "It'll be okay. I'll see Tony, and Manfred, if I can manage it, and I'm going to ask Guy Burlingame to scare me up a gig. We could use a little cash."

"Is it the money, or are you beginning to miss it?"

"Greed, darling. And need. We're getting down to the nitty-gritty." She suddenly swung around and stared at him. Her eyes were so intense they seemed to have darkened to midnight blue. "I don't like to leave you."

"You know, Karen," Edward said. "You must never feel the slightest reluctance to go off on your own, for a few days or for as long as you like."

"Sometimes I think you'd almost like me to take off."

"Only to relieve me of guilt," Edward said.

"What guilt?"

"For your taking care of me."

"First of all," Karen said, "I'm not taking care of you, we're taking care of each other, and secondly, I'm the one who feels guilty."

"Whatever for?" he asked.

"For making *you* feel guilty."

They grinned at one another.

"So," she said, "how about if your guilt cancels out my guilt and we just get on with it?"

"All right. This conversation is straight off Persis's Nichols and May record."

"Meanwhile, if I feel like making another thirty-city tour of the U.S., I'll let you know. Right now I'm finding it tough to imagine being away from you for a lousy week."

"That long?" he asked mournfully, but his eyes were twinkling. She gave him a quick rap on the arm.

Karen caught up with Tony in Indianapolis. Marylou was singing at the Market Square Arena where Karen had performed with Denny Harper's tour. It was a peculiar experience, standing back by the risers, watching her old friends, Nicky, John, and Billy, lit up on the stage with a guitarist she didn't recognize and Marylou. The singer's limited range had been carefully exploited to create the semblance of melody, and her outfit was fabulous, a skintight purple bodysuit with strategically placed silver designs that flickered teasingly in the spotlights. Tony had done his work well.

For a moment, Karen yearned to hop up there for just one number, just for the fun of it, no commitments. But then she took a closer look at Marylou. She was always on the move, jerking her body across the stage like a self-propelled marionette. There was no rest up there, no standing still even for a moment. Today's audience was the Sesame Street generation, accustomed to a barage of constantly changing images. Marylou would give it to them, leaping and dancing until she dropped, just as Karen had done. The difference was that for Karen, the joy and the exhaustion had come from the music itself, not a crazy puppet show.

When it was over, Karen headed for the dressing rooms. She was struck by the subdued emotional climate of Marylou's fans. They stood in an orderly pack with their pieces of paper, hoping for autographs. There was none of the almost hysterical excitement that had met Karen after her performances.

Karen slipped into Marylou's dressing room and quickly latched the door behind her. Marylou sat in an exhausted heap, her hair glued to her head, the purple bodysuit stained with sweat. She gaped at Karen, then with fearful eyes turned to Tony who stood in the corner beside the door.

"Nice job, Marylou," Karen said. "I'm glad I finally got a chance to hear you."

Marylou tried to answer, but her response came out like a croak.

It took a moment for Karen to figure out why Tony looked so odd. Instead of a suit, he wore jeans and a plaid shirt. "How did you get past that mob without being recognized?" he asked. "Oh, never mind, it's easy, you look like shit."

"Thanks," Karen said. "I'd like to speak with you privately."

"No," Tony said. "If you remember, I wasn't permitted that privilege at our last meeting."

"Do you really want Marylou to hear what a snake you are?" Karen asked him. She stared him down until she saw the light dawn. He reddened and went to the door.

They walked back out onto the huge arena floor that was actually a basketball court. Technicians were dismantling equipment on the stage in a clamorous ritual that Karen knew was completely efficient despite the seeming pandemonium.

"I could sue you for slander," she told Tony.

At first, he did not reply. With hands in his pockets, he watched chairs folded, litter cleared. "I wanted to hurt you," he said finally.

"Well, you succeeded. I suppose the whole industry is convinced that I'm an unreliable druggie," Karen said.

"Warm's a very discreet guy."

"Oh, please, you know damn well these things never stay under cover. I don't think I've ever wanted anything professionally as much as that musical."

"It was a ludicrous idea." Tony's hand came out of his pocket and sliced at the air, a karate chop.

"What you did was the worst kind of betrayal."

"It was my job to keep you on track, and you have to admit I did it pretty well until you fucked everything up."

"Well, it's not your job any more. It's over."

"What do you mean?" Tony asked. "What's there to be over?"

"I mean I don't ever want to see you again. There is no connection between us, not even hate." Her voice was very calm.

"You're giving me the creeps," Tony said. "Aren't you going to yell?"

"No. Listen to me, I don't want to hear your name, I don't even want to read it in the newspaper. You don't exist."

"Jesus, Karen." Tony's head tilted sideways as if he'd been struck in the face. "I loved you and you left me," he said.

"Love! What on God's earth do you know about love? All you know about is sex and proprietary interest."

"Other words for love," he retorted.

"Yeah," Karen said. "My lawyer will call your lawyer. Now, move aside. I'm going to see the band."

Edward spent his first morning after Karen's departure typing a chapter about Julius Southwick's romance with Carmen Villanova, which had ended, farcically, with Carmen's announcement that she was in fact a lesbian. Despite the revelation, Julius had emerged from the affair with some dignity, in part because of his good-humored reaction and also because most of the men he knew envied his temporary conquest of the ferocious Spanish contralto, lesbian or no.

Edward blew on his icy fingers and snatched the last sheet from the typewriter. He gazed out over the moors. It was very quiet. Talk to me, Julius, Edward thought. I'm lonely without her.

You've been blessed, biographer, Julius obliged from the neat pile of pages beside the typewriter.

Why the past tense? Edward asked.

Why indeed? Julius echoed.

I don't think I want to talk about it, Edward thought.

This is your conversation. Do as you wish.

Edward picked up the smooth pale-rose rock Karen had brought him from one of her excursions into the hills and plunked it down on his manuscript. I'm hanging up on you, Julius, he thought. Then he stood up, stretched, and went into the kitchen. The solitary hum of the refrigerator made the room seem even emptier. He felt that he could easily skip lunch, but instead, he dutifully fixed himself a sandwich and settled at the table to eat, newspaper beside his plate. It seemed pointless to sit outdoors when Karen was gone. In her absence, even the flowers seemed to droop.

Remembering her admonitions regarding exercise, he decided to take a long walk. The day was fine, and Karen would be pleased when she called tonight. So he drove into nearby Helmsley where he could pick up the trail to Rievaulx Abbey.

The three-mile walk was a favorite of Edward's because of its diversity. It began along a farmer's track that skirted the ruins of Helmsley Castle, then bordered a meadow that was already fragrant and green with barley. The earth felt spongy beneath his feet, comfortable for walking if a bit damp. He scaled the stile at the edge of the field and was soon plunging down into the wooded ravine. The soil beneath the trees was black, and the leaves, an intense yellow-green, looked like the tender wings of grasshoppers unfolding and beginning to stretch. Here and there, wildflowers edged the path, and a startled rabbit darted across the way. Edward took deep breaths and strode along wishing he could sing. He tried a few bars of "Oh, What a Beautiful Morning," but offended himself with the sound of his reedy voice. He moved on in silence, finally emerging out onto the road. He walked awhile, encountering only a hay wagon and a minivan filled with teenagers, then turned right along the creek. Purposely, he did not strain for a view of the abbey, but teased his eyes until time for the full impact. And as always, he was not disappointed. Around the final bend rose a steep, densely wooded hill, at the foot of which stood Rievaulx in ruined splendor. The stone walls never seemed the same. Edward had seen them drab and forbidding in a September rainstorm. Once last winter, Karen and Edward had come here after a blizzard to find the place glistening like gilt treasure cast away by the gods to lie abandoned but majestic in the snow. Today, against the green of the hill, the graceful stone arches looked very pure, almost translucent.

Edward picked his way up through the crumbling stairways to the chapel. The roof had long since disintegrated, inviting sunlight to pour down onto the thick grass floor. Underfoot, medieval gravestones were set in the earth like tiles, their inscriptions worn smooth by seven centuries. Edward stared up through the arched windows and wished fervently for Karen. How could he ever describe to her how the light illuminated the stone with such radiance it seemed aglow with some mysterious internal fire?

Suddenly, a stray cloud covered the sun, and in an instant the life disappeared from the stone, leaving it dead and gray. Edward shivered. He untied the sweater he had knotted around his shoulders and slipped it on. A shadow flickered in the corner of his eye. He turned, surprised. He had thought he was alone in the ruins, but no, there was someone, a cloaked figure, like a monk.

"Hello!" he called out. But there was no reply except the hollow ring of his own voice bouncing from the cavernous walls. He felt a chill reach down the back of his neck and along his spine. "All right, now," he said aloud, and began to search. He made his way through all of the intricate archways, but still there was no one.

In a few minutes, a noisy group of German tourists arrived, and with them, the sunshine. After a brief rest, Edward made his way back to Helmsley for a solitary dinner at The Black Swan.

When Karen telephoned that evening, he told her he had walked to Rievaulx.

"Was it lovely?" she asked.

"Yes," he said but did not elaborate.

Guy Burlingame sat across the table at Jim McMullen's, sipping his whiskey sour. Karen, meanwhile, eagerly consumed a hamburger and eyed the extravagant spray of flowers at the end of the bar.

"They can't make modern buildings or burgers in England," Karen said. "Ah, this is wonderful. And where does Jim get his flowers?"

"It's good to see you," Guy said. "You look fine."

"No complaints?" Karen asked. "That's a first. There must be a pimple *somewhere*."

"I owe you an apology."

"What for?"

"Somehow, the word of your alleged drug addiction never passed my ears. If I'd gotten wind of it, I could have squelched it on the spot. I must be slipping."

"Manfred is discreet," Karen said. "I met with him yesterday, he and this financial type in a three-piece suit. They seemed pretty excited by what I've done so far."

"So you've been working just for the hell of it?"

"Edward convinced me it would be worthwhile as a learning experience, if for nothing else."

Jim McMullen walked past their table, combing a thick shock of hair back with his fingers in a gesture left over from his modeling days. On his way back, he stopped to place a hand on Karen's shoulder.

"I like your asters, Jim," Karen said. The man looked nonplussed. "Flowers. Asters are flowers," Karen explained.

"Oh," McMullen replied with a laugh. "Goes to show you how much I know. Do we get to hear you sing this trip?"

"Sure. Where is it I'm going to be, Guy?"

"Pretzel's, in SoHo. Tonight and tomorrow night at ten."

"I'm gonna sneak out of here and come listen."

"Thanks, Jim," Karen said. "At least there'll be one person in the audience."

McMullen left them. Karen liked the man because he was particularly kind to the elderly. As usual, today's lunchtime was filled with blue-haired ladies and the occasional old gentlemen who had defied the odds. McMullen was at this moment helping one such fellow up out of his chair to be escorted to the men's room. Karen wondered if he might be The Kaiser, boyfriend of Edward's mother.

"Hello," Guy was saying.

"Oh, am I dreaming?" Karen said. "Must be jet lag."

"I was asking if tonight's gig is a toe in the water to be yanked out forthwith—or are there plans to dive in again?"

"We need the money," Karen said. "I thought my semifortune would last forever, and we've practically used it up already, what with the house and now building a stable for my horse. I'm so grateful to you for setting me up tonight. It's astounding how much they're paying me."

"I'll never have trouble getting you a gig here or anywhere else. The world misses you."

Karen smiled. "The world is fickle. It'll forget about me soon enough."

"And you don't care?"

"I'm writing. I get up very early and go for a ride, then I do breakfast with Edward, and it's off to work. I garden, too. It's a full life."

"And nobody hears your songs." Guy reached over to pick a thread off her sweater.

"Edward does. And Persis, his sister, if she's visiting, and Milly and Vincent, and you would, too, if you'd ever come see us."

"Oh, my darling, I react to fresh air with instant swollen glands. I have to remain within the polluted environs of a large urban settlement."

"You went to Lady Mariah's."

"She's still inside the twenty-mile limit. But I must confess, I felt quite ill after I'd been there an hour. I could feel my skin shriveling from a paucity of carbon monoxide. You have a tiny line between your eyebrows." He traced it with his finger. "Or is it the light in here?"

"Well, Guy, after all, I'm not the little ingenue you used to know."

He peered at her, moving his head back and forth to make a full inspection.

"You look like a snake when you do that," she complained.

"Uh-uh-uh-uh-uh," Guy said. "You're not getting enough."

"I beg your pardon," Karen said.

"How's your sex life, Wells?" Guy asked.

Karen tried to hold his gaze but failed. She focused on the vase at their table. "Fine," she answered. "As if it's any of your business."

He held up his hands in apology. "It's only because I'm so fond of you that I'll let you off the hook, my darling. Only remember there's a shoulder here in case of need."

She smiled at him. "I know that. Thanks. I didn't mean to be surly."

They spent the rest of their conversation discussing mutual acquaintances in the music world. Karen gobbled up the gossip as eagerly as she did her hamburger. Finally, Guy had to rush off, but Karen was content to linger over her coffee. Leave it to Guy to take one look and zero in on her sexual deprivation. She stared into her cup and thought of Edward.

For the first few weeks after he had been examined by the doctor and declared fit, he had tried to satisfy her by other means than intercourse. For a little while, the arrangement was gratifying enough, but soon the one-way nature of the situation began to discourage her. She felt like a dog being taken for its daily outing. So lately their physical contact consisted of hand-holding and warm hugs. Edward's kisses were so drained of fire that she had begun turning her head aside to catch them on her cheek. And yet, his eyes were always full of love.

"And here she is, Karen Wells!" There were drum rolls and a haphazard rendition of "Who Stole the Moon?" as Karen walked out onto the stage. The applause in the crowded club rolled on and on, pouring over her like honey, sweet but full of its own sticky demands.

Finally, she held up her arms and waited for the room to quiet down. "It's been a while," she said and shook her head as the clapping began again. "You're very kind. Now, listen, we've got some new material. I promise I'll sing some of the oldies, too, but if you don't mind playing guinea pig, we'd like to try some stuff out on you." There were enthusiastic hoots. Karen grinned, beckoned to the keyboard player, and began an upbeat but gritty song called "Cookin'."

There's certain things about you, babe
That make me want to touch you
Procrastination's not my style
Not my way of lovin'
So we're gonna get down to it now
Let's show you how to do it
Light your match and twist my knob
And we'll preheat my oven.

At first, she felt stiff and restrained, but soon the music reached into her and drew out the old confidence and buoyant artistry. Afterward, accompanying the triumph was a sense of loss: for the satisfaction of singing with the support of fine responsive musicians, for the giddy exhilaration of all that adulation, even for flickering memories of Tony and the sexual excitement of their postperformance celebrations. But when she thought of Edward, she longed to be home with him.

On the plane, she read the review of her performance in *Orbit* magazine.

> The Voice (a.k.a. Karen Wells) is back, or at least she showed up at Pretzel's on Friday and Saturday. Now and again, an artist rises above the confused and mostly mediocre cacophony of the pop music scene. Karen Wells does not merely rise, she shoots straight up like a rocket to glow in the upper atmosphere as have a mere handful of others before her (Streisand, Midler, Janis Joplin come to mind). Her range, both emotional and musical,

has stretched. She delivers a song of quiet intimacy ("Belonging"), raunchy sexuality ("Cookin'"), and romantic longing ("Silver Clouds") with equal integrity. Her lyrics are grittier, her melodies more complex. She has matured, and yet there was a bittersweet quality to her performance that leaves an afterthought of regret. Perhaps this is because Ms. Wells reputedly has no plans to record her new music, nor has she booked future concerts. Despite her artistic generosity last weekend, there is a determined sense of privacy that keeps her just out of reach.

Welcome back, Karen Wells. Tell us, please, that you are here to stay.

"Lord," Karen whispered.

She took one look at Edward and accused him of fasting. "You didn't eat a goddamn thing, I can see that," she complained.

"A slight bout of Montezuma's revenge. But better now."

"You're flushed." She reached up to lay a hand against his forehead.

"Oh, perhaps a degree or two, nothing crucial."

"Edward, if you're not frozen solid, you're ill. We're getting you to the doctor tomorrow."

"I'm fine. Honestly, much better. Relax now. You just got home. Don't we have something more interesting to talk about than my state of health?"

She could see he was becoming agitated at her attention, so she stopped fussing and followed him into the living room where he had set up the dinner table by the fireplace.

"Now tell me about the show," Edward said. He sat with his right side facing the fire so that half of him glowed red-orange.

Karen took a swallow of wine and read him the review. "Gooey, huh?" she said.

"What did it feel like to be back in the spotlight?"

She thought for a moment. "There was a bit of a rush at first. Nothing like having a mob of fans cheering and pounding their feet on the floor. And I liked singing with a group of musicians who know what they're doing. But basically it was . . . irrelevant."

"What a strange sort you are," Edward mused, and shoved a roast potato around on his plate.

"In a way, I wonder if you wouldn't like me to get back into it," Karen said.

"What makes you say that?"

"Because you worry that I'm too dependent. Edward, do I strangle you?"

He set down his fork and took her hand. "My darling, I think you are definitely too dependent, and I take reprehensible advantage of the fact. No man is as pampered as I, and I missed you dreadfully."

"I'm coming over there," Karen said.

"That's perfectly all right with me," Edward said, and held out his arms.

But it was Karen who became ill. When she woke the following morning to ride Belle, she stepped out of bed and fell in a heap on the floor. With the room rocking and pitching around her, she managed to crawl back on her mattress and lay there, alternately tossing off blankets and piling them on again, until Edward appeared in the doorway at eight o'clock.

"My dear," he said, and came to sit on the edge of the bed. He took her hand. "You're burning."

"Something I picked up in New York, I guess," she murmured. Everything ached so painfully that even speaking was an effort. Words tugged cruelly at the muscles beside her mouth and accentuated the pounding in her head. Edward's cool fingers seemed to sear her flesh like dry ice.

"Close your eyes," Edward said. She felt his weight lift off the bed.

The rest of the day was blurry, but she knew the doctor came, bringing his black bag and his round face into her room. As he pumped up the blood-pressure sleeve, his face seemed to expand like a scarlet balloon.

"He's going to explode!" she shouted to Edward, and began to whimper. Edward stroked her forehead. "It's all right, darling," he said in his calm voice. "You're going to be fine."

"Our walking tour!" she cried. "We're going to miss it!"

"No, no, that's a long way off. You'll be mended long before. We'll have a lovely time. Now sleep, sleep."

And she did, for almost two full days. When she finally woke with a clear head on Tuesday evening, Edward was sitting in a rocking chair in the corner of her room, reading. She gazed at him for a while, watching how the light from the lamp reached into the thick curls of his beard and lifted out tiny shards of silver and auburn. It was odd how the hair on men's heads did not match the hair of their beards.

Edward sensed her eyes on him and looked up. He smiled with that wide half-crazed grin that affected her like a caress between the legs.

"Hello," he said. "How do you feel?"

She tried to sit up. "As if I'd been thrown off a horse."

"I just took your temperature. No fever."

"You did?"

He nodded, closed the book and came to her bed.

"What time is it?" she asked.

"Nine-fifteen, Tuesday evening."

She thought that over. "I don't think I've ever been this sick. Doctor Humbersham was here, wasn't he?"

"Yes. You told him to fuck off."

"I didn't!"

"When he was listening to your heart with the stethoscope. It's all right. He took it in good part. Are you hungry, darling?"

"No. I mean, maybe. I guess a cup of tea, but mainly I would love to brush my teeth. Can you help me up?"

"No. You're staying in bed. I'll get your toothbrush."

He brought her a basin, a glass of water, and her toothbrush. The toothpaste was striped, red, white, and blue. "Tacky stuff," Edward complained.

"Patriotic, though," Karen said, and tried, with Edward holding her, to brush her teeth. But her hand felt as if it was attached to her arm by a very thin thread. It bobbed and drooped and refused to cooperate.

"Wow," Karen said. "What's this, some rare neurological disease?"

"No, it was a nasty flu, and now you're weak. I'll take care of this. You just lie back against the pillow and open up."

"No."

"Don't be difficult." He sounded so stern that she obeyed at once. He went at it systematically, starting with the back molars and working his way forward. But before he could finish, she began to giggle. Finally, he had to put the toothbrush down.

"What if a visitor from another planet came in here and saw you doing that? He'd think it was some weird sexual rite. Edward, you're so *earnest*. And me with my mouth gaping open like the Lincoln Tunnel. Oh, dear . . ."

He brought her tea and toast and watched as she tried to eat. She managed half a slice of toast.

"If I feed it to you, will you eat another?" he asked.

She shook her head and closed her eyes. "Can't." She was nearly asleep already. "But you could read to me a little. Whatever you're in the middle of. Whatever of which you're in the middle."

He removed the tray, kissed her cheek and sat down in the corner with *The Oxford Book of English Verse*. Searching for something serene, he flipped to Keats and began, "Thou still unravished bride of quietness, / Thou foster-child of Silence and slow Time . . ." She was asleep before he reached the end.

It took her a week to recover. She sat up in bed with maps and guide books spread out over the bedclothes, plotting their trip.

"You can't trek all over Yorkshire in your condition," Edward protested.

"But we have to go next week before you start the last section of Julius. Otherwise, we'll have to postpone it until the fall."

"Maybe we ought to," he said. "Here, drink your juice." She swallowed it thirstily. "All right. Now, what about this trip? Can we modify it? How about taking the car and doing short day walks?"

She thought about it. "If you promise we get a real tour when the book is finished."

"Agreed."

"We'll walk from Osmotherly to Ravenscar. That's the route the Vikings took to deliver the dead bodies of their warriors to the sea. It goes right up over the North York Moors. The army uses it now to train troops. They make them do it in thirty-six hours or something, and it's fifty-plus miles. But the Vikings did it in twenty-four."

"Oh, I think we ought to see if we can match the Vikings. If we make it, I'll buy you a brass brassiere and a helmet with horns. Ready for some reading?"

"Just a little, and a very short nap today. I want to get out of this bed."

"Soon. Now lie down. I'm going to begin *Return of the Native* this afternoon and see if I can finish reading it in twenty-four hours like the Vikings."

"If you do, I'll buy you a brass jockstrap."

They started out on a fine May morning, driving first through the medieval town of Richmond with its cobbled streets and then up into the dales along the River Swale. The lanes were very narrow, winding, and often enclosed with tall stone walls or now and then aged farmhouses that abutted the road. The dales swelled up on either side, rounded and green and almost tamed by man, but not quite. Now and then the car passed beneath summits so windblown that trees would not grow, so wild and aloof that even the stone fences that latticed the lower hillsides like intricate jewelry could not reach them.

"I can't wait to get up there," Karen said. "I'll bet there won't be one other person anywhere."

"You're a solitudinarian," Edward said.

"So are you. And an escapist, besides." She drove over a humpbacked bridge that barely accommodated the width of their car.

At Thwaite they stopped at an inn for lunch. The array of food was staggering. On each table were lemon tarts, Yorkshire cheesecake, a plumcake, and thick slices of brown bread. Their omelets came with fried potatoes, peas, and a salad. Karen ate eagerly.

"Why do you say I'm an escapist?" Edward asked.

"It's the wrong word," Karen answered. "I'm thinking of your fascination with the past, with Bloomsbury. Maybe it's more that you feel out of sync with your time."

"Who wouldn't? You're exactly the same, refusing to read the newspaper. That's a rejection of the present tense."

"Well, I get freaked out by too many pictures of war, famine, and dead babies. For you, Bloomsbury offers rules, a comforting sense of order. On the surface, at least."

"Only on the surface, I assure you," he said.

"But it's a coherent system, which is more than this decade can offer. Admit it, Edward, Bloomsbury's your sanctuary."

"I'll admit it for the sake of argument. But what's your escape, then?"

Karen thought a moment. "You," she said. Edward looked dismayed. "Sorry, dear, is that too great a burden?"

"I just don't want to let you down. But I also believe you find enormous comfort in your work, your garden, the moors, all these things. I wouldn't like to think, however, that we're retreating from reality."

"Well, maybe there's something to be said for retreat," Karen went on. "When everything is right out there screaming at us over television, radio, in newsprint, there's a sensation of being raw. What's so terrible about drawing a curtain on things so that we don't walk around feeling assaulted all the time?"

"Most people don't notice, Karen."

"I can't believe that."

"All right," he said. "Remember when I took you to that antiwar film in York?"

"I'm losing my appetite."

"When we walked out of there, you were trembling with horror and furious with me for taking you."

"The only possible response to that bloody picture."

"But darling, nobody else was 'freaking out,' as you say. There were some sober faces, but by and large people were chatting and arguing about which pub to go to."

"What are you saying?"

"Perhaps that we have to develop a skin thick enough to cope with the real world."

Karen pushed her plate away. "What about the farmers who live up here in the dales? Aren't they escapists, too?"

"I don't know how connected they are to what's occurring in the rest of the world."

Karen glanced at her watch. "Look, Edward, we're not going to do any walking at this rate. You know once we get into one of these, we could be sitting at this table for the duration."

"You're right," he said, and stood up. "Violence in pornography kept us going until five A.M., and now I can't remember which side I took."

"You rat, of course you remember." She followed him out into the sunshine. "And that electrician came at noon to fix the refrigerator and we were both still in the sack. He thought we were complete degenerates."

Their walk began along a muddy track beside the river, then up an abrupt incline into the hills. The discussion continued while the terrain remained level, but soon they needed their breath for steep work. They climbed for nearly an hour, keeping pace with one another. Finally the stubby bushes thinned and the path became a pale brown line through heather and mossy grass. The wind pressed their clothes tight against them and whipped Karen's hair about her face. Edward put his arm around her as they stood looking across the top of the world. Shadows from the clouds sped along the ridges and scurried eastward toward the sea. The air tasted sweet in their mouths. When they sat down, the earth was soft and dry beneath them.

"When it's time for me to die," Karen said, "bring me up here."

"And carry your body to the sea from Osmotherly?"

"Yes." She leaned her head against his shoulder. A sheep had strayed near, but when Karen turned to look, it scampered away, displaying a blue patch on its wooly rear.

"I like the ones with the blue bottoms," Karen said.

"Yes, the red dye makes them look wounded."

They lay back in the grass. "Do you think it's possible to make a musical out of *Wuthering Heights?*" Karen asked.

"Is that what you're doing?"

"Sometimes I think so."

"Well, why not?"

Karen fell asleep in the warm sun, and when she woke, Edward was on one elbow, staring down at her.

"I wish you would kiss me," she murmured, then shook herself awake. "Forget I said that."

But he leaned over and kissed her on the mouth.

She smiled and sat up. "Come on. We'd better get cracking so we can find a place to stay before dinner."

In the night, in their tiny twin-bedded room, Karen woke to hear Edward throwing up into a basin. She switched on the light and asked what she could do to help him. He shook his head, finished, and looked at her apologetically. "Sorry. Couldn't make it to the bathroom."

"Do you think you're done? Shall I take this?"

"No, no. I'll do it." But he was gray under the eyes. Karen pushed him gently back into bed and went down the hall to the bathroom, returning with the clean basin. She sat next to him and placed her hand on his forehead. His skin was cold and damp.

"What is it, Edward? Did you eat something?"

He shook his head. "It'll pass."

Karen felt the chill from his skin reach into her spine and creep slowly up her back. "It's happened before."

Edward nodded.

"You didn't catch this from me?"

"No."

"How long has it been going on?"

"Since you were in New York."

"Did you see the doctor?"

"Yes."

Karen waited, but he did not answer. "Don't torment me. What did he say?"

"He said he wants to do some tests."

"Not in Prawnby, surely."

"No. He's sending me to London."

"When?"

"Next week, as soon as we get back."

She placed her palms together in an unconscious simulation of prayer. "How could you not tell me?"

"You've been so ill, and then there was the trip. You were looking forward to it so. I didn't want to spoil it."

"And you were waiting on me hand and foot when you were sick yourself."

"It's not incessant."

Karen picked up his hand and held it to her cheek.

He smiled. Without his glasses, his eyes looked liquid and a little vague. "Embarrassing," he said.

"Don't you dare be embarrassed," she said fiercely.

"Not the vomiting, being ill in general. Curious. I wonder why that is."

"Isn't it more that one feels burdensome, putting people out? That's how I felt anyway."

"Not precisely. It's more general. Humiliated in the face of the huge majority of healthy humanity. As if it's a weakness one is somehow responsible for." He reached for his glasses.

"Oh, no, you don't." She retrieved the glasses and set them firmly on the bedside table. "You're not going to work yourself up into one of those marathon analytical sessions. You should be sleeping." She smoothed the blankets around him, switched off the light and got back into bed. Soon she could hear that he was asleep, but she stared into the darkness and sensed the breath of malevolent shadows that crouched in the corners of the room.

At breakfast, it was obvious that Edward could not continue the tour. He sat with plate untouched, and from the deep line between his eyebrows, Karen guessed that he was in pain.

"Don't you think we ought to go home?" she asked.

He objected, but feebly, and rested while she packed their bags. Soon they were winding their way back down the Swale Valley, Karen driving gingerly so as not to jostle him.

"It's very hard," she said at one point, "that you didn't tell me."

"I would have, as soon as we got home."

"I suppose I thought we were always honest with one another."

"I wasn't at all prepared to be honest with myself. Please don't be angry."

He sounded so sad that she softened immediately and gave him a smile. "Okay," she said, "but I'm going to get you back with a whopping big lie one of these days, and I won't tell you when."

"I look forward to it."

She began to sing, knowing that it always lightened his spirits to listen to her. When her voice tired, he began an inquiry into his own fascination with excellence: Baryshnikov, Turner, Bach, Shakespeare, and others, finally circling back to Karen Wells.

She laughed.

"No, I'm quite serious. I'll never forget listening to your record that first time in London. I'm sure it was an important element in my attraction to you."

Karen whispered hoarsely. "What if I get permanent laryngitis. You going to kick me out?"

"I said it was *one* element. I also liked your tits."

"That's what I admire about you, Edward, you're such a scholar."

They got home before three o'clock, and she put him straight to bed.

While Edward rested in a hospital bed recovering from the ordeal of testing, Karen was called in to hear the verdict. She stared at the doctor, a fancy Harley Street specialist.

But her mind had come to a full stop at the word *mass* and refused to function despite the fact that the man's thin lips were still moving. Karen was caught in a groove like the needle in a record. *Mmm-ass, mmm-ass, mmm-ass. What's all this about a mass? / I'm not in your med-school class. / Pardon me for being crass, / But shove it up your pin-striped ass.*

". . . never enjoy conversations such as these," he was saying.

Lord, he was looking for sympathy. *Think of what this must be like for me,* the aggrieved face was saying. *This is an acknowledgment of failure. Think of the humiliation.*

Karen lowered her lashes, fearful that he could not miss the hatred that was streaking out at him from her eyes.

"Can anything be done?" she asked finally.

"Not in surgical terms. It's too large. But there is always the possibility of slowing it with chemotherapy, perhaps even shrinking it." He waited, watching how his words struck her as if each one were a dart. "How do you expect him to react when he's told?"

"I don't know."

"Would you like me to tell him?"

"No!" She held up a hand as if to ward him off. "No, I'll speak to him."

"If experience is any guide, he will wish to make arrangements. It's always more complex than one might imagine."

"Yes, I suppose dying is a rather complicated affair."

The doctor blinked, trying to decide if she was being sarcastic. She stood up and gripped the back of her chair. "I'll be in touch." She left and headed for Regents Park.

She walked briskly along the paths, peripherally aware of the elderly people seated on the benches and the young women with little children. It was the sudden scent of lilacs that finally defeated her. Their odor seemed to advertise everything that was beautiful and valuable and fragile in her life, creating waves of memories that filled her mind—of her own childhood in the springtime, wildflower hunts in the woods with Michael, the delicacy of the shape of Edward's ears, his voice calling her at lunchtime to come out of the garden, words gay as flower petals tumbling across the yard in the breeze. She covered her face with both hands for a long time. Then she dried her eyes with one of Edward's handkerchiefs and sat down on the edge of a bench, gingerly, as if she had been bruised.

It wasn't that she hadn't suspected. She had been having dreams of Michael, long, convoluted nightmares that always ended in loss. And it seemed that every morning when she brought Edward his breakfast in bed, he had shriveled as if he had been visited by a succubus in the night. But suspicion was not confirmation. The words in that office this morning were like heat-seeking missiles flung at her from between tobacco-stained teeth. No matter if she had cowered under the heavy mahogany desk or behind the metal file cabinets, these cruel messages searched her out relentlessly, targeting what was warm and vital and piercing it. She and Edward were both mortally wounded.

She had pledged to tell Edward today, if only to shield him from the inhumanity of those brutal arrows. It was no use planning speeches. She knew that whatever words she chose now would dry up in her mouth at the sight of him.

Karen had always detested hospitals, instinctively recoiling from the atmosphere of sickness and helplessness. In her twelfth winter, she had crashed her toboggan into a tree and broken her arm. The orthopedist, suspecting a possible concussion as well, pressed her to stay overnight. But Karen had slipped her parka over her good arm and walked out, parents protesting but trailing along behind. She had always thought that if she had a child, she would give birth to it at home.

She walked down the wide, shining hallway of the third floor. Sisters glided past in their habits, carrying trays and clipboards. Karen stopped outside Edward's room and read the name *Vaughn, Edw.* on the door. How many times had she stood offstage and waited for the signal to go on? Hundreds, maybe thousands of times—and never had she felt such dread. She crossed herself and plunged into the room. But he was asleep. There was color in his face, and one foot poked out from under the sheet. His toes looked substantial and comforting. She pulled a chair up next to him and watched his face. His eyes twitched under the lids. She wondered if he was dreaming. This was her Edward, not some specter perched on the brink of the grave. Perhaps, after all, she could keep him with her still.

He opened his eyes, yawned, and smiled at her. "Hello."

"Hi," she said and took his hand. "How do you feel?"

"It wouldn't be a bad hotel if only they'd keep their hands out of my rectum. When do they propose to let me out?"

"Tomorrow."

"Can we go home?"

"We'd better discuss that."

Edward took a long look at her. "You've seen Dr. Nickleson."

She nodded and kept her eyes on his, willing the tears to stay down below her larynx where she could feel them swelling.

"You understand that I want to know everything," he said.

"Yes. It's not great news."

"Go on." He watched her mouth carefully.

"There's a large mass, but they don't feel they can remove it. Dr. Nickleson is suggesting chemotherapy which he thinks may either slow it down or shrink it."

"Does that mean staying in the hospital?"

"I think so, yes. We would have to work that out."

They were both silent for a moment. "Edward, there's no word for what I feel."

He smiled at her. "I know that, darling. You mustn't fret."

"Mustn't fret . . ." she echoed. I might throw myself under a train, she thought, but okay, I won't fret.

"I suppose the thing to do is compose a list of questions," Edward said.

"I would like to talk with some other people, for other, you know, maybe, opinions."

"Yes, but I'm so fogged up." He yawned again. "They gave me something and I can't stay awake. How am I supposed to finish my book if I'm all dopey?"

"Maybe we should go to New York, find someone there."

"We'll see. Karen, I can't think." His eyes had closed. "We'll talk about it. There's no rush."

Several minutes later, when she thought he had fallen asleep, he said, "Will you be here?"

"Of course," she answered. Soon he was breathing deeply. Karen rolled her chair close to the bed and gently placed her arm across his body as if to protect him. She wondered how he could sleep, and then she too began to grow drowsy and drifted off, wishing that she would never wake up.

They visited several specialists after Edward was released, carting with them the bulky envelopes that described the thing growing in Edward's belly. At first, Edward focused his questions on the chances of survival. But it soon became apparent that no one believed he would survive. After that, he concentrated on how much time he might have left and the quality of those weeks or months or years. The chemotherapy would be experimental. It would make him feel wretched, far worse than he did at the moment, but it could buy him time. How much time? Edward wanted to know. But no one could tell him that.

"There's someone you should see," Nicky Stein said over the telephone. "He's right there in London."

"I'm awfully tired of watching these people stare off into the woodwork when we ask them how long he's got," Karen said.

"No, this was Ella Gould's doctor. He's a maverick and a brilliant oncologist. I checked him out with the brass at Sloan Kettering. A South African Jew transplanted to Harley Street. Go see him, please, and then call me."

"All right," Karen said with a sigh. "But sometimes I think these visits will do him in quicker than any tumor."

"Call me," Nicky reiterated.

Dr. Moss was a small man and stocky with a cheery round face and bowed legs. He had a pronounced South African accent, which made Karen think of tennis rackets rather than stethoscopes. With Ella Gould's name as a reference, the doctor had set aside an hour the following afternoon.

"I don't want to hear anything anybody else has said to you. Just tell me what you feel, what's happened over the past months."

Edward told him about the chronic vomiting, the diarrhea, the pain that had begun only recently. "For such a large mass . . ." Edward began, but Dr. Moss held up his hand.

"No, no, that's opinion. I don't want anybody's opinion, yours included. Just facts."

Karen and Edward looked at one another. Edward's eyes were twinkling behind his glasses.

"Come in here and take off your clothes," he said. Then, to Karen, "You wait right there. We'll be back."

They were gone for nearly twenty minutes. Then Dr. Moss appeared with Edward in tow, indicated that Edward should sit, and began to read the X-rays. Karen noticed that he placed the covering letters face down without looking at them and confined himself to the hard data. Finally he closed the envelopes and folded his hands on the desk.

"You want bullshit, you came to the wrong boy," Dr. Moss said. His gaze was direct, but not unkind.

"Go on," Edward said.

But Karen wanted to stand up and shout, "Not me! Lie to me!" Instead, she reached for Edward's hand. He squeezed it.

"That damn thing's glommed onto important stuff in your gut. Can't carve it out. You don't have a lot of time."

"What about chemotherapy?" Edward asked.

Dr. Moss gave a hearty sigh. "Yes, there's that, such as it is."

"Will it give me more time?"

"Might. Sure as hell make you miserable."

"How much time do you think it would buy?" Karen asked.

"A few weeks, maybe months, two, three."

"How miserable is miserable?" Edward asked.

"Nausea day and night, weakness so you won't get out of bed. Actually, it might even kill you quicker."

"You're not a chemotherapy devotee," Karen said.

"For many people, and for certain types of cancer, yes. I'm not saying you shouldn't. I'm just telling you what to expect."

"I appreciate that," Edward said.

"I figure you've got to decide how much those extra weeks or months are worth to you. Some people want to breathe as long as they can, even if they're gagging into a basin at the end."

"I have to finish my book," Edward said softly.

Karen and Dr. Moss looked at him.

"How far along are you?" Dr. Moss asked finally.

"Two-thirds, maybe three-quarters of the way. It sounds as though chemotherapy would prohibit my working."

"I believe so," Dr. Moss said.

"What would you do?" Karen asked.

"I've wondered about that," Dr. Moss answered, looking her full in the face. "I know what I *think* I'd do, but that doesn't mean a rat's tail."

"What do you think you'd do?" Edward asked.

"Sell my house, buy a real pretty sailboat and hire somebody to haul me around the Caribbean with my wife and kids. And when I quit breathing, they could just shove me overboard."

Edward nodded.

"Now, look here, if you decide to go the chemo route, I'll back you all the way, you understand? There's ways of doing it right and ways of doing it wrong."

"Would I have to be in the hospital?"

"Mostly."

They all sat in silence for a while. There was no signal from Dr. Moss that he was eager for them to leave, though the waiting room was packed.

"How much time would you say I have?" Edward asked.

"Wouldn't want to say."

"I understand that, but . . ."

Dr. Moss interrupted. "Only because human beings are damned unpredictable. I could tell you four months and you could surprise the hell out of everybody and make it for ten."

"That little," Edward said.

Karen saw that Dr. Moss was shaken. "I'm sorry. If you were thinking years . . . It won't be years, not even one. I can tell you that."

"That's precise enough," Edward said. He reached for the papers on the desk. "Thank you for your time. You've been more helpful than you could possibly know."

Dr. Moss came around the desk and took Edward's hand. His nose barely reached Edward's breastbone. "If you have any questions or if there's anything I can do, you let me know. I'll be around." He showed them to the door. "We're not as smart as we think we are," he said, and turned away.

Karen knelt in the garden and dug a neat border around the pansy bed with her trowel. The sun seemed to fill the sky with yellow light, crowding out the blue so that it was only visible in a thin line hovering along the rim of the downs. The garden had responded to her ministrations by surrounding her with blazing colors. Insects buzzed, creating interesting harmonies that teased her ears. It seemed inconceivable that anything could be wrong on such a morning. The thought had occurred to Karen before, back in New York, as she read an account of a volcanic eruption in Central America while she sat sipping coffee and peering out the window at the sun glistening off the East River. The dead bodies of children were being pulled out of mud slides, and here she sat under a glorious sky. At such times, nature seemed indefensibly callous. Surely tragedy ought to be accompanied by worldwide thunderstorms, tornados, tidal waves, or at the very least, clouds and drizzle.

She plopped down behind a peony bush where she could watch Edward making notations on his manuscript. Since they had returned from London, he had been working incessantly without regard for stomach pains or debilitating bouts of nausea. A large porcelain basin sat on the ground at his feet so that he would not be forced to waste precious time in the bathroom. Karen would hear the sounds of retching and then the tapping of the typewriter resuming at an increased velocity. She longed to ask him to rest, but she knew the request was futile and she understood why.

In fact, Edward had enlisted her help in making telephone calls to his research contact in London to check certain facts and in tracking down the housewife in Prawnby who was retyping the manuscript. Karen proofread the pages, saw that they were corrected, and sent a copy of each chapter to Edward's editor in New York and to Andrew MacGregor in London. This morning was the first time she had been free to weed the garden in three weeks, and only because Edward was stuck on the section in which Julius confesses his infatuation with Vanessa Bell. A discrepancy had arisen between Julius's dates and those in Virginia Woolf's diary, describing the same party as transpiring on two different nights.

"Well, did you find the culprit?" Karen asked him at dinner.

"Yes, it was Julius. There were two parties that week. He got them mixed." Edward tried to eat his mashed potatoes, but Karen could see it was an effort.

She kept her voice light. "Did Virginia have any observations about our Julius?"

"Of course, quite a dissertation. At the beginning of the evening, she thought he looked like a farmhand but wasn't as sensible. Then she decided his doe-eyed wistfulness was compelling. And finally she acknowledged that his mental prowess surpassed her original impression. His understanding of Shakespeare, the sonnets in particular, was illuminating, she thought, and she liked his sense of humor. Julius could be almost as acerbic as Virginia. But what finally endeared him to her was his telling her that despite his infatuation with Vanessa, he thought Virginia to be far more beautiful and Vanessa rather coarse."

"Poor Virginia." She watched Edward set down his fork and told herself there was no point in urging him to eat. Her own hunger turned to sickness in her stomach. She cleared the table and brought them a pot of tea. "Edward?" she said tentatively.

"Whatever it is, the answer is yes."

"I hope so," Karen said. "I've been thinking about Persis."

"In what respect?"

"That we haven't told her what's . . . well, about your prognosis."

"There's no need to do that now."

"When we called her after the appointment with Dr. Moss, you said you were coming along very well."

"I don't wish to alarm her, and the fact is, I'm doing fine under the circumstances."

"But she's your sister and your friend. Shouldn't she know what those circumstances are?"

He held up a hand. It trembled slightly. "Karen, you must let me do this in my own way."

"She would come and help with the book, you know she would. There's still the whole last section . . ."

Edward stood abruptly. His chair toppled to the floor with a crash. "Don't do this now. Don't undermine me. I can't bear it."

Karen stared up at him in horror. "I'm sorry," she said. "Oh, my God." She put her hands over her face. After a moment, she heard the front door click shut.

When he came back, Karen was curled up in a corner of the sofa, her guitar beside her. She called to him and he appeared in the doorway, a spearlike shadow against the dim light of dusk.

"Please forgive me," she said. "I had no right to interfere."

He came into the room, but only just barely. She went to him and stood without making any attempt to touch him. "Please forgive me. It won't happen again." He held out his arms and she went into them. She thought she felt his breath shudder on her hair as if he were crying, but when he spoke, his voice was calm.

"Come over to the couch with me," he said, "and I'll tell you what I saw outside."

He explained how he had sat under the ilex tree and watched the evening stars come out over the moors. He had stared very hard into the sky, hoping to catch one suddenly come into view, but each time it was as if the tiny lights were teasing him. Suddenly a new pinprick would glitter in the corner of his eye and draw his attention away while yet another became visible in another part of the atmosphere.

"I didn't catch a single one," Edward said. "Games with the universe. I suppose one shouldn't expect to win."

Karen didn't answer.

"It's I who should be asking your forgiveness," Edward said. "I behaved abominably and I'm sorry."

She leaned against his shoulder and waited, but he said nothing about Persis. His foot brushed the guitar leaning against the couch. "Have you been singing?" he asked.

"I tried, but nothing happens. Do you know the constellations?"

"A few. Orion. Ursa Major and Minor."

"Let's study them this fall," Karen suggested.

"I'd like that," Edward said.

She hesitated a moment, then went on. "I want to do whatever I can to make things easier for you."

"I know that. I also realize I'm being selfish."

"What on earth do you mean?" Karen asked.

"You need to talk more openly about what's happening to me. But I find it very difficult, Karen. Perhaps it's denial. I suppose it is, or maybe I'm not yet ready. I think you're a brave person."

"I often deny it myself," Karen said. "You can't face reality *all* the time, not when it's so unfair."

"You give me enormous comfort."

"Do I?"

"Yes. I was thinking out there under the tree, something else. I can't see that I've brought anything positive into your life. You've practically given up performing, retreated from your old world, even from your country. It seems you've given me a new life at your expense."

"For a smart person, you can be incredibly dense," she said. "Think about it. When you first knew me, was I a happy kid?"

"You were . . . busy."

"I said *happy*."

"No, I don't suppose I would have called you that."

"How about these past months up here, and even cramped together in that hole in London?"

"You have been contented, haven't you?"

"It goes beyond contentment. With you, I've had peace, freedom, joy . . . Oh, for God's sake, I sound like a Hallmark card. And we're not even mentioning the musical, which I lay totally at your doorstep. Tell me truthfully, Edward, how many people do you know who've been this happy, even for half a minute?"

He thought it over. "I think perhaps my parents before my father grew old and cranky. No one else."

"I rest my case."

"What about children?" he asked.

"I pretty much put it out of my mind." She hesitated a moment. "But there are times when I wonder how it would have been."

"Me, too. Recently, in particular."

"I suppose it's too late," Karen said, but the statement was more like a question.

"Yes."

"They should have caught it that first time, when you went down to have your penis looked at."

"There was no reason to believe there was anything critical the matter," Edward said. "Lots of men are impotent, and very few because of stomach cancer."

"Still . . ."

"Karen, that train of thought can drive us both mad, and I wish you'd relinquish it."

"You're right, you're right." Her eyes had grown used to the darkness. Edward's face was a collage of gray and black shapes pieced together against the square window. She could see beyond his shoulder to the stars winking in the treetops outside. "I wish we'd known in time to start a baby. We would have raised it right, with fresh air and books and music and lots of laughter . . ." She sighed.

"I do speculate on what we would have produced," Edward said.

"Would you want a boy or a girl?"

"A girl," he said instantly.

"Why is that, I wonder?"

"Oh, I imagine it has something to do with intimidation. With a boy, I'd be expected to play catch and such things."

"I hate to tell you, darling, but little girls demand equal time on the playing field these days."

"I suppose so. Just the same, I'd prefer to sire a small version of you rather than a pint-size me. When my niece learned to crawl, she was always grabbing hold of my pants cuffs. I quite enjoyed that."

"Edward, maybe we should try. We could just try . . ."

He was silent for a while. Then he said quietly, "It's very difficult to be a parent alone."

"I wouldn't mind. It would be a part of you. It would be a comfort."

"Karen, darling . . ." He reached out and smoothed her hair. "There's something I've wanted to ask of you."

"Anything."

"It's about your music."

She waited. Edward reached out to touch the neck of her guitar. "It's a banal analogy, I suppose. Still, I can't help but regard your songs as a kind of offspring, your children in some sense. After all, they've emerged from inside you, they are completely unique, and they allow for a kind of permanence."

"From a pretty lonely union. You're not their father."

"But in a certain fashion, I am. For some time, your work has come out of our life together, particularly the material for the musical. When I'm . . . no longer here . . . you will write out of loss, I know, but it will still be from us. Our children. In the same way that my book is our child, if I can only finish it in time. Am I making myself the least bit intelligible?"

"Yes, Edward, but I know you're also trying to find a way to help me through it. You think that if I work, I'll survive the grief."

He smiled at her. "You invest me with such nobility of purpose. I was rather hoping you'd produce an album devoted to life in Yorkshire with Edward Vaughn. You could whisk me off into immortality on your creative shirttails."

"It's been very hard for me to sing."

"I know that."

"I can't think of what it will be like . . . afterward."

"Nevertheless, I want you to promise. Write some songs, just for me. And I want a real pledge. Look me in the eye, hold my hand, and swear. No bullshit."

She smiled and took his hand. "All right, Edward. I swear. No bullshit."

She could feel his body relax as he drew her to him. They sat for a long time without speaking, together in the gray light.

20

Edward began to deteriorate so rapidly that Karen feared the manuscript would never be finished. She set up a bed in the living room where he stayed all day, typing on a special table Karen had commissioned from a local carpenter. The pain had become far more intense, but Edward refused to take the medication because it blurred his concentration. Sometimes Karen would hear him moaning as he worked, but still the pages mounted. After supper, which was now left mostly untouched except for clear broth or juice, Karen half carried him upstairs to his room. She slept with her door open so that she could hear him when he was sick in the night. He would never call for her, but she always heard him stir, and she groped her way down the hall to help him to the bathroom or hold the basin. Then she would crawl back to bed, expecting that sleep would come immediately. But despite her exhaustion, she often lay there for hours, unable to get warm again, fearful of her dreams and incapable of imagining the future.

One morning in early September, she came back from her ride later than usual and found a man in a black suit sitting with a notepad beside Edward's bed. Karen stood in the doorway, supposing him to be a doctor.

"This is Harold Bolling, dear," Edward said. "Mr. Bolling, Karen Wells."

The man stood and shook her hand. He seemed nervous. "I have your record album," Mr. Bolling said. "It's very lovely."

Karen blinked at him as if she did not understand his words.

"Mr. Bolling is a solicitor," Edward explained. "He's helping me to make some arrangements."

"Oh," Karen said. She felt intense hatred for the man. "Would you like a cup of tea, Mr. Bolling?" she asked.

He smiled, and a dimple appeared to the right of his mouth. Karen stared at it until it disappeared. "I'd like that," the man said. "Thank you."

In the kitchen, Karen could hear the low rumble of voices. It was easy to identify the rhythm of Edward's speech; he was talking in paragraphs. When she took the tray in to them, the sound abruptly stopped. It seemed to her as if Mr. Bolling was trying to shield the notepad from her eyes with a subtle movement of his hand. Karen poured the tea, fled outside and began to walk, along the edge of the meadow beside the fence and up the narrow track that led to the moors.

She knew that she must not worry Edward with notions of false hopes, she must not cry and cling to him. She knew he was asking her to respect his privacy, now more than ever. She was still deeply troubled by his isolation from Persis. Since his outburst at the table, she had kept quiet. But even last evening Karen had heard him speak with Persis on the telephone, assuring her in a cheery voice summoned from nearly depleted reserves of energy that all was well, that he did not need her, that she would come at Christmas as usual. Knowing she was expected to lie, Karen made excuses to avoid conversations with Persis. But what if Edward were to die without ever seeing his sister again, without ever saying good-bye? Persis was Edward's last defense against his fate, Karen knew. As long as this crucial person was unaware of the truth, the truth did not exist.

Stumbling ahead with the long yellow grass of autumn billowing against her legs, she searched for courage. She tried to think of Edward lying dead, with his long hands crossed on his chest. But her mind repelled the image and the wind blew it away, leaving her with the memory of his face as he had watched her in the broken elevator that first night, his curious, gentle, bemused eyes and the incongruous maniacal grin. She fell to her knees and lifted her face. "I hate you!" she cried to a sky that was cloudless and impervious like an immense glazed bowl. Startled sheep scampered away at the unearthly sound erupting from the girl with the wild eyes and hair the color of the golden meadow.

When she came back to the house, Edward called to her right away. She washed the dirt from her face and from under her fingernails where she had gripped the earth and went to him.

"Hello, darling," she said. "Mr. Bolling's gone?"

Edward nodded and patted his bed. "Come sit a minute. I want to talk to you."

Her feet and legs moved as if hinged with metal pegs. She was a robot woman, hollow inside except for a few miscellaneous wires.

"I've instructed Mr. Bolling to do a will for me." Edward's voice was careful, asking for restraint. Karen looked at him calmly. "I've made you my beneficiary. Not that there's much. But perhaps there will be some royalties from the book, and the apartment in New York, it's a cooperative, you know, and has surely appreciated considerably since I bought it." He took her hand which, for once, was colder than his own. "The lease on this house, of course, belongs to you. There are a few stocks that will be enumerated for you in the document, nothing of much value. I've left some books to Persis. And there's one more thing. I don't want a funeral."

Karen kept her eyes on the sheets, using every muscle in her body to maintain control. She was beginning to tremble. "All right," she murmured.

"I know how difficult this must be for you," he said.

"Oh, Edward, for *me?*" she blurted.

"Yes. And I know it's useless to ask you to go away."

"Do you want me to go?"

"If it would help you through it more easily."

"How can you even think it?"

He smiled, and there was the faintest suggestion of the old grin. "I said useless, didn't I? It would surely break my heart if you left."

"Edward," Karen said. "I don't like to bring this up again, and I'm scared I'll make you mad at me. But it's so important, so, so important."

"You mean Persis."

"Yes. Please. Think of how you'd feel if the situation were reversed, if Persis were sick. Think of how grateful I would have been for the chance to say good-bye to Michael, even knowing I was going to lose him. Oh, God, I hate to give you more pain, but it's for you, too. Don't you want to see her again?"

Edward's eyes filled with tears and he turned his head away. "Could you bring me my table, please? I'd like to work."

Karen put her arms around him very gently. His beard smelled clean, like leaves. I can still touch him, she thought. "All right, darling," she said. "Just give me a minute and I'll get you set up."

One morning, after being up all night with Edward while he was sick, three times changing his pajamas and linens, Karen fainted. Edward waited for his morning tea, and then grew concerned when she did not answer his call. He hauled himself slowly out of bed and by holding on to the wall, made his way downstairs to the kitchen, where he found her unconscious beside the refrigerator.

"Oh, my dear," he whispered. He managed to dampen a towel and then sat cross-legged next to her. He drew her head onto his legs and put the towel against her forehead. Her eyes opened, stared up at him vaguely, and then she sat up, alarmed.

"Edward, what are you doing on the floor?"

"I could ask the same of you."

"I have no idea. I guess I sort of passed out."

"Not much 'sort of' about it," Edward said. "We're hiring a nurse. This morning. At this rate, I'm going to live longer than you are."

"God willing," Karen said, rubbing a lump on her forehead.

"Did you hurt yourself?" he asked.

"Not seriously. How in hell did you get down here by yourself?"

"Waltzed," he said.

"With the wall, I bet."

"Precisely." They were both cross-legged now, facing each other. "What a pair," Edward said, and began to laugh.

Karen got up and pointed a finger at him. "Stay right there. You can have your tea where you are so you'll be fortified for the return trip."

"If you'll join me."

So they sat on the floor beside the refrigerator and drank a pot of tea.

"We had a nurse for my father," Edward said. "She was a lovely woman, heavily made up but impeccable. And very kind to Father. Mother had her suspicions, which turned out to be quite accurate. Nurse Monica was a transsexual."

"Oh my," Karen said. "Did they fire her?"

"On the contrary. She was a fine nurse, the best they'd had. They kept her on until she'd saved up enough money for an operation. Mother bought her a beautiful dress as a going-away present, and Father was inconsolable."

Once Karen got Edward ensconced in the living room again, he said sleepily, "Call Persis, will you? She'll come help you out."

"Very ill," Karen said, and cursed the cable that made her words lurch and burp crazily across the ocean floor. What a way to tell a person that her brother is dying.

"Edward said the doctors were encouraging," Persis protested. "That he was in remission."

"He lied."

"Then *you* should have called me."

"He wouldn't let me."

"You should have told me anyway."

"You're right, I should have."

"Karen, really, I'm so pissed."

"I'm sorry. I've tried, honestly, but he's been very stubborn. God damn it, just come over and we'll have a civilized conversation. I can't tell you anything this way."

Persis arrived at the York station on schedule. She embraced Karen who immediately began to cry.

"Oh, damn, I'm sorry," Karen said. "I mustn't cry. It's hard on him. Oh, God, Persis, I'm glad to see you."

"You must absolutely cry," Persis said. "I could murder you both."

"What was I going to do? He begged me."

"All right. I'm here now and I've been frantic all the way over. Let's have the whole story."

As she drove, Karen tried to prepare Persis for what she would find. "He's terribly thin. It's hard to understand how he keeps on. Everything either comes up or goes right through him. He's so brave, Persis, he never complains, and he refuses to take the pain medication because it makes him woozy and he's determined to finish the book."

"How much more does he have left?"

"Two chapters, and he thinks the last one will be tough. Beginnings and endings, he says. It's terrible for him to work so hard, but I'm not permitted to fuss, even when he's having pain. I don't care if he finishes that damn book if I can have him with me even just a few more days. He's killing himself, and there's nothing I can do about it."

"Perhaps it's keeping him alive," Persis said.

Karen glanced at her in surprise. "I never thought of that."

"Does he sleep much?"

"No. Sometimes he'll vomit all night long and then apologize for being a bother. At least now we've got the nurses."

"I'm glad of that, because you look like . . . like shit."

Karen gave her a wan smile. "Spoken like a true poet."

"Well, words fail," Persis said. "Terror and jet lag, you know. But something like a raccoon comes to mind, with those huge black circles under your eyes. I can't believe you didn't call me, either of you. I'm going to break his nose."

"Go easy on him, Persis, please. Keeping it from you was like keeping it from himself. He just wasn't ready."

But there was no danger of Persis exploding once she saw her brother lying frail and emaciated in the living room. Karen watched with admiration as Persis instantly concealed the horror in her face and drew a chair next to the day bed. "Edward, you're a horse's ass."

"Surely that is not a revelation at this late date," Edward said. "I'm glad to see you."

"You look awful, but not as awful as she does," Persis said with a nod toward Karen.

"I've been beating her with my bedpan," Edward confessed. "I get such a thrill, but she does, too, incidentally; these things work both ways. Tell me about your flight."

"Oh, it was full of suspense. There were five young men, very handsome Mediterranean types in expensive suits with bulges in their breast pockets, sitting in the rows directly behind me. I had my eye on them in the airport, but when I heard them muttering Arabic on the plane, I assumed we were in for a quick trip to Libya. Somewhere mid-Atlantic, they began to argue. It got pretty heated. So I just put on my earphones and watched the movie which I presumed the airline was showing to distract us from our imminent hijacking."

"What was the movie?" Edward asked.

"Something like *Lust, Drugs, and Violence in Fort Lee, New Jersey*. There wasn't an actor in it over thirteen years old."

"What happened to the hijackers?" Karen asked.

"When we got to Heathrow, they were met by an appalling assortment of young women, all screaming and throwing things, flowers, chocolates, underpants. It was a rock group."

Karen watched Edward laugh and felt a mixture of gratitude and jealousy that Persis's presence could cheer him so. After a while, Nurse Hornsby, a short, square woman with an elaborate gray hairdo sprayed stiff as a helmet, came bustling in.

"Mr. Vaughn must rest now," she proclaimed. "Excuse us, please."

Edward rolled his eyes at Persis, but he looked exhausted. Persis went into the kitchen with Karen while the nurse dealt with Edward's rumpled sheets.

Persis sat down heavily and faced Karen across the kitchen table. "I got here just in time, didn't I?"

"I don't know. He's been this way for three weeks. It's so good to have you here."

"I guess I knew somehow. I could have called the doctor myself, though I don't suppose he would have told me anything. I could have wormed it out of you. I just didn't want to know."

"You were wonderful in there. He hasn't laughed like that in such a long time. How did you do it?"

"Generations of Yankee stoicism," Persis said bitterly. "It makes me feel like puking."

"Well, I admire your self-control, and Edward's. It must be in the genes." She twisted her hands. "I certainly don't have it. I get so maudlin."

"Don't be ridiculous. You've been living through it for months now. Anybody would get worn down. But you're going to lean on me a little."

"How long can you stay?"

"For as long as you need me."

"I'm probably going to cry again, sorry," Karen said. "I'll cut it out once I'm used to having you here."

"It's okay with me, honey," and she took Karen's hands and held them tightly.

Edward banished Nurse Hornsby the next morning and asked her to send his sister in. After a moment, Persis arrived with a huge mug of coffee in her hand.

"Lord, doesn't anybody else drink coffee in this godforsaken place?" she asked him. "The coffee pot has barnacles on it, and Karen had to go to three stores before she could find a decent brand."

"Where is she now?"

"As soon as she got back from the typist, she went for a ride on Belle."

He nodded. "Good. I want to talk to you. I'm concerned about her."

"She says she's doing better since you got the nurses."

"No, I don't mean that. I mean what's going to happen to her later, after I'm gone."

Persis looked stunned.

"Persis, she's unable to read the newspaper because she can't tolerate bad news. I learned long ago not to give her sad books to read. *Anna Karenina* nearly did her in. She went around pale and ill for a week after that one."

"Why do you think that is?"

"I suppose it's partly just her nature. But additionally, life dealt her a blow by taking her brother away from her. She's never gotten over that." He heard a noise and glanced at the doorway, but it was just Nurse Hornsby throwing open the kitchen window. Edward moved restlessly as if the sheets were creased beneath him. "I'm worried."

"Do you think she might harm herself?"

"I want you to look after her."

"Of course I will," Persis said.

"I don't mean for a few days or a few weeks. Until you feel confident that she's all right."

"Edward, I'm very fond of Karen. I'll move in with her if that's what it takes, and stay here until we're both as gray as that terrifying nurse in there."

"Thank you, dear." He closed his eyes. "Would you take off my glasses for me? They're digging into my ears." She removed them and set them on the bedside table. "I'm very tired." He fell asleep almost instantly, but Persis stayed beside him and watched his face, wishing she were an artist so that she could draw him and etch the shape of his mouth and nose into her mind so as to never forget. She longed to take his hand and hold it to her cheek, but instead she touched his hair very lightly and left him to rest.

As Edward had predicted, the last chapter was indeed tough. His pain had become almost incessant, but still he refused the pills. It finally became necessary for either Persis or Karen to stay with him while he wrote, propping him up when the pillows slipped, removing pages from the typewriter, holding the basin when he was ill, and sparing him any excess movement other than moving his fingers on the keys. He spent two days working on the final paragraph. The second afternoon, Persis sat next to him on the bed, actually holding up his wasted body and steeling herself against Edward's involuntary moans.

"Could you wipe my eyes?" he asked. "They seem to be watering."

"Surely." Persis did as she was asked.

"Now, prop me up again, will you? Wretched feeble flesh, I'll never be a sumo wrestler."

"You'd look silly in those diapers," Persis said.

There was a sharp intake of breath as a spasm of pain shot through Edward's abdomen. "All right," he said after a moment. "Now, let's see. It's only these last few sentences. Julius as the spokesman of his time . . ."

Nurse Hornsby marched in just as Edward cried aloud with another pain. "Enough!" she exclaimed. "Mr. Vaughn, you will take your medicine and you'll take it now!" She grabbed the pills off the bedside table, emptied two tablets into her hand and held them to Edward's mouth. He shook his head.

"He doesn't want them," Persis said.

"What's the matter with you?" the nurse asked Persis in a fury. "You're killing your brother. And the wife, too. What is it, are you after the money from this precious book of his?"

Edward began to shudder, but this time with laughter. "I don't expect you to understand," he said.

"He's delirious," the nurse said. "Help me open his mouth."

"I'll do no such thing."

At this moment, Karen appeared in the doorway. "What's going on?" she asked.

The nurse wheeled around and shouted at her. "Why don't you have mercy enough to just dig a hole in the garden and shove him in it? Why prolong the agony?"

She dashed the pills to the floor and squeezed past Karen. After a moment, they heard the front door slam. One of the pills was still rolling. They listened to it in silence until it stopped, then Persis began to giggle. Pretty soon all three of them were laughing helplessly.

"Ahh, I feel much better now," Edward said. "Poor soul, I don't think she has a literary bent." He rested his fingers on the typewriter keys. "Now, ladies, let's polish this sucker off."

Persis looked up at Karen. "He's been hanging out with you too long."

Edward woke in the darkness wondering where he was. He thought he heard street sounds, sirens, the roar of a bus moving away from the curb, someone shouting on the pavement below. Gradually, the country quiet surrounded him, and he remembered. Julius, he thought, life has exceeded all of my expectations. I'm grateful for what I've had, greedy for more, but mainly I'm frightened. They say that when it happens, it's like passing through a long, dark passageway with light glowing at the end, that it's not the least bit terrifying. I wonder, was it that way for you? But there was only silence and the low sigh of the trees as the wind slid down from the distant hills.

The fever began the next day. When Karen came back from her morning ride, his bed in the living room was empty. Karen raced up the stairs with her heart clogging her throat.

"What is it?" she asked Nurse Hornsby who was just coming out of Edward's room with a tray.

"Fever of forty-one degrees. Not that I'm in the least surprised."

"What's that in Fahrenheit?"

"About one hundred and three," the nurse said. "Excuse me, please. I must fetch some things from the kitchen. Mr. Vaughn must be kept hydrated."

"But what is it for? Why does he have—"

"The doctor will be here shortly." The nurse pushed past her and went down the stairs. Karen glared at the receding head of cast-iron gray curls and wondered how the woman slept. Perhaps it was a wig, and underneath was a very small shiny metal ball. Karen swayed and clutched the banister.

He was sleeping. For the first time in many weeks, his face was flushed with color. Karen laid her hand against his burning forehead and his eyes opened. "Hi," he said. Karen had never heard him say "hi" before, but perhaps the double-syllable "hello" was simply too much for him to manage.

"Hi yourself," Karen said. "You've got a temp."

"Mm."

"Are you in pain?"

"No. Thirsty."

"Old Ironsides will be up in a minute with some juice."

"You help. Not her."

"Of course, my darling."

"Ironsides. Cute."

"Shh."

When the juice arrived, she ejected the nurse and slipped the straw gently between Edward's lips. He drank eagerly for a moment, then shook his head and turned away. Karen could hear the rumble under his ribcage as the liquid hit his empty stomach.

"Borborygmus," Edward muttered.

"What?" Karen asked.

"Look it up," he said, and fell asleep again.

The doctor arrived late in the morning. After examining Edward, he conferred with Persis and Karen.

"A secondary infection of some kind. Since he has no immunities to speak of, his system is prey to all kinds of things. I've started him on an antibiotic."

"But that won't help if it's viral," said Persis.

"I'm afraid not."

Karen held her hands knotted together at her chest. Her fingers were white. "Dr. Humbersham, remember how he took care of me when I was sick?"

The doctor nodded.

"Is he going to make it through this?"

"Difficult to tell," the doctor replied.

"Oh," Karen said. The sound was like the whimper of a wounded animal. Persis's arm went around her.

"I'll ring you up later on," the doctor said. He reached out and gave Karen's shoulder a pat. He opened his mouth as if to say something, then shut it again and left.

"It's my fault," Karen said. She sat huddled at the kitchen table. Her hands flew wildly about her face. "I got sick and then he got it, only I'm strong and he was weak and he couldn't get over it."

"Karen, don't be absurd," Persis said. "You had the flu. Edward's got stomach cancer. You don't catch stomach cancer."

Karen stood up and began pacing back and forth. "He was fine. We were walking the dales and it was so lovely, but I made him sick. I was poison . . ." She threw her arms out as her voice grew frantic. "It's me!" she shouted. "I should have stayed away! I forced myself on him and now I've killed him!"

Persis caught Karen and pinned her arms to her sides. "Stop, now stop. I won't listen to this outrageous nonsense. First, you're going to have a drink, and then you're going to sit here and listen to me. But you have to promise to shut up. Otherwise I'm going to slug you. They do that in the movies to calm hysterical women, and I'll do it to you, I swear I will."

Karen looked up at Persis and said calmly, "It's just like it was with Michael. I let him go away and he died."

"Just how do you think you could have prevented that?" Persis asked, still holding tight.

"I could have shot him."

"What?!"

Karen's eyes were glazed but she spoke quietly. "I mean in the foot or something."

"They would have put you away."

"But Michael would be alive."

"I hope you don't have any plans to go upstairs and shoot Edward in the foot."

"No. It's too late."

"Karen," Persis said, leading her to the chair. "Sit down. You're losing it, darling. You stay out of that bedroom for the rest of the day, and when that doctor calls back I'm going to get you a prescription for Valium or whatever they use over here."

"I've got plenty," Karen said. "It doesn't help."

"Then we'll try brandy. And if that doesn't do it, I'll belt you in the jaw. Are you hearing me?"

Karen nodded. She had begun to look like herself now, but she was slumped in the chair, used up. Persis poured her a drink and watched as every drop disappeared.

"Now. Better?"

Karen nodded.

"What about your music? I haven't heard you sing once since I got here."

"I break down when I sing. It's too, too . . ." She pointed to her heart. "I feel too much with the music. It's unbearable."

"I want you to understand something," Persis said. "All that trash about poisoning Edward and ruining his life. You don't really believe that."

Karen didn't answer.

"You brought him to life," Persis said. "He was a drab illustration out of one of his beloved musty old books. If you hadn't come along, he would have died without ever really existing. And he most certainly would not have written that biography."

Karen watched her thoughtfully.

"He feels the same, you know," Persis said. "He thinks he's brought you nothing but grief."

Karen groaned.

"The two of you are a couple of bozos."

The fever lasted for three days. Karen went into Edward's room and watched him lying still as the life was seared out of his body. Once, when his face contorted, she asked if he was in pain.

"Yes," he whispered. "Karen, you haven't forgotten. What you promised about the music. No bullshit."

"I haven't forgotten." Her heart began to pound, a frantic crashing in her chest. "Let me get you something for the pain."

"No. I want you to know something." His voice trailed off into exhaustion. She leaned close and waited until he had summoned the strength to speak. His breath warmed her face. "I'm not afraid any more," he said. Then he whispered something.

"What is it, darling?" she asked.

"Sing to me." He opened his eyes. They were dark and full of pain.

"I'll be right back," Karen said.

When she returned with her guitar, he was motionless except for the barely discernible rise and fall of his chest. Karen played softly, willing herself to keep control, willing her throat to stay open so that the sounds would come out sweet and comforting.

"Someday I will give you the moon. / I'll wrap it up in a silken sash / And lay it glowing beneath the tree. / You'll hold it in your hands and laugh at me. / I'll give it to you soon . . ."

Her voice seemed to float in the damp, sickly air of the room, words like blossoms drifting. *"And lay it glowing beneath the tree. / You'll hold it in your hands and laugh at me. / I'll give it to you soon,"* she sang. But he could no longer hear her.

After a while, Karen picked up the wire-rimmed glasses from the bedside table and placed them gingerly on Edward's face. Then she bent over, kissed him on the lips and whispered, "So you won't stumble if it's dark."

21

The trouble was, the fact was always there. It lurked in the shadows of her bedroom, waiting for her to awake. It slid into her consciousness like a snake and filled her with horror. She would not have believed that grief could be so physical. It was as if this fact of Edward's death had invaded every corpuscle, every cell, so that each breath was labored, each movement agonizing. And yet lying motionless maddened her. She trekked back and forth between his empty bedroom to the living room where his chair still held the hollow of his body. She stood in the kitchen and heard the echo of his soft voice prodding her for every detail of her morning ride.

She longed for sleep, and yet with sleep there were the dark dreams that left her twisting, sweating, sobbing. And if, rarely, she slept without dreams, she awoke only to be crushed yet again by merciless reconfirmation of the fact.

Persis stayed on. She urged Karen to ride with her and take long walks, guessing that Karen would heal more quickly through intense activity. After the first month had passed, there were no more cries in the night, no more sudden episodes of tears that struck without warning. Persis noticed that Karen's cheeks were often wet after their outings on the horses, but Persis had her moments, too.

Persis invited Guy Burlingame for a weekend. On Saturday morning, the women coerced him into a walk across the vast sweep of the

Hambleton Hills. Guy wore wing-tip shoes, a three-piece suit, and an electric-blue pocket handkerchief. At the sight of him gingerly sidestepping the sheep droppings, Karen laughed. Persis and Guy glanced at one another with pleasure.

There was a week of unusually warm weather toward the end of October. One morning, Persis looked out the window to see Karen on hands and knees digging and weeding under the ilex tree where Edward's ashes were buried. She had planted flowers on either side of his grave, so the little hill was ablaze with bright autumn blossoms. Persis watched her for a long time.

In early December Karen sat in Edward's chair by the fire with a mug of hot chocolate cupped in her hands. "Wouldn't you like to go home for Christmas?" she asked Persis.

Persis looked up from her book, her glasses, the half-lens type, perched on the end of her nose. With the shadows flickering against her face in the firelight, she looked very much like Edward. "Only if you'll come with me," she told Karen.

"You've been wonderful, babysitting me all these weeks, but it's a hardship for you. You have a life back in New York. How long can you just hang out here?"

"I'd like to see my mother, that's the only thing," Persis said. "Other than that, I'm perfectly content to stay here. It's a fine place to write poetry."

"It must have been hard on them," Karen said. "His never saying good-bye to the rest of the family." The fire cracked and popped, sending a spark out onto the floor at their feet. She flipped the cinder back into the fireplace with an expert twist of her foot.

"He knew Mother was frail," Persis said, "and I think he hoped she might die before he did. But he could have sent for Frank."

Karen's expression had lost its customary blank look. When she talked about Edward, she came to life. "I've thought about that a lot. I believe it was because he had already said good-bye within himself. He was resolved. It would have been too painful to reach back into that life again. It was only you he could bear."

Persis considered this and nodded. "Will you come with me at Christmas?"

"All right," Karen said, and she retreated again somewhere beyond reach.

The morning they were to leave, Persis heard music floating out of Edward's room. She tiptoed to the door and saw Karen sitting on the bed with her guitar, head bowed, hair like a silken curtain over her face. The song's melodic simplicity reminded Persis of a madrigal:

I won't talk to you of love,
I'll find something else to say,
But don't smile and take my hand
And don't look at me that way.

Your eyes say it's far too late,
I don't want to cause you pain,
I won't talk to you of love, but
Please don't look at me that way.

Persis went downstairs to call Guy Burlingame. He was out, but she left a message with his secretary, saying, *She's singing again.*

New York was all dressed up for Christmas. Karen had insisted upon staying in a hotel. Edward's and Karen's apartments were still sublet, and Persis's was tiny. Besides, Karen protested that Persis needed some time alone. "I'm fine," she assured Persis. "You've been my keeper long enough. It's time to get back to normal, don't you think?"

Persis looked at her closely, then hugged her. "Okay, but check in with me. Every day. Let's set a time."

"Oh, for God's sake."

"No, I mean it," Persis said. "Otherwise, I'm going to make you stay with me and *you'll* have to sleep on the floor."

"Oh, all right. One P.M. You might even be out of the sack by then."

Persis left her in the lobby of the Sherry Netherland. Karen dropped her luggage off with the bell captain and went out onto the street. An enormous glowing snowflake hung over Fifth Avenue. The sidewalk was packed with shoppers as far as the eye could see. Karen supposed she ought to join them, but her enthusiasm for the act of giving had died with Edward. There had been such joy in buying him things. He pretended disinterest in the gaily wrapped presents, but he was always so blatantly delighted with the contents. Last winter, she had bought him a red cashmere scarf at Harrod's that he had worn to breakfast every morning in January. "Keeps away catarrh," he had said. She turned in to the park and walked north through the zoo. The animals had been deported during reconstruction, so there were only a few people, most of whom stood under the Delacorte Clock waiting for it to chime the hour of four. She felt her robot legs carry her up behind the museum and onto the circular path around the reservoir. Gulls circled, crying mournfully over the gray water. At the edges, ducks picked through the debris of last summer: beer cans, a dirty tennis ball, a bloated plastic bag. Underfoot, the track was frozen into puddles of soiled lace. Without curiosity, she watched a rider thunder past on the bridle path below. Karen had sold Midler last year. The event had saddened her at the time, but today she felt no remorse. Her heart was a robot, too, a simple machine capable of supporting only one emotion now, and that was grief.

Her outer skin told her that it was cold. She turned and started back downtown toward the hotel.

She spent the night awake. The impersonality of the hotel room appealed to her; there were no tormenting memories here. Although she moved restlessly around the room and even lay down now and then, most of the time she stared at her reflection in the mirror. Her face seemed strange, with eyes like enormous open mouths, hungry and dark. At six A.M., she murmured, "I tried."

Midafternoon the following day, while Persis was still trying to get through to Guy Burlingame in London, Karen was on a 747 flying northeast over the Atlantic. She reached the Yorkshire house in a limousine at three A.M. She gave the driver an extravagant tip and unlocked the front door. It was so cold inside that she could see her breath, but she did not turn up the heat or start a fire. Instead, she poured a large glass of wine from the refrigerator and went upstairs. Still wrapped in her fur coat, she sat on the edge of Edward's bed, took several bottles of pills from her pockets and emptied them into a heap beside her. She stared at them and sipped the wine. "So what do you think, Edward?" she asked. Her breath made clouds in the icy room. She lined the pills up in neat rows. Her fingers brushed a lump in the fabric. She reached under the bedspread and pulled out one of Edward's socks, a blue one from a pair Karen had given him. It must have clung to the spread in the laundry. She held it to her face for a moment, then pressed it out flat and stared at it. It seemed reproachful somehow, lying there curved in the shape of a frown.

"I know I promised," she said to the sock. "But it's too hard."

There was no answer. After a while, Karen picked up the pills one by one and dropped them down inside the sock. At six A.M. when Guy Burlingame burst into the room, he found her sitting cross-legged on the bed with a pad in her lap.

"What in God's name are you doing?" he asked.

She looked up at him. Her face was streaked with tears. "Writing a song for the last act," she said. "It's pretty good."